GOODBYE STRANGER

Blake Rudman

A HellBound Books Publishing LLC Book
Houston TX

A HellBound Books LLC
Publication
Copyright © 2023 by HellBound Books Publishing LLC
All Rights Reserved

Cover and art design by Tee N Art
For HellBound Books Publishing LLC

No part of this book may be reproduced, stored in a retrieval system,
or transmitted by any means, electronic, mechanical, photocopying,
recording or otherwise without written permission from the author
This book is a work of fiction. Names, characters, places and incidents
are entirely fictitious or are used fictitiously and any resemblance to actual
persons, living or dead, events or locales is purely coincidental.

www.hellboundbooks.com

Dedicated to my beautiful daughter, Selah, as this book was written during COVID-19 when you were a magical hopeful thought soon to be a reality. You're a supreme blessing, and the world is your oyster.
Love, Dad

GOODBYE STRANGER

Chapter One

Danielle Harrington

The memorial service was set to begin in an hour, but my husband Preston and I drove up to the church early. When we arrived, there was already a line of paparazzi at the bottom of the hill, held off by private security and a few harried police officers to help control the flow of traffic. Preston slowed the car for a moment. When one of the guards nodded and waved us through, Preston zoomed past the crowd.

"Vultures," he muttered. We hadn't taken a limousine, opting for our black SUV instead. Even with windows tinted in double black, the die-hard photographers jumped around us like they were chasing royals. On an occasion like this one, they were bound to hit the celebrity jackpot if they kept looking.

I sniffed and used my pinkie to capture an errant tear before it could smudge my mascara and the rest of my makeup. The impending funeral service reminded me of the moment I'd first heard of Rob's gruesome death.

"How's Rob's family going to get through this mess?" Preston asked.

"I don't know. It's got to be so difficult for them to lose him," I answered, digging in my purse for a Kleenex to stifle a new round of tears.

"No, I mean how will they get through this traffic?" he clarified.

"Run a couple of them down?" I teased, momentarily pulling myself from my melancholy.

He chuckled. I got a glimpse of that smile that lightened his rugged features: high forehead, Roman nose, blond hair, and strong chin. He hadn't smiled much lately, not since shortly before his friend's death. I was sure he was struggling big time with the death of his close friend. And at the same time he was having to face the reality of his professional football career being over. Maybe even something deeper was going on that he wasn't ready to talk about yet.

I checked my reflection in the mirror to make sure I was still presentable for the funeral. I had worn waterproof mascara on my dark brown eyelashes. My large brown eyes looked a bit bloodshot but acceptable. I brushed a strand of my wavy shoulder-length brunette hair back into my bun, securing it with a bobby pin.

"You look great, honey," Preston said. "You're the best looking of all the players' wives."

The church was at the top of a winding path. I could see why this place had been chosen for the ceremony. Live oak trees with low, sweeping branches obscured the sanctuary itself, so there was a chance at the mourners having some privacy. Preston parked our car in the lot across from the church.

Wandering the property to avoid the empty church for a while, we came to a cemetery.

"This place gives me the creeps," I said.

Preston slipped his hands into his pockets. "No one is going to jump up out of the grave and get you."

"I know." Despite the typical New Orleans humidity, the March morning was cool, and I shivered as a slight, tepid breeze brushed my bare arms.

The grounds were well kept, with flowers next to most of the polished headstones on the above-ground tombs. I was still trying to wrap my mind around Rob being laid to rest at barely thirty-eight years old. How could someone so young, so full of life and energy, so close to our family be . . . dead?

A movie ran through my mind of every scene I could remember that included Rob: the first time I met him, when Preston had introduced me to him after a home game. That had been over fifteen years ago, when both Preston and Rob were rookie players learning the ropes together, the excitement on both of their twenty-something faces at the chance to play on the same team in the NFL. Rob's knee injury, when he had spent weeks hobbling around, a frequent visitor at our place as we fed and nurtured him back to health. By that time he had been traded to another team, but the men's friendship was solid enough that they still frequently sought out each other's company. Poker nights. Weekends at the Gulf. The time Rob and Preston found an old set of Jarts—the ones with the pointed tips— and challenged each other in backyard matches. Trying to set up Rob after his divorce with one of my old college friends. That flame had flickered out a little too fast. And then, more recently, the partnership at the restaurant.

A car crash, a sudden illness . . . those things wouldn't have necessarily been a better way to die, but they would have made more sense than him being murdered in a robbery. He still had a few years left to his football career, and with millions of dollars in the bank, I couldn't imagine he hadn't offered whatever he had in exchange for his life.

Since the days right after Preston and I first started dating seriously, I'd always made him promise me that if someone tried to carjack or mug him that he would give them whatever they wanted. He was recognized everywhere he went, and that made him a target. No playing hero. It was more important to come home alive than risk getting killed over something easily replaced.

The part I couldn't even bear was that someone had beaten Rob to death, cracked his skull open. I wondered if he had begged for his life or if he had even had the chance. I'd seen the crime scene photos online. I couldn't fathom why anyone would want to do that to him. You hear about violent crimes all the time, but it's completely different when it's someone you know. The trail of blood on the kitchen floor was a stomach-turning image I could never forget.

And the fact that the victim could have been Preston . . . I shuddered and immediately shut out that thought.

I had pictures on my phone of Rob during a cookout at our house only a month earlier, carrying our daughter Isabel on his shoulders. I preferred to remember him that way, but I wasn't at all sure that would be possible.

"I'm glad you weren't the one who found Rob," I said.

Preston simply nodded. He had a faraway look in his blue eyes, probably envisioning such a horrifying scenario. Marco, the assistant manager, had found the body when he came to open. Apparently the robbery had taken place the night before. According to what the police told the family, Rob had already been dead at least seven hours by the time his body was discovered. Marco had already vowed he would never be able to work there again.

"How many siblings did Rob have again?" I asked, changing the topic.

"Two brothers, four sisters."

"Wow," I said. "I can't imagine." I forced myself to think of something other than death and mourning. "Hell. I'm at my limit with our two. One more kid and one of the little angels is getting adopted out."

He nodded at that. One of the few things we'd always been on the same page about is how many kids we wanted. We have twins, a boy and a girl, and as much as they worked my last nerve, I'd kill or die for them without question. The fact that we'd had two kids at once made us even more certain that two was the perfect number.

"Rob's family are Irish Catholics."

"How are you doing with all this?" I asked Preston. "I mean, really? It happened at your restaurant, and we haven't even talked about . . ."

"I don't know what to think, honestly, baby. It's still a shock. I'm going to unload the restaurant. It's not supposed to be a bad neighborhood, but if it's not, how do you explain this? Maybe the area has changed over the years, though none of the staff complained about it. I'd never have bought it if I thought something like this could happen. Other than that? We'll see."

I bit back what I had been about to say. Preston knew damn well that my question had nothing to do with him getting rid of the restaurant. He'd been talking for a while about leaving the business. It was one of the things he and Rob hadn't been able to agree on. Since Preston had retired a year earlier, he'd had loads of endorsements. It's not like money was a consideration. I wanted to know how Preston felt about losing a friend and partner he'd known for the last twenty years. Preston had told me so many stories about playing high school football together with Rob. Their friendship had drifted a bit when they attended separate colleges but had become strong again with their shared NFL connection. Then to have his friend die in such a brutal way.

"When I was a kid in high school," he said, interrupting my thoughts, "sometimes I would take my girlfriend up to the local cemetery and we would screw. A little action right now might be a good diversion." He slid an arm around me, his hand brushing my ass.

I gave him a look. His eyebrow was raised, a little mischievous grin on his lips. I'm all for inappropriate timing as much as the next girl, but I certainly didn't expect it right then. Preston had a strange way of mourning—more of a coping mechanism to handle such intense feelings, I surmised. I couldn't help but smile back, though. Even at a time like this, my man's libido remained on perpetual overdrive.

With my luck, though, someone would be bound to catch it on camera. Sure, we'd have fun. When we were barely drinking age, he used to have a thing about sex in public places. Over the years we did less and less of that. We had never been caught doing anything, but . . . almost being caught was a big part of the thrill. No matter what he craved in the moment, however, I knew he would regret it if his Boy Scout image was sullied.

I scanned the tree line and the road beyond. "Not out here. Where would we go?"

"Church restroom?"

"I haven't been to church in years, Preston. Isn't there some kind of going-to-hell clause if you do perverted deeds in there?"

"Oh, perverted. I like that. You're going to have to fill me in on what you've got in mind."

"Rain check?" I asked, placing my hand on the middle of his chest.

"Danielle, maybe this isn't the best time to bring this up, but I want you to pack yourself an overnight bag when we get home because I'm taking you for a getaway this weekend. I've arranged for childcare and everything. I just need you ready to go Friday at five p.m."

"Preston?" I was genuinely surprised and delighted. I gave him a giant hug and kiss. "What's the occasion?"

"Just celebrating us." He gazed into my eyes, and I felt myself falling in love all over again.

He leaned down and kissed my lips. Just then, I saw the first of several cars slowly drive up the road.

***

By the time the memorial was about to begin, the church was packed to capacity with friends and loved ones. A decision had been made to have a separate memorial later in the week for Rob's fans. Cameras were forbidden inside, and guests were warned beforehand that they needed to surrender their cell phones at the door.

Things went as well as they could for such an affair. Preston made a passionate eulogy about brotherhood and how Rob was the kind of man anyone would have wanted as a friend. Several other players shared similar stories with the congregation about the man he was as a sportsman, a friend, and even a few humorous stories from on and off the field. His ex-wife Kelly also spoke, and she had only kind things to say about him. Her voice cracked as she read the speech she had prepared, but she held herself together until the very end of it. When she went back to her seat, she burst out in tears. They had been in each other's lives on and off since the divorce, and I wondered if she regretted their split.

Rob's parents were in attendance, and I felt the emotion surge in me at his mother's heart-rending cries at the end of the service. She approached the closed casket, and the moment she touched it, her knees buckled. Rob's two older brothers grabbed her just in time. Their father lingered a step behind, eyes blurry with tears. He seemed to struggle to catch his breath. He laid his hand on the casket and closed his eyes, a silent prayer or a goodbye soft on his lips.

I'd heard that cry of a bereaved mother before, and there is something the same about it each time, no matter who it is—purely inconsolable grief and hysteria. The sound made me flinch. Every fellow funeral-goer I could see from my vantage point wiped an eye or a nose or struggled to hold back their emotions. Nobody should ever outlive their child. It hurt my soul to watch these two parents in such agony. Preston bristled beside me. Reaching for his hand, I felt his fingers curl through my own. His touch was cold and clammy.

***

By the time we left the church, the cool morning had melted into a typical hot, sunny Louisiana afternoon. Preston powered the windows down for some fresh air the moment we were inside the SUV.

He grabbed his seatbelt to buckle himself, but it stuck and required a full ten seconds of yanking before it came loose and he was able to buckle in. "Danielle, can you take this in to get the seatbelt fixed? It drives me crazy."

"Yeah, sure," I said, only half hearing his request.

I guess he'd forgotten about the gauntlet that waited for us at the bottom of the hill. The paparazzi hadn't moved one bit. If anything, it seemed like more of them had shown up. He slowed our car to keep from hitting one of the photographers, and as he did, another one rushed around to the driver's-side window and pushed a microphone in Preston's face.

I powered up my window, almost smashing the fingers of one overly eager asshole who tried to approach me. I heard him cuss at me through the glass.

"Preston, would you like to make a statement regarding the death of Rob Anderson?" the reporter on his side of the car asked.

My husband took off his sunglasses and looked directly into the camera, a few paces behind the guy with the microphone. "I would just like to say we're all saddened by his loss. He was an excellent player, an even better man, and he will be sorely missed. We were fortunate to have him with us for as long as we did. I don't believe any of us that knew him will be quite the same without him."

I was shocked.

Maybe I shouldn't have been, but Preston didn't give statements to the press. It was part of the playbook of having grown up within a clan of well-renowned sports champions. He especially never spoke to members of the press off the cuff. Any statements were carefully curated through a manager and publicist beforehand. He always told me there were plenty of things he would like to speak openly about, but he remained aware of the dangers of misrepresentation and liability. He hadn't maintained a flawless reputation by making any statement lightly, regardless of how innocuous it might have seemed at the time.

And then I was even more astonished. My husband sniffed and wiped a tear from his scrunched-up eyes. Was he crying?

***

A gathering was held at Rob's brother Timothy's house, which was a relief because he lived in the same neighborhood that we did. The house was a gated mansion on a few acres of land. The place was beautiful, with a view of a lake behind it, and with the back doors of the living space open, people were free to walk in and out to the back patio.

It wouldn't be right to dodge out too quickly, but I was looking forward to the idea of slipping out and going home. I was already emotionally drained by the time we got there.

It was odd to see Preston surrounded by all his teammates again. Guys who spent the offseason in other cities around the country had made the trip down for this important funeral of their former teammate. They stood in the den, talking, everyone in black. Preston was at their center, still the leader even though they had been without him as their quarterback for months. He told a story about him and Rob, one that he'd probably told before but that entertained his friends nonetheless.

He was that kind of man. People were drawn to him, always had been. Sheer magnetism. My mom used to say he was the kind that could get any girl into trouble. I met him my first year of college. He was already being wooed by the league and was showing promise on the college gridiron. Really, he could have had his choice of girls. There was no reason he had to pick me. Don't get me wrong, I'm a good-looking woman, I'm smart, and I know who I am and what I can do. It's just that when a man has that many women floating around him at any given time, you can't say for sure that you'll be the one to get his attention. I was a girl who liked sports almost as much as he did, and I think that intrigued him. More importantly, I didn't have the time or the temperament to fawn over him. That was the mistake the rest of them made.

"Want a drink?"

The voice shook me from my thoughts. I turned to see my brother-in-law, Tyler, standing behind me. Also an NFL quarterback, he always returned to his hometown of New Orleans in the offseason, though we didn't necessarily see him often.

"Oh, hi," I said, giving him a quick hug. He handed me a glass. By that point, it would be the third drink of the afternoon. "I didn't see you at the service."

"I was there," he replied. "Joanna stayed home with the kids today, so I ran a bit late. Olivia has the flu, and we're hoping Sydney doesn't get it."

"Oh no," I said. "Hug her for me, would you? Poor baby. I haven't seen my nieces in too long."

"Well, when the kids aren't contagious anymore, you're welcome to drop by anytime."

I took a sip of whiskey, pausing a moment as the warmth spread through my throat and into my chest. "Damn. That's good."

"I know, right?"

Tyler stood beside me, and we watched as other people walked by. It felt oddly like we were the wallflowers, while everyone else mingled. As much as the Harrington brothers were different, I found myself able to have companionable silences with them both.

"Pretty happy crew for one of these things," Tyler commented.

"I guess. Or maybe they're all half drunk."

"Couldn't hurt." He grinned.

Tyler was the physical opposite of my husband. He had dark brown hair and brown eyes, and where Preston was the extrovert, Tyler was a bit more reserved. The two of them had had a contentious relationship for years. Tyler never quite matched up to the family's legacy, or to be specific, Preston's football career. While Tyler was among the top eight quarterbacks in the league, most people who knew the game argued he would never be good enough to make it into the hall of fame. Over the last season, his team's lackluster performance had even spurred talk of a trade. If that happened, he would go to an inferior team, and at thirty-three, that could spell the unofficial end of his career. Tyler's triumphs on the field did not match up to his big brother's, even though they were tied at two Super Bowl wins apiece. Preston had earned the unique honor of twice beating one of the all-time great quarterbacks, Brooks, from New England. Though when Preston was asked, he publicly stated he believed his brother was the stronger quarterback; football, like any game, required an element of luck, and that may have been the only thing that kept Tyler's solid success from being full-on greatness.

It had to be difficult for him, doing the best he could, only to be told that his best would never be good enough to measure up. I knew very well what it was like to be caught in the shadow of a great man, a mere footnote to someone else's place in history.

Preston always claimed that their antagonistic relationship went all the way back to their childhood, but the difference in achievements didn't help. Sibling rivalry and the inability to measure up to their father's astronomical expectations had made it difficult for them to bond properly.

"How's Preston dealing with all this?"

I glanced at Preston from across the room. He was talking with one of his old teammates and Crystal, the teammate's girlfriend and my best friend.

"I'm not really sure yet," I replied.

"The Harrington clan has never been the best when it comes to talking about hard things." Tyler shrugged. "I'd ask, but he'd brush it off."

"He was crying when we left the service."

"Yeah, that's already been all over the internet." Tyler scratched his chin. "I don't know. Just seems to me that he can't help but take the spotlight, on or off the field. Regardless of their friendship, today was supposed to be about Rob and his family. The press will just spin this as being about Preston."

I didn't know what to say to that. The same thought had occurred to me, but I didn't want to validate his impressions. Tyler and Preston already had enough issues with each other without me getting somehow pulled into the middle of their ongoing bullshit.

I also wasn't sure Preston was doing anything on purpose; maybe talking to that reporter had been a spur-of-the-moment impulse.

Tyler took another gulp of his drink, finishing off the glass.

"Excuse me," he said. "I have to go say hello to some people."

He left my side. I mingled for a while and tried to forget the whole uncomfortable exchange.

***

I recalled the last time I had seen Rob, which was one week before he died, on an ordinary Wednesday afternoon.

Rob had reddish-brown hair, big brown eyes, and a sensual mouth that easily broke into a wide grin. Over the years I had grown to think of him like a brother-in-law, but I knew what other women saw in him. He had the height and toned physique you came to expect in a football player. What set him apart was the graceful way he moved, how he fixed on you with his eyes when speaking. When he focused on you, no one else in the room seemed important.

According to my college friend who'd had the brief fling with him, he was good in bed, too.

I had just come home from work that afternoon, and the kids were upstairs doing homework. I heard the doorbell ring, and since I was close by, I had answered it myself instead of waiting on the maid.

"Hey, beautiful," he said to me with a wink.

"Hey yourself," I said. "What are you doing here?"

"I needed to drop this off for Preston. Is he home?"

"Not yet, but come in, you can wait for him."

"I'm going out of town for a little vacation at the end of the month, and I need to make sure that everything is handed over before I leave. Give him this, will you?"

I took the package from him, a box about the same size as a book and wrapped in plain brown paper. "I'm expecting him in a little while if you want to wait."

"Yeah, that would be fine."

I led him back to the kitchen and we chatted about the restaurant. He had told me how excited he was about a new menu he was planning. The new offerings would be Asian/Jamaican fusion dishes. He was telling me that hybrid culture cuisine was the next new thing, popping up in the trendy parts of the city.

I made coffee (a bad habit for the late afternoon, but I did it every day), and he hadn't minded having a cup with me.

"Tell me something. Are you looking to retire soon? Because you sound more excited about the restaurant than you are the game."

"You know, I had that injury last year and it got me thinking. Do I really want to keep doing this and risk more injuries? At best, I say I have about two to three years. Which, sure, is a lot of money. I've invested well, so it's not like I am hurting for anything. I'd like to have kids one day, which means getting into a serious relationship again. I'm getting tired of the single life."

"Yeah, but it's not going to take long for you to find somebody. There are a lot of women who wouldn't mind getting married to an attractive millionaire."

He laughed. "Yeah. Gold diggers top the list! Not *everyone* was lucky enough to find the girl they were meant to marry in college. Anyway, I want to be able to be an active father one day, not one of these sixty-year-old men with a twenty-year-old wife begging her to shut the kids up. I don't want to be walking with a cane within ten years. I know so many guys who wake up every morning in pain or who take five pills a day not to be. I'm thinking next season should be my last."

"You told Preston yet?"

"No, because I know he's going to try and talk me out of it. He has his own regrets."

I nodded. We had never talked about it, but I knew Preston missed the game and the attention that came with it. Part of the reason he did so many appearances and endorsements had nothing to do with money. It was about maintaining his place in the limelight.

"What about Kelly?" I asked. "Do you ever regret not having kids with her?"

He took a moment to think about it. Something in his eyes softened at the mention of his ex-wife. "No. Don't get me wrong. I will always love Kelly. One day she is going to be a great mom. If we had stayed married, sure, I would have wanted that. Now that we're divorced, I'm glad we didn't. She holds grudges, and I can't see her not pulling the kids into it eventually."

Preston had been running late that night. After an hour of waiting, Rob yawned and looked at his watch. "Well, I guess I had better be going. Tell Pres I will be in touch."

"Will do," I said as I walked him back to the door.

"I'll see you when I get back in town, sweetie." He kissed my cheek, and I watched him walk out to his car. He drove off, and I never saw him again.

I left the package in Preston's office, on his desk. With the events of that following week, I didn't think to ask if Preston had opened the package or if he'd even noticed it.

***

Once we were home from the funeral, I asked Preston if Tyler had spoken with him after the service.

It had been a long day and I was getting ready for bed. I was changing into my nightgown; he was already in bed, fiddling with the television remote.

"I saw him and said hello, but we didn't really speak," he said. "I was talking to someone else, and when I turned around he was gone."

I came out of the bathroom. Standing in the doorway, I looked at my husband. He looked sleepy but not upset.

"You'd tell me if you were . . . I don't know . . . if you wanted to talk about what happened?"

He shrugged. "My best friend died. I don't know what to say about it. No one expected this, and I'm still trying to wrap my head around it. And no, I don't want to talk. I just need this next weekend to relax with you away from home."

"Okay. I don't want to be a nag; I'm just trying to check in. Making sure you're all right."

I slipped into bed beside him. "Consider that done," he said and reached over to turn out the light.

Chapter Two

Danielle Harrington

On Thursday night, Preston had a little glimmer in his eye when he asked if I was ready to get out of town. He said that he'd planned out our whole weekend. "Everything is ready. The kids will be staying with some friends, and I spoke to your assistant at the gallery. She can handle things for a few days."

"Where are we going?" I asked.

"I can't tell you, darling," he said with a smile. "What would be the fun in that?"

Our weekend retreat turned out to be in Dallas. Preston had arranged for the wife of one of his football buddies who had kids the same age as ours to pick up Ethan and Isabel from school. They would be having a fun weekend with friends, so I didn't have to worry about them. Preston asked me to have my bag packed and to be ready to leave from our house at three on Friday afternoon.

Promptly at three o'clock, a BMW with one of Preston's friends driving arrived to transport me to the airport. After going through security, Preston met me at the gate with a kiss and a bag of Swiss chocolates. Our seats were in first class. Though it was only a two-hour flight, we had time to relax and catch up on the goings on of the last few days. It hadn't even occurred to me until then that we'd worked so hard all week that we'd barely had time to talk to each other. We held hands and enjoyed our time together.

Once we arrived in Dallas, we were whisked off to the Omni Hotel. I'd never stayed there before but had heard about the luxurious accommodations. We had an entire suite, complete with a shower for four and a hot tub. In addition, a bottle of chilled champagne and a platter of chocolate-covered strawberries awaited us. I kicked my shoes off, jumped onto the middle of the bed, and stretched my arms out.

"I can't reach any of the ends." I chuckled. "You could get lost in this bed! It must be double the size of a king."

Preston smiled—not the kind of smile he used for the press or even the weary one I often saw after a long day, but that delighted expression that warmed the blue of his eyes. "It's custom, I'm sure. You really think you could get lost?" he said, taking off his shoes and jacket. He laid down beside me. "I think it would be fun to try. See what we can do with all of the space."

Preston's arms came around me, and we were soon kissing and touching. He felt so good. There was nothing quite like the safety of being in his arms. "What made you think of this?" I asked. I held his face in my hands.

Preston pulled away for a moment. I detected a seriousness to his eyes. "I'm so fortunate to have you and our kids. It just feels like everything moves at the speed of light. It would be so easy to forget that this beautiful life we have started with just the two of us. I don't want you to ever think I don't appreciate all you do and what we've built together. So"—he leaned in for another kiss—"sometimes I've got to find a way to remind us both."

At nightfall, we took a walk outside. We sat poolside and enjoyed a drink together. Few people were around, but those who were didn't seem interested in us. Later, we retreated to our room. Preston offered to order dinner, but I had other thoughts in mind.

I led him to the hot tub. Between the steam and the champagne, I felt wonderful and the slightest bit dizzy. Preston fed me one of the strawberries. I felt silly trying to look sexy while he did it. Then I saw how he was looking at me—with a loving anticipation that reminded me of when we first met. No matter how silly I felt, I knew I was special to him.

We made love that night. I remember how gentle he was about it, taking his time to tease me. I loved when he took his time; at home there was always the need to hold back, to not be too loud and to double-check the lock on the door. And of course there was always Preston's phone to contend with. I was pleased that I hadn't seen him glance at it once since we'd landed. I let myself feel and emote all the things I wanted to whenever we were together.

I remember drifting off to sleep with him beside me, his chest against my back. "What a great night," I said to him just before I dozed off.

"One of many more," Preston said. I slipped into a deep, restful sleep.

***

Preston Harrington

I had been wanting to get away for weeks, just to relieve the pressure I felt. Of course, bringing Danielle with me just made things easier. She did deserve a getaway. This way, she wouldn't ask me any questions about where I had been. If anyone was curious, we were spending some much-needed time away as a couple. Didn't most people wish they were lucky enough to get out of town whenever the urge suited them?

My wife has never been able to drink much champagne. She loves it, but it seems to affect her brain and get her drunk faster than other drinks. Now, a good meal would have balanced things out and she would never have gotten as tipsy. But since she wasn't eating much, I made sure to add a little sedative to her glass—nothing that would hurt her; just a little something to boost the natural effect champagne had on her.

I was glad to hear Danielle slightly snoring next to me, which told me she was in a deep sleep. I couldn't take the chance that she would wake up and find me gone. We would be in town together for another night, but I'd made plans for us to see *Hamilton*. I knew Danielle would be excited about that and would limit her drinking to be more alert. Anyway, if I wanted time alone, it would have to be tonight.

I rose carefully from the bed and changed my clothes. A pair of jeans and a plain white shirt were all I needed. I'd brought cowboy boots, but I decided against them and put on sneakers instead; I wanted to blend into the crowd as much as possible. No one at home knew our little weekend trip was to Dallas. Knowing some random fan might recognize me, though, I wore a dark wig.

I took a taxi from the hotel, paying in cash, and rode to a spot I was familiar with. I'd visited this bar once before when I was in town for business. The loud country music drowned out the flat-screen televisions that played NASCAR or MMA but not football.

Wanting to experience a little night life, I made my way to the bar and ordered a whiskey. A pretty blonde girl sat down beside me. I pretended not to notice her at first, and I think she was doing the same.

"You're not from around here," she said quietly. I looked more closely at her features. I wasn't sure if the blonde hair color was real, but if it was a dye job, at least the color suited her. She had a sensuous mouth that she highlighted with a velvety red lip color. Her eyes were a shade of gray green, the kind that changed easily in the light. The shape of them, rather than the color, reminded me of Danielle.

"No, I'm not," I said easily. "How about you?"

"Transplant," she said brightly. "Originally from Nashville."

I nodded and motioned to the bartender. After ordering a pitcher of beer for us, I sat back. I often found that it was better to let a woman talk rather than ask too much. Most of the time, they were used to men that hogged the conversation, so they appreciated the nice change to talk about themselves.

"You like Dallas?" I asked. A basic, easy question. No threat in that.

"I do. I miss family sometimes. Then I call them on the phone and remember why I moved out here in the first place."

We both chuckled at that. People who didn't get along with their families were less likely to stay in touch with them. And if she were lonely in general, maybe she would be open to other things.

"I'm only here for a couple of days on business," I lied. "But this looks like a nice enough place to get some drinks. Maybe find a little company."

"Oh, company," she said with a little nod.

"What's your name?" I asked.

"Kayla," she said with a smile. "Kayla Johnson."

"Charles," I said. "Charles Smith."

We passed the better part of an hour with small talk, thankfully none of it about sports. I pegged her as someone who not only did not recognize me, but one of those people who had no interest in any kind of sports, much less football. Her profile was a typical one: a divorcee, new in town, and she liked to hit the bar at night to have an excuse to get out of the house. Here was something that I could work with.

"My place is not far," she said, batting her eyelashes. I took a beat to respond. It looked like she was holding her breath for my answer.

"Sure," I said with a grin. I reached for my wallet to pay our tab in cash. "That sounds great." The night was still young, and I could have as much fun as I wanted before I needed to be back to the hotel. Danielle wouldn't wake for another seven hours. I would be by her side before then, pretending that nothing had happened.

Chapter Three

Danielle Harrington

After that weekend getaway, Preston and I settled into a pattern of what felt like normalcy. Toward the end of the month, I got a call and an invite to go out with my friend, Crystal.

Crystal Wells and I had been friends for a decade. Though divorced now, she had previously been married to one of Preston's teammates before he got traded. These days she was dating another football player, and though she claimed it wasn't serious, she had been with the same man for three years.

"I'll never get married again," she assured me. "Too much trouble. I much prefer just being a girlfriend."

Despite what she said, I thought being married again, to the right man, would make her happy.

"You say that now, Crys. What about when you're older?"

"What about it?" she replied. "By then I'll be chasing younger men."

I just shook my head. She was half joking and half serious. Personally, I believed it was a waste for anyone to be alone. I wasn't going to push my opinion on her, though. She'd heard it before.

We often met up for lunch or a workout, but on this day we had an appointment at an exclusive spa. Their client list was made of mostly celebrities and the well connected, so we had been lucky to get priority booking for an appointment. Lying face down, we were both getting massages.

"This feels so good." I sighed.

The masseuse who was working on me spread some delicious-smelling oil on my back and limbs. It was a blend of light citrusy scents with an undertone of jasmine.

"It's been awhile, right?" my friend said, moving her shoulders a bit. The masseuses left us to have a moment to relax, and Crystal turned to me with a mischievous grin.

Crystal was a beautiful woman, but if you had seen her pictures from when she was twenty, you wouldn't have recognized her. By thirty she was a bleached blond, her boobs had been done, and at some point, implants had been added to enhance her cheekbones. You would never have known that her hair had been mousy brown, her chest flat, or that she had been the typical "girl next door" from a Midwestern town. What I most admired about her was if you asked her opinion, she would give it to you without any sugar coating.

"Tell me what's going on with you," she said. "You've been really quiet these last few weeks."

"Well, the art gallery has been busy, so there's that. You know, I really am glad I have had something to preoccupy my time, even if it's part time. There's a new showing at the end of the month. It's been hard watching all the media coverage about Rob. Yet it's all the same information in the same loop, no new theories and no suspects. People come into the gallery and think that I should be fine talking to them about what happened. They don't seem to get that he was a close friend or that the way he died is still haunting me."

"Rude," Crystal declared. "I wonder how they would like it if a random stranger approached them about the death of someone they cared about. People don't think at all."

"Meanwhile," I sighed, "I think I may have misjudged my husband."

"How?"

"I thought he was okay, but over the last few weeks he's spending a lot of time alone. I literally do not know where he goes. When he comes back, if I ask him, he gets angry about it, like I'm trying to find something out that isn't my concern. I mean, we did have a great weekend away together where we reconnected, but other than that, I've gotten to the point where I have stopped asking questions so I can keep some semblance of peace in the house."

"Uh oh. Honey, you don't think he's out getting laid?"

I laughed. "I mean, I know anything is technically possible, but I don't think so. He's well fed at home. I can count myself as lucky because I am not one of these women who have a husband that doesn't want sex. Quite the opposite. The only complaint I have is that sometimes it feels like we just aren't close. Even though he seems like he's been trying to make up for it lately—the two of us spending more time alone, even going out of town together—I still don't exactly feel the way I used to. I don't know if it's just time passing or if our relationship is in a different place."

"How do you mean?"

"If we're lacking anything, it's intimacy, not sex. I could do with a little less pillow biting and more pillow talk."

"Does Preston know that?"

"I've tried to tell him. He listens, but he's not getting it."

"Yeah, that's men for you. I understand what you're saying, but I think I've given up on hoping men will ever get the emotional stuff we want from them. I really couldn't give a damn about what a man's got to say on any subject as long as he's still busting my headboard."

***

I thought back to my dating days with Preston. He was so attentive, right from the beginning. I'd never met anyone like him who seemed to care about every detail in making me happy. And even though he was legitimately the most popular guy on campus—with his good looks, athletic prowess, and smile that could light up a whole room—I always felt special, like he had eyes only for me. Never did I feel like he was flirting with other girls or playing games to make me jealous.

Around the time my birthday rolled around that first year we were dating, he planned a special date where he took the time to place notes in various places around campus, leading me on a scavenger hunt from one clue to the next. The final clue I opened up instructed me to dress up and head to Neyland Stadium, where the University of Tennessee football team played. All by myself at that point, I walked tentatively toward the darkened pitch, fingering my gold necklace and wobbling a bit in the heels I seldom wore. This location was Preston's home away from home, but I felt slightly creeped out walking through the tunnel by myself. My phone's flashlight directed my path.

When I was ten yards from the opening onto the field that the team ran through on game days, I heard a power surge and a loud snap as someone activated the stadium lights. Dim at first, they grew brighter by the second. When I reached the grass, I intuitively made my way to a shape in the middle of the field.

As I got closer and the lights continued to brighten, the shape became a table set with two place settings, a glass of wine next to each, and a bouquet of flowers in the middle. A folded note on the nearside plate directed me to face the field goal at the south end of the field. When I did, a beaming Preston came jogging toward me dressed in a suit and tie. He planted a long kiss on my lips, pulled out my chair for me, and then seated himself across from me at the table. Two waiters, who I recognized as Preston's teammates, delivered one course at a time to us. The delicious steak dinner was followed by slices of cheesecake for dessert.

After gifting me with a beautiful aquamarine ring, the birthstone for the month of March, Preston presented a bag with my tennis shoes in it so I wouldn't have to wear my heels as we took a romantic after-dinner walk around campus. He knew how much I loved taking walks. That evening sealed my heart. I was Preston's girl forever and always.

The other most memorable date was the one where he asked me to marry him. I was initially directed to wait on a street corner for a particular taxi that brought me to a nearby airfield. An employee at the airfield walked me out to a small airplane with Preston and a pilot inside.

We flew to Nashville, where a waiting car whisked us off to a performance at the Grand Ole Opry and then dinner downtown at Jeff Ruby's Steakhouse. Again, Preston had been thoughtful enough to pack walking shoes for me, as we took an after-dinner stroll next to the river. We enjoyed the lights and sounds of the city, and when we reached Riverfront Park, a group of six singers appeared out of nowhere, serenading us with the song "I Love You Truly."

When the song ended, Preston crouched down on one knee and presented me with the very engagement ring I'd admired when we'd been shopping one time and chanced upon a jewelry store. I hadn't even thought he'd paid attention to what I liked.

Now, glancing at that beautiful half-carat diamond, I couldn't say exactly when I started to get a little concerned about how Preston was spending his days. Crystal's unease about Preston had stuck in my mind. Twice when I thought he was home, I called the nanny and she said he'd left the house hours before. I wouldn't usually have cared about him going out on a day he had off; I just had a gut feeling that I should start paying closer attention.

I had my own part-time work at the gallery plus running the kids to activities, so I wasn't about to try following him. I did the next best thing.

I called his agent's office and spoke to the executive assistant, Joslyn.

"Would you mind sending me a copy of Preston's itinerary? He doesn't like to admit it, but he's horrible when it comes to keeping track of his schedules."

"No problem at all, Mrs. Harrington. I'll email you a copy. Would you like me to send him a duplicate as well?"

"No, that's okay."

"I will send you his schedule weekly," Joslyn offered. "I find it helps a lot of our clients if their partner has a copy."

I smiled. Was I one nosy wife among many, or were these other people just married to the forgetful sort? I'd never done anything like this before, and while I felt a little ashamed, I also sensed a thrill in it, like sneaking out of a candy store with sweets in my pocket I hadn't paid for.

Within minutes, I had the email. The attached document was a virtual calendar that showed Preston's agenda for the month. As expected, many of those dates had to do with meetings for possible new ventures. There was time marked off to deal with the newest of his endorsements, including a commercial for a national pizza chain.

After the fifteenth of May, the entire calendar was blank, except for one event.

I looked up in disbelief. It was already the 25th.

I sent Joslyn a quick question. She replied almost instantly.

No, Mrs. Harrington, it's not a mistake. Preston requested we leave the last part of the month open.

What had he been doing for the entire month then? I thought again about my conversation with Crystal. Preston didn't have any reason to stray, but what if he was? I couldn't be the only woman with a seemingly faithful husband who had gone outside the marriage for the thrill of chasing a new woman. Maybe he needed more attention than I was giving him. Maybe it wasn't even that complicated. Maybe he just enjoyed sniffing a new skirt.

The only thing left on his schedule was for the following week: a charity event at a children's hospital that the two of us attended every year.

What infuriated me was that I didn't fully know if anything was wrong. It's not like I could just ask Preston and expect a level answer. What if he wasn't doing anything wrong but simply craved time alone? One of the things I had never wanted to be was that woman who nagged her husband about cheating when he hadn't strayed, all to have him snap one day and mess up with some random girl.

I kept quiet. I didn't ask about Preston's schedule or what was going on. One way or another he would say something I didn't like and we would get into an argument. I was relieved when he asked me to go to the one event he did have scheduled. Maybe it wasn't an answer to what was going on with him, but it made me feel a bit of normalcy.

Chapter Four

Danielle Harrington

One of the many charities Preston and I support is St. Michael's Children's Hospital. He had endorsed them from the beginning of his career, back when he was still a wet-behind-the-ears quarterback, hungry to prove that he was worth the hype surrounding his draft. Ultimately, he donated so much money that they renamed one of the cancer wings of the hospital: it became known as the Preston Harrington Memorial Wing. As always, this was one of the few of his events I liked to tag along for. I enjoyed visiting with the children on the ward.

After attending the fundraisers for so many years, we were both familiar with the usual suspects who showed up for any event at St. Michael's. They invited a hodgepodge of figures from across the sports world, and like Preston, many were veterans when it came to fundraising. His agent had made all the arrangements as usual, informing us of what time we were expected to be there, which patients we would go and see, and what kind of protocols for gloves and protective garb we would encounter on the ward.

The event usually began with a quick Q & A session with the press. Reporters would be allowed to ask a few questions about each athlete's contributions to the hospital and why it was personally important to them. It was usually a light-hearted affair, and some of the guys even brought their own kids to participate. After that, they would go visit the children, give presents, read stories, and sing songs. It was meant to be an uplifting day for the children. I enjoyed visiting these brave little ones, and so did Preston. Many athletes were happy to give of their time and energy, but I had a feeling that others were there strictly for the positive publicity and the photo op.

When we arrived, the sports stars were already being seated at their tables. Members of the press were getting cameras and lighting set up, some flipping through notes or checking their phones.

"Dani, look at this," Preston whispered. "Do you see who's over there?"

I looked to the left. Tyler sat all the way at the end of the table, smiling but looking vaguely nervous.

"Why the hell would he be here?"

"Preston, come on. Maybe he wanted to help some kids too? It's a charity. Relax. Let's do our usual thing and get out of here."

There were times when I was less than happy with my husband, and that day was one of them. He grabbed his cell phone, punched in his agent's number, and went outside to talk to him. His agent, Kurt Barrett, had been with Preston since before we were married.

I didn't bother following him; I stayed and watched everyone get set up. Tyler noticed me and smiled in my direction. I nodded back. It then occurred to me that this appearance was something Tyler might not have arranged himself. Maybe the hospital administration had reached out to him, thinking it would be nice to have both the Harrington brothers. Either way it was just for a charity, and I didn't imagine that Tyler was doing it out of spite.

Preston came back after about five minutes. He smiled anytime a camera slid his way, but I saw his face was flushed. I can only imagine the reaming Kurt had probably gotten. Preston could be a downright asshole if he thought anyone was getting in the way of his spotlight.

"Hey, let's just be nice, okay?" I whispered out of the corner of my mouth. "If you really think there is something wrong about him being here, you can ask him later."

"Of course."

Preston took his place on the panel, and soon enough the questions began. He was placed at the far left while Tyler was on the far right. I think it only happened that way because everyone else was already seated. I wonder if anyone figured out that the two brothers were better off not sitting together.

Each athlete took questions, but the conference was stolen by a basketball player who had brought his three-year-old daughter with him. She broke in while other people were talking and happily asked the adults her own questions. Everyone thought it was precious and played right along. I was relieved when it was over and we could move on to the reason I really wanted to be there: to go upstairs and visit the patients.

***

By the time we got to the children's ward, Preston was in better spirits. There's really nothing like being around sick little ones to make you stow your own shit. I ended up visiting some kids on my own, preferring to stay away from cameras. Frankly, I never liked getting recognized in public for being Preston's wife—I mean, I did have a life outside of him, and I didn't live it in the spotlight for a reason.

I sat for a while with a five-year-old girl named Brittany: a green-eyed little child with a button-shaped nose and round, pink lips. Her skin was so thin and pale that I could see the veins in her head and neck. We talked about her favorite show, a Japanese cartoon about unicorns fighting an evil wizard. She let me polish her nails with a shade of purple with silver glitter. I had to wear a mask to even go in her room. Her little hands were so delicate and her nails so tiny that I struggled to keep my own hands from shaking. I tried to not let these things get to me, and I was mostly successful. She smiled and laughed as we talked, so I hoped I had put up a good front.

I tried not to stare at all the machines around her or the IV in her left arm. I held it together as long as I was in the room. Once I said my goodbyes and was out of her sight, I ran for the bathroom. I didn't want her or any of the other kids to see me cry.

I took a few minutes and washed my face. When I entered the corridor, I heard music. Someone was playing the guitar.

I followed the sound down the hallway and to the left. Several people surrounded one room, including several reporters. Curious, I had to look.

In the middle of the commotion was my brother-in-law playing guitar for a little boy who was beaming with joy. He was wearing the jersey for Tyler's team. Apparently the boy was a fan. None of the children had been told beforehand that anyone was coming to see them, so it was a sheer coincidence he had chosen to wear Tyler's team colors that day. I knew Tyler played guitar but was surprised to see him doing it in public.

After the song was done, everyone clapped. The little boy cheered.

I smiled as I watched him interact with the child, teasing him and telling silly jokes. Tyler had two young girls, but it occurred to me he would be a great dad to a little boy, too. Maybe he and his wife would try one more time for a son.

"Tyler, how's it feel to be here with your brother today?" a reporter asked.

"It's great. With our hectic schedules, my brother and I don't get to do much together, so a day like this is the perfect opportunity to come out and do something good for the community."

I blanched. It was a seemingly innocent comment, but the media could spin that seven ways from Sunday. They were always trying to build up antagonism between the two brothers as it was. Preston wasn't going to like this at all.

"Would you say that your career has affected the way you and your brother get along in private?"

Tyler's jaw clenched. I noted a flash of anger in his eyes. This question hit him where it hurt. Then he shook his head slightly and smiled. "I would say that there's never been a rivalry and never will be. I have two older brothers anyone would be proud of."

"Do you think you will ever be able to match up to Preston's—"

I could have punched the reporter right then, but Tyler cut him off before he continued with his nonsense. His voice remained modulated, but there was no mistaking the look in his eyes. "Today is about the kids. We can talk football stats at another time."

***

I caught back up to Preston about fifteen minutes later, and though he hadn't been there to see the incident with the reporter, I could tell he knew about it somehow. His mood had changed. The shift was imperceptible to the strangers around him, but to me it was as clear as the wind signaling an oncoming storm. I saw the way he tracked the clock on the wall, the look in his eyes, and his quick movements. He was anxious to leave.

We were in the car before he spoke to me.

"They asked me questions about my relationship with my brother," Preston said.

"What did you say?"

"I said, 'No comment.'"

"Shit, Preston. The reporter started it with Tyler. Your brother said there was no rivalry and that he would be happy to talk about football later."

Neither one of us spoke for a while. I think he realized the real fuck-up was his own. Tyler had handled the situation perfectly. A "no comment" from Preston would just look like he was disagreeing, that he had something to hide.

"Whatever they're going to say, it can be smoothed over by your publicist." I attempted to soothe him. "It's really nothing. Even if people think there is something going on between you two, some kind of rivalry, it won't matter as long as you don't do anything to feed into their perception."

"Are you trying to handle me?" Preston asked. He only took his eyes off the road for an instant, but the glare he gave me did nothing but piss me off.

"I'm reminding you of what you already know but don't want to think about."

"I want to know why he even had to be there! If he hadn't, this wouldn't be a problem."

"What did your agent say?"

Preston shook his head. "He said he had no idea who invited him down there. I mean, come on, this has been *my* event for years. He just wanted to get the attention."

"Really? Everything's about you. What, can't the hospital take anyone else's money or respect someone else's time?" I regretted it the moment I said it, but it was too late to take it back. I knew this was going to make things uncomfortable, but I had no intention of apologizing because it was true.

***

One of the problems with being married to anyone for fifteen whole years was I knew all my spouse's weaknesses. By the time we got home it was obvious that Preston was giving me the silent treatment. Of all the things he could do to me when we got into a disagreement, being ignored was the worst. I didn't like petty arguments. Sometimes, there were things I felt the need to stand up for. This was one of those times for one good reason—I wanted my husband to understand this whole thing wasn't as important as he made it out to be.

He ordered pizza and had dinner with the twins in front of the television, watching a movie. When Ethan and Isabel asked if I was joining them, their father said I had work to do, maybe another time. I kissed my babies on the top of their heads (which Ethan cringed from, of course), grabbed a couple slices of pizza, and retreated to my office space. I wasn't going to argue with him in front of the kids, so I got on my laptop, hoping to distract myself with games and social media.

I tried to comfort myself. Preston didn't spend enough time with the twins, and I thought I should look at this as a good excuse for him to do something fun with them. He'd excluded me, but I was determined not to let it hurt my feelings. He probably hadn't meant it that way anyhow. One of the few things I didn't like about him was his occasional thoughtlessness when it came to things like that.

I came down later to make sure that the twins got their baths and were off to bed on time. When Preston came to bed just before midnight, he wouldn't even look at me. He slipped into bed and laid down.

"I can't believe you're really upset about an offhand comment Tyler made. He probably didn't mean anything by it. Have you even thought to ask him what he meant?"

He shrugged. "You're defending him a lot all of a sudden."

"I just think that by the time the next news cycle hits, no one will care."

"My career has been based on my reputation. It's more important now than it used to be. I can't afford for people to tie anything negative to who I am."

"Okay, fine," I said. I snapped off the light and laid down with my back to him.

"I was going to tell you before," I said. "I want to take the kids to my mom's for the Memorial Day weekend. I think maybe I should take them by myself. Maybe a little time alone will help you sort things out."

It was only three days, and the original plan was that he would come up to my mom's with us. What I really wanted was for him to tell me he was sorry and maybe we could at least agree to argue about it tomorrow. I wanted to ask him about what he had been doing all the times he said he was going to work when his schedule was clear. But I knew better than to bring that up—it was a nuclear option. There are just some times it's not worth the added bullshit.

"Okay, that sounds like a good idea." He kissed my cheek and rolled over to go to sleep.

Chapter Five

Preston Harrington

Danielle and the kids headed out early the next morning. I saw them off with kisses goodbye and admonitions to the twins to be good. Isabel grinned. Ethan just shrugged. They both knew their grandmother would spoil them, so being good was probably not a part of the equation for the weekend.

Once they were gone, I decided to take a run.

It was still cool and misty outside, and dark enough that I figured no one would pay attention to a guy in a hoodie on a jog. Our community is gated, and the neighbors were used to seeing me come and go.

I hadn't jogged through the neighborhood in years. I put in my ear buds and scanned the houses on either side of the street. The whole lane was eerily quiet. There were lights in the houses of the early risers, but no one was out on the street. The times I drove past, I hardly paid any attention, always focused on getting back to my own house. But as I ran, I noticed that some of the houses had changed, especially one on a particular street.

What caught my eye was a two-story Victorian about five blocks from my own house. It was gray, trimmed with white, and freshly painted. I had the vague memory that it had previously been some other color, maybe white or a pale yellow. I paused for a second, staring, because it reminded me of a house in the neighborhood where I'd grown up. I hadn't thought about that old house or the people who lived there for many years—for good reason.

***

Jim Davis was one of the kids I knew all the way through school. We had known each other since I was in first grade and he was in third, when we went to the same elementary school. I wouldn't say we were particularly friends, but we had played sports with each other. I'd never had problems with him until I got on the football team in middle school. Jim lived in an old Victorian a couple of streets over from the house where I grew up.

The year I turned fourteen, Tyler was nine years old. My little brother was virtually my shadow, following me whenever I let him. We had a special closeness as kids. Gregory, our older brother, was already in college at Ole Miss and playing football, poised on what looked to be a long and promising career in the game.

Once Greg started getting offers from the NFL, attention was drawn to Tyler and me in a way we didn't expect. People had always respected our father, who was well known as a former quarterback and a sports announcer. Harrington was a name that had come to be recognized for excellence in sports. He was on the air every Sunday during football season, laying out the truth about players, coaches, and teams.

Once people were viewing Tyler and me with new respect, like maybe we could carry on what our dad had started and our older brother was making good on, those expectations, even the ones unspoken, added a pressure that had not been there before.

My father is proud to tell anyone that he never pushed any of his sons into football, only supported us once we knew it was our goal. Our love of the game was ingrained into us by our lifestyle, the fabric of our family memories, and of course, in our DNA. I can't speak for Greg or Tyler, but I never truly imagined any other life for myself.

A few kids from my school took the opportunity to hassle me. Some of them said the coach gave me too much playtime just because I was a Harrington.

But other neighborhood kids turned out to be an even bigger problem. Jim and his cronies went to Rosedale Middle School, a few blocks away. The divider line between middle schools was literally two or three blocks in either direction. That was bad luck for me, because it meant this kid still lived in my neighborhood and could easily find me.

About a month prior, my team had faced off against Jim's school. In the third quarter of the game, the score was almost even. I was running to make a touchdown when Jim came at me like a freight train. I was knocked backward, fell, and hit my head hard. I remembered looking up and seeing stars. They took me out of the game, and I got as far as the bench before I started throwing up. I can't remember anything else during that game or the rest of the afternoon. I remember waking up in bed later that night. My dad explained what had happened and reluctantly told me that my team had lost.

Jim got pulled off his team soon afterward, and apparently they had been losing ever since. Rumor was that my dad complained to school officials that Jim was too big to be playing with the other kids, and that they removed the boy because of it. I didn't know if that was true or not. If so, my father didn't tell me.

Jim was his team's secret weapon—brawn without brain—and they couldn't function without him.

One day, Jim and four of his buddies were waiting for me after school, all of them taller than I was. I didn't have my growth spurt until a couple years later. Coward. He knew he couldn't take me by himself, but there was no way I was going to beat their whole pack.

"You think you're hot shit, like you're going to be somebody. You're not anything," Jim called out to me.

I ignored him and his gang and started to cross the street. Already approaching the last residential block before my own street, I was hoping I could get home instead of having to fight all of them.

That hope was short lived. I was in the intersection when I was shoved to the ground. My books fell and scattered over the concrete. I got up and looked at them one to the other. I wasn't sure which one of them had pushed me, but Jim was laughing the hardest.

"Oh, you think your brother is a big deal too, huh? I heard he's going to get his ass kicked in the game next week. Just like you're about to get now."

Four on one they started beating on me, right in the middle of the street. I took a fist to the cheek, a kick to my butt, and a knee to my lower back.

As I squirmed to get away, I threw in a few punches and kicks, desperately trying to protect my eyes, midsection, and privates. After what seemed like hours but was probably only several long minutes, the brilliant gang determined that beating me up in the middle of the street wasn't the best idea. But they still had more horror in store for me.

"Hey, guys. Back here," said Jim. They surrounded me and, half dragging my unwilling legs, forced me to walk to an area between a couple houses that was sheltered from the street with foliage. In one of the houses lived an older lady who was usually home. Surely she would see me and send help. But soon we were in an area where no windows faced me and even a passing motorist would not look.

"Hey, guys, I've got a better idea," said Jim, smiling. "Watch this."

I realized my worst nightmare was coming true when Jim pushed me down, unzipped my zipper, and then grabbed my pants leg. I held tightly to my belt loops, but again with four guys working together, they easily removed my jeans and underwear. Their laughing and taunting dug a pit of hate deep in my soul.

I rolled over and curled into a fetal position, covering my privates as best as possible, which made the boys laugh even louder.

"Hey, star football player, did you want these?" asked Jim, holding up my clothes.

"Yeah," I muttered quietly.

"What? I didn't hear you. Speak up a bit."

"Yeah!" I yelled, which made the boys laugh all over again.

"Well, I think you need to earn them. Guys, what should we do to let him earn back his clothes?"

"Make him bark like a dog," shouted one kid.

"OK. Bark like a dog, Preston, and we'll give you your clothes back."

I didn't trust them for one second and stayed quiet, not even wanting to look at their faces.

"Hey!" Someone—I assume Jim—kicked me. "I'm talking to you. Do you want your clothes back or not? If you do, bark like a dog."

"Ruff . . . Ruff," I said without spirit, playing along in hopes they'd tire of this game.

"Is that good enough, guys?"

I was surrounded by a chorus of nos.

"Well, you heard it, Preston. That wasn't good enough. Give us a real bark. Only if you want your clothes back."

I said nothing.

"Preston!" Jim kicked me again. "I told you to bark."

"Ruff! Ruff!" I screamed.

The boys again laughed. "C'mon, Jim, let's go play football at the park. He's had enough," said one of the boys.

Finally, someone with mercy.

"OK. We'll go. We'll leave the big football player alone. But I think we'll take this little trophy with us."

"No!" I screamed and grabbed for one of the pants legs that was dangling from Jim's hand. But the boys ran off with my bottoms, leaving me bare naked from the waist down and a block from my house.

My first thought was to scurry out of there before any of the boys decided to come back. I sprinted to the nearest tree for shelter. I broke off a lower leafy branch to hold in front of me and then made my way from backyard to backyard, about ten yards at a time where I would stop behind some tree or bush, check for people or dogs, choose a new goal to dash to, and then run with all my might toward the next protected area. I wished I hadn't chosen to wear a bright red shirt that day.

At one point I heard someone yell, "Hey, kid, get out of my yard!" *So now you see me? Where were you a few minutes ago when I was getting my ass kicked?* I felt nothing but hatred toward humanity.

With only three houses to go, I had to get past a group of three elementary-aged boys who were playing in the backyard. I knew these boys. They were friends of Tyler. Thankfully Tyler wasn't with them at the time. But they were running all over the yard with their arms extended to the sides, like they were airplanes or something. How could I get past without them seeing me? The front of the house wasn't an option. I waited a few minutes behind a tree but realized the longer I waited, the more likely some adult would see me and my bare butt. I decided to dash across the yard and into the next one that had a huge bush to hide behind. The young boys hooted and hollered, clearly entertained by my lack of clothing. When safely hidden behind the bush, I called over the nearest boy.

When he got near enough, I grabbed him by the sleeve so he couldn't run off. "If any of you ever tell anyone, and I mean anyone, what you just saw, I'll kill your dog. So you had better go back to your playing and forget real quick that you ever saw me here. Do you understand? And you make sure and tell the other boys. If any of you ever tells, it's your dog that dies." The kid whimpered and looked like he would be sick. "Promise me." I yanked harder on his sleeve. The kid was so flustered by this time, he could barely speak. "Promise me!" I demanded.

"I p-p-promise."

"Good." I released his sleeve. "Now, go play."

Finally I reached the house next door to mine. I ran the last distance into the backyard of my own house and peeked in the window to see where in the house my mom was. Luckily, she was in the kitchen and her back was turned. I hurried to the front door and ran up the stairs before she could see me.

Once safely in my room, I put on some clothes, curled up on my bed, and sobbed. I knew I was too old to cry, but I couldn't help it. As I relived the scene in my head—the pain, the shame, and the humiliation—my tears turned to rage. I would figure out a way to get revenge.

Something else happened that day too. Something I never planned to tell anyone.

But for now I had to clean up before my mom came up to ask me about my day. She would have demanded to know what happened. I forced myself to get into the bathroom to wash out my cuts. When she did ask later about my black eye and cut lip, I told her I'd tripped and fallen, which I figured was close enough to the truth anyway. Tyler gave me a funny look, but I didn't tell him either. No one would ever know the depth of my shame.

When I look back, that summer was the beginning of secrets that were too big for me to share with my little brother. I've always thought that was part of growing up. You become distant to other people and learn to take care of yourself without help from anyone.

I didn't go to school the next day, which was a Friday. I was pretty sure the boys would be waiting for me again. I told my mother I was sick, and though she didn't seem to quite buy it, she didn't argue. I was lucky that my father was out of town for work. He didn't believe in days off unless we had a high fever, and he always checked for a temperature.

I wasn't scared of dealing with Jim. I just needed some time to figure things out. On Friday afternoon, my mother played cards with her friends. It was my luck that she wasn't hosting the game that week. I would have most of the day alone. If I was lucky, I wouldn't need more than an hour to get things done.

∗∗∗

Jim came from a nice enough family. His father was a doctor; his mother stayed home. Watching his house was easy. They lived across the street from the park, so I went out there and sat hidden beneath the shadow of the trees, watching.

The family owned two cars. When I got there, the sedan Jim's father drove was gone; his mother's white jeep sat out front.

After about a half hour of waiting in my perch across the street, I saw her come outside. I smiled when I saw her get in her car and leave.

We lived in what people considered a secure neighborhood. No one was naïve enough to leave doors unlocked, but they were comfortable leaving a window or two open, especially around the back of the house. Home alarm systems were available, but I didn't know of anyone in our neighborhood who used them. It made my plan that much easier.

I crept in through the window of what must have been a den. Two sofas and a television flanked a wooden coffee table. A few toys were scattered around, including a teddy bear and a handful of GI Joes on top of an end table.

I made my way through the first floor. The house was eerily quiet. I reminded myself that I didn't need to waste time. Jim's mom might only be on the way to pick up something quick from the store or at the dry cleaners. If she came back and found me, things were going to get messy.

The kitchen would have everything I needed. I had seen something once on a movie I watched with my older brother that I wanted to try. I thought about just turning on the gas stove and leaving it, but I realized that might not work. As I recalled, the actors had turned on the stove and left it for several hours before anything happened. Someone might come home and turn it off. I couldn't control the result if I chose that route.

So I switched gears to something I had learned in science class at school. All I needed was some oil. My teacher had mentioned how flammable oil was. This would be my own personal science experiment. I rummaged around and found a large bottle of corn oil in a kitchen cupboard that looked like it would do just fine. I took the bottle and trickled it around the house, leaving a trail from the kitchen floor and all the way through the back, to the den. The pillows, the teddy bear, and the overstuffed couches would make excellent kindling. I poured more oil there, emptying the last of the bottle onto the cushions and then tossing it aside.

I smiled as I lit the first of the matches I'd brought with me from our kitchen cupboard at home. The crackling sound of the flames licking up the oil was pure ecstasy. I watched as the fiery stream snaked its way across the floor and slowly crawled up the wooden floor in the hallway. *Faster, faster*, I egged it on in my mind. Once the wood caught, it was like magic. Fire hissed as it flicked down the trail of oil, black smoke curling toward the ceiling. As a last measure, I did go ahead and turn on the gas stove burners. Why not?

Then I scrambled back to crawl out the window I had entered through and stealthily made my way back across the street. Mouth dry, heart pumping hard, I climbed into a live oak tree. From my perch, I remained obscured from the road by tree limbs and shadows.

The first curls of smoke were nearly impossible to detect from afar, but I knew where to look and watched as they crept along, folding around from the back to the sides of the house. Soon smoke poured out anywhere it could find an outlet in the front of the house. Then came the sound of shattering glass. With the windows broken, the air that rushed inside fed the hungry flames. Black smoke surrounded the house and flowed out into the street.

I had never known excitement like that. I felt strong, invincible. I had to cover my mouth with my hand to keep from laughing out loud. As the flames grew, so did this feeling of power inside me. I had created something powerful with my two hands and a few matches. I felt a kind of pride in knowing that.

There was no saving that house. By the time the fire trucks arrived, flames had engulfed the second floor and caught hold of the attic. Thick black smoke poured from every opening. People gathered on the street and the opposite sidewalk watching it burn. I could hear their general murmurs, though I couldn't make out the words. They were pretending to be horrified, but I was certain that underneath they were as entranced by the sight as I was.

I noticed the white jeep making its way back to the house. Jim's mother. She stumbled out of her car and looked up at the house in what must have been disbelief. I could see her mouth was open. Her body shook.

Two of the firemen on the scene turned when they heard her screaming. They were prepared to hold her back for her own safety, to keep her from running into the house. They shouldn't have bothered. "My baby! My baby, my baby!" she cried.

Then Mrs. Davis collapsed on her knees in the middle of the street.

A few neighbors emerged from the crowd to pull Jim's mom off the concrete. A woman fell to her knees and embraced her for a few moments before another neighbor pulled her to her feet. I couldn't hear what exactly was being said, but my guess was that the firefighters were trying to confirm if anyone had been in the house when the fire started. With her own hysteria and all the noise around her, I had a difficult time hearing what Mrs. Davis was saying.

I had never bothered to check upstairs. It was possible someone was home. Could it have been Jim? I wasn't sure, but I doubted it. In my mind's eye, he was hanging somewhere around the school, pissed off because I had never shown up and he had missed his chance to kick my ass again.

He was probably completely unaware of this drama: his mother screaming in the street like some crazy person while everything they had was destroyed. Boy was he going to have the surprise of his life when he returned to—where his home *used* to be.

I thought of the GI Joes and the teddy bear I'd seen in the house. Maybe a smaller child had been inside? I didn't know if Jim had a brother or sister, had never felt the need to ask. It wasn't the kind of detail I would usually pay attention to.

I stayed in my hiding spot for a long time, savoring each stage of the fire. The firefighters took a couple hours to put out the blaze, collect their equipment, and leave. Mrs. Davis was taken away by either friends or relatives who had come to the scene. Eventually the crowds dissipated as people hurried back to their own homes. Once they were all gone, I climbed down and slowly started up the street toward my house.

The fire was the talk of the town for months. I learned that a person had died in the fire—Jim's younger brother. The Davis family moved away without saying goodbyes, except to their closest friends. One of the kids at school said he heard that they had left the state—relocated to Colorado, where they had other family. I never saw Jim again. I was surprised, even a little disappointed, that none of Jim's friends bothered to pick on me after he was gone. I don't know if they suspected a connection between me and the fire, but I wasn't scared of them anymore. I was just waiting for them to try something, because if they did, I planned to make them very sorry.

At least I never had to see Jim again. I could settle for keeping the secret. I paid attention to each newspaper article about the incident. I even cut a few of the pieces out and hid them in my nightstand. Jim's little brother had been a five-year-old named Eric. According to Mrs. Davis, he'd had a bad cold the morning of the fire. She had given him the last of the medicine she had in the house—which most likely made him sleepy—and then headed out to the store to get more cough syrup and some groceries. She had been planning to make soup for him. He had died of smoke inhalation. They found his remains inside his bedroom, upstairs at the back of the house. By the time they arrived on the scene, firefighters had no way to reach him.

The police believed the fire to be a clear case of arson, but from all accounts they had no evidence that linked the fire to anyone. I had taken care that no one saw me. Though I was nervous about it for a few weeks, nothing happened. By the middle of summer, the investigation went cold. The newspapers didn't have any new information about the fire to print. The blackened wreckage was torn down, a new house built in its place. Within seven months another family had moved in. The Davises and the fire that killed their youngest child seemed like a distant memory. It was such a deep secret that I nearly convinced myself it had never happened at all.

Chapter Six

Preston Harrington

After I finished my jog, my plans were to spend the day alone. I love my family, but there were times when it was hard to be around them and put up with the noise in my head. Life had been stressful enough lately without keeping one step ahead of what everyone else thought.

Since last year, I'd had a hard time keeping my focus. I hadn't realized how much the game kept me centered. These days as I worked, I wasn't getting the same kind of gratification. Anxiety had been building up inside me for a while.

Now early evening, I got in my car and drove around. I had no place specific in mind, but I ended up at a favorite watering hole. I was about to get out of the car when I felt my phone vibrate in my pocket.

I expected it would be Danielle checking in. Instead, it was my brother sending a text:

Hey, hope you're good. Would like to meet up soon.

I shook my head. After his appearance at the hospital, this was the closest thing to an apology I could expect from him. Did he think I didn't realize that? I fired back a quick reply so he wouldn't bother me again:

Remember Grinder's? I'm getting a beer tonight. Call me next week.

I shoved my phone in my jeans pocket and went inside the bar.

Grinder's is my favorite bar from back in the day. We made a lot of memories there. I had my first (legal) drink there when I turned twenty-one. Later I would always drop in whenever I was in town. There used to be pictures of me and my friends behind the bar. It's one of those places where the food is as good as the liquor. Danielle loves their fries.

As I walked in, I took a casual look around. I wore my baseball cap low. I wasn't in the mood to get recognized, but it was a possibility whenever I was out. One lonely drinker sat at the far end of the bar. Several college kids were gathered in the center of the room, watching a basketball game on a big screen that took up half a wall. There was always some form of sports on, even if it was a soccer match from overseas. A couple kids glanced over to see who had entered the bar, but I looked the other direction.

I took a seat at the middle of the bar. The bartender wasn't anyone I had met before, a dark-haired Italian with a familiar smile. I gave my order and pulled a twenty from my wallet, happy to not have to chat with the regular bartender who was usually there. This guy looked like he could be the son or brother of the regular guy.

When he slid me my drink, I looked down to avoid conversation and took a long sip. I was there simply to get out of the house for a minute. As much as I wanted time to myself, the quiet had begun to irritate me.

Danielle hadn't bothered to call me when she made it to her mother's, but she had sent a text. She attached a picture: a selfie with the kids, her mom, and a couple of her cousins sitting around a firepit in the backyard. The kids were roasting marshmallows. Everyone looked happy and relaxed. It was a small reminder that I wasn't needed there.

I texted back a smiley face.

I noticed a glance from the guy at the opposite end of the bar. He was nursing a whiskey and watching the replay of a game that featured none other than my brother Tyler. I guessed he was probably on number four at least. There's a look you see from guys when they haven't hit that magic number of drinks that will make them start acting stupid but they are inching really close to it: glassy eyes and restless hands that played with his napkin and the bowl of peanuts beside him.

"Hey," he said.

I didn't look up.

"Hey, you over there?"

I looked from left to right. "You mean me?"

"Yeah. What do you think about Tyler Harrington?"

I turned away, staring straight ahead. I could hear the barkeep was in the back, emptying out crushed ice. I could see a few pieces bounce across the tile floor.

"What about him?" I asked.

I looked at the man this time. He was of medium height and frame, with red hair and a thin beard and sporting a flannel shirt, jeans, and an old leather jacket. Ordinary Joe.

When he looked back at me, I looked into my beer again.

"I mean, you've heard the rumors, right? Do you think they're going to trade him next season?"

"Well, I don't know. My guess is good as yours."

"See, I look at it like this. His brother is retired now, and there won't be any competition between the two of them anymore. I think Tyler was the better player between the two of them. And he didn't always whine when stuff didn't go his way. Seemed like he cared more about his teammates. Know what I mean?"

"No, not really." Did this guy recognize me, I wondered? Was he egging me on?

"Uh huh," the stranger replied and knocked back the remainder of his drink.

Just when I thought that was going to be the end of it, the asshole started up again.

"I met him once, after a game, and he signed an autograph for me. Didn't run off, either. Hung around for a few minutes and had a real conversation about the game. That was when I knew he was genuine. That brother of his, though? That Preston is a real piece of work."

"I don't pay attention to tabloids," I said, getting up. "You have a good night, though."

I left a tip and headed out. I'd parked in the back, and I took the alley as a shortcut.

I heard footsteps behind me, and I turned around. The stranger was right behind me.

"Can I help you with something?"

"I knew that was you," he replied, chuckling. "I'd know your face anywhere."

"The fuck is your problem, man? I came here to have a drink, that's all. Why don't you go bother somebody else?"

"I just wanted you to know you were shit for a player. Everyone knows it. The media, the fans. You're just so busy believing your own hype because the commentators have been kissing your ass for years."

I'd had enough of his attitude. I grabbed him by the throat.

His eyes got huge and his mouth opened wide. He tried to grab at my arms, but I squeezed tighter. Lifting him up, I backed him into the brick wall. I pulled him back far enough to beat his head against the brick. He kicked my shin, but I didn't flinch. I slammed his head into the wall.

He tried to fight back. He landed one hit square on my chest, and I shoved his head into the wall twice more. Upon the third hit, I heard it—a satisfying crack.

He shook. His eyes rolled back in his head. I stood there, still holding him upright. A vile sound came from his throat, one I recognized. The death rattle.

His hand fell from my jacket sleeve. His body went limp. His head lulled forward, and a drop of blood and spittle escaped his still-open lips. I let go of him, and his weight sagged to the ground. A trail of blood from the back of his head smeared the wall. It had taken only a few moments for him to enter the alley breathing and to die slumped at my feet.

I looked toward the mouth of the alley. No one was there, but that didn't mean someone might not come through.

"You shouldn't have fucked with me," I whispered.

I bent down, yanked his watch off his wrist, and stuffed it into my jeans pocket. Then, after pausing a second, I also grabbed his wallet to hopefully make this situation look like a robbery gone bad.

Noticing a dumpster nearby, I shoved it over, barely concealing the guy. I needed only a few minutes—time enough to get to my car without being seen.

I walked away from the dead guy, hands in pockets, and wandered onto the street. Another street backed up to the parking lot. I went the long way around. Once I was finally in my car and had pulled out into traffic, I laughed. I couldn't believe this had happened in such a random way.

My heart was pumping fast. And something else . . . I was fucking *hard*.

I thought I'd drive around a bit. After I'd traveled several miles down the freeway, I stopped to use the restroom at a 7-Eleven in a suburb I'd never heard of before. After slipping on a cowboy hat from my back seat and pushing it down low on my forehead—no one expected an athlete to wear such headgear—I walked casually through the store without giving the clerk, who was busy ringing up a Slurpee for a customer, any eye contact. Checking my clothes in the mirror, I found a smear of blood on my dark blue jacket. The smear looked black, nothing that you would see if you didn't know it was there. I would get rid of the jacket later. I had two other similar ones at home. Danielle wouldn't even miss it. I checked through the dead guy's wallet, grabbed the cash and driver's license from inside, and stuffed the remainder at the bottom of the trash underneath a wad of paper towels.

I emerged feeling calmer but still buzzed. The unseasonably cool air only added to my feeling of being intensely alert. I filled up the tank, grateful this station let me pay at the pump this late at night, and got my car back on the road. Still on an adrenaline high, my thoughts rushed. Had I left anything behind? There had been no cameras in that alley, but surely some were active in other places. No one inside the bar had paid attention to me. Except for the dead man. Would anyone miss him right away? He hadn't scratched me, but I thought of DNA evidence and fibers . . . it seemed there was always something like that.

I was both thrilled and terrified.

It had all happened so fast. I hadn't intended to kill him, maybe to just rough him up. He was there, I was there, and all the built-up anxiety had found its release. I felt more alive. I could swear that everything seemed brighter—the lights on the road, the sound of traffic. I was aware of everything, even the pumping of my own blood.

I needed a way to trace my thoughts, to keep everything on track, at least until I could record it in my book. I had started making these voice memos on my phone.

Previously when I'd followed my urges, I hadn't thought of a way to memorialize things. Using my phone to record was simpler, since I didn't always have my book handy. I felt better after I got things off my chest so I could understand the order of things.

I recorded everything I could remember about the evening starting with my conversation with the guy in the bar. I included his name, too, since I'd read it from his license. Steve Bishop. Ordinary name for an ordinary guy.

I spoke into my phone: "I still haven't calmed down yet and it's been hours.

"While I'm recording this, I am in my car, parked on the waterfront. I came out here to stare at the waves, watch the boats go by. All this time, I thought I would feel so empty without football. It turns out that other things satisfy me just fine.

"I wonder what is in store for me next. I realize—have realized for a while now—that I'm just not like other people. I'm more powerful than others. I have the power to choose who lives . . . and who doesn't. I'm the Joker from Batman. Except better. I don't wear clown makeup, and no one knows who I am. At least they don't know *that* guy."

This game was one I enjoyed immensely.

Chapter Seven

Danielle Harrington

I came home on Sunday night instead of Monday morning because I missed Preston.

When I got home with the kids, he wasn't there. It was already late, so I made a quick dinner and got Ethan and Isabel to bed.

"Where's Daddy?" Isabel asked, face turned up in a frown.

"Working late, sweet pea." I kissed her cheek. "He'll be home a little later. Come on. Time to get in your jammies."

Truth was, I didn't know where he was; I could only guess. You don't tell a kid shit like that. You just lie and hope you're doing a good enough job that they won't realize anything's wrong until they're on some therapist's couch when they're about thirty years old.

But I couldn't keep the nagging worry from popping into my head: was Preston seeing another woman? Why wasn't he home late on a Sunday night? My confidence in our relationship was wavering. Preston was a handsome man—and famous. Surely he had lots of opportunities in his life to meet beautiful women. And if he were seeing someone, how would that affect the kids?

As good a home as we gave our kids, I routinely worried about fucking them up emotionally. My parents had never been the best example of parenthood; they were strict about rules but not at all affectionate or attentive. I felt like I was always trying to either do things to make them happy or acting out because they could be so controlling. I worried that maybe I wouldn't know if I were a head case.

Preston had similar issues, only a little worse. He said his mother was prescribed Valium when he was small, and soon moved up to four-martini afternoons. Don't get me wrong, I loved him. But other than being sports royalty, I wasn't sure his family was a shining example of normalcy.

Once the kids were in bed, I went downstairs and opened a bottle of red wine. I needed some time to escape from my thoughts. I took the bottle and my glass up to my bedroom. I turned on Netflix and watched a comedy show I had only seen part of, a stand-up comedienne who made her living on jokes about her ex-boyfriends and the deteriorating state of the world. I tried to stay awake, but I was entirely too comfortable. By the time I finished my third glass, there was no use in even pretending I could stay awake. I closed my eyes to rest them for only a moment and was out like a light.

I woke suddenly later that night; I felt the heaviness of a weight at the edge of my bed.

"Pres?" I whispered. My throat was dry. I sat up.

My husband had his back to me. Still dressed, he half turned. The blue glow of the television lit his profile. He smiled.

"Hey, baby. I was trying not to wake you."

"It's okay." I rubbed my eyes. "Where were you?"

"Just out. Got bored being here alone. I forgot how quiet it can get."

"Yeah. As loud as it was at Mom's, it wasn't the same without you either."

He reached over and pulled me into his arms. We kissed, and I felt his stubble scratch my cheek. I caught his scent, the familiar mix of soap and his aftershave. I closed my eyes to enjoy that smell. It made me feel safe and home, and a little horny.

"What brought you back early?" Preston asked, smoothing a tendril of hair behind my ear.

I shook my head. "I can only take so much of relatives, you know?" I preferred to leave it at that. I didn't want to tell him that I'd been worried for some reason I couldn't explain. It seemed silly to even think that way. I couldn't tell him that when I was halfway to my mom's house, I was ready to turn the car around and come back home just because I had the feeling something wasn't right. I didn't, only because I knew I would look like a jackass for flaking out on my mother and making the kids endure a three-hour car ride for nothing.

He laughed. "Yeah, I hear that." After a pause, he said, "I brought you something."

"You did?"

"Yeah, I've been kind of a jerk lately, so I thought I'd try to make it up to you a little."

"Oh, Pres, you didn't have to."

"Here." He presented the small wrapped box, gazing into my eyes expectantly, like he truly hoped I would appreciate what was inside.

I unwrapped the small box to find a beautiful sapphire ring in my exact size with two tiny diamonds on either side of the blue sapphire. "Pres, it's beautiful!"

"Well, I know how you love the September birthstone and thought you deserved to have one even if your birthday is in March."

I slipped the ring on my finger, having now forgotten why I was upset with him. He was such a thoughtful husband! "How about I run some water and you join me for a bath?" I said. "We haven't done that in a long time."

"Damn, um, would you mind having the bath . . . after?" he teased, kissing my earlobe. "Because I don't really want to wait. We're right here," he said. He traced his tongue along my neck. "Baby, you even taste sweet."

Our clothes were off in no time.

I pulled back from him, just a moment. The lights were low, leaving shadows beneath his eyes. I could see the sparkle in them, that look I had known for so long. Something about the way he looked at me then was familiar . . . and still unknowable.

"What do you see," he whispered, "when you look like at me like that?"

I drew my hand across his bare chest. "How much I love you."

He grabbed me by the waist, pulling me into his arms. Holding my wrists lightly, he leaned above me. Though only his fingers touched me, I could feel the heat of him. He paused for a moment, and I thought maybe he was searching for the right words to say. He'd always been better with actions.

He smiled. "I'm glad you came home. I need you."

It felt good to be in his arms again. We had an active sex life, but that night, I felt like we were more connected with each other again. He took his time with me, something he hadn't done in a while. Maybe my hints about needing to feel closer to him had reached him after all.

Afterward we did take a long bath together. I was so relaxed, and I didn't feel the need to talk or fill up the time.

Once we were back in bed, I fell asleep with his chest pressed against my back.

****

"You look great today," Crystal said, "I mean it."

Crystal and I kept our regular date. On this week we were having lunch. I honestly wasn't feeling like working out, though I didn't want to admit that to her when she worked out five days a week without any complaint. Most weeks I only did one. When she said that she had a yen for a good drink and some hamburgers that day, I was all for it. Grinder's had some of the best, and I hadn't been there in a long time.

"Oh, thanks," I told her. Crystal wasn't one to easily throw out compliments, so she meant it.

"What's up?" she asked. "I know you haven't had anything done."

I laughed. "No, I'm just actually getting some sleep again."

"Things slowed down at work?"

"After this last showing, yes. I swear, I am glad we don't have to do another one that size until next fall."

"You ever think you might just need more help at the gallery?"

"Probably," I admitted. "But then I would hover and worry about if things were getting done right, so what's the point? I think a three-person staff is enough for right now. Pres has been doing things with the kids for the last couple of weeks, so that's made things easier. I mean, I have a little time to myself after work."

She nodded. "You ever think about what it would have been like if you two hadn't had kids?" she asked.

It was a strange question, but I thought about it. "I don't know. I mean, our kids have been the center of everything. I don't know if we would even still be married. Why do you ask?"

"It's the funniest thing. Suddenly, Alan is talking to me about wanting kids," Crystal said.

The waiter brought our drinks a moment later, and I listened to Crystal talk about her fears: how marriage was a nonstarter for her and she wasn't interested in raising kids alone. In a way, she felt much like I did before I met Preston. I was more career oriented than family minded back then. I liked to think of myself as having found a balance in between. I could understand what Crystal said about not being sure whether Alan was the right man and thinking he still might not be the one she wanted to have children with anyway.

"No one is going to be perfect," I said carefully. "I think he's a nice guy, but if your gut is telling you something different, I won't try to convince you otherwise. For instance, I sometimes wish Pres were a little more affectionate with the kids. Even though he's not, I know he adores them. I've no doubt he'd kill anyone who tried to hurt them."

"If that's Preston's only issue, you two are doing well," Crystal said and smiled.

"I'm lucky. Anyway, you should take your time to think about it. He may want an answer right away, but if he's rushing you . . . I mean that gives you one answer about him right there. He's going to need patience. If the two of you are taking things to the next step, then he can't afford to be inflexible with you."

"Yeah, which is what bothers me," she said, tossing her hair over her shoulder. "I think I need another drink."

While my friend tried catching the eye of the waiter for a second drink, I glanced up at the television. The news was on, showing a crime scene.

The bartender walked over to us. I smiled.

"Mrs. Harrington," he said. "Glad to see you stopping in."

"It's been a long time, Louis. How have you been?"

"Pretty good," Louis said. "I am so glad to see some of our old customers like you. In fact, my son says he was at the bar a few nights back when Preston came in."

"Oh?" I frowned.

"Yes, it was his first time seeing your husband in person. I think he may have been a bit starstruck. He couldn't bring himself to ask for an autograph."

"Ah, that can still be arranged! How's business going?"

"As well as can be expected. You didn't hear?"

"Hear what?" I asked.

"A gentleman got murdered out around back a couple days ago," he said. "You can imagine it's been a little slow since then."

"Two days ago?"

"Yeah. I think it was the same day Preston stopped by. Anyway, ladies, let me know if you need anything else."

I stared after Louis. Why hadn't Preston mentioned he'd been here?

"Yikes," Crystal said. "I hadn't heard about that either. That gives me the creeps. Life in the city, I guess."

***

While driving back home, I pondered why Preston hadn't mentioned Grinder's to me. Had he forgotten about it by the time I got home from my mom's?

Preston and I used to go to Grinder's all the time, especially before we had the twins. It was kind of our place. Usually he mentioned anytime that he stopped by there. In fact, I was used to him texting to ask if he could get me an order of fries whenever he stopped in. Grinder's was one of the few places I would bother to get fries. If I was going to waste the calories, there was no use in not getting my favorite.

As soon as I got home, I pulled out my laptop and did a quick internet search. The story popped up immediately:

Steve Bishop was found in an alley adjacent to the bar overnight. An employee at Grinder's discovered the body when he took trash out to the dumpster. The medical examiner ruled the time of death around midnight the previous evening, apparently from blunt force trauma to the head. An autopsy to determine the exact cause of death will be conducted this week.

Bishop was married with three children, ranging in age from seven to fifteen. A source close to Bishop's family states that he was a regular at the bar and went there twice a week.

A string of petty robberies have occurred within the vicinity over the past month, and Bishop's body was found without his watch, cash, or any other valuables on his person. The police stated that they are not at liberty to speak further about any leads on the case while their investigation is still ongoing.

Chapter Eight

Preston Harrington

For the first week after I killed the man at Grinder's, I was relieved and surprised at how easily it had all gone down. The body was found later that night, and though it made the news, it wasn't a major item. People got killed in the city all the time. Outside of the immediate circle of friends and loved ones of the victim, no one else would care. I watched the news clips, and though they talked about the man having a wife and kids, none of his family appeared on camera. They gave a canned response about hoping that people would honor their privacy through this difficult time. I smiled at that. It was all so trite. They didn't care either. Maybe they were waiting on a decent insurance settlement.

In some ways, killing was just so easy. Especially when you were a master at it like I was. I would laugh sometimes about the articles the press would write about me being such a nice guy, a family man. Well, I was a family man, but nice guy? If only they knew! Danielle was happy to be back home, and I made sure I was on my best behavior. I spent more time with the kids, got home in time for dinner every night, and made sure we were having sex most nights of the week. I was being a stellar husband because I didn't want her to make any waves.

On Friday, our daughter Isabel was at her best friend's house for a sleepover. The child's mother, Angie, was a good friend of Danielle's, so the plan was to let Isabel stay part of the afternoon, that night, and then pick her up around eleven the following morning. With Danielle at work, my son and I had the afternoon to ourselves.

"Want to go to the fair, kid?"

"Yes!" Ethan enthused, grinning and throwing both fists in the air.

The fair was an old-fashioned one, cheaply put together, the kind of thing a kid should enjoy at least a few times in their childhood: with a carousel, Ferris wheel, bumper car ride, and a roller coaster with only two loops. I always marveled at how these low-rent outfits seemed to pop up out of nowhere, do business, and then move to a new city within a couple weeks' time. I enjoyed the one that used to come through town when I was a boy. I would take Tyler, and we would spend the whole day.

By evening we would come back with sticky hands and faces from all the candy and junk we had eaten, happy and exhausted. I smiled, thinking how even one cotton candy always made Ethan so energetic, like he was amped up on speed. I was grateful that I could keep up with his running around. Having to work out regularly as part of my job had its benefits. But there were still times when I wished I could have accepted the end of my career better.

My brother Gregory hadn't let his injury stop him from having a full life. It began with the most minor of symptoms that suddenly grew worse: numbness in his hands and fingers. When he went in to see his doctor, he was diagnosed with spinal stenosis. The nerves along his spine were being squeezed. Surgery and physical therapy were to follow, but any chance of playing in the NFL was out of the question; at one point the doctors predicted he might not have normal function. The worst-case scenario was paralysis below the neck. Despite the odds against him, he fought his way back to health.

Greg never let the injury stop him after that. Once he was fully recovered, he moved on to a regular job and a life that suited him well. He'd even made himself a wealthy man in the bargain.

My injury affected my outlook differently. I developed a pinched nerve in my neck, which my doctor believed was caused by a herniated disc. I ended up taking off a whole season to have the problem corrected. After surgery, they started me on anti-inflammatories and later a mild pain killer. I'd been told it was a common injury and that many players had it and did fine on the playing field. I went through a course of therapy prescribed to build up my neck and arm strength.

When I got back to the gridiron, I wasn't the same. The real wake-up call was the opening game of the season, when I was unable to make a single touchdown pass. My so-called recovery had not returned me to full strength. Turning my neck too quickly caused a stinging pain in my neck, even with the medication. And the strength in my arms had not completely returned, which made the situation even worse.

While I could still perform many of my signature moves, I couldn't count on completions of the long balls. The seventy-yard bomb became more of a prayer than a promise. I turned my focus to short routes and audibles. With my physical prowess decreased, I had to use my experience and preparation to make up for what I lacked. I started to rush through plays.

Not being able to turn my head quickly enough created a blind spot. It took me an extra second or two to spot an opening on the field, precious moments that meant the difference between a solid offense and a shaky defense. My worst fear was that one day, I wouldn't see an opponent coming at me until it was too late. Players rushed with the speed of Mack trucks, and I had to be ready for the possibility of a crash.

The surprising thing was that, although fans and commentators noticed my different style of play after the injury, I now excelled at short routes and successfully completed two seasons, even setting a new touchdown record my second season back. And best of all, I led my team to the Super Bowl each of those two years. We lost miserably that first year but won the second time around.

The fear of getting another big hit never left me, though, and even while scoring dozens of touchdowns, the pain was affecting me more and more. One more injury would be enough to finish my career for good and possibly do enough damage to impact my daily life. I readily popped pills and accepted Toradol injections from the trainer on game days.

By midseason, I knew that my internal clock was ticking down. Sure, I would always be thankful that I could still do all the normal things a healthy person could, even with a few extra aches and pains. There were trade-offs for the career I'd had, along with the fame and prestige. Pain was to be expected, especially past a certain age. I decided to retire after that final Super Bowl win. Friends, colleagues, and loved ones liked to remind me that I had a storied career and that I had retired the oldest quarterback currently in the league, even with the injuries I sustained. But that knowledge didn't lessen the sting of never playing professional football again.

Back in the present moment, Ethan and I went on the rides first. The bumper cars were his favorite. I took a few pictures and wondered if Isabel would later regret being at her friend's house instead of with us. If she wanted to go, I wouldn't mind taking her later in the week.

Ethan's other favorite was the fun house. He jumped back and forth in front of the mirrors, laughing at the twisted forms that followed him from one spot to another. His childish joy was infectious, and I couldn't help but laugh with him.

"Look, Daddy, I'm a monster!" Ethan cried, baring his teeth and grunting.

"What kind?"

"A werewolf," he said as he crept forward on tiptoe, his arms away from his body, bent at the elbows, wrists limp. His stance reminded me of the zombies from an old music video.

"You don't look that furry to me," I teased.

"I change under the moonlight," Ethan said, his voice an ominous whisper. "That's when my fangs come out too."

I laughed, and the sound reverberated oddly through the space. I followed behind him, my reflection twisted among the many mirrors: a huge head and curved torso, big eyes and a little mouth, a bent back and smile full of teeth standing sideways like leaning tombstones.

By the time six o'clock rolled around, we had been to every ride at least twice and some a few more times than that. I had signed a few autographs for people who recognized me, but mostly people had left the two of us alone today. The weather had been warm during the day, but now I sensed a little chill in the air. Guys I played with from northern climates always laughed at how wimpy we southerners were about a little cold. But, hey, I couldn't change my upbringing. "It's time to go, buddy."

"Can we come back, Dad?"

"Maybe, I'm not sure how long they'll be in town for, but we'll see."

We were on our way to the parking lot, about a couple feet from my car, when someone called my name.

"Preston, Preston Harrington! Can I ask you a few questions?"

I turned on my heel and looked behind me. A man a few feet from us was holding a recording device. The first thing I thought was that he had to have been following me for a while to get so close; either that or he had staked out in the parking lot for hours and had been waiting for me to return. I couldn't figure which possibility made me angrier. Why had they come to ask me questions about the murdered man outside Grinder's right in front of my son? Could I pretend I hadn't heard the reporter? I wasn't prepared with my answers concerning that night. My fury was climbing exponentially by the second.

I got control of my voice enough to respond to the guy. "As you can readily see, this is a family day. I have my son with me. Can we not do this right now? If you would like a real interview, you can call my representative and set something up."

The guy twisted his lip. "Would you like to go on the record with a statement about how your brother described your relationship recently?"

My face relaxed so much, I was afraid the guy might notice. He was inquiring about my relationship with Tyler? I almost laughed. But then I remembered how upset I still was about Tyler.

The reporter was a tall, thin man with glasses and curly hair. Dressed in jeans and a T-shirt, he blended in with the rest of the crowd. I realized then that I had seen him earlier in the day, in different spots. I hadn't thought anything of it. I should have realized before that something was off about him. Why would a young guy be out at a fair, without kids or a girlfriend with him? All it took was one overzealous person with connections to make a phone call.

If one reporter was present, usually others were wandering around also.

I hustled Ethan into the car and slammed the door behind him. Then I gave the reporter my full attention.

"Let's get something straight. You're not going to harass me in front of my kid, especially not with tabloid fodder about what my brother did or did not say. That's my kid's *uncle*. Does that seem right to you?"

"Hey. How you tell your kid about this is not my business. It's not tabloid news, and it's in the press anyway, so he might as well be prepared. I'm only doing my job."

I simply stared at him for a moment. I wondered what it would be like to grab him by the neck and choke him. Right here in the open, with people watching. He was an insignificant gnat. I could kill him or ignore him, but either way his life would not matter. Maybe I would hunt him down and do it later. Show up when he least expected it, while he was alone in his apartment, and snap his neck. Better yet, beat him with a pipe until his skull cracked. Until he bled and his body went still. Something about knowing I had the will of a god and the strength to carry it out was both utterly satisfying and calming.

I smiled. "No comment," I said and backed away.

Chapter Nine

Danielle Harrington

One of the players on Preston's old team was getting married, and the bachelor's party was that night. I sighed when he mentioned it because I had known about it for weeks; it had simply slipped my mind. It wasn't one of these events where they were going out of town, thankfully. I had heard about a couple of those parties getting way out of hand, especially when travel and heavy drinking were involved. I wouldn't have felt comfortable telling Preston not to go anyway. He still loved his teammates, and it meant a lot to him that whenever anything like this was going on, he was still invited.

I stayed up and watched a movie with Ethan, a comedy he liked and had seen before. I put him to bed later than usual, but since it was the weekend, I didn't mind being flexible. It was rare that I got time to spend with him one on one, so I was enjoying it.

I slept lightly that night. I had unpleasant dreams, but I couldn't quite remember them in the morning. By the time

I came downstairs, Preston was up. Ethan was with him, eating cereal.

"Morning, sleepyhead." Preston kissed my cheek. "Now close your eyes."

"Wha—"

"Just close them." He placed his hands lightly over my eyes, placed a cup of warm liquid in my hand, and directed me a few steps to the other side of the kitchen. "Now you can look."

I glanced down first at the cup in my hand and saw a latte with a design in the cream—not quite as professional looking as the coffee art at a coffee shop, but still, thoughtful. And then I saw the beautiful, shiny latte maker on my countertop.

"I know how you like your lattes. Now we can make them at home together."

"Preston, how thoughtful!"

He spent a few minutes showing me how to load in the coffee beans and cream and his best attempt at making an artful design on top. "We'll have to study up on how to make those designs, but until then . . . lattes at home!"

I threw my arms around his neck for a big hug. "Thanks so much, Preston! I love it!" I YouTubed on my phone for tutorials on how to make latte coffee designs. "Say, how was the bachelor's?" I asked, looking up.

He grinned. "Uh, I guess it was what you expect. I mean, I'm happy for the guy and all, but I must admit, I kind of wonder if I'm getting a little too old for the drinking those guys were doing. I missed you, for sure. I have a couple funny stories for you later, when only the grownups are in the room."

"That good, huh?" I laughed.

"Definitely."

"Well, that's going to be awhile then, because I have to pick up Isabel. Will you be around when I get back?"

"Sure, honey," Preston said, smiling.

"Ethan, would you mind coming with me to go pick up your sister from Angie's?"

He looked from me to his father. Preston nodded.

"Uh, sure," Ethan said.

"Go get dressed, sweetheart."

He padded out of the kitchen. I waited until I was sure he was safely out of earshot before speaking.

"I'm just glad you came back in one piece," I teased my husband. "I don't want to hear about any sleazy women laying their hands on you."

"No, ma'am." Preston grinned.

I went upstairs, got dressed, and was ready to go in about twenty minutes. I would have to watch the YouTube latte video later. I was outside getting my son strapped into his seat when Kurt Barrett's car pulled up.

Kurt had a full head of silver hair, and big and bright blue eyes that followed you whenever you entered a room. He had been a sports and entertainment agent for his entire career and had represented Preston for most of his. A salesman at heart, he was the kind of man who could talk you into anything if you let him. He didn't show up in person unless there was serious business to be laid out.

"Good morning," he said as he approached me.

"Same to you," I said. In a softer tone, I asked a question. "Preston didn't get in touch with you last week, did he?"

"No, he hasn't returned any of my calls or texts recently, so I thought I would drop by."

I made friendly conversation with him for a moment, and then he made his way up to the house. As much as he liked Preston, I had never known him to drop by unannounced. What bothered me was that one of the few things left on Preston's schedule was for him to follow up with Kurt. I was surprised he hadn't done it.

***

My trip to Angie's was brief. I picked up my daughter and brought both kids straight home. It only took about forty minutes. Preston wasn't at the house when I got back, and neither was Kurt.

I didn't know what to think about that. Either they'd had a successful talk and both of them were going about the rest of their day, or it had gone badly—and Preston had decided to go do some shit by himself, as he usually did when he was displeased about something. Since he had promised to be home when I got back, I suspected this meant he was pissed about whatever Kurt had to say.

The kids settled in front of the television set, and I looked around for things to do to burn off my anxiety. I have a habit of cleaning when I'm nervous. We have a maid, but I still have a few things I like to do myself, laundry being one of them. Going through dirty clothes seemed a little too intimate to be left to a stranger.

Maybe part of growing up poor is that once you have enough money to afford certain things, like maid service, you feel uneasy allowing people to do everything for you.

There were already a bunch of clothes in the hamper, so I slowly sorted and separated them. Most were Ethan's things, including a couple of shirts that were so muddy I debated just throwing them away. One of Isabel's shirts was almost as bad, but her stains had been from a run-in with a chocolate ice cream cone. Sometimes with kids clothes it wasn't worth the effort; bleach lost the battle eventually. I put the soiled whites to the side and figured I would save those for last.

Among the remaining stack was a few of my jeans and skirts, and three pairs of Preston's slacks.

Over the years, I have gotten used to finding all kinds of things in his pockets, so searching them is par for the course. I find treasures like lighters (for the occasional smoke), pocketknives, and even one of his phones. On this day, I turned his pockets inside out.

A pack of gum and a black matchbook fell out. The red cursive lettering spelled out: *Grinder's*. I threw it on top of the dryer and stared at the matches. I remembered now how that waiter had mentioned Preston being there recently. I had forgotten to ask Preston about that.

Then I saw something else: a spot of brownish red on the inside edge of the matchbook. I couldn't be sure, but it looked like a drop of blood.

*****

Preston Harrington

I invited Kurt in and offered him a drink. It was early for one, but I already knew what kind of conversation we were going to have. I stood by the window and looked out at the pool in the back, trying to keep my nerves at bay.

I had woken up that morning with a nagging pain in my neck, one of many injuries I'd suffered on the field that had finally convinced me to hang up my cleats. Most days I felt a sort of stiffness that tended to dissipate throughout the day. On this day it was a full-on throbbing. I'd taken some pain reliever, and though I had already had one drink, I resolved to take a Vicodin if the pain didn't recede over the next hour.

"I'm not going to take up too much of your time," Kurt began. "I wanted to touch base with you because you're canceling a lot of engagements."

"Okay. So that's a problem?"

Kurt shrugged. "Time off is not a problem at all. I just wish I had known about it beforehand so I could have been more strategic about planning things with a couple of these companies. Papa's Pizza canceled a shoot that cost them a lot of money, and though that may have been okay once, I'm sure a repeat wouldn't be advised. I can tell you Eagle Insurance is stricter about people being there when they want them. Last thing we want is for anyone to get the impression you're hard to work with."

"All right," I said. "Can we still block off my appearances for next month then? I just need some time with my family."

Kurt paused a long time before answering. "We can do that, and I don't have a problem with it. But personally, I would like to know what's wrong."

"What do you mean?"

"Because this isn't you. I think you forget how long I've known you. You've always been a hard worker, and you don't take time off without a reason. Hell, there were times I wished you would have taken time off because you were sick or nursing an injury. If there's something going on, I'd like to know about it, not for business's sake but as a friend. I would like to be able to help."

I was listening intently. He truly meant what he said, but I realized that what he had to say didn't matter to me. I didn't want to tell him about what I felt or complain to him that lately I was in one form of pain or the other, still thinking about the past or fighting the physical effects of my injuries. I wanted time to myself while I figured out what I was going to do about it.

"I wasn't trying to screw up anyone's schedule," I said. "Fine. Clear my schedule for next month then, and if anyone asks questions, tell them I am spending time with my family."

Kurt stood. "All right, I will do that. You may end up with a fairly packed schedule the following month . . ."

"Let's not worry about that until later."

"Can I ask you something else?"

"Sure."

"I have the feeling you have been struggling with your retirement. You haven't been the same. Do you think that maybe you need to speak to someone about it?"

"Kurt, really? Come on. You want me to talk to a shrink?"

"Over the years, I have had several of my clients struggle with the same transition you are going through. I know of a therapist who works specifically with current and former athletes. It's about having a sounding board, someone to listen to you who isn't working on assumptions and judgments. No one has to know about it; if you need a way to get yourself feeling better, I think it couldn't hurt."

"Feeling better? Who's to say I'm not fine in the first place?"

"Look, I wasn't going to push this subject," Kurt continued. "We haven't been talking much lately, and I'm a little concerned."

"You're worried unnecessarily," I told him. "If I were having trouble, I would take care of it."

Kurt looked defeated. "All right. I would never push, but I wouldn't be doing my job if I didn't mention it to you. If you were my own son, we would be having the same conversation."

We talked a little longer, but I made it clear that I was not interested in therapy. My thoughts raced. What had made him consider approaching me about it? I hoped he wouldn't ask any more questions because the last thing I could tolerate was anyone nosing around my personal life. He thought of himself as a family friend and I didn't need him raising questions, especially not to Danielle.

At the end of our meeting, I asked him to show himself out.

I took in a deep breath and reminded myself that he'd only walked away from me because I had let him. It was my choice to let him go home to his wife. If I'd had my way, without consequence or mess to clean up, then things would have turned out differently.

Chapter Ten

Preston Harrington

Only a few of my memories are free from darkness at the edges. Most have an overwhelming sense of heat and hate and desperation. Like I'm tumbling into the vast unknown. An abyss. As I've had more time lately to think, I've realized this about myself.

Time was now slipping by, and relentlessly. Sure, the late thirties are still young, but it's not the same kind of youth when the forties are only a couple years away. The more I think about it, the more I realize that whatever that darkness is, or why it has always been there, I was always attempting to push it down or somehow ignore it. Even the happiest times in my life were never quite what they should have been. I have never been sure how to measure "normalcy," whatever the hell that is. I am better and worse than most in a lot of ways, but I have never managed to be average. Time gives you a different perspective, but it also tends to soften the hard edges of things. You tell yourself things weren't as bad as they were.

I met Danielle at a party I never intended on going to, on a night when I wasn't supposed to be out. It was my second year of college, and it was a Sunday night. I was going to have a tough football practice the next day, and I should have been in my apartment sleeping. I had a roommate named Tom, and he prodded me into partying that night.

"Just for a few beers, man. It will be fun. Promise we'll be back before too late." Tom was a tall, lanky kid. You always knew when he was shining you on, but more than likely you figured it would be fun.

We gave ourselves only a couple choices. Either we were going to invite a few people to hang out at our place or we could go out to a house party. Too many people recognized who I was to try anything else. I had to be selective about the people I was around. Any public outing could quickly turn into someone asking for a signature and a picture, since everyone assumed I would someday be a star in the NFL. We ultimately decided it would be easier to show up to the house party than to have our own.

Most of my friends on campus were other football players; we played and practiced together, watched videos, and studied plays. No one else understood how hard the game was or how rewarding. We mostly kept to ourselves, just because it made things easier.

Tom was one of those guys who was popular with a lot of people across the board, someone who seemed to know some out of every tribe. Like in high school, clear lines were drawn between nerds and jocks, loners and popular kids. When asked why everyone knew him, Tom said he was that rare individual whose personality cut through superficial boundaries. More likely it was because he sold weed.

"You need to be, like, among real people," Tom said on the ride over. "There's got to be more to life than football."

"Sacrilege," I said with a laugh.

The Beta house was maybe four blocks from the university. It was behind a gate, covered with so much ivy that you couldn't see the house from the street, except for the Greek letters on the brick front of the building.

"Ever been here?" Tom asked.

"Maybe last semester?" I had a vague memory of being at a party for the team after a victory. The booze had been flowing considerably that night, and my clearest recollection was waking up the morning after with a wicked hangover.

Inside the house was what you'd expect: the converted mansion had a common room on the main level where everyone hung out, some sitting on sofas, others standing, most on different levels of being drunk or high. A fireplace was kept lit for the ambience.

The place was wall-to-wall people, like being in the crowd at a concert. The music was so loud, a person couldn't think, yet ironically you couldn't hear much of the song except the driving bass line.

As soon as we were inside, I started for the back of the house where I spotted a keg in the backyard with a bunch of guys gathered around it, already about three sheets to the wind. As I moved past the kitchen to reach the back door, I grabbed one of a few bottles of beer left floating on ice in the kitchen sink.

"You didn't want to drink from the punch bowl either, did you?"

I turned and saw a pretty brunette with doe-like brown eyes standing behind me. She was thin and of average height, wearing a black dress, not super tight, but enough that not much was left to the imagination. I stared at her for what felt like a full thirty seconds. I was rewarded by a smile and a faint blush of her cheeks. I liked that she held her space and didn't look away or do that nervous fidgeting some girls did the moment you looked at them.

"I have a feeling that's what might have gotten me the first time I was here, but I can't remember enough to be sure."

She laughed at that, a light, sweet sound, and tossed back her long, wavy locks. "Well, pass me one then?"

I did, and her fingers brushed mine when I gave it to her.

I was about to ask her a question, I don't know what, because she was beautiful and my mind was swirling in circles. As I was about to open my mouth, another guy walked in. I looked away long enough to pop open my beer, and next thing I knew, this guy had his arm around the girl's waist.

"Oh hey, there you are," he said to the girl. "I was wondering where you were. I see you met the best quarterback we've had in years."

The girl looked at me and blinked. I could tell she was trying to place where she had seen me before but couldn't quite figure it out.

I smiled. This girl genuinely didn't know who I was! It had been so long since I had met a girl who wasn't more interested in my team and my family than in me. I couldn't remember the last time a girl had showed true interest in me as a man and not because I was a quarterback for the Volunteers. I was the top college draft in the country. Women looked at me with dollar signs in their eyes, calculating whether they had a chance at me and what they needed to do to lure me into a relationship.

"We were watching him play last week," the guy added. "This is Preston Harrington. You know. His father played for the . . ."

"Oh, right," she said. "Nice to meet you. I'm Danielle. This is Josh," she said.

"Middleton," Josh added, and offered his hand for a shake. I took it. Danielle stood back from us both, as if she found the whole exchange mildly embarrassing.

"It's nice to meet you," Josh went on. "I'm from New Orleans too. Last time I went back home, I went to my little brother's high school game. Your brother Tyler was on the opposing team, and I have to say, that kid knows his stuff. Afterward I went up to him to congratulate him on his success. Where is that kid going when he finishes high school?"

"Oh, he won't be coming here," I said with a smile. "He's going to follow our father's example and go to Ole Miss."

Josh started to go on about the game and how he hoped my team would blow away the competition in the next game. He said he would bet good money on us because he knew we could get the goods. I don't even know how long he went on like that. He was a true fan.

Danielle drifted away from us both. I barely got a glimpse of her as she went back down the hall and out of sight.

I let him talk, get it all out of his system before asking another question. "Is Danielle your girlfriend?"

"Working on it." He raised an eyebrow. "She's hot, isn't she?"

"Lucky man," I said.

***

For the next two weeks I made my goal to find out as much as I could about Danielle. She was obviously different from the other women I had met in school, and I wanted to get close to her. She was on my mind constantly, but I didn't know even the simplest things about her.

I mined Tom for information first, and though he didn't know much to tell me, he knew enough for me to use as a starting point.

"Her last name is Sorenson," Tom said. "Friendly girl. Dates around but hasn't had a serious thing for any of the guys on campus, far as I can tell. She might have a boyfriend back home, but if she does, then I've never heard her talk about him. Scholarship kid. She doesn't come from money."

"And you know this because?" I asked.

"Her friend Cindy is a regular customer, so when I do drop-offs, Danielle is usually at home with her nose in her books. She mentioned something once about having to keep up her B average."

After I found out where she lived, I checked out the place. I had to make sure she wasn't living in someplace cheap. Depending on what part of the neighborhood you landed in, some of the off-campus housing could be questionable. Not everyone could afford the condos and houses closer to the north side of campus, even with roommates splitting the rent. As it turned out, Danielle and Cindy shared a nice apartment, a two-bedroom upstairs in the back of a building with only two other tenants. If I timed it right, I could sometimes see the girls going in and out. Cindy worked as a barista at a nearby coffee shop on late nights and weekends, which meant Danielle was often in the apartment by herself at night.

Always maintaining a safe distance, I would borrow my roommate's car—a silver sedan nondescript enough to blend in—to keep tabs on her. Being near her intensified the ache I had at night, the longing. I would lie awake thinking about her. I fantasized about what it would be like when we were finally together. That was something I was going to see through. I already knew she was not simply any woman. Danielle was different. I wanted to know all there was to know about her. I was going to have to figure out how and when I was going to make my move.

About a week after the party, I observed Josh coming to Danielle's house. He arrived with a bouquet of flowers. Danielle came to the door, and they spoke. From my vantage point, they appeared to have a friendly exchange. She invited him in.

Another excruciating twenty minutes passed with the two of them behind closed doors. I gripped the steering wheel tight and stared straight ahead. Was he inside that house touching her? Did he think he had the right to be with her that way? None of the windows were open, so I was unable to even sneak a glance at them. I wished that the panels were thin enough to see their shadows.

At the same time, I knew if I caught a glimpse of Danielle in his arms, that would only make things worse.

Finally, Josh left. I searched his face for a trace of emotion. He didn't have the relaxed smile or walk of a man who had just gotten laid. At least I told myself that he didn't. He would have been grinning from ear to ear. Instead he stared into space, his brow furrowed. If he hadn't been so preoccupied, he might have seen me.

All kinds of thoughts ran through my mind. The important thing was to keep it together. I needed an excuse to bump into her again. I would find a way to make it look natural. With the right planning, I could tip the circumstances in my own favor.

But soon I came to realize that I had made a mistake, one that would have had dire consequences in any competition. I had underestimated my opponent.

***

Sometimes when you're looking for an opportunity, one pops up in a better way than you would ever have planned out yourself.

Josh Middleton stopped me one day. I was in the library, gathering up books for a report I needed to work on for my Western Civilization class. I was leaving as he was coming in. He greeted me. "You going to be here long?" Josh asked. It should have been obvious.

He was too loud and enthusiastic, and the librarian, standing only feet from us, gave him a glare and a little hissing sound from her lips. I couldn't help but smile.

"No. You?" I asked.

"No, man, if you can wait a minute. Want to go grab a beer?"

One thing about the campus is that people usually gave me space. When someone I didn't know well approached me, it was always a little of a surprise. Apparently, because we had met at the party, Josh considered us at least casual buddies.

Any other time I would have said no. I didn't know or like this man. He was apparently seeing the girl I wanted. Instead, I smiled and turned on the charm, the kind I used for interviews and photo ops at the end of a game. "Sure, I can wait for you."

I didn't have long to wait. He was only returning books. Once we left the library, we talked about where we would go. There were two bars within walking distance, and I chose the one I liked best. I can't even remember the name of it now, but it was a dark little hole that played loud classic rock over the speakers. We sat at a booth in the back, shared a pint, and talked.

It might have been more accurate to say that he talked a lot and I listened, throwing in a phrase here or there to help push him forward. It was easy. As the pint grew empty, he was open to nearly anything I asked. What he wanted to talk about was Danielle, and I was eating up every word. He might have been my competition, but I understood well how that girl could get in a man's head.

"Here's the thing," he said, running a hand through his hair. "It's not like she's blown me off, but she doesn't seem that interested. I don't know what I'm doing wrong. I ask her to go out, and she's like, okay, sounds like fun. Other than that? I'm not sure if she just doesn't like me or if she is trying to see what she can get out of it."

"What do you mean?"

Josh shook his head. "I don't know. Some girls like to hang around and see what they can get until the next guy comes along. Get you to wine and dine them, and then when they see a dude with a nicer car or a bigger house, they're gone."

Now that statement struck me as funny. Here he was basically accusing Danielle of being a gold digger. What the fuck did he have to offer any woman? He was average in every way I could tell: height, weight, looks. Brown hair, eyes that could have been blue or green but were most likely a watery hazel. He had thin lips and a straight nose that was small enough to look feminine. This guy had never broken a bone playing any sport, and I doubted he would be good at one. The muscle he did have was built up from the gym, not anything that would have required real stamina or skill.

I didn't know what his money situation was like, but I would have been ready to bet it wasn't much better than hers. Even if he could give her things, he wasn't much to look at. Anything that's not ordinary can make a man stand out, give him his own swag. This guy had nothing of the sort. It was hard not to reach across and just slap him. Instead, I acted sympathetic.

"She didn't strike me that way, but what do I know, I only talked to her for a couple minutes. If that's the case, why are you with her?"

His eyes glazed over. He looked down at his beer for a moment. There was barely any left in his mug, though he didn't reach out to pour another. He sighed. "I don't know, man."

I saw the truth then, beneath the fake bravado and the shady, sideways putdown of a girl he thought could do no wrong. He was in love.

***

Since Josh had been the one who reached out to me, it was easy to take things from there. I called him one afternoon when I knew he would be out of class. We had exchanged phone numbers and talked several times since then. When we hung out, I paid for the beer. His insights into Danielle, even the smallest bits of information he learned about her, were more than worth the cost.

Over time I could see that I was building trust with Josh. After awhile I didn't even need to ply him with alcohol. If I asked him something, he would straight out tell me. I became confident in my ability to manipulate him. He was a simple ass.

"You heard there's going to be a party at Sarah Morrison's house?" I asked. "Saturday night?"

"Yeah, I heard."

"Well, are you going?" I prodded. "Look, I was thinking about what you said. Maybe it's not that Danielle doesn't like you, maybe she's just . . . a little uptight. You might have to work on her awhile to get what you want."

Josh started to make some noises of protest, but I stopped him. "I'm not saying that means you can't get her, it's just sounds to me like you're in for the long haul where

Danielle is concerned. In the meantime, I think you should get out and have some fun, you know? Release some pressure. There's always pretty girls around when Sarah throws a party, and I heard half the cheerleaders will be there too."

He laughed, and I knew I didn't need to persuade him anymore.

***

Sarah Morrison shared her house with two other girls, Jessica and Mindy. They liked to entertain, and I was familiar with a few of the people invited. Though I didn't go often, I always heard about it whenever they were having a party over the weekend. I had a sort of permanent invite whenever the girls were having a get-together.

I knew Mindy the best out of the three, though I hadn't spent much time with her since our last year of high school. She was from my old neighborhood in New Orleans. When her parents divorced, she had moved with her father to Tennessee. Tyler had dated Mindy's younger cousin, Natalie. She had been his first serious girlfriend. My little brother was a Harrington to the bone, always able to woo the pretty ladies.

Josh could have used some of that mojo. When he arrived at the party, I noticed him talking to a girl. Though he smiled, he looked completely uncomfortable. I hung back for a bit, not wanting to interrupt. I then came to a realization that upset me.

Josh might have been a bit of a geek, but I had never seen him as uneasy around Danielle as he was with this girl. In fact, he was much more confident with Danielle. This girl he didn't know made him antsy. It bothered me that he had already been around Danielle long enough to have gotten past that first anxiety a man has around a new girl.

If he couldn't flirt and pick up someone new, it was going to cause problems for him.

I waited until the girl drifted away—maybe she wanted an excuse to be away from Josh—and walked up to him.

"How's that going?" I patted him on the back.

"Nowhere," he said with a smile. "Nice girl, though. Not my type."

"And what is your type?" I asked. "Other than Danielle?"

"Pretty, smart. Funny. It's one thing when a girl doesn't get your jokes, but it's a bad sign when she has no sense of humor."

"Well, don't let that bother you. She might not want to seem too eager." Short of more drastic measures, I'd half hoped he would get interested in someone else. Knowing he was out with other girls would probably end things between him and Danielle, especially if I presented her with proof of it. It didn't seem like he wanted to bite. One solution was slightly messier than the other, but I didn't care.

Josh looked away before finally meeting my eyes. "Maybe just not her."

"Well, she's not the only girl around. Want to smoke?"

"Sure, why not?"

"Come on." I nodded to the stairs. "There's a balcony outside Sarah's room. It's already crowded as fuck down here."

He shrugged and followed me. I had to suppress my laughter. Josh was already making this so easy for me. I had been trying to steer him toward other women for a good two weeks and he hadn't been that interested. The week before that, I had decided that if he wasn't going to back off of Danielle, I was going to have to take care of it myself. I was tired of trying to slowly prod him into seeing the error of his ways. He wasn't going to stop seeing Danielle, so I was going to put a stop to *him*. I already knew how I was going to do it.

I didn't intend on getting drunk or smoking anything. I take care of my body and limit any habit that would be detrimental. I did need him to be comfortable around me. The best way to make an opponent drop their guard is to let them think they're in control.

More importantly, I needed to make sure he was drunk, because that was going to make killing him easier. I'd gotten a couple of blunts from my roommate, because I figured that would help the process along. Josh could smoke both if he wanted.

Sarah's room was unlocked, and the doors to her balcony stood open.

"How'd you know about this?" Josh asked.

I shrugged. "Sarah and I might have, uh, a history. She wouldn't mind me being up here. I mean, I've been here before."

"Ha, nice," he said.

We sat on the patio, and I drank one beer as I watched him chug down a few. I smiled when he lit up the blunt, though I was disappointed he only took a couple of puffs on it.

The problem with guys like Josh is they expected so much from life: the best woman, success in college and career, a good life in general. He wasn't willing to do the extra work to earn those rewards. Josh got by on his average grades, the promise of a career in his family's business, and his sophomoric advances toward women.

I had worked hard to earn my place on my team and had been poised to choose whichever offer I wanted from the league since freshman year. I not only admired women, but I studied them. I noticed what they liked and what they responded to, not just what was easy to say to get them to fall in line. Unlike Josh, I was absolutely committed to doing whatever it took to make Danielle mine. If that meant clearing the field, so be it.

When Josh got drunk, the bastard always started to talk. On that night, he was spouting pure nonsense. I wasn't sure I could tolerate listening to him for a whole night. I was only halfway listening. I heard him say, at the end of a long and rambling speech, "I think I love her."

"Love who?" I asked. I knew who he meant. Hearing him say it would only solidify my resolve to do what I knew needed to be done.

"Danielle. I mean, I don't think she takes me seriously, and she can have whatever man she wants. I keep telling myself I'm going to change her mind, and it doesn't happen, but I keep hanging around and holding on for just, I don't know, the possibility that she'll realize I can be good for her."

He got up and started to pace. I think it made him nervous that I didn't give him a reply. I sensed that what he really wanted was a pep talk. Any good friend would have told him that things were going to be all right and that all he needed to do was hang in there until he wore her down. I had seen that happen with other couples before. I'd given him some version of that speech several times, disingenuous as it was. I wasn't going to rehash that bullshit again.

When I did speak up, he was surprised at what I had to say.

"If she wanted you, I think she would have shown you by now. If what you're telling me about the two of you is true, she's placed you firmly in the friend zone. Maybe she enjoys spending time with you, the same way she likes going out with her girlfriends or having a pet to keep her company. Once a girl figures out she just doesn't want you, there's no coming back from it. You're not the kind of guy who would push the issue, so basically, you're screwed.

You should move on to another woman, one who shows more interest in you. Maybe try one who's not so far out of your league that you never had a fucking chance in the first place."

He gaped at me for a moment and then laughed. It was a gut-shaking chuckle that doubled him over. When he stood again, he had tears in his eyes.

"Pres, you almost had me there! I thought you were serious."

"I am very serious."

He straightened up. It took a beat for my words to sink in. "What the hell's wrong with you?"

I stood up and got in his face. "Maybe Danielle can't put her finger on why she doesn't like you. So I'll tell you why she doesn't. You're a sorry excuse for a man, and she can feel that. Any woman could."

I was moving toward him then.

"I don't know what your problem is, but you need to back off." He was trying to look tough, but I saw the fear in his eyes. I was taller, bigger, and stronger than him. Even if he had been clearheaded, he wouldn't have had a chance.

"Sure, make me," I said.

He punched me. Big mistake.

He got one hit in, but I'd come prepared to the fight. I had a small length of pipe hidden in my jacket. It was six inches long but had a good weight to it. I'd wrapped masking tape around one end for a better grip. The business end was hollow. I hit him hard, but he threw his arm up, absorbing most of the blow. It still made an impact on his head, just behind his left ear, but he didn't lose consciousness.

"Mother fucker," he said, his voice at once confused and angry. His forehead was bleeding, and he squinted, stumbling, like the world was spinning out around him.

I then got pissed because this bastard still thought he could fight me. He tried to land another punch, but I easily sidestepped him. I shoved him backward.

With one eye closed, he wiped at his forehead with one sleeve. "You'll never get away with this," he said.

I had to finish him before he drew more attention to himself. I rushed him, the same way I would have charged at a player on the field. One good push and he fell backward over the balcony. I didn't bother to look down. I heard the solid thud of his body on concrete when he hit the ground.

For a moment it seemed there was no other sound than his body breaking, and then someone inside the house screamed.

My plan had come together so well. I'd made the decision exactly how his life was going to come to an end. I felt wired, powerful; I wanted something to be, and I had made it happen. There wouldn't be anyone standing between Danielle and me anymore.

I slipped into an adjoining bedroom and down the stairs while everyone seemed to be rushing outside to Josh's aid. I went out through the kitchen door and walked over to where I had parked my car. As I drove toward my apartment, I saw an ambulance rushing toward Sarah's house. I couldn't imagine that Josh would be alive after a hard fall like that. If he was, he wouldn't be around for long.

I knew it would be a sleepless night. Instead of going directly home, I drove past Danielle's apartment. I saw a light on in her room and could see her outline from the window. She sat at her desk, reading, completely absorbed in her studies. A lamp on the opposite side of her desk reflected light on the window that made her look like she had a halo, too bright for me to stare at for long. I thought about how much I wanted her and reveled in the fact that she would soon be mine. When I did finally bed Danielle, knowing the obstacles I had overcome to get her would only make it that much sweeter. She would never have to know how far I had gone for her. But on this night, I didn't stay watching her for long. By one in the morning I was back at my apartment.

Josh was in and out of consciousness for a day or so after he fell. He lapsed into a coma, one that the doctors said he was unlikely to emerge from. The last I heard, he was still on life support because his parents didn't want to accept the hard truth of their son's condition. If he ever came out of it, he would most likely be a vegetable.

Chapter Eleven

Preston Harrington

After my meeting with my agent, Kurt, was done, I decided to take care of some other business that needed handling. Maybe Kurt didn't think so, but I still had things to think about other than commercial shoots and promotional work. Some days I enjoyed that kind of activity, and others I didn't have the patience.

I woke up the next day with my neck still sore and stiff. I was especially relieved to not be making any public appearances that day. I try to hide pain, but I don't know that I have ever been effective at it. Worse yet, the camera tends to reveal what you don't want it to see.

I still had the restaurant I needed to sell off, as well as dealings regarding some of my properties to attend to. I had wanted out of that investment for a long time. My partner Rob had worked with the planning of menus and the promotion of the business, while I had been more of a silent partner. The site was already closed, but finding a new buyer wasn't going to be easy. A few people were interested, and I was certain my realtor would find someone suitable who would take it off my hands for a reasonable price.

Between phone calls, a couple of quick meetings, and driving around town, I couldn't help but be distracted. My mind was on the game. A year had passed since my retirement, and I still missed the gridiron. It had been everything to me.

People imagined that the satisfaction of playing in the NFL was due to the adoring fans and the excitement of game days. In reality, it was the entire process. Planning, preparation, and skill combined with timing and a bit of luck were all necessary for a win. You were fighting not only an opponent but also battling yourself, working to make both mind and body faster, quicker, better. It wasn't all about strength and speed, either, though those were the tools needed to be effective. You had to know your plays and how to react to your opponent's moves. Studying the other team meant hours of research and watching replays, knowing the mind of the other quarterback and his players as well or better than they knew themselves.

The glory of winning was only the recognition that came from giving all it took to make it to the top of your game and career. Once you were there, the push to innovate never ended. The better you got, the more the public expected you to achieve.

I still loved that my old teammates kept me in the loop with their lives and everything that went on in their careers, but if I were truthful, their stories were uncomfortable for me to hear. No matter how much they wanted to include me, I was no longer a player. There were no more Super Bowl rings in my future, no more saving the game and putting the critics to shame.

I recalled my first Super Bowl. I had been so pumped up and ready to set the sports world on fire. Nothing was going to stop me. Sure, the hostile assholes in the press tried to sink my spirits, pointing out how tough our opponents were and how Vegas favored them and all the other BS those twerps loved to peddle. My inexperience, supposed "stubbornness," and reputation as a risk-taker were all cited as reasons that would lead to my humiliation. "Just keep talking," I kept saying to myself almost every day during the two-week buildup to the big game, determined to make them all look like fools.

But right from the start, our whole game plan fell apart. They weren't buying the play-action fakes at all and remained in coverage, blanketing our receivers. They didn't need to blitz to cut through my line and keep pressuring me. I was sacked three times in the first half, knocked down a half dozen more. Some hits were after I got the ball off, too, and the damn referees seemed to have swallowed their whistles. Regarding one blatant cheap shot in particular, my teammates were screaming for a roughing-the-passer call from the sidelines, but the league knew the fans loved big hits and often let things slide in big games. One of those hits was helmet to helmet, and I was wobbly getting up from that car wreck.

In the locker room, the atmosphere was tense. Down by seven, our team was still confident but naturally concerned about the outcome. They depended on me, their superstar quarterback, and the O-line knew they were letting me down and I was getting pummeled out there. But I refused to bitch about it. There was no way in hell I was going to let either my opponents or my teammates see any sign of weakness from me.

As Coach approached the team to talk, he glanced at his assistant and, seeing the look on his face, asked, "Where's Preston?"

The assistant whispered in his ear. Coach quickly shrugged him off. He approached the team, his voice counterpoint to the dull roar of the crowd in the stands now reacting to the superstar halftime entertainment the NFL had laid out for them.

Every player tuned out everything but Coach. "Guys, this game is ours," he said. "We've been in a lot tougher spots than this one." He scanned the room, turning his back a moment, and then spun around. "The only thing they can do is make us believe what they say about us—that a superstar quarterback can't carry a mediocre team." The silence was deafening; he knew he was hitting them where it hurt. He made eye contact with all of them at once. "Those bastards! Are we mediocre? Mediocre?" he demanded.

The point sunk in. Every man rose to his feet and roared, "Hell no!"

As the team mingled, filled with rah-rah good spirit and camaraderie, Coach went to the men's room, where he found me crouched over a toilet, my face ashen after having puked my guts out. "You okay, son?" he asked.

I looked up, my eyes meeting his with steely determination. "Yeah, I'm fine," I managed to say. I felt the same as I had often in my football career—starting in high school and a couple times in college. I'd been hit too hard in the head a few times, so what was one more?

Coach said, "Look, we're only down by seven. If you're banged up bad, we can bench you for a quarter and still win it in the fourth."

My reaction, before I even realized what I was doing, was almost violent. In a rage, my voice much fiercer than I probably intended, I shouted, "No! No way. I'm fine. I'm just getting my second wind!"

"Christ, Preston. You're getting killed out there, and they rang your bell more than once pretty damn good. I want you to tell me the truth; if you're hurt bad, there's no need to be a hero. You're young. This probably isn't your only bite of the apple."

Everything he said was true—but it all went in one ear and right out the other. I was one hundred percent convinced that I was invincible and indestructible. I stood up, gave him a brave wink, and walked away to join my teammates.

By the time we trotted out and back to the game for the second half, we were ready to make history. We wanted the victory so bad, we could taste it. My team was looking to me to lead them to that victory, and I wasn't about to let them down.

I took even more hits in the second half, and though a dull pain thudded somewhere deep inside my skull, I used every ounce of willpower I had to shake it off and ignore it. While the third quarter was touch and go with the team even falling behind by ten at one point, the fourth quarter was a real thriller. We were down by five when the two-minute warning whistle rang in our ears. All of my concentration was on that football, and with only two minutes to play with, I marched us down the field and nailed our Pro Bowler tight end in the back of the end zone with a bullet for a game-ending TD with zero left on the clock.

I was named Super Bowl MVP, after earlier having been awarded MVP for the season. My ego was sky high, and my future seemed endless.

Not surprisingly, of course, my thoughts soon turned to my last day on the field, many years later at the end of a long, brutal, and glorious career . . .

We were playing in Santa Clara. I'd been on that field before, but not in years. On this clear, bright California day, the pressure was on. This was the Super Bowl again, and the sportscasters and even knowledgeable fans were already expecting the game to be a tough one, an almost even matchup of strengths and weaknesses between the teams. One thing the other team didn't have was the rock-solid defense we did. They were good, just not as good as us. I had studied them enough to gauge their moves; their predictability was a weakness I was happy to exploit.

I knew we could beat Carolina. We had come in well prepared; it was mostly a matter of focus. We'd put in the hard work to ride the wave all the way to the playoffs, and I was determined that we weren't going to stop.

Carolina dominated in the first half, but in the second, with everything on the line, we pulled together. The game was probably my best one that entire season, though it was the least of my performances at a Super Bowl. Once we hit that third quarter, our opponents couldn't get any momentum. The tide had obviously turned in our favor, but we kept our shoulders to the grindstone and didn't get overly confident. We pulled ahead with a 22–10 lead, securing a win and one last championship ring to top off my career.

The contest received mixed reviews. Some said I had pulled a lackluster performance, even going as far as calling me a game manager, a side-handed insult meaning that my team had done all the work. Others praised me for being on point. They said I had returned to previous form, emerging victorious and ready to go into the next season with fire on my heels.

The truth was somewhere between those extremes. I had given my all to the game—blood, sweat, and devotion—but there would be no next season in the future. I knew it was going to be my last game going in, which made it that much more bittersweet. I'd battled against injuries all season. My energy was lower than it should have been, my stamina on the field waning. Yet I was able to hold it together long enough to do what I wanted: to exit on a high note, still playing the game well and delivering my team to victory.

Afterward, accepting that my football career was over was a daily struggle. At times I thought I was fine with it, but other days it came back like a form of grief that colored the rest of my life. I had many things to be happy about: a beautiful wife, a home, kids. But if I was honest with myself, I had to admit to an emptiness inside me, one I couldn't fill with work anymore. I wanted to go out and find someone to take out my aggression on.

Shaking off thoughts of the past, now done with the phone calls and meetings for the day, I decided not to go back home for a bit.

I own a house outside of town, in an area surrounded by empty fields and farmland. It was one of my first big purchases when I joined the league, back when I was twenty-one. I had the purchase planned out before I ever saw the house. By keeping part of my signing bonus in cash as well as cashing out portions of my first six paychecks, I secretly amassed enough money to buy something that no one would ever know about. Maybe I didn't need to be so cautious, but I had a need to keep certain things all to myself. I paid for the property with my stashed cash. The gentleman I bought it from was a retiree who had been anxious to dump the home and move with his wife to Florida. He told me that he had family there, including a house he'd inherited. I sweetened the deal with some extra money, on the provision that he would not tell anyone who had bought the land from him.

"Well, who are you again?" the man said, grinning with a yellow-toothed smile. "I haven't seen you before. Besides, my memory isn't for shit these days, and for that kind of money, it can get much worse. If you want it a secret, you've got it."

I wasn't sure if he truly meant it. If he hadn't reminded me a bit of my grandfather, I might have ended him and buried the body out back. But he had family, and I couldn't afford for anyone to come looking for him. Instead, I decided to trust him. He moved out within a week, as we agreed he would. I heard nothing from him again, but I kept tabs on him over the years.

The man died of natural causes a few years later. I found his obituary online. Not until after his passing did I start using the house for what I intended.

No paper trail on that property led back to me, and it was the only one of my properties Danielle didn't know about. I had it furnished completely different than my other properties which, of course, had Danielle's influence. This was all me: dark woods and colors. I even walled over a couple east-facing windows. Too much damn sunlight. I wanted basic, nothing pretentious. I'd grown tired of my public persona, which had become a burdensome façade.

This place was all for me. Nobody else. While not Shangri-La, I didn't have to share it with anyone. It was my own getaway from the world.

I took care of keeping the house clean myself. Desert landscaping—with rocks, patio stones, and low-maintenance bushes—kept me from having to worry about a lawn. The house itself was white metal siding with green trim, a seemingly pleasant family home. There was even a swing on the front porch, which swayed gently in the breeze.

The house itself was of modest size: three bedrooms, all upstairs. Downstairs was a living room with a brick fireplace, kitchen, dining room, and den.

I kept the kitchen stocked with nonperishables, snacks and drinks, but not much else because I never knew how much time would elapse between visits or how long I would stay.

It was the perfect place for me to escape to when I needed privacy. The nearest neighbor was a mile away. A turn off the access road and a quarter mile would bring you up to the house, but it was a place difficult to find unless you knew where you were going. Though the stone wall surrounding the property was visible, the house was deep in a shaded glen, obscured by trees until you reached the gate.

On this afternoon, I decided it would be best to be alone. I didn't want to wear the mask of the friendly, respectable family man who was happy to be retired from the career that had once defined him. I learned when I was young that the darker side of my personality—the violent urges, the anger—was not something I could let others see. These were secrets I would take with me to the grave.

When I was a kid, I liked to taunt my younger brother Tyler; I liked that he knew about some of the things I did. It was my way of keeping him in line. More than that, I took pleasure in knowing that someone realized who I really was and that he would fear me because of it.

I didn't feel things in the same way other people did. Some things I knew I should care about, I truly didn't. I worried about my parents noticing my lack of feelings about certain things.

I studied people's reactions, and mimicking the appropriate social cues became easy for me. A death in the family? I'm so sorry for your loss. Is there anything I can do for you? You're sick today? I hope you feel better. Did that person hurt your feelings? I'm sorry that happened to you. It's all the same platitudes. I had a hard time believing other people meant it when they said such things. Once you understood it was about making an uncomfortable situation slightly more bearable, the correct words flowed easily. I knew how to use the appearance of caring. I just never felt it.

My lack of emotions set me apart, in a good way. Other people let their feelings rule them. My detachment allowed me to use a more surgical approach to getting what I wanted. I learned the art of using other people's emotions to get what I wanted from them.

*****

I went inside the house and got comfortable. I watched the replays of some recent games, matching the current players' performances to my own and that of my teammates. Seeing their shortcomings and thinking about what I could have done better or differently was easy. I could judge them as cruelly as I had sometimes been judged. I laughed at their poor decisions and rookie mistakes.

I was feeling unsettled. It had been weeks since I had ended the stranger at the bar, and I was going to need to do something else soon. I felt uneasy in my own skin. I needed to find a way to calm this agitation. I couldn't afford to be reckless. I had to control myself. And so far, that meant only one thing.

I had a special room that I went to when I needed to calm down, a place where I kept my memorabilia. It was the last bedroom upstairs, all the way in the back. At first look, it would appear to be an office, with a mahogany desk, a leather chair, computer, and printer. The walls were lined with bookshelves. I liked books, but these were ones with subjects I wouldn't be seen reading anywhere else. Other people might remark about the great number of books in my collection that were about men and women who shared violent predilections: Gacy, Bundy, Ramirez, and Wuornos, to name only a few. All those wore the title of serial killer. I found comfort in their stories. Why? Did I get off on gory death? No, I didn't think so. I spent a lot of time alone thinking about it and concluded that what excited me was the uncertainty, the thrill of the deed and the even higher turn-on of the escape. Others of the books were simply thrillers by Stephen King, James Patterson, Gregg Olsen, and others. I wasn't crazy, after all. I laughed aloud at that thought. Or was I? Getting away with crimes proved my own ingenuity and the stupidity of those who crossed me.

I didn't exactly have much in common with most of these people in my books. These were people who were caught, punished, or who had even been executed or died in prison. Many were losers, having grown up unloved, lacking in the bare necessities. I could not identify with the lives most of them led. What I did understand was the need to show superiority through the power of the kill. I knew what it was to use charm and familiarity to put my quarry at ease, only to move in and take what I wanted. They were less elegant in the commission of their crimes and obviously less fortunate, but in some ways, I considered these my brothers in arms.

I couldn't exactly put my finger on it, but I could relate to them in ways that others could never understand. Killing for "us" was not about a one-time thrill or accomplishing some kind of mission. It was an essential part of who we were; the specter of death empowered us. Our strength was built on the lives we stole away.

One thing about the books is that authorities always speculated about the reasons behind acts of violence. I believe a killer truly freed from the weight of guilt didn't need reasoning or a traumatic past to point back to.

I often thought that was a response of people who were afraid, seeking to understand something outside their reach. They looked too hard for tidy explanations to every human behavior considered deviant. A few killers had nothing in their past that would explain their love of bloodshed. My theory is that some people just had a taste for it, one that evolved as they progressed through life.

I sat down at the desk and ran my fingers along the smooth wooden surface. I took pains to keep this room clean. I polished the desk each time I visited, though I considered skipping that part of the routine this time. I didn't find any trace of dust. A light scent of lemon cleaner still hung in the air.

I unlocked the bottom drawer and took out a metal box.

Over the years, I had collected something from each of my kills. All except for Josh Middleton; I'd had to flee that scene in too much of a hurry. There had been no chance to grab anything of his. Afterward, I had even considered going to the hospital to see him but thought better of it. He was in a vegetative state, and the likelihood he was wearing his school ring or anything else I could get to was slim.

My cache of items looked unrelated: a lady's necklace, a man's wedding ring, a med alert bracelet, a green silk tie. I had added the watch from the guy at Grinder's, Steve Bishop. I touched each one slowly. I was transported back to each kill these totems represented, savoring the memories. Nothing compared to the intimacy I found in reveling about each one. Watching a person's eyes change as they realized their life was slipping away. I thought more about that and pondered why it was so intriguing for me. The power of life and death in *my* hands. No football analysts to assess my performance down to my every flinch. No sports writers to root for me or deride me. Nobody else's opinion mattered—not even the victim about to die. Only my own. I felt more alive than ever when in the act of inflicting death.

Each victim experienced denial until that moment, and then the realization when they understood I was the reason they would be leaving earth.

It's almost like that moment before a woman draws in that little breath, the gasp before her body begins to buck and shiver. That second right before she's about to orgasm when she can't believe what you've done to her. Well, they don't call orgasm a *little death* for nothing.

I leaned back in the chair and took my time, pleasuring myself. I closed my eyes and vividly recounted each kill in succession. I licked my lips, envisioning that moment when their lives ebbed away. I groaned when I came, the sound bouncing off the walls.

Despite what conventional thinking might suggest, I didn't believe my enjoyment of murdering had anything to do with sex. Yes, in some ways it was the same as my sex life with my wife. Similar in intensity, similar in the sense of release, but in no way was it the usual man-woman sexual experience. Some elements of killing were so unique, so dark, so forbidding that it thrilled me to think about it. Sex was always a lot of fun, but this defied description.

Later, once I got cleaned up, I put the box away, almost reverential in the gentle movements of my fingers. After all, these were not mere keepsakes, these were treasures I had earned, and no other person could ever grasp their true significance.

I was now ready for another much-anticipated part of my visit. My favorite weapon rested in the drawer beside the box. It was a length of pipe. Back when I was in college, a plumber had come to my apartment to fix the sink. He left behind an extra piece of straight pipe made of iron, having miscalculated the length. I had wrapped one end with masking tape for a better grip. The open end was great for cracking bones or dealing a fatal blow. The weapon felt right in my hand, the perfect heft. I liked that it was easy to disguise. I put on a sports jacket and slipped it under a sleeve. It was thin enough to remain concealed until it was too late.

I'd had to clean it many times over the years. The end of it had begun to turn brown with what looked like rust but was actually blood that remained.

"Yes," I whispered. "You and I have to go out again soon."

When I was done, I felt better.

I locked up and went back downstairs. An old game was still playing on the screen. I had a couple of vodkas and fell asleep on the couch shortly before nightfall, lost in pleasant dreams.

Chapter Twelve

Danielle Harrington

Preston was gone for the rest of the day. My best guess was that Kurt had pissed him off. I was hoping that was all it was, but I was concerned. I texted him but got no reply. That's what really bothered me.

At nine, I put the kids to bed. I sat up, worried, and though I told myself that I wouldn't, I texted Preston again. It was unlike him not to reply to me at all, even a few words. I remember one time he had texted me back: *I am alive honey*. I wasn't pleased by the sarcastic answer at the time, but I would have been relieved with even that much.

I started to think about all the times he had showed up late or not at all when he was supposed to be home. In the year since he retired, I had noticed his comings and goings a lot more. When he was still playing, there were a few times when he would go unaccounted for or show up at home later than seemed reasonable. He would blame it on workouts or studying the game or some other thing . . . but how often had he been truthful about where he had been? I was not the kind of woman who liked to have her husband on a leash. I didn't have the time or the energy to chase a man. I was beginning to wonder if maybe I hadn't paid enough attention. Maybe this had been going on for the last few years, but with my own work and the kids, I had lost my focus on what he was up to.

Back when he was still playing, I had come home early one day to find him burning his shirt in the backyard. He had said that during a practice, another player had tackled him and ended up getting a bloody lip, and some of the blood had gotten on his clothes.

He always preferred to burn old clothes; he wasn't one to donate, and he didn't like the idea of someone going through our trash looking for souvenirs. I'd heard stories of people dumpster diving to get old clothes from a celebrity's trash. Some jackass could sell them for thousands of dollars online. I didn't argue the point with him. As gross as it sounded, a sports jersey with blood on it was probably the kind of thing that would be a find for certain people.

I'd shrugged that off as my husband being a little overly fastidious. He didn't get rid of many clothes anyway, so it wasn't a common occurrence. But after finding the matches from Grinder's in his pants pocket, I couldn't help but wonder what else had gone unnoticed, what he might have burned without me knowing it.

I decided I would check the yard. Checking the steel drum Preston kept to burn things, I found new ashes. Bending over to get a closer look, I was able to find a small piece of cloth with a button on it. Though the fabric was charred, I found a tiny shred of fabric with a silver button still intact. It looked like the one from his navy jacket. His favorite.

I went back upstairs and looked through his closet. The navy jacket was nowhere to be found. I knew for sure he hadn't been wearing it the last time I saw him. The button matched other similar jackets he owned. I would know because I had ordered all four for him, all from the same maker.

Someone had been killed at Grinder's recently. The thing I couldn't shake about Preston not telling me he had been there was that Grinder's was a spot we used to love to go. I couldn't imagine any reason he would go there and not mention in passing that he had stopped in. Could it have slipped his mind, or was there some other reason he hadn't mentioned it? I worried about his safety and about mine. That neighborhood must have gone downhill lately. The thought also crossed my mind that he could have met someone there he didn't want me to know about. A woman perhaps? I shoved that thought to the back of my mind but noted to myself to pay better attention to details regarding Preston.

My thoughts then drifted to Preston's friend and former business partner Rob, and how the two of them had been arguing back and forth about the business right before Rob was killed. Preston was loosely connected to not one, but two murders. He had been at Grinder's within a day of that random murder and, of course, knew the victim Rob well. I wondered if that freaked him out to be in the vicinity of such heinous activity more than once in a short time span. Maybe that's why his recent behavior had been a bit off.

I knew Preston could not have had anything to do with Rob's death. But did he know the person who had killed Rob? Thinking such dark thoughts made me shudder. I felt like I might be going crazy.

Maybe Pres was having a more difficult time with these two recent deaths than I realized. Maybe he needed help—therapy or something. Preston was a good man, a good husband, an NFL star, for Pete's sake. He loved the kids, and he loved me.

Even as I tried to comfort myself with that thought, I also considered that some people were awful to other human beings but good to their own families. Preston could never kill anyone, but maybe he had gone so far as to fight with someone. If that was the case, he needed help. Anger management, probably. Perhaps therapy.

But why had he recently burned his favorite shirt? I forced myself to think of possibilities. If Preston had gotten into a situation where he'd hit someone hard enough to draw blood, why hadn't anyone come forward? Why hadn't the injured party asked for money or sued for pain and suffering? Preston was unlikely to get a pass. On the other hand, many people would go out of their way to provoke a public figure like Pres if they thought it could help them get some cash. If my husband had paid his lawyer to make something like that go away, I would have heard about it.

I didn't want to believe that Preston would harm anyone or that he would cheat on me with another woman. But could he? Could he have done either one? Would a person burn a shirt simply because they had cheated? To get rid of a perfume scent or lipstick stain perhaps? That sounded far-fetched to me. Soap and water would do the job much more easily.

My thoughts then drifted into an area I did not want to go. What were the chances of someone being loosely connected to two different murders in a short span of time? Would burning a shirt make sense if Preston had witnessed a murder? How about if he—

No. Absolutely not. Even the possibility of Preston being the guilty party in a crime so monstrous made me nauseous.

Did anyone want to believe their husband could be capable of absolute evil? I wondered. Maybe when you loved someone you simply refused to see their betrayal until you had the evidence in your face. I decided that was exactly what I needed—evidence. Either I was right or wrong, but I needed to know exactly what was going on. If it turned out that I was paranoid, well, I could be the one to go into therapy for it.

My God, maybe he was just having an affair. It was sad to think of that as the better of two evils. We had been married for fourteen years, and though it would hurt like all hell, I could imagine us working that out. We had too much history to throw out of the window for some nameless fling in a hotel room or a girl who chased him for money and the occasional afternoon tryst.

If Preston had hurt someone, what was I going to do? There were the kids to think of and our lives were intertwined. What was going to happen if all this time he had been . . . ?

I shook my head. This was all nonsense! It had to be.

I decided I needed to take some action, for peace of mind if nothing else. I sat down and did a quick Google search of how to covertly track where your husband has gone. The process looked simple enough. I only had to buy a cell phone plus an extra high-capacity battery bank and then download a free app onto the phone. I would hide the phone somewhere in his car and it would give me a complete history of everywhere he went. Perfect!

I made myself an Amazon account based on a new email I set up, ordered the products to be delivered to my work address, then deleted the history from my laptop. I doubted Preston had ever or would ever look at my history, but I thought covering my tracks was the best plan. I was a pretty good private eye! I thought, the guilt seeping in a moment later to steal my exhilaration. But really, I was only seeking the truth. If Preston never went anywhere questionable within a reasonable amount of time, then I would throw away the cell phone and, with it, my doubt.

I told myself that he would probably come home during the night, maybe a little drunk, explaining how he had let time pass him by while hanging out with some of his friends. I would see that all these things I was thinking were ridiculous. He would tell me all about his day, confessing that he had mixed his pain pills with alcohol and, while the effects weren't good, he was okay. It just took longer than normal for him to come back to himself. I would ask him about his pain, and he would shyly admit that it was getting out of hand. We would talk about options for him. There were a lot of different medications that he could try. Maybe he could explore alternative medicine. I knew other players' wives who said acupuncture had worked wonders for their men. Preston would argue, I would persist, and he would cave to my wishes.

I would be pissed about all of this but relieved that he was okay and that the problems we had were workable, normal, the kind encountered by all married couples. We would somehow get through them together.

He would take me in his arms and tell me that he loved me, and we would make up in our favorite way—by having sex. He would hold me afterward and we would fall asleep, and I would not ask him all the questions that seemed too odd to mention.

That was what I wanted to happen. It didn't occur to me until I had my fourth glass of wine that a similar song and dance had happened between us many times before. I wondered how long it would take for my Amazon order to show up.

***

Morning came, and still no sign of my husband.

Isabel, ever the daddy's girl, wanted to know where he was.

"He's working, baby."

"Is he on a plane?" she asked, eyes wide as she stared at me over her cereal bowl. She was only seven. Since his retirement, she had gotten used to him being home more often, and these last few weeks had to have been confusing for her. He had no set schedule anymore but came and went according to his whims, but children needed structure. I reminded myself to bring that up once Preston got his sorry ass home.

"Yeah, he is," I blurted. "If he's not delayed, his flight should come in late this afternoon."

"Okay." She nodded and went back to eating her breakfast. What was I going to say if he wasn't home by the time they were back from school? In this case, honesty would have been much worse. I topped off my lie with a smile. That might have been the crappiest moment of an already trying morning.

I loaded both the kids into the car and drove them to school. I barely even remembered the trip. I was home within twenty minutes. Nearing panic mode, I got on the phone.

I called Kurt's office first.

"No, he hasn't been by here. I haven't seen him since yesterday," the agent said, then paused. "Is something wrong?"

I pretended not to hear his question. "Was he agitated when you left?"

"No, he wasn't." Then a pause. "I mentioned a couple of things he didn't want to get into, but he didn't seem upset to me."

"Do you know where he's supposed to be today?"

"Nothing's scheduled, which was really the point of our conversation. He's had too many days like that lately if he expects to keep making money on his sponsorships, much less get new ones. He has one appearance scheduled for tomorrow."

I didn't need to know more than that. I hung up with him and started to call around. I started with some acquaintances, wives and girlfriends of other players from his team. I tried to keep it low key and not sound hysterical, like some crazy bitch who was trying to find out where her husband was, but my low-grade panic was developing into something a little worse. I imagined his car in a ditch, his body pinned underneath a mass of crumpled metal. I couldn't even remember a time when he had been gone for an entire day and night with no contact with me at all—not since we were married, and probably not after we started dating seriously, either.

I didn't want to call the authorities. A normal person could contact the police, and if he turned up on his own, it would be no big deal. That was not the case with Preston, and he would be so angry if I did that, exposing him for public scrutiny. A mistake like that could mean a loss of income on top of public embarrassment. The last thing we needed was some bullshit scandal about him fucking another woman or being out on a drunken binge.

The last person I called was Preston's brother, Tyler. I explained to him what was going on. He didn't say anything at first, just listened. My voice broke by the time I was finished explaining. I wiped a tear from my cheek.

"I don't know where he is, and I'm not even sure where to start looking for him. I don't know what happened, but some strange things have been going on and I need to talk to somebody."

"Okay, so let's do this. I have today off and I'm not that far from you, Danielle. I'm on your side of town for an interview with *Sportsman's Quarterly*, which just wrapped up an hour ago. I have some time to meet up if you want to talk. Can you get away for a bit?"

"Sure, I can have someone stay with the kids this afternoon," I told him. "Text me your address and I'll be there."

Chapter Thirteen

Tyler Harrington

I was interested to hear what Danielle had to say. I couldn't help but wonder what it was she had seen about my brother that was beginning to alarm her. Any woman would be suspicious about her husband being gone for two days without any word, but it made me wonder where he was and if he might be hurt. To my knowledge, he had never gone so long without calling his wife. I tried not to dwell on it. Danielle was already upset, and the last thing I wanted to do was alarm her more than she already was.

My brother Preston had always been the favorite, the golden boy. People wouldn't likely believe me, but I never envied that burden. There was pressure when people expected you to be perfect. What did I envy? His ability to come away clean from anything, no matter what kind of situation he got into; that was a life skill I had yet to master.

By the time I was nine years old and Preston was fourteen, our older brother Gregory was attending college at Ole Miss. Preston and I shared a close bond. I liked to tag along and do the things he did, whether that was playing ball or bike riding with other kids in the neighborhood. Most of the time he didn't mind. Like any older kid, there were times when he wanted to hang with friends his own age and I wasn't included.

In our own way we were oblivious to our family legacy at that point. I don't remember my father as a quarterback but as a sports announcer. We got free tickets to any game that Dad announced, and sometimes we were lucky enough to go. At times, travel affected us being able to be in school, and whenever that was the case, we stayed home. My father is proud to tell anyone that he never pushed any of his sons into football, only supported us once we knew it was our goal. Honestly, he never would have had to. Our love of the game was ingrained into us by our lifestyle, the fabric of our family memories, and of course, in our DNA. I can't speak for my brothers, but I never imagined any other life for myself.

During the times when Dad was on the road, we had a bit more freedom. He wasn't a harsh disciplinarian, though he was the one around our house to hand out punishments. Certain rules—like how late we could stay out with the neighbor kids or finishing homework before the dinner hour—were stretched a bit. We grew up in New Orleans, in a good neighborhood. Many of the families who lived in that area had been there for generations. My parents were Mississippi transplants, but they'd moved to the area right after they got married. The block we lived on was shaded by old magnolia trees and a few dogwoods. There was a park a block away. The only place I didn't like to go was the old Lafayette Cemetery, which was west of our house.

We were free to roam the neighborhood; we rode our bikes or walked to our friends' homes without our parents worrying for our safety. When the streetlights flickered on, we were expected to make our way back home.

Looking back, our absence probably gave our mom a little more time to do whatever she needed: clean the house, cook dinner, and have some time with her own friends. As long as we were both bringing home good grades and not talking back to her, Mom was convinced that we were doing just fine.

That summer, I remember there being a cat beneath the front porch. It was a skittish stray, a calico. I've always liked animals, but my parents wouldn't put up with pets. My mother complained about animal hair and carpet stains. I tried to lure the cat out a few times. Once I left her half a can of tuna. I came back later and found the can had been picked clean. The few times I finally got her to come out, she looked at me for a moment and then quickly retreated to the dark safety of the crawlspace beneath our house. "Fluffy," I called to her, just a random name. She always moved so fast, a ball of white and brown spotted fur. Even though she was timid, I could see her green eyes glowing at me from under the crawlspace. She rewarded me with a soft meow.

"Why do you bother?" Preston asked me one day. He was standing on the porch, glaring at me with a look of disgust on his face. He watched as I kneeled to feed the cat a bit of leftover steak. She didn't even come all the way out from her hiding space. I felt the touch of her cold nose. At that point she was bold or hungry enough to snatch the food from my fingertips before making her getaway.

"It's feral," Preston said. "Probably has rabies."

"No she doesn't!"

"How do you even know it's a she?"

I didn't bother to say I had seen her belly. She looked like she would have kittens soon. I knew Mom would probably call the pound on her once she realized there would be kittens in the near future.

"I just figured she was a girl. I don't know."

A few nights later, we heard mewling sounds and then screeching. The cat was giving birth. It was a full week before we saw the cat and her brood, though we could hear their meows from time to time. The high-pitched cries of the kittens were loud enough to become annoying.

My mother threatened to call the pound, as I expected. I begged her not to. I'd caught a glimpse of them: a litter of four, and of course too young to be separated from their mother. The shelter would probably be the end of them.

My mother sighed. "All right, we'll do this. Go get a box and gather these cats up. Maybe you can find someone nearby who wants them. If you haven't found anyone who can take them by the end of the day, then we'll have the pound collect them in the morning."

I managed to round the felines up, though it took the better part of an hour.

"I'll go with you," Preston offered.

We took our bikes out and canvassed the neighborhood. Mrs. Charles's house was the first. She loved pets and was always either adopting or fostering them. As it turned out, she had two dogs and three cats, too many to bring any new pets into her home. A few of our friends' parents declined, mentioning that it would be trouble to have a cat with such young kittens. As the afternoon drew on, it was depressingly clear that we weren't going to find them a home. If Mom would have let us keep them a few weeks, we'd have had a better chance of giving them away one by one. She wasn't going to allow it, even though I'd suggested that earlier in the morning.

"Come on," Preston said. "I've got another idea."

I wasn't sure what he planned. We were walking toward home, but my brother had an odd smile on his face.

"What idea?" I asked.

"You'll see," he said.

When we came to the open gates of the cemetery, I swallowed over a lump in my throat. This was the one place I didn't like to explore and had never been by myself. Some of the older kids liked to hang out in the graveyard after dark.

"Why do we have to go in there?" I asked.

"Listen, don't be a sissy, come on," he snapped.

Preston walked his bike inside and left it propped up against a moss-covered magnolia tree near the entrance. I did the same.

In New Orleans, few people get buried in the earth. The city is below sea level, so the crypts are constructed above ground. Some of the stone crypts are made like tiny houses for the dead, complete with roofs and inscriptions on the front. Some had stone angels standing beside them. Others were only big enough to hold the casket, covered over in stone. In this place, the wealthy and the poor resided together.

There was an unnatural stillness to the place. The wind was softer. The trees swayed lightly in the humid breeze, moving the moss along with it.

Preston was holding the box with the kittens. I heard their soft mewling. My brother turned to me, smiled, and ran.

"Preston, stop," I yelled after him. My voice echoed back.

I heard Preston's laughter but wasn't sure where it was coming from.

I turned and looked around. This place was a virtual maze of uneven shapes and gray shadows. Stubborn weeds broke through the stone and crept along the edges of some of the crypts. Preston knew this place much better than I did. For me, the cemetery was a grim maze.

I listened for footsteps. My brother's sneakers didn't make a sound. It was late, and the gathering shadows weren't helping my already overactive imagination. We would be in trouble if we took much longer. Worse than that, I didn't want to be in this place once nightfall came.

I realized that calling to him wasn't going to help. He was hiding from me. I listened, and after a few minutes heard a faint mewling. I followed the sound until I found Preston.

He sat on the ground with his back against a crypt. He smiled at me. He had put the box down beside him, and a couple of kittens had climbed out and were wandering around. Fluffy was in his lap. She looked up at me as I approached. She opened her mouth, making a sound too small for me to hear.

"There you are, little brother," Preston said.

And with that, he snapped Fluffy's neck.

I screamed. Preston just laughed.

"Why'd you do that?" I cried. "You killed her!"

"So what if I did?" he said with a shrug. "If we gave it to the shelter, it was going to be put down anyway."

"I'll tell Mom!"

He stood up and tossed dead Fluffy onto the ground. I stared at her wide-open eyes, the angle of her neck that was all wrong.

"No you won't." Preston's voice was a low, gravelly whisper. "You won't say anything. You don't want to be a snitch, do you, Tyler? Because bad things happen to people who don't know how to keep their mouths closed."

His threat made me suck in my breath. I had never seen him look at me like that before. I could tell he absolutely meant his threat. He wasn't talking about roughhousing or even a good punch. He wanted to *hurt* me. His hands curled into fists at his sides, and his feet were planted slightly apart. I couldn't see his eyes, other than that they were narrowed. I wasn't sure that I really wanted to see the expression there.

If something were to happen, would anyone know? He could throw the cat away and no one would ever find her. Who would believe me if I said he had done anything wrong?

I decided to run. I found my bike and rode home. I was halfway there before I even thought of the poor kittens. I had a pang of guilt. I was sure that he was going to kill them too, but I hadn't thought of trying to rescue them.

I got home before Preston. Mom wasn't home. I went upstairs and locked myself in my room. When I came down a couple of hours later, my brother was with her in the kitchen. I stood in the doorway, staring at them both. I wasn't sure what to think. What if he told her that *I* had killed the cats? It wouldn't be the first time he had blamed me for something he had done, though this would be the worst.

"There you are, honey. Pres said you didn't feel well. Are you okay?"

I looked at my mother's worried expression. Preston stood behind her, grinning.

"I'm fine, Mom."

"Well, you sure?"

"Yeah," Preston spoke up before I could reply. "We ended up taking the cats to the pound anyway."

"Ah," she said. "I know you're disappointed, but you did try to give those poor things a chance. Someone might still adopt them over the next couple of days. Well, we should have some dessert with dinner tonight. What would you like, Tyler?"

***

I didn't tell my mom anything because I knew she wouldn't believe me. Preston could always talk his way out of trouble, like the time he stole a switchblade from the hardware store and slipped it into my backpack. I was caught with it and accused of being a thief. I was grounded for a full month for that stunt.

I knew it would be the same way about this. I did still have a nagging doubt about whether to tell my mom or not. Either way it all seemed like a moot point, something that wouldn't do anything but get me in trouble.

After a few weeks passed, I had convinced myself that I was overreacting to think that Preston would actually hurt me. He acted like nothing had changed. I was still the little brother that he liked to joke around with. But I felt different, and that was the thing I couldn't get around. For a long time I felt scared of him; I would think of that moment in the woods and his eyes when he asked me what I was going to do. Sometimes my memory of that day seemed like a dream, something I had only imagined.

That was the summer that life started to change. In many ways, the changes were quite normal. I kissed a girl for the first time that June. On the 4th of July weekend, I fell out of a tree and sprained my wrist. In August, animals started to go missing from the neighborhood. At night, when the house was quiet, I wondered if anyone thought to look for their bodies out at the cemetery.

That year, Preston easily made starting quarterback for the junior high football team; he could thread the eye of a needle with a football. He was soon the star player, but this made him cocky, which made him a bit reckless.

He risked getting hurt by holding onto the ball too long, taking chances that were completely unnecessary. Preston loved to toy with the other team. He'd often wait until that last second when a sack seemed inevitable before getting rid of the ball. The danger was part of the thrill for him. Then his risk-taking backfired. Come the last game of the season late in the fourth quarter, with the division championship at stake, the coach warned Preston to stay focused and not showboat. But Preston had to be Preston. One minute to go, and within striking distance of the end zone, Preston could have made a quick throw to the right corner, but he chose to carry the ball himself straight down the middle, opting for a dramatic surprise finish. On the five yard line, he was gang tackled by three opposing players, each the size of a bull moose. Preston went down hard, his helmet crashing into the ground with a sickening thud.

The whistle blew. Preston did not rise. A murmur went through the stands, followed by hushed silence, and Dad rushed down onto the field to join the knot of concerned players and officials surrounding my motionless brother. I was made to stay in the stands with Mom, I suppose to comfort her, but I was as scared myself. Preston, to me, had always seemed invincible. I couldn't believe that anything bad, at least physically, could ever happen to him. He was the golden boy, and him getting seriously injured seemed unthinkable.

Like some kind of miracle, though, Preston suddenly shook off the cobwebs, somehow clearing his head enough to get on his feet. The crowd roared in a mixture of admiration and relief. Though still a bit wobbly, Preston refused medical attention and then insisted they put him back in the game. The coach refused at first, saying that the boy's health was more important than any game. But with some strident urging from my dad and a promise that he would take full responsibility for any negative outcome, the coach reluctantly allowed Preston to finish the game. I wasn't surprised one bit when he delivered the winning touchdown on the very next play. No one keeps Preston down for long.

Chapter Fourteen

Tyler Harrington

The address I texted to Danielle was of the hotel where I'd had my interview with *Sportsman's Quarterly*. Located up the coast, it was called the Meridian Arms and was both out of the way and had a great little restaurant. It was a small place but upscale, catering to the wealthy and well known. I breathed a sigh of relief when my sister-in-law arrived. I didn't know what to expect from this meeting with her, but the two of us having a talk was long overdue. When she agreed to meet me, I realized how serious she was and that she was deeply worried about my brother. Though I had my own concerns about Preston, I wasn't sure what I could say to comfort Danielle.

A hostess seated us in the hotel restaurant. Other than a young couple with a baby and a pair of elderly ladies, we were alone. Our timing hit between the lunch and dinner crowd. We sat at a booth in the back next to a window that boasted a view of the beach and ocean below. It was a gloomy day, with the gray skies reflected onto the dark, churning water.

Danielle looked like she had rushed out of the house that morning. She wore jeans and a plain white sweater. Her hair was pulled back in a ponytail. I rarely saw her without makeup and heels, but she wore neither on that morning. She looked different—younger, more vulnerable. There was no hiding the shadows beneath her eyes.

"Hey." I hugged her and planted a kiss on her cheek. I felt something wet on her cheeks. Tears? As I drew back, I noticed her eyes were glassy. She had been crying. We sat down and the server approached us. We ordered iced tea. I waited until we were alone before speaking.

"You okay?" I asked.

She tried for a smile, but it faded at the edges of her lips. It seemed the attempt to feign happiness was too hard at that moment. She nodded. "Yes. How about you?" she asked. "How are the girls? How was the vacation?"

"Oh, they're fine, but a handful as always. And the vacation was great. The girls loved seeing Yellowstone. They're excited about camp this year. Me and their mom, not so much. It always sounds like a good idea until it's time for them to leave."

"Yeah, I can imagine," Danielle said. "It's the scary part of kids getting older, trying to figure out how much you want to let them do on their own and what they aren't ready for."

"Exactly. They will go, and I'm sure they will love it. Those first few days will be nerve-racking for me, though."

The waiter arrived with our drinks, and I told him we needed some time before we ordered. I opened my menu, just to have something to do.

Danielle stirred her tea, and I heard the ice clinking inside the glass. She spoke softly, so quietly I almost wanted to ask her to repeat herself. I had heard her. I was simply surprised at what she said. I looked up to meet her eyes.

"Do you think Preston would ever . . . be unfaithful to me?"

"What? Do you think he has been?" I gazed into her beautiful brown eyes, as big as a doe's. I'd always seen the beauty in Danielle. Yes, I loved my wife and kids, but Danielle was beyond gorgeous. How could my stupid brother even consider cheating on her?

"Well . . ." She bit her lip and looked down at the table. "I'm not sure."

"I mean, I wouldn't think any guy could cheat on you, but he is good looking and quite popular, so, I don't know. Do you have any evidence?"

She paused, looked upward with a sigh, and then down as tears streamed down her cheeks. "I'm sorry."

"No, I'm so sorry," I said, cupping her hand with mine. "But again, maybe he's just been having a hard time with retirement. Unless . . . you've found something."

"No, no, it's not what you think." She paused, sighed again, and took a deep breath, as if trying to get up the courage to say what she'd found. "I was almost hoping you'd say yes, you knew him to be unfaithful, because . . . the alternative is so much worse."

I scrunched my eyebrows and spoke slowly, squeezing her hand. "What is worse? What do you mean?"

"Has Preston, uh, have you ever known him to be . . . violent?" Danielle whispered the final word so quietly, I could barely hear it. Her eyes fixed on mine to ascertain my full reaction.

"I'm . . . wait, has he hurt you?" Rage built in my soul. I was horrified at the thought of Preston hurting Danielle in any way. I instinctively searched her face for bruises.

"Not me," she said carefully. "He's never raised a hand to me or the twins. I'm asking about how he treats other people."

"How do you mean?" I said slowly, wanting to know but dreading her response.

"I've seen blood on his clothes before, and it wasn't his. It's happened more than once. He burns clothes sometimes, which he's told me is a habit, but I've begun to wonder about that lately. He lied to me about where he was on the night a man got killed outside of Grinder's, but I know he was there. I went there with one of my friends, and the bartender mentioned Preston had been at the bar that night."

"Was that about two weeks ago?"

"Yes," Danielle said. "Exactly."

I took out my cell phone and scrolled through my messages. "Have a look. I texted Preston, and he said he was at Grinder's. I remembered that because we haven't talked since. That was two weeks ago."

Danielle looked at the text briefly. She handed the phone back to me. "Well, we know where he was for sure, don't we?"

She was already upset, and I didn't know how to tell her these things. I hadn't been able to make my parents believe me when I was a kid. Now it was important that I make a case to her, one she could believe. What made it that much more difficult was I knew she had always loved him, and she wouldn't *want* to believe it.

It was one thing for her to have fears and concerns about her husband's behavior, but I knew well that it was a different thing for me to speak out about them. Her instinct would always be to defend him, despite her own troubled conscience.

"So, he *is* violent," Danielle pressed.

"When he was a kid, he acted out in ways that were disturbing. He was very careful because no one really knows about what happened but me."

"Why?"

"I was a kid, and nobody would believe me. You know how Preston is; he's always been charming. That was part of the problem. My parents couldn't imagine him doing the weird things I was accusing him of, like hurting other kids that had bullied him in the past. None of them spoke up because they were terrified of him, rightfully so. They didn't tell any adults. There was no one to back up my story. He had a thing about killing animals, people's pets even. He killed some kittens in front of me once when the two of us were alone."

"Bullying," she said. "This is a lot worse. Tell me about the animals."

"Are you sure you want to hear this? It was a long time ago."

"Yes, I feel I need to hear."

I told her about seeing my brother snap the neck of Fluffy, and how pets around the neighborhood started coming up missing not long after that. I kept my description as brief as possible. Many questions remained unspoken between us because neither of us knew the answer. Had Preston continued being violent in his adulthood? I had always hoped that it was something he had outgrown. As we became adults and got on with our lives, I wasn't around him anymore to know. And truthfully, I hadn't wanted to know. If he had been violent since then, how bad was he? Could he have graduated from killing animals to killing people? Had Preston murdered the man outside of Grinder's that night? I hadn't ever wanted to fully consider that Preston was capable of such atrocities. It was easier in my mind to think that Preston was fine; he'd grown up.

Now I wondered if Danielle was considering that Preston had been the one to kill the guy outside Grinder's. My mind spun with the possibility that Preston might have injured or even killed more than one person out there. I felt physically ill. I couldn't ignore this anymore. I felt somehow complicit in Preston's dirty work, like I was guilty right alongside him. Knowing Preston, he never did anything only once—he worked at it until he was as good as humanly possible. Why would killing be any different?

Could I help him? I was his brother, after all, and now, besides Danielle, perhaps the only one on the planet who suspected my brother was capable of such evil. But how do you get help for someone who was so good at lying, convincing people that he was right, and hiding his actions? The fact that Danielle simply asked the question was enough for me to convict my brother. He was surely guilty of unspeakable crimes. There had to be a stopping point when enough was enough and people stopped accepting his lies. There had to come a point where Preston had to pay for what he did.

The waiter came back and asked to take our order. I ordered a salad, and Danielle said she would just stick with the tea. I'm pretty sure neither of us had much of an appetite, but the distraction gave me a few minutes more to formulate an answer. I'd always wondered about my brother. From the reading I had done on the subject, I knew that for him to outgrow his thirst for blood would be rare. Still, Preston was a successful man, one who earned the respect he'd obtained over the course of his career. No one else had any consideration about his behavior being left of normal.

"I'd hoped that things were going well for Preston," I told her. "His career is one thing, but I mean personally. The two of you always seem to have a really strong relationship."

"I thought so too," she said. "I have been trying to figure out if he had a history of violence, but whenever I've been with him, I've never seen anything. Let me ask you." Danielle leaned forward. She fidgeted with the cloth napkin beside her plate. "Do you think he's always been like this? Prone to a short temper and acting out?"

"I think he's always had some *tendencies*," I told her. "It got much worse after he started getting injuries on the field. The first concussion was when he was fourteen years old. Then he got a second concussion a few weeks after that and he got much worse. At the time, no one thought of a concussion as a big deal; they didn't do anything about it. The biggest concern was whether he could continue to play, and once they decided he could, that was the last anyone spoke about it. That was when I saw real changes in him, when he started hurting animals and other kids."

"Wait. He hurt other kids too?"

"Well, if he got bullied, then he would seek revenge, you could say."

"Seek revenge?"

"By beating up the bullies."

"And your parents never knew about this? Or were concerned about the concussions?"

"My parents never knew he beat up on any kids. I was afraid to tell them myself—afraid of Preston, I mean. And I don't blame them for not being more concerned about brain damage because even the doctors didn't realize how serious those injuries were. Enough research has been done now that they know better. Chronic traumatic encephalopathy or CTE, the doctors call it. I'm sure you've heard how the NFL changed the rules because of concussions, not allowing certain kinds of hits and tackles anymore."

"Yes, I remember when people started talking about how serious CTE is. I can remember Preston getting at least one serious concussion when we were in college," Danielle admitted. "Of course, he had more later on. Shit. So tell me something. Did you live in fear of Preston when you were a kid?"

I shrugged. "Yes and no. There were times when everything seemed fine between us and hadn't changed. But just as quickly, he would turn around and threaten to kick my ass if I told anyone about the latest kid he had beaten to a pulp. I didn't test him. He meant it and, trust me, he would find a way to make it sound like it was all my fault."

Danielle shook her head. She put her hands flat on the table, taking a deep breath in. She seemed close to tears again. She stared out the window for a moment, but when she turned back, she looked me in the eyes. "This is why you've been distant. I mean, Pres and I have had conversations about it before, but I mean, of course you would feel put off. It makes more sense now." She stopped short, as if she meant to say more but decided against it.

We had always had talks about family before—about my kids and theirs, what was going on with mutual friends and with our parents. For a long time, Preston had not been a topic of conversation between us, except in indirect ways. I sometimes had the impression she reached out to me in hopes that Preston and I would eventually talk more. This was the deepest conversation we'd had yet. Knowing that she had come to me with this information made me certain; she might not be ready to accept the full truth yet, but she was desperate to know what her husband was doing.

"I don't know how Preston feels," I told her. "I would be lying to you if I said it didn't affect how I relate to him now. When we talk, I feel like I never know if I'm seeing him or his façade."

Danielle's phone vibrated, and she picked it up off the table to glance at the incoming message.

"I wish I had something to say that would make any of this better," I told her.

"Well, I didn't ask you to make me feel better, just for the truth," she said. "And it feels better than lies do. On some level you always know it when you're being played. Speaking of which, Kurt just texted me. He says Preston called and checked in with his office today about an appearance that was moved up on his schedule."

"Well, at least he's nowhere hurt."

Danielle put a hand over her chest. "Yeah, there's that. I don't know. I might have to strangle him myself. How would you feel about having one less brother?"

We both laughed. I felt a mixture of relief and sadness. My brother wasn't hurt, but these questions were not about to go away. It was finally about time that some of these things came to light. My hope was that Danielle wouldn't go back to pretending everything was okay now that she knew where he was. I also wondered if there weren't other clues she had picked up on during all the years she had been married to him. Maybe, like my parents, her love for him had blinded her to things that should have been obvious. Someone needed to expose the truth about him.

"What are you going to do with all this, Danielle? You feel comfortable asking him about what's been going on?"

I really wanted to ask her if she felt *safe*. I didn't want to think Preston would hurt her. If push came to shove and my brother's secrets were about to be revealed, would he put his wife's life above his own?

I hoped Danielle would act wisely. She might think Preston loved her, but I believed Preston was incapable of those kind of emotions.

"I can't believe this is my life," my sister-in-law said. "Comfortable isn't the word. I just have no fucking choice."

"If you need anything, call me. I mean it, day or night. I'm concerned about both of you."

She shook her head. "That's very sweet, but I don't know what you could do."

"You might need someone just to listen," I said.

"Not like I can tell anyone else this." Danielle grabbed her purse. She looked me in the eyes. "When I do confront him, I'll keep your name out of it."

***

Danielle Harrington

On the ride home from the hotel where I'd met up with Tyler, I had too much time to think. I tried diverting myself as I made my way through the traffic. Music wasn't doing it. I played an audiobook for a while, but I couldn't concentrate on it. Instead it became a droning background noise. I knew I'd have no idea what was said later, so I turned it off.

My conversation with Tyler kept playing out in my mind. I was glad he'd been honest with me. I had found out enough of what I needed to about the boys' childhood.

Knowing that Preston was all right was one weight off me, but my conversation with his brother raised so many other questions. It was hard for me to imagine him hurting animals or maliciously attacking other children. How well did I really know this man that I loved? How well could you truly know *anyone* for that matter?

Was he so good at hiding the truth that I never even realized he was capable of such violence? If Preston knew how to hide his thoughts and actions that effectively, how deep did that deception go? Did this mean that he had never truly loved me, or the kids? Was our family just part of the charade, the price he paid to look normal to the outside world? Was his need to be alone simply an excuse for him to be away from me long enough to satisfy his appetite for violence? I started to question everything. As much as I loved him, what else was going on that I didn't know?

I tried to push away the feeling that the life I'd been living was a scam. One question led to another, driving me into an even darker hole; while I didn't know the truth, there were too many possibilities to consider, each one more frightening than the other.

My life before Preston had been pretty ordinary. I hadn't come from a wealthy home the way he had. Even with two paychecks, my parents at times struggled to pay bills or make the mortgage. In an odd way, there was a freedom to that. I wasn't expected to do anything other than go to school and do a decent job on my grades. No one would ever compare me to other people in the family. I had no public reputation to live up to, no family business to set my sights on after I graduated high school.

Growing up in a home with such high expectations definitely influenced him. Preston had told me before that sometimes he felt that he was always expected to be perfect, to be on stage with everyone. I felt a lump in my throat. He'd told me that in reference to his years in high school and college. It was a pressure that caused him to seek perfection, to make sure his actions appeared above reproach. I wasn't sure how that played into him using violence as an escape. There just had to be more to it, and I needed to understand what was going on with him.

I didn't want to believe Tyler, even after what I had seen. I had the gut feeling that he *believed* he was telling me the truth.

But how much of his truth was colored by his relationship with his brother? I couldn't say that his jealousy didn't impact what he believed. Besides that, there might be deeper issues between the brothers that neither would talk about. I couldn't completely accept what he had said without knowing more. It didn't seem wise to completely ignore what Preston had said about Tyler, either.

When Tyler spoke to me, I heard how careful he was. He was frightened for—and frightened of—his older brother. At the very least, he believed Preston was a threat, even if he was wrong.

There were things in my own childhood I didn't quite remember or had remembered wrong according to my parents. How much of his story now was based upon a childhood memory that had shifted and evolved to match the beliefs he had about his brother and their relationship? Tyler would have been only nine years old when the kitten incident took place. At that age, his parents and his brothers were still a large part of his world. Having the approval of the brother closest to him may have been important and any slight taken as a threat or a rebuke.

Preston had told me so many times that his younger brother was jealous and had been as far back as he remembered. I didn't want to believe Tyler would feel that way, but I understood well that jealousy could affect the way he remembered things. Maybe he didn't even realize it.

I couldn't say how Preston acted with animals. I didn't think he liked them in general, but then a lot of people didn't. The kids had been asking for a puppy or kitten on a regular basis. He hadn't budged. When I asked him about it, he said animals were unsanitary and bothersome.

Once I got home, I still had a few hours before Preston would be expected for an appearance, and I would make sure I would be there. Until then, I had to fill the hours somehow. I went upstairs to my office and closed the door. I needed some time to get my wits together. I was sure my husband was lying to me, but I didn't know the whole story yet. He wouldn't hurt me or the kids. That hadn't changed.

At least that's what I told myself. Even though I knew he wouldn't be coming home yet, I kept one ear out, waiting to hear Preston's steps on the stairway or his car coming up the driveway.

I powered on my laptop and typed a phrase into the browser: *CTE Brain injury.*

Tyler had brought up concussions and brain injury. The topic had been a hotly debated one over the last few years, and the NFL had gone to great pains to change the rules to limit injuries. It was a matter of better equipment but also of taking it seriously when players were concussed. New safeguards had been put in place back in 2017. Preston had suffered every single one of his concussions before then.

I counted back the years and thought about the times he'd had concussions throughout his professional career. If I put those together with the ones that Tyler knew about from when Preston was a kid, I came up with seven.

Seven concussions. Preston likely had even more minor ones that neither Tyler nor I knew about. How many little hits did a professional player take, from high school and up? If a player didn't experience symptoms after getting hit, they probably didn't even ask for help. Preston never asked for help with his pain until it became intolerable; I knew that much from his neck injury.

I remembered the acronym but not what it stood for: CTE (chronic traumatic encephalopathy). Always the student, I dug in to understand the mechanism behind the disease. I found that after a person suffers repeated hits to the head, an abnormal protein develops in the brain, causing neurological damage. It's a degenerative disease, and the results are awful: aggression, anxiety, memory loss, even suicidal thoughts. According to the article, the disease was first discovered in wrestlers. More research revealed that football players and soldiers suffered with this disease at an alarming rate. Something close to 98% in football players, no matter what level of the game they played. High school, college, and professional football players all had the same percentage of CTE. Even when football players wearing helmets got hit in the head multiple times without getting concussed, the nerves in part of their brains got slightly damaged.

What I found most unnerving was that there was no way to diagnose a living person with the disease. Behavioral changes and a history of concussions could suggest it, but until an autopsy was performed, there was no way to verify the abnormal protein that caused the disease was present.

The ringing of my cell shook me from my morbid thoughts.

"Hi, Mommy," my daughter's voice came over the line.

"Hi, baby. Are you being good over at Aunt Crystal's house?"

"I am," she said dramatically. I could imagine she was rolling her eyes. "Ethan is, well, I guess he's okay. He got on Aunt Crystal's nerves earlier, but she said she's over it."

"What are you guys up to?"

"Right now she's showing us how to make cookies. She even let me put in the chocolate chips."

"Awesome," I said with a smile. "You mind if I talk to her?"

"Sure," she said. I heard Crystal's voice in the background, and then Ethan's. Then both twins were laughing, always a sign of mischief. When my friend came over the line, she sounded breathless.

"Hey, Danielle. What's up? I'm sugaring them up before I return them to you."

"About that," I said. "Any chance you would mind keeping them tonight?"

"Um, no, I can keep them."

"We're not on speaker phone, are we?"

"No. Hold on," she said. More talking in the background. Isabel said something about watching her favorite program.

"If I turn it on, you have to sit still, okay?"

A few moments later I heard a door close. "Okay, I'm in the bedroom now; they can't hear me. Did you find Preston?"

"Yes. Haven't seen him yet, but he called into his agent's office, and they called me. Still don't know if he will be back tonight for sure, but if he is, I don't want the kids . . ."

"Understood," Crystal said and cut me off. "You do what you have to do; the kids will be fine. You know I love them. I've got to say, I'm going to be sideways pissed the next time I see Preston, knowing that he's treating you like this."

I hadn't told her anything other than Preston had been gone for a day and night and hadn't called me. If she knew what was really going on, she wouldn't have taken it well. So far, I was glad that she hadn't pushed for more of an explanation.

I felt so alone. I couldn't tell anyone about what was happening. My mother would insist that I go back home. The only one who even had an idea was Tyler, and I already figured there was only so much he was able or willing to do. He wasn't going to sacrifice the Harrington name for anything.

Chapter Fifteen

Ed Birch

As a former FBI agent, I went to one of the best military schools, and upon graduation, I was recruited into Quantico for training. I'd had a solid career in the bureau for over ten years. People would describe me as a tall, thin, dark-haired man who wore my hair in a military cut. I had boxed as a teen, and my nose had been broken twice, giving it a slight hump and a beak-like shape. Few of the scars I got were from my time at the bureau, but I liked to let people think they were. It added to the feeling that I wasn't a man to be messed with.

One mistake was all it took to get me to ruin the career I had worked hard for and for the people that mattered to lose trust in me. While on a stakeout one night, I got bored and had a drink.

I couldn't forgive myself because I knew better. I had been waiting to see a suspect arrive on scene. Hours in, I was fidgety and restless. I let myself get distracted by my own worries instead of focusing on the job. One drink, I told myself. A sip from the silver flask I'd started keeping in my breast pocket. An hour passed, and I emptied the whole thing.

Sometime the following morning, between one fifteen and one thirty a.m., the perpetrator slipped into the building I had under surveillance.

Several other agents were posted at different points around the building, and I was radioed of the suspect's approach. I should have gotten the jump on him quicker than anyone because I was closest to the point of entry.

A few seconds of delayed response time was all it cost me, but in that space of moments, a serial killer managed to claim one more victim. My commanding officer smelled the alcohol on my breath that morning and had me tested. My blood alcohol was just below the legal limit to drive; but *any* alcohol in the system while an agent was on the job was more than enough for censure.

The victim's eyes still haunted me to this day. She was a beautiful girl in her early twenties. So full of life. I would see those doe-like eyes in my nightmares . . . and in my daydreams. I would imagine her tossing her long, wavy brunette hair and the tinkly sound of her laugh. I would imagine that promising life cut short . . . because of my negligence.

The higher-ups showed no mercy on me. The circumstances that had led up to it—the death of my only son due to SIDS, and the subsequent disintegration of my marriage—nor my own contrition were taken into account. After I was fired, the most painful thing to come to grips with was that all the good I had done in my entire career was erased by one bad choice. Now I was deemed forever untrustworthy.

I went back home and tried to pick up what was left of my existence. That meant selling my house; Lisa, my ex-wife by then, wanted no part of it. We'd had a five-bedroom house outside Gastonia, North Carolina—a beautiful place with a view of a creek and a few acres of surrounding land. The backyard was decked out in a swing, a children's playset, and a treehouse left behind from the previous owners. When we moved in, Lisa and I had been looking forward to our own children enjoying those things. The house was meant for a family. The green stillness of the land only made my acute sense of loneliness worse. I moved out as soon as I was able.

The next several years were largely aimless ones. AA had helped me to clean up my act. I subsisted off my savings for a time, living in a small house in Indiana. I eventually started working again, first as a security guard, and then as private security.

My old friend from back home, James Riley, asked me to come to California. We'd gone to military school together but had taken decidedly different paths. James had gone to law school and become a prominent entertainment attorney.

"I'll fly you out," James offered. "I need you to handle some security for me. Boring as hell to you, probably, but it's for some very high-level people. Celebrities, their spouses, people who are willing to pay a lot of money. It could get you on the map. The good thing about these people is once you get a couple of high-paying clients under your belt, you gain credibility with that entire community. You may even find one or two that you like working for regularly."

I was sitting in my kitchen when I got the call, staring out into the backyard. My German shepherd was chasing a ball, perfectly happy in the afternoon sunshine.

"I appreciate the opportunity," I said. "Celebrities don't sound like my thing, though."

James chuckled. "Uh, no, but money is everyone's thing, right? You don't realize what you're turning down here. We're talking about a couple thousand dollars a night to walk around with a rock star. If anybody tries to get their hands someplace they're not supposed to be, you get to break their jaw, no questions asked. I know you. Don't tell me that you wouldn't like the opportunity to punch somebody these days. With your background, you will be considered *elite* security, and you'll have premium pay."

"All right then," I said. "I guess I'll find someplace to board my dog for a few days."

I went out to Los Angeles, and what was supposed to last for a week turned into a month. Soon I realized that this job was a ticket to a different life. I rented a house and had my cousin fly to Los Angeles to bring my dog to me.

While security wasn't exactly fulfilling, I decided I could definitely put up with it. The city was a nice change for me. It became easier to shake off some of my old sadness in a new environment, and the money I brought in didn't hurt. I even started dating seriously again, something I thought would never happen.

Eventually, I started thinking about what my future would be. I knew there would come a time when I wouldn't want to protect actresses and rock stars. Many of them had their own drug problems, and while my demon had always been the bottle, I knew Hollywood wasn't the best environment for me.

Getting my license as a private investigator was the next logical step.

James came in handy for me again when I needed it. He helped set me up with jobs working with clients, specializing in cases that involved rich, powerful people.

The cases I worked were often run of the mill: people wanting the goods on their cheating spouses, someone wanting an extensive background check on a potential new lover, parents wanting to know what their teenagers were up to when they were away. The one thing they had in common was that none of these people could afford their business to become a public matter. Some were already stalked by paparazzi and anyone wanting to turn a quick buck.

I took one or two cases every other month, and they paid handsomely. In the meantime, I lived a new life. I was able to forget the life I previously lived when I was with the bureau. *Almost.*

Occasionally, I still had a nightmare that brought me back to those days. I'd been pulled off the bureau in the middle of my last case, and my predecessors had never tracked the serial killer down. I still felt guilty about it, that my actions might have hindered the one slim chance they had of catching the bastard.

Late one evening, I got the phone call that would change my life. Once again it was James, coming through with a new job. This time, I was watching television, with my dog on the couch beside me. My girlfriend, Anna, was in the kitchen, humming as she cooked.

"This is pretty much a sure deal," James told me. "You'll have to go to New Orleans to meet with the client. He wants to see you face-to-face and have you sign the confidentiality agreement," he said.

He paused. In that one moment before my friend took another breath, I felt it—what I used to call the tingle. A feeling, like static electricity, that crawled its way down my arms and into my fingertips. Law enforcement people liked to refer to it as a gut feeling. It was plain old intuition, honed to a fine point through years of observation. Something was up.

"I know this attorney, and he usually levels with me about exactly what his clients want," James said. "He didn't want to tell me anything at all, but I finally got him to say it. The job is for Tyler Harrington."

"The football player?" I asked.

"One and the same. He needs someone followed. Probably thinks his wife is having an affair or something."

"Well, shit," I said, scratching my chin. "This should be interesting."

***

I did a little research into Tyler's background over the three days it took to arrange a meeting. I always did a cursory check into my clients. It paid to know who one was dealing with. Tyler had a stellar career, not as good as his brother Preston's, but still noteworthy. He was married with a pretty wife and two young girls. He had an apparently idyllic life. Though he was probably nearing the end of his career, he was still the kind of man who would have a well-fulfilled life after his time on the gridiron was over.

I drove out to Tyler's house from the Louis Armstrong New Orleans airport to meet with him and his attorney. His executive stone-front house was surrounded by a lush green lawn. As I walked up the winding sidewalk with flowers on each side leading from the driveway to the cement landing, I noticed that the large window in front of the house was half covered by a blind. The football player answered the door himself, and after introductions were made and pleasantries exchanged, we sat down at the dining room table to get to business.

One of the things about meeting actors was that I usually found them to look different than most people thought they did. Men and women alike were often unrecognizable without a makeup artist to enhance their best features. Most were taller or shorter than I guessed; some looked older or younger in person. There really was something to be said for professional lighting and camera angles that favored the "good side" of someone's face.

Tyler Harrington would be the first sports figure I had worked for. He was exactly as I expected: tall and muscular with brown hair and dark eyes. He didn't appear to be any more or less the athlete he was on television, even while dressed in an expensive suit.

"Thanks for coming out to the house, Mr. Birch. My wife is at work and the kids are at school, so I thought this would be the most private place to talk. As you probably understand, discretion is my utmost concern," Tyler said.

"I've worked with all kinds of people before, as I'm sure your attorney has told you," Birch replied coolly. "And you won't have to worry about discretion. I need to know who you would like me to follow and why."

Tyler looked over at his lawyer, who nodded.

"I'll let you two gentleman talk alone," the lawyer said. He got up and disappeared down the steps to the lower level of the house.

Once the lawyer was out of earshot, Tyler spoke up. "I need you to follow my brother, Preston Harrington."

"All right," I said, taking a notepad from my pocket. I could have taken notes on my phone but found that people were more comfortable when I used pen and paper. "Tell me why."

Tyler adjusted his tie. He cleared his throat. "Recently, my sister-in-law, Preston's wife, Danielle, told me that she found some items that might put my brother at a crime scene: a blood-spattered matchbook, a piece of one of his jackets burned in the backyard. One of the employees at the bar said he was there that night."

"Crime scene?"

"A murder. There are other things. Time where Preston has been unaccounted for. He goes off without telling anyone what he's up to. One of his best friends died recently. Rob Anderson was killed in what was apparently a robbery from the restaurant he co-owned with my brother.

It feels like a lot of weird coincidences lately. Not enough to positively say that he's done something, but more than enough to make us both uncomfortable."

"We?" I asked.

"My sister-in-law is very concerned," Tyler said. "She brought up the topic with me, and we've been talking about it."

"Do you think your brother would be the type of guy who could commit a murder? Or do you think he's just running around on his wife?"

"Well, I do know that when he was a child, he was violent with other children. He killed animals. He did both in front of me and then threatened that he'd hurt me if I ever told. He made it clear that he was going to do something worse than just beat me up. I never told anyone most of what happened, and the few things I did tell, no one believed me.

"I had decided it was a phase and hoped he'd moved on from it. As adults, we lead very separate lives. We're cordial but not close. For the sake of the family, I never got into things with him. But after Danielle came to me with her concerns, it brought back memories I would have preferred to forget. But now I can't. If he is seriously out there hurting people, then I've got to do what I can to stop him or I feel complicit in the guilt."

"Does Danielle know that you've taken this step? Would she be on board with this?"

"No on both counts," Tyler replied. "Danielle wants to believe in his innocence. She's told me before that she needs solid proof before she's willing to do anything about it. This is about more than convincing her. I want to know what he's doing, and if he is out there killing people, I want to know enough information to get the authorities involved. If anything, I want to keep her out of the loop with this as long as possible. I hope I'm wrong about Preston, but I don't think so. I'm also motived to protect Danielle. She doesn't deserve to be in the middle of all this."

Tyler took out his phone and searched through his photos. "Here's a picture of Danielle, just so you have a frame of reference."

Glancing at the picture, I felt my breath tighten. I took the phone from him to better study the photo. I swallowed hard, trying to not visibly react, yet I felt sweat beads forming on my forehead. I cleared my throat and grabbed my collar to loosen it. She was the spitting image of that other girl—the one I had failed to protect. I cleared my throat again and coughed.

"Are you OK? Can I get you a glass of water?"

"Yes, please." I set the phone down with the photo facing downward. The picture was seared into my memory anyway.

When Tyler returned with the water, I willed my hand to not shake as I gulped the whole thing down and wiped my brow with the back of my hand. Those big, brown eyes. The dark, wavy hair. The girls looked similar enough in my mind to be sisters.

I forced myself back to the present moment, knowing I was already all in on this case.

"I'm happy to help you," I said, trying not to sound as overeager as I felt. "If you have a suspicion that something is going on, it usually is. Of course I hope nothing is wrong, but it wouldn't be right for me not to warn you. That said, you should give some thought about how anything negative I find will impact your family."

"I understand," Tyler replied. "I think I've been preparing myself for it for a long time now."

Chapter Sixteen

Preston Harrington

I hate unprofessional people. I built a life on maintaining a reputation based on following through with promises and completing even the smallest tasks to perfection. When I see people who don't care about their jobs, who waste others' time, it pisses me off.

Gio Martinelli showed up at our commercial shoot for his pizza chain two hours late. I was irritated because what should have taken an hour or two at the most ended up taking most of my afternoon. I already knew my lines. All of the crew was ready; everybody knew what they were supposed to do and where they were supposed to be. Where was he? I couldn't understand how he thought it was okay to come in several hours late. Kurt gave me shit about rescheduling, but here it was we couldn't shoot because the restaurant's owner was nowhere to be found.

It couldn't have happened on a worse day. I hadn't been home or even called Danielle. I'd planned on being in and out in a couple of hours and on my way back home to her. This was going to mean I would be away longer, and I knew she was going to be angry.

Martinelli was the Pop in Pop's Pizza. The public knew him as a hard worker, a small-town guy who had bought a hole-in-the-wall pizza place and turned it into a rags-to-riches story. Over ten years he had turned his stores into a franchise and later into a respectable national chain. Pop's was known for its high quality and family-friendly atmosphere. It was part of his company's mission statement, and he stressed the importance of the family unit. All his stores were closed on Sunday so his employees could be with their families. He'd publicly stated that he felt the bedrock of any successful family was religious faith. The campaign tagline for Pop's read: family, food, fun.

I had done several commercials with Martinelli before, and he'd always shown up without any problems. They were spending a lot of money on this commercial; we were on a closed sound stage with at least a hundred people milling about: camera crew, sound engineers, production and personal assistants, a handful of actors, makeup and hair people. The set was a replica of the inside of a Pop's Pizza store, with a front counter and kitchen, complete with working ovens and registers. Everyone was being paid while they were on standby. My concern was that time was being wasted. I needed to get home.

After I found out about some of his personal beliefs, I was glad we never were more than acquaintances. I didn't want any of his beliefs to cause me any blowback. The last thing I wanted was for people to associate me with a bigot.

During a television interview once, Gio had made a statement about how he didn't want to hire gay employees at his company because he felt their relationships weren't sanctified by God. I wanted no part of that bullshit. There was some talk about it in the news for a few weeks, with some customers and members of the gay community boycotting. Of course, a small but loud contingent of people also showed support for Gio's beliefs and what they liked to call "traditional family values."

At the time, I talked to Kurt about getting me out of the endorsement deal with Pop's. Our contract was ironclad, but the good thing was that it was about to run out. I only had three months left, and I'd already made the decision I wouldn't be renewing. I literally couldn't wait for my time with this company to end.

Finally, Gio showed up and we got the taping started.

The story behind the commercial was simple: I was supposed to be a new employee at the Pop's Pizza store. I was tossing around pizza dough like footballs, "accidentally" hitting coworkers and a couple of customers before the owner was supposed to come in and stop me.

"Hey, Preston!" Gio yelled. "What are you doing?"

The director yelled cut. "That's not the line."

"Oh?" Gio said, scratching his head. "What's it again?"

The director shook his head. "The line is, 'Hey Preston, what are you doing with the dough?'"

They redid the shot several times. The pizza chain owner couldn't seem to do it, making up a different line every time he was supposed to speak. He shrugged. "Sorry. Guess I'm not feeling it today."

I tried to help him, whispering the line to him before the camera started rolling again. Gio was the only one who seemed not to realize what a shitty job he was doing.

"When I want you to do that, I'll ask," Gio snapped.

I wanted to say something else for him then, but there was no time. I fixed a plastic smile on my face as we tried the scene again.

After Gio screwed up three more times, the director called for a fifteen-minute break. He grumbled profanity as he walked off.

I headed out toward the back of the lot; a catering truck and craft services was set up for the actors and crew to pick up anything they wanted to eat. Two of the extras in the commercial were standing off to the side of the catering truck, waiting for their orders. They were both still in their costumes as Pop's Pizza employees. One guy was tall and skinny with dark curly hair, the other a shorter, stockier young man with sandy blond hair. I pegged them both as college students. You could usually pick out the extras on any set because they were often enthusiastic to be there and usually hung around craft services, taking advantage of the free food.

"Man, I don't care that he was late," the dark-haired guy said. "I hope we go into double time. You see it was taking him awhile to get his lines straight."

"Oh, it's not that he's late, it's why he's late," the lighter-haired one said. "Have you seen the latest story on TMX?" he asked, whipping out his cell phone.

"No," the other guy said. "We're supposed to have our cell phones off," he said, looking around nervously.

"Yeah, well, they're supposed to be off during taping, and we haven't shot anything they can use so far," he said. "Check out the website. Look familiar?"

The taller guy snatched his friend's phone away and stared at it, frowning. "The hell. Is that him? Gio?"

"Looks like," the shorter one shot back. "In the flesh."

I grabbed a bottle of water and headed back to my dressing room. As soon as the door was closed behind me, I logged onto the TMX website. I had never been a fan of gossip websites, but if Gio was the subject of one of their hack jobs, I needed to know about it. Not only was I the spokesperson for the chain, but I had bought into thirteen or so of their franchises around the country.

The story was trending and easy to find. The headline on the story read:

Pop's Pizza Magnate Caught with Underage Girls

Gio Martinelli, owner of Pop's Pizza, was caught in a compromising situation with two girls under the age of eighteen. An anonymous source sent these pictures to our editor last week. We were able to verify the identities of not only Martinelli but the two girls involved, ages sixteen and seventeen. Because they are minors, we will not reveal their names, and their faces have been blurred in the picture.

Martinelli has been married to his wife, Lydia, for twenty-five years and they have four children together. He is known for his clean image and his self-described "faith-based business" that caters to families in a kid-friendly atmosphere.

We reached out to Martinelli for comment but had not received a response at the time this article was posted. We will keep you up to date with any new information on this developing story.

The picture beneath was Gio sitting on a bed between two naked girls, their faces and body parts covered over by black strips. This was just bad. I couldn't figure how he had the nerve to do it. Despite my many sins, I had never cheated on my wife. The fact that these were young girls made it that much more disgusting.

This was bad all the way around. He could be charged with statutory rape. This was the kind of dirt the press loved, giving them something to talk about for the next several news cycles. He could kiss his image goodbye. I had my own investment in this company to think about, and

I wasn't happy with the idea of being seemingly connected to this mess.

I made a quick phone call to my accountant and left him a message. I might not be able to get out of my sponsorship role with Pop's for a few months, but there was nothing that would keep me from selling off the franchises I owned. I wanted it done right away, and I didn't care if it meant taking a loss.

On news like this, the stocks would probably plunge anyway.

I returned to the sound stage and noticed the crew was standing around. A few of them were talking in whispers, but I caught snatches of conversation. The news had spread through the entire crew within a few minutes.

I heard a door slam, and Gio walked back out, with the director trailing behind him. All eyes were on the pair. No one spoke as Gio stomped his way onto the set. Apparently he had been summoned into the director's office to have an unpleasant talk about what had kept him from the set and why he couldn't remember a few lines. My guess was that he probably wanted Gio to straighten up or scrap the shoot for the day. In my opinion it wasn't a bad idea.

While Gio was technically running the show, he probably was smart enough to know it would be a major mistake to piss off the people doing the commercial. He had stockholders to answer to, after all, who were likely to be unhappy for other reasons.

"Places, people," someone yelled.

"What are you looking at?" Gio addressed me, fuming. "I know you probably heard what happened. Like you've never done anything wrong in your entire life? I wouldn't believe it for a second. I'm sure you've had girls throwing their panties at you since you were a kid."

"I don't mess around with other women, but what I do, I don't get caught for," I whispered. I punctuated my remark with a grin.

His brow furrowed. He turned away from me. I wondered if he had considered how screwed he would be if any of this ever came out. This guy was a loser. I formed a plan in my mind. *If you're nervous about the director chewing you out, wait until you get home, buddy.*

We started taping again, going over the lines.

"What are you doing with that pizza dough, Preston?" Gio asked. I felt the heat of the lights and the scrutiny of the silent crew around us.

I kneaded the dough, enjoying the pliable feeling of it between my fingers. "Oh, getting it ready for tossing!" I replied without missing a beat. I had the short script committed to memory. While I played with the dough, I imagined my fingers squeezing his neck, his eyes going wide as he struggled for breath, his fingers struggling to pry my hands away.

"Whoa, Preston, you're tossing those a little too hard!" he noted. It had taken the entrepreneur multiple attempts to finally get into his role, but once he did, he made it sound natural. I looked at him, and in my mind I was replaying the image of him with those two girls in bed. I wondered if he'd violated other young women and how long he'd been getting away with it.

"Well, we need to make sure we get these pies out there, Gio," I said, and with false modesty tossed a mound of dough at a coworker, who caught it, rolled it flat, and added sauce and toppings before putting it into an old-fashioned brick oven.

"That's good, Preston, but take your time." Gio patted my shoulder for effect. "We don't rush anything at Pop's!"

It took everything for me not to recoil. I thought about my pipe and how I loved the thought of bringing it down on his skull. I'd watch his blood splatter hit the wall. I wondered what he would think in that last moment before the world faded from his sight. Would he wonder what had caused me to do it? Would he plead for his life with his last few gasps of breath? Maybe there was a special place in hell for people like him.

"Cut!" The producer yelled. Finally, we were wrapping the shoot.

I was relieved when it was over. Gio might think he was free to talk to me and anyone else he wanted to, but so what? I could more than handle the asshole. If he decided to come for me, he'd regret it. In fact, it might be fun to teach him a lesson, just for the hell of it.

I retreated to my dressing room to change out of my black Pop's uniform and back into my own clothes. I sighed and attempted to massage away the pain in the back of my neck. It had started throbbing toward the end of the shoot. I knew I had some ibuprofen in my car's glove compartment. I was anxious to take a couple pills and head back home for some sleep. If I were lucky, my wife would still be at work for a few hours, giving the medicine time to kick in.

I opened the dressing room door and stopped in my tracks.

"Danielle."

***

Danielle Harrington

"Hi baby," I said.

Preston looked surprised. For a split second I saw a flash of irritation in his eyes. Then he smiled, and he looked like the Preston I knew, the one who I always believed to be gentle and kind. He reached out and grasped me in a quick, tight embrace. Out of habit, and maybe because I couldn't help it, I squeezed him back. The scent of his cologne and aftershave were comforting, even if I knew I shouldn't be anywhere near him.

"I'm so happy to see you! I was going to call you earlier, but," Preston said, lowering his voice, "today was a nightmare on set, and by the time I got back here, my phone was dead."

"What about last night?" I asked.

"Can we talk about that in the car?" he said, arm around my shoulder. He gently steered me toward the exit.

"Of course," I said with a tight smile. If he wanted, I could play this game with him too. He had reasons for not wanting to say anything while people from his commercial shoot were still milling around. Of course my ultra-private husband wouldn't want strangers to hear what might sound like a disagreement. The walk across the lot was also going to give him time to think of a convincing lie, I was sure of it. Meanwhile, I tried to silence all the questions and worries that had been swirling through my head all day.

"How'd you know I'd be here?" he asked.

"I wondered if you would ask me that. Kurt said you would be filming today," I said. "I thought it would be nice if I picked you up."

A few people nodded as we walked by, and some of them smiled. A young couple, both extras who had finished work on a different set asked for Preston's signature, and he obliged. He talked to them for a few minutes. As always, he shined in the spotlight. Would he ever stop craving the attention? I didn't think he would. By the time we reached my car, he squeezed my hand and smiled. "I brought my SUV. I'll follow you back to the house, Dani."

"All right," I said. "Don't get lost, Pres."

He chuckled at my sarcasm.

I led the way as we pulled off the lot. I tried to keep my hands from shaking, gripping the wheel so hard I could see the veins underneath my skin. I did half expect him to drive off and leave me once we were in traffic, flip a U-turn when I was stuck at a light and couldn't follow. Maybe part of me half wanted him to. People broke up every day. I had already made the decision that I couldn't go on in this state of suspense, unsure if the man I married had hurt people . . . possibly *killed* people. I still could barely think such an awful thought. I had the constant feeling of being sick to my stomach, my heart fluttering. I needed to know if I could trust him or not. And would our kids be safe around him? I felt I could protect myself one way or another, but the kids? But he loved the kids, I counseled myself. He could never harm his own children.

The only other time I had experienced such uneasiness, albeit for a very different reason, was during an incident early in Preston's professional career. He had been in the middle of a tightly contested road game when he took a cheap shot (the replays clearly showed it was a late hit, not to mention intentional helmet-to-helmet contact) from a 325-pound monster. I was horrified as my man had to be helped off the field several tense minutes after the ref called a fifteen-yard penalty for roughing the passer.

I still remember the feeling of my heart thudding to the pit of my stomach and the awful, chilling fear that clawed at my guts.

The NFL's priority in those days was getting players back on the field as soon as possible after an injury, especially a superstar quarterback, rather than erring on the side of caution and benching him. Nobody seemed at all concerned about the irreparable brain damage players could suffer from repeated violent blows to the skull, which could literally jar the brain within its cavity. A quick injection of a pain killer and a player could be ready to return to the field in minutes.

True to form, between Preston's persuasive powers, "Damn, that really rang my bell," he had quipped, laughing it off, and the team's desperate need for his QB prowess, his injury was deemed minor and he was proclaimed fit to continue the game after sitting out only two plays. I noticed later after the game how much he slept for the next few days and even vomited once in the middle of the night. But I didn't make too much out of it at the time; I knew he would get angry if I tried to baby him.

Of course, what was happening now was not the same kind of fear, but it was the kind of life-changing worry that could burst our family's bubble. After all, our life path of success had always seemed to lay before us so clearly.

At the moment, I wasn't sure about anything, but I kept telling myself that knowing one way or another would be better than suffering with this uncertainty. There would be a path to a solution once I knew what I was dealing with. At least I hoped there would be.

We made it to the house at the same time. I used my key to get in through the garage door, which opened into the kitchen. I left the door open behind me. It had been a long afternoon, and I wasn't sure how long my nerves were going to hold up.

"It's awfully quiet," Preston said, standing in the doorway. "Where are the kids?"

"With Crystal," I said. "She's been promising to spend a day with them for a while, so I figured today would be fine."

"Oh." Preston's brow wrinkled. "Well, I hope they have fun. You know," he slipped his arms around my waist, "how about we have some fun of our own? How often do we get a quiet house?"

We kissed, but his touch made me sad, and angry, and a host of other emotions I didn't want. I kissed him back but also took a careful step backward, leaning against the kitchen sink. It was hard to push him away at that moment. If I wanted to pretend that everything was okay, the best place to do it would always be in his arms.

"You didn't tell me what happened yesterday," I reminded him.

He sighed. "I'm so sorry, honey. I'm embarrassed."

"Why?" I asked.

Preston waited a beat before responding. "I wasn't having a great day. My neck was bothering me, and you know, Kurt didn't exactly help my mood, either. I went out for a long drive and ended up at the Marriott bar. I had a few drinks and ended up taking a room upstairs. I wasn't good to drive home."

"Why didn't you call me to pick you up?"

"It was late, and you would have had to call the nanny to come be with the kids. I didn't want to bother you. I meant to call you, but I fell asleep. Next thing I knew it was morning and I barely had time to get down to the commercial shoot. I grabbed my phone, thinking I would call you, but it wasn't charged. The shoot took forever. I was going to try my cell one more time when you showed up."

"I see," I said. "So you couldn't have used the hotel phone, or even had the concierge call to let me know where you were?"

"I should have taken care of that, I know. It was just a bad night and I wouldn't have been good company to you anyway. Listen." He put his hands on my shoulders. "I know I should have called you, but I can't undo it. I'll do better next time. I didn't do it to slight you in any way, honey."

He looked at me with those blue eyes of his. Despite everything, I still wanted to believe him. I wanted to let him kiss me again, and maybe take me upstairs. Pretend none of this was happening. I knew that whatever was happening wasn't going away. I owed it to myself, to him and to our kids, to get to the bottom of it.

"Tell you what," I said. "Why don't you go in the living room and relax? I'll put together a snack for us. I'll be there in a minute."

Now I was the one stalling. I needed something to do with my hands. Tyler's words came back to me: *he's always had tendencies*. If Preston had always been this way and I was only now finding out, what did that say about him? What did it mean in terms of our relationship? Did he really love me, or was I just part of the appearance of respectability he needed to cover up who he really was?

Preston smiled and gave me a swat on the butt. I could tell he thought the situation was handled. I was angry that he thought it was that easy. Then again, hadn't I always easily acquiesced in the past?

I hadn't eaten a damn thing when I went to see his brother, hadn't bothered since the day before. But even still, the rumbling in my stomach had a lot more to do with tension than hunger. I put together a plate for us: crackers, cheese, grapes, apple slices. I grabbed a bottle of wine and headed out to the living room.

When I got there, Preston was perfectly comfortable. He sat on our leather couch, feet up, with Sports Corps on the television. I put the food down on the coffee table.

"That looks great, thanks," Preston said. "They had food at the shoot, but you know how it is. It was a lot of junk, but anything good for you takes forever for them to make. I just skipped it."

"Yeah," I said, smiling. "Figured that. Gonna get one more thing."

I brought back a wine glass for myself, a bottle of whiskey for him, and a tumbler. I put it onto the table in front of him. He looked up, and again I caught a look in his eyes, a flash of emotion he hadn't wanted me to see. How many times had he looked at me like that before and I had just missed it? How often had I attributed his need for space or the fact that he seemed withdrawn to being overworked or introspective? He was charming and extroverted, but there was so much more to the stillness between his words and glances than I had allowed myself to dream of.

I finally understood there were things he wanted to make sure no one would see, especially those closest to him.

"I think you're going to need something stronger than just a glass of wine, so that's why I brought you some whiskey. I need an explanation, a *real* one, about what's going on with you." I sat down on the sofa opposite of him. "I'm waiting."

"Danielle, what do you want me to say? I should have called . . ."

"No, not that. I want to know why you went to Grinder's and didn't mention it to me."

He shrugged. "Yeah, maybe I did. I don't understand. What is this? I can't get a beer without checking in?"

"When you go to our favorite bar and someone winds up dead the next day, that might be something worth discussing."

I took in a breath and waited, hoping to see some kind of change in his expression. He was deadly calm, his eyes blank. When he spoke, his voice was calm. He sounded like he was reasoning with someone unhinged. He tilted his head slightly, frowned as if my words utterly confused him.

"Darling, you're going to have to explain to me why you're so agitated about this. Why is it so important to you?"

"How could someone being murdered outside our favorite hangout spot *not* be important? I'm worried about you."

Preston took a sip of his drink in lieu of answering right away, so I tried a different tactic. I reached into my jeans pocket and pulled out the button, still attached to bit of charred fabric. It landed on the coffee table between us with a soft metallic thump.

"Explain this," I demanded.

Preston was expressionless. "I'm not even sure what that is."

"Oh, you don't recognize it? The remains of your favorite jacket, which you burned out back."

"You're worrying me right now. I haven't burned anything in a long time. And even if I had, what's the big deal?"

I picked up the button and stuffed it back in my pocket. "You're really going to stand there and pretend you've got no clue what I'm talking about? Really? You sure this is what you want to say to me right now?"

He blinked. "Honestly, I wish I knew what this was about."

"Did you get into a fight with someone? Tell me what happened that night at Grinder's. Did anything happen between you and the guy who got killed there?"

His mouth dropped open, and then he laughed. "Please tell me this is some kind of joke."

"You may be sitting here trying to get me to think I'm crazy, Preston, but I fucking know better. I am your wife. Something here is not right. You want to play this game where I'm the one who's crazy, think again."

"Danielle, I don't know anything about that man. What are you talking about?"

"Do you want me to spell it out for you?" I asked.

Preston paused before answering. "You're going to have to because I don't understand what you're insinuating."

"Did you hurt that man? Or did you get so angry with him that you . . . k-killed him?" I had a hard time saying the word aloud.

"What? I won't even dignify that with an answer! That's ridiculous."

"Oh, ridiculous is it? I will not have you treat me like this in my own home!" I screamed. "Tell you what. You want your space to do whatever it is you're up to, go for it. You're not going to treat me like I'm stupid. I am the one person you're supposed to be honest with. But that's just fine . . ."

He stood up. "What?"

"Look. Don't talk to me. While we're on the subject, don't touch me, either. When you decide to come clean with whatever is going on with you, we can have a real talk. Trying to play with me like I'm crazy just isn't going to work."

"I can't make you accept it if you don't believe me," he said. "I've got no clue what you're talking about."

He got up and walked out of the room. A few moments later, I heard the door to the guest bedroom slam.

Chapter Seventeen

Sharon Middleton

I visited my son twice a week. I used to go every day, but after the first five years of doing so, my physician told me that seeing him daily was causing my own health to deteriorate. I, who had always been a stubborn woman in my own right, realized there was some truth in this. The people closest to me thought I was crazy for going to see him at all. My son had been in a coma for twenty years after an accidental fall from a balcony.

He had sustained multiple injuries: broken ribs, a punctured lung, and both his legs broken. Even his nose, straight and perfect like his dad's, had been busted in the fall.

I reminisced over the days when he was a small child and sick in bed. He seemed to catch every flu, cold, and childhood illness. I felt if only I could watch him, keep his body cool, everything would be all right. I was aware that wasn't the case anymore, but the familiar ritual was all I could do to soothe myself.

The doctors told me that they had spotted neurological trauma early on but had underestimated the severity of it.

At first, they gave Josh a hopeful diagnosis. Their working theory was that he might only be under for a few days. They ordered scans and tests to make sure.

Once the results came back, the attending physician admitted that Josh's prognosis was very poor. They warned that if he did wake, his mental function would be severely affected. Most likely he would be a vegetable. With each day he didn't wake, the odds that he would never wake up grew larger.

For the first six months of his coma, I watched him in the hospital. During his perpetual slumber, his body was indeed healing. The casts on his legs were eventually removed. The bruises faded. The swelling and dark circles around his eyes eventually went away. He was pale and still, and in a way, that was even worse. He was as lifeless and cold as a statue.

After his time in the hospital was over, Josh was moved to a skilled nursing facility. The staff there were tasked with moving him to prevent sores, cleaning him daily, and keeping him fed through a PEG tube directly into his stomach. Since he was breathing on his own, I was not forced to make the decision to take him off of life support. There were many times when I thought that might have been more merciful. I hated even thinking that way.

The staff at the nursing facility were different than the ones at the hospital. They were kind to me, but they didn't pretend to have any hope of recovery. I tentatively asked one of the nurses if she had ever seen anyone get better. The nurse looked at me with wide brown eyes and a soul-deep sadness that answered my question without the woman speaking a word. When she finally did speak, her words were carefully measured.

"The patients I have seen in his condition haven't usually recovered."

I had lost a lot since the early years after my son's injury. My marriage had already been on the rocks, and when Josh got hurt, it killed what little patience I had for my husband. Medical bills bankrupted us. We lost our home, our cars, all we'd spent our adult lives working for. After the house was put up for auction, my husband moved out of state. One of my cousins told me that he moved back to Montana, where he still had family ties. I hadn't heard from him since.

My sister offered to let me stay in the guest house behind her home, and that was where I'd lived for the last fifteen years. If not, I wasn't sure where I would have gone. My younger son, David, was already living out in California with his wife and baby. He helped me as much as he could, but I hated to ask him for money because I knew it was a struggle for him.

When I went to see Josh, I would read to him. His favorite stories were horror and science fiction. I would check a few books out from the library every two weeks and bring them on each visit. Sometimes I imagined I saw his brow furrow, his lips purse. There was an explanation for this, too; involuntary movements, I was told. I continued to read, to talk to him and squeeze his cool hand because I believed some part of him was still aware.

I checked my calendar that day, and realized that in five more months, it would be the twenty-first-year anniversary of his accident. I burst into tears. What was the use of all this suffering? Why wasn't I able to turn away and stop thinking about him like his father and the rest of the family had?

I went to see my son later that day, and for once, I didn't have the heart to read to him. I sat, holding Josh's hand, staring out into the rain on this gray, dreary day. That afternoon, I made another silent plea to God, one of millions down through the years. It was simple, heartfelt, and desperate. So were all the other prayers that hadn't made a damn bit of difference.

Let him wake up or let him pass away, because I can't bear this anymore.

I stayed for an hour. Once that time was up, I gathered my coat and scarf and left my son. Walking down the long corridor, I was dreading the trip home through the rain. There was a shelter at the bus stop, but it didn't stop cars from splashing water onto the sidewalk as they streaked by.

I had just reached the doorway and was about to step into the rain when I heard someone calling my name.

"Mrs. Middleton, Mrs. Middleton!" the nurse cried.

"What is it?" Fear struck me, tying itself in knots in my throat and stomach. In that moment, I regretted my prayer and the desperation that caused it. I was shivering when the young woman reached me.

The nurse's dumbstruck expression turned into a beaming smile.

"Mrs. Middleton, come, you've got to see!" She grabbed my arm. "It's a miracle!"

Chapter Eighteen

Danielle Harrington

Sports Corps held an annual fundraiser to benefit children with learning disabilities. Preston and I had been going to the event for the last five years or so. It was a black-tie gala with a banquet, charity auction, and awards ceremony. The fundraiser charged twelve hundred dollars a plate, along with a five-hundred-dollar fee to reserve a table. On top of that, attendees were asked to bring their checkbooks and be generous. The event attracted the best of the sports world, along with various celebrities and philanthropists who wanted to show off their charitable giving. Photos of the attendees and mention of how much was raised toward the cause would be all the talk of social media and television tabloids the following day.

At some point I remember looking at the calendar on my phone and thinking that since it was early June, we would have several events to be attending. Between March and June something was always going on, and Preston participated in at least four of five fundraisers each season.

This year, Preston had been chosen to be the keynote speaker. He was also being honored for his charitable work.

Among sports celebrities, he was considered highly notable for his focus on charities that primarily helped children.

I'd halfway forgotten that this night was coming up until Preston mentioned it.

"How soon?" I asked.

His brow wrinkled. "Saturday the 15th. Two weeks from now. I can't believe you forgot."

I paused before answering him. "I've had other things on my mind."

"And while you're at it, could you make an appointment to get that seatbelt on the SUV fixed? It keeps getting stuck, and it drives me crazy."

"Sure," I said to appease him, knowing that with everything I had on my plate these days, his seatbelt still ranked pretty low.

We were in the kitchen. The kids had already eaten and were in the living room, playing a video game. I was working on my fourth coffee of the day. Preston seemed to be hanging around. He'd finished his meal but sat beside me, toying with his cell phone. My best guess was that he wanted to talk but wasn't sure how to start a conversation. I was anxious but doing my best not to show it.

I hated the long silences and the uneasiness between us lately. I was sure that even the kids were picking up on it. I couldn't go back to feeling normal around him without some answers. He hadn't given me any. Though he was sleeping in our bed again, we weren't touching each other. Really, we weren't speaking much. I missed our closeness. I didn't know what he expected from me. Pretending things were fine wasn't going to solve anything.

"Will you have enough time to get things together?" he asked.

"It will make the planning a little tight, but yes," I said. I didn't offer any other comment. It would make getting a custom dress next to impossible, but he didn't need to know about that. Appearances were always important to him, and that meant I had to make sure I was the woman whose look drew the most attention.

"It's been awhile since we've had a night out," Preston said.

"Yeah, it has."

"If we have to be out anyway, we might as well enjoy it."

I smiled. Usually, I would tell him any night that we got to go out for the evening and have the babysitter with the kids was one we couldn't waste. We would get a nice hotel room, order champagne, and spend the night making love.

I wasn't sure what he was expecting. I would make sure I looked good, I would smile and speak at all the right times, be the wife I had always been in public. The rest? As long as his silence lasted, I was ready to hold out.

Preston must have known better to push things with me right then. He went in the living room to be with the kids.

I went upstairs and took a shower. I put on my robe, dried my hair with a towel, and looked over the banister into the living room.

He was playing video games with the kids. Ethan was shouting at the screen, and Isabel was laughing. Like his dad, my son hates to lose, and he will demand as many more games as it takes to win again. Preston was grinning. "Son, we'll do another round," he promised. Isabel rested in the crook of her dad's arm, her own game controller tilted to the right.

The way he interacted with the kids hadn't changed a bit. That was something I was grateful for.

I decided to use that stupid malfunctioning SUV seatbelt as an excuse to slip into the garage and place the new cell phone with a GPS into the car. If he asked, I was just "checking" on the seatbelt. I'd downloaded the app and attached the battery bank but had dragged my feet on placing it in the vehicle. I also grabbed the kitchen garbage as a further reason to be in the garage. I usually wasn't this paranoid, but in my nervousness I was overthinking everything.

I approached the SUV but then glanced at Preston's Corolla. This was the car he used as backup when he traveled to places where his image didn't matter so much. Which car? On a hunch, I decided to hide the phone in the Corolla. I got the trunk open and shoved the phone and battery as far back in the compartment as I could reach, then covered it with a blanket. Thankfully, the trunk was a mess. Preston apparently didn't check back here too often. If he ever discovered the phone, I'd be dead. Perhaps literally.

I dumped the garbage and then went back inside. Instead of joining my family, I walked down the hall and into Preston's office.

I kept my own office locked most of the time because I didn't like the kids going in there if I wasn't with them. Preston usually did the same because there were expensive things in there, including a display case that held trophies and memorabilia from varying points in his career. On this night, the door stood ajar.

The entire left wall was covered by customized oak cases with glass shelving, meant to show off his treasures under the best light possible. He had them lined up by importance; at the top were trophies earned over his NFL career, below those were plaques and certificates for charity work, and on the lowest rung were college and high school trophies.

The right wall held his bookshelves. These were filled with biographies. Most were sports-related texts, though he did keep a few history books, too. I always thought these were more for show than anything else. I never saw him read any of these. There was usually a stack of paperbacks on his bedside table, and those were the only ones I ever saw him read. He liked action and mystery novels, which he considered his guilty pleasure.

In the middle of his room was his desk, a huge thing made of carved oak. Two computers sat on top of it—a laptop and a desktop. I was looking for the last package Rob had dropped over to the house, a few days before he died.

The desk had at least twelve drawers. It was an old-fashioned thing with square lines and elaborate woodwork on the legs.

I remembered leaving Rob's box on the desk, but Preston had never mentioned it, and I hadn't seen the package again. I was hoping to find it or the contents.

I wished I had opened it myself to begin with. Something had been going on between the two of them in those last weeks. They'd always had disagreements about the restaurant. What business partners didn't? But this had been something more. I'd never gotten either one of them to be honest about that. In retrospect, I should have paid more attention. Maybe Preston wouldn't have told me, but Rob and I were close enough that he would have if I'd questioned him about it. At the time, I hadn't wanted to be involved in any arguments between them. I'd told myself they would be able to solve it without my interference.

I went through the drawers but didn't find anything out of the ordinary. Preston was overly neat. Everything was carefully arranged down to pens and pencils. I found a few unused notepads. Otherwise, the desk was empty.

Maybe he wasn't keeping anything important in that desk on purpose . . . after all, he did keep it unlocked.

I looked at his desktop computer. I didn't know the password to get in, though I figured I could crack it if given enough time. That was one thing I wasn't willing to try while my husband was in the house.

I heightened my senses and noted that Preston was still with the kids. I could hear them laughing and the loud sound effects as they played a video game.

I could always say I had been looking in his desk for a blank piece of paper or a pen, after all. Cracking his password and getting into his laptop wouldn't be as easy to explain.

I went to my room and laid down. I had so many thoughts I didn't want to entertain, each one leading down a darker path than the one before. I dozed off and didn't wake until I felt Preston slip into bed beside me. I kept my back turned to him. Without speaking, he slipped an arm around me. I didn't move. With his chest pressed against my back, I was already too close to the edge of the bed to put any more space between us.

I was lulled into sleep again, feeling his warmth against me. I woke a few moments later to feel his hardness against my back. He'd moved his hand so that his palm rested between my thighs.

"Baby," he whispered. His tongue flicked out to touch my earlobe.

"Pres," I whispered. His hand moved upward, gently stroking me. I sighed deeply. It was all the encouragement he needed.

He turned me over. He straddled me, knees on either side of my hips. Our room was dark, but through a bit of moonlight visible through a window I could see him in shadow. Naked and powerful, all muscle and masculinity. Though he was above me, his hands were at his sides. His head bent toward me. How many nights had he kneeled above me like this? I was always so happy to have him, to feel him.

And in that moment, I looked up at him, and felt . . . sadness.

He stroked my cheek. "Tell me you love me," he said.

"I do," I whispered. "I love you." I meant it with every fiber of me, but at the same time, it felt like a betrayal. Tears came to my eyes. He didn't seem to notice. He slipped his forefinger in my mouth, and I sucked it. Meanwhile, he was pleasuring me with his other hand. I know he felt it when orgasm took hold of me.

He pushed away the covers and leaned down, kissing me long and deep. I wrapped my arms around him and closed my eyes. I'd missed him so much, and he knew what to do to make me weak for him.

Later, we laid in each other's arms. I didn't want to move. I feared that something awful would happen to make this our last time together. We shared companionable silence for a while. My head was on his chest. He ran his fingers through my hair. It was hard to believe that this man was anything other than gentle and loving. I wanted so much to believe that he was the man I'd always thought he was.

"I hope you know you can tell me anything," I said. "I mean, anything. I want us to be close like we used to be."

I had been listening to the steady rhythm of his heartbeat. I heard it skip once and then beat double time, like a dancer making up for a missed step.

"How do you mean?"

I rose up on one elbow so I could look at him.

"I mean, I want all of you. The things you don't tell anyone else. The shit you feel when you're trying to hold back. I want to know. I feel lately like there's something going on that I don't understand, and you keep locking me out."

He drew me back down and kissed my forehead. "You worry too much," he said softly. "Anything that's wrong, I will take care of."

I fell asleep. When I woke the next morning, he was already in the shower. The clean scent of his soap was carried into our room on the steam of running water. For a moment, before I had time to think about it, I felt normal and safe.

It didn't occur to me until then that while he hadn't admitted anything was wrong, he hadn't completely denied it either.

***

After I got the kids off to school and Preston left to play golf with some buddies, I was in panic mode. I had thought about it, and I wanted a custom-made dress for the Sports Corps charity event. Seven days was cutting it extremely close when it came to having a gown made, but an off-the-rack dress wouldn't do. So I did what I always do when I need help with such things. I called Crystal.

"Well, I'm glad you told me," she said over the phone. "I am having the last touches on my dress made, and who knows, my lady can whip something beautiful up for you. I'm going to the banquet too. Trust me, you may be responsible enough to get things arranged a month ahead of time, but I doubt most of her customers are."

We met at an address downtown during my lunch hour. The shop was an exclusive one, and there were instructions that customers could only be seen by prior appointment. Since Crystal was going in for her last fitting (and was a VIP customer), she had called and explained that I would be coming along with her. The dressmaker, Emily, said that would be fine.

Emily greeted us at the door. She was a petite, bouncy woman with long brown hair she kept up in a bun. An employee came out and offered us a bottle of champagne while we waited for Crystal's dress to be brought down.

Between Crystal and me, she's usually the heavier drinker. But on this day, I downed two glasses before she'd gotten around to her first.

"Are you nervous, honey?" she asked. "I know this event is a big deal, but we've been to a million of them. You know you'd look flawless in a burlap bag. Why are you worried?"

I shrugged. "You're right. It's silly of me."

I didn't want to explain. It would be better to pretend that I didn't have any problem bigger than getting the right dress to wear on a night out with my husband.

Emily came back with Crystal's dress, and I had to admit that I was impressed. My friend worked hard for her body, so I couldn't say I envied her. She was simply gorgeous: the form-fitting, emerald green dress was satin and shoulder-less with a cowl neckline. It skimmed every curve. The flowing train was the perfect touch, the epitome of old Hollywood chic.

Crystal gushed. While she and the dressmaker discussed accessories and the kind of jewelry that would best accentuate the outfit, I checked my cell phone.

I was surprised to see a brief text from Tyler. It read:

You won't guess what happened. The newspaper is calling it a miracle.

There was a link attached, which I clicked on. Once the article popped up, I had to read over it twice. The picture of the man in the article was vaguely familiar, but I didn't who it was until I saw the name.

Coma Victim Wakes after Twenty Years Slumber

While Joshua Middleton slept, the world has changed around him.

Twenty years ago, Middleton was a student at the University of Tennessee. He was looking forward to a career in his family's furniture business and was enrolled as a business/accounting major.

Middleton's mother, Sharon, says that her son was a fun-loving young student who enjoyed a very social college life. "He had a lot of friends," she said. "Everyone who knew him was very upset about the accident. He wasn't the kind of kid who would go out and get drunk, but he must have had too much that night. His accident changed all our lives as we knew it."

The accident was a fall from a second-story balcony during an off-campus party. Middleton suffered various injuries, including numerous broken bones and a punctured lung, and was unconscious at the time he was brought to the hospital. He was originally given a fair prognosis, but as the days passed and Middleton did not wake, doctors began to worry.

Dr. Aaron Carrey has been Middleton's doctor since he was injured. "In Josh's case, we were perplexed about why he wasn't waking up. CT scans showed that he had some brain activity, so we knew that he could regain consciousness. We spotted damage in the area of the brain controlling speech and language, but we couldn't tell how that might affect his ability to communicate until he was awake.

"Unfortunately, once a patient is in a coma, their chances of waking from it decrease as time goes on. We advised the family that if he did wake within the first few weeks, he would likely be in a persistent vegetative state. Over the years I have read about coma patients waking after many years, but it's never happened to one of my own."

Middleton has been at Greenview Skilled Nursing Facility, where he has been cared for since the year after the fall that caused his coma. He's currently being evaluated for multiple therapies. He will need physical therapy in order to build up his strength so he can walk again. Though he has been able to say a few words and even write brief messages, he will need therapy to help him regain his ability to speak normally.

"It's going to be a long road ahead for my son," Mrs. Middleton says. "At least now, we have hope. Josh is awake, and I'm ready to be here for him for whatever he needs."

I put away my phone and sat there. It was hard to believe. I hadn't even thought of Josh in years, and now I felt guilty about that.

The dressmaker said something about a pattern sample for a black lace dress in my size, and I tried to pay attention.

***

Back when we were in college, Josh had been one of my best friends.

He was whip smart and funny. He was a cute guy, though not exactly my type. We would hang out and study, sometimes go to parties, when he could pull me away from my studies long enough for me to have some fun without compromising my schoolwork. I appreciated that he never made me feel like I should be guilty for studying as hard as I did, or that I was somehow weird for not partying as much as some other students did.

Here was the thing about Josh, though. After a certain point, I realized that he had a crush on me. Though I liked him fine as a friend, I wasn't interested in him. It was probably unfair that I continued to hang around him, knowing that it was never going to turn into a relationship when he really wanted one with me.

I only had a few friends, and in a way, I didn't want to let him go. For me, school was a rat race, and I was always running behind something; keeping up with the reading, notes, and trying to make sure I kept a consistent 3.0 to maintain my scholarship and financial aid. I was probably more fearful about that than I should have been. I was a kid with parents who had worked hard to help me get there, and my nightmare would have been fucking up my grades. I was determined that my family was going to be proud of me.

Josh would drop by my place with a snack for me when he knew I was studying, or pull me away for a couple hours to hang out at a local coffee shop. I remember jogging with him in the morning when our schedules allowed it. I liked that he was always a gentleman with me, never pushing anything.

One day, my roommate happened to be home when Josh dropped by on one of his impromptu outings. He usually didn't give me much warning when he was going to come over, but it turned out to be a welcome distraction.

Cindy waited until he was gone and then turned to me. "So, are you guys together yet?" she asked.

"No."

"You know that man likes you. I mean, I don't get what the problem is. He's obviously into you. He's not half bad. I mean, he beats out the last couple of my exes. I'd offer to take him off your hands myself if he wasn't obviously in love with you already."

"Love? He's my friend. He doesn't think of me like that," I told her.

"Yeah, right," Cindy replied. "I catch that puppy dog look he's got in his eyes whenever he looks at you. Guys don't invest their time unless they're interested."

I didn't want to admit to myself that I was going to have to eventually tell him something. That day came when he showed up at my apartment with a dozen roses on a random afternoon.

"I think you've gotten the wrong impression from me, and if you did, I'm sorry. These are lovely, but it wouldn't be right for me to accept these from you. I just . . . I want us to be friends."

He was crushed. I remember the look on his face. He got quiet and made some excuse about having to be somewhere for an appointment. He didn't speak to me for about a week, but after that, he came back and pretended nothing had happened. He was essentially the same, except that I noticed he was more careful about keeping his physical distance from me. He didn't touch my arm or stand in my personal space. I figured this was his idea of just being friends: the two of us doing all the same things without him placing any pressure on me to be romantically involved.

He called me up one evening, just a random check in. I was in my room, going over one of the chapters for my art history class.

"What are you doing tonight?" he asked.

"The usual," I said. "Exams this week."

"Yeah," he said and paused. "I'm going to a party tonight. Hanging out with some of the guys there. Think you'll be up late?"

"I'm guaranteed to," I told him. "Why?"

"Uh, I might stop by later with snacks. Depends on how things go."

"Meaning, if it's a really good party you might end up seeing me in a couple days instead," I volunteered. "Don't worry about it. Maybe you'll meet someone there."

I wanted to tell him that I hoped he would meet someone because he was a fucking sweetheart and he deserved a girl who could focus on him. I wanted to tell him that I was still his friend and always would be. And that when he found someone, I was going to be so happy for him. But none of that was what he probably wanted to hear, so I didn't say it.

He paused for a moment. "Not likely. Preston Harrington is coming with me, though, so that will be fun. You know, I was thinking when I met him he'd have a stick up his ass, coming from a famous family and all, but he's not. I met his brother Tyler first, and I thought that maybe he was . . . I don't know, the exception to the rule. I've hung out with Preston a few times now and he's always been cool."

"You didn't mention that," I said.

He chuckled. "Figured you wouldn't care. If you were a football fan, I might have bragged about it."

We spent a few more minutes making small talk about school. He mentioned the girl that was throwing the party, and I told him about a few rumors about her exploits. We both laughed at my description of her. After we settled down, there was a moment of silence. I heard him take a quick breath, and I imagined that he was smiling.

"Just in case I don't see you," Josh said, "have a good night, and don't work too hard. Whatever it is, I guarantee it will still be there in the morning."

"Which is what I'm afraid of," I said.

"You know what I mean. No need in pulling an all-nighter."

"Josh?"

"Yeah?"

"Don't worry about me. Have fun."

That was the last time I heard from him. The next day, the news about Josh's fall was all over the campus and the local news. I felt awful. I had encouraged him to go. Maybe if I hadn't put him off, he'd have left the party and come to my house before he got himself wasted.

Everyone was in shock. The police were quick to call it an accident, and no one challenged their theory. Josh knew a lot of people, and I had never come across anyone who didn't like him. During the week following the accident, the students got together to raise money to help Josh's family handle the medical bills. All anyone knew for sure was that it looked serious and Josh hadn't been conscious since he fell.

During the second week after his fall, there was no change, and the rumor that spread across campus was that he was near death. There was a vigil planned in the student hall. I would definitely be there and debated over whether I should go all afternoon. I hadn't told anyone, not even my roommate, about that final call I had received from Josh. No one knew of my secret guilt; I knew it was irrational, but I couldn't shake it.

I was in the back of the student hall, listening to one of Josh's classmates make an impromptu speech, when I felt eyes on me.

I looked to my side. Preston was standing a few feet away. We locked eyes and he nodded. I'd run into him at a party a few weeks earlier, and Josh had introduced him to me. Once the vigil was over, he approached me.

"I'm so sorry about Josh," he said.

"Oh, thank you," I said. Preston smiled, but the expression in his eyes was serious.

"I felt like I needed to do something for him," he said. "I guess this is the best thing to be done for now."

I nodded. "I hate feeling helpless."

Preston slipped his hands in his pockets, rocking back on his heels. As he looked at me, he fixed me with his stare, and I was taken with how clear and blue his eyes were. "Want to get out of here? Maybe get a cup of coffee?"

"Sure," I said. "That would be nice."

People continued to talk about Josh and pray for his recovery; it was like he was already dead. As the days stretched into weeks and months, people got on with their lives. It was easier to forget. In a way, his fate was worse. Josh was clinging to life, but it was clear that he was going to become a burden to his family.

I had moved on, never stopping to wonder if Josh had met up with Preston as he said he'd planned to that night.

***

I was so upset by Tyler's text that I barely paid any attention to the drawings that the dressmaker gave me to look at. I told her that I liked the first one—a stunning black dress that wasn't my usual conservative style. It was going to be a big night, but I had also decided I didn't have time to be overly finicky about the dress. If the damn thing was going to be ready on time and fit me correctly, I'd consider it a win.

I pretended everything was okay. I hugged Crystal and bypassed our usual lunch, promising that I would make it up to her later. I said I had some errands I had been trying to put off, one of which was a doctor's appointment, and then had to get back to work. I wasn't sure she bought my excuse. She'd known me a long time and had always been good at reading my emotions. One way or the other, she did me the kindness of playing along with the story I gave her. If she hadn't, I think I might have burst into tears or screamed at her.

I got in my car and texted Tyler back:

That's a crazy story. I can't believe it.

A few minutes passed before Tyler's answer appeared on my screen:

I know. I knew him. I remember when he first got injured. You remember him. Right?

I sat with my finger hovering over the screen of my phone. Did Tyler already know that Preston had been acquainted with Josh? He probably did, but maybe he was waiting for me to confirm it. Even worse, anything on text could be shown as evidence later.

Is this what my life has become? I thought. *Am I worried about whether Preston had something to do with Josh's fall, and if there's evidence of it? Have I reached the point where it's not so important what he did, as long as he didn't get caught for it?*

I shoved the cell phone back into my purse without sending a message. There were a lot of reasons not to answer his question. If he asked me later, I could say that I didn't see it or that I forgot about it. There was no reason to tell him anything else. I still had my reservations about my brother-in-law. If he couldn't pin one thing on Preston, it didn't mean he was above blaming him for something else.

One thing bothered me to my soul. I wasn't sure if I had ever asked Preston if he had been there the night Josh fell, but I clearly remember Josh telling me he'd meet Preston there. Twenty years had passed, and it could be that I had asked and he had said he wasn't there. If he did say he wasn't, I knew there was a possibility that he was lying to me. Preston could look at you without blinking and convince you the sky wasn't blue if he wanted to.

Chapter Nineteen

Josh Middleton

I felt like I was floating.

When I opened my eyes, all I could see was white. Figures were indistinct. I blinked. My eyes felt so dry, almost as if they had been sewn shut. It took awhile, just staring, before I understood what it was I was seeing. A wall. *Wall*? Was that the correct word? I didn't think it was exactly, but close enough. There were little marks in this wall . . . in this . . . *ceiling*. The word was suddenly in my mind. The word slipped away, but I had the feeling that I knew what this ceiling or wall meant in the grander scheme of things. It meant that I was inside.

But who was I? And what was I doing here . . . wherever this was? This was not my bedroom. How old was I anyway? Where was my mom?

Mom. I remembered the thought of her and how she made me feel more than how she looked. She was always ready to put a bandage on my boo-boos, make me food that I liked, and even play catch with me in the yard occasionally. I could remember her putting cool washcloths on my forehead when I was sick with a fever. She would stroke my arm and then pull up the covers so I didn't get cold. I felt such peace when I thought about her. She protected me. From what? I couldn't remember, but I knew that her memory made me feel safe.

Dad? I only got snatches of memories about him. I recalled random scenes: him at a park with me teaching me how to do a slide tackle for soccer, his face smiling from the crowd after I finished a swim race, in the yard demonstrating the correct technique for throwing a football. His face was fuzzy, though. And somehow I didn't feel that he had been a constant in my life for some reason. Did he come and go? Was he not home much?

And someone else important to me. A brother. David. He must have been younger because I felt some sort of protective instinct for him. I think I must have enjoyed spending time with him but sometimes got annoyed with him. That's the feeling I got—like I wanted to spend time with him, but not too much. I think we played catch with the football together.

Anyone else? I had vague memories of a dog. A dog who liked to play catch as much as I did. Except he was always the one catching and would bring back a slobbery ball for me to throw again. Those were happy memories.

I could recall some lady about my mom's age. An aunt? All my other people memories at the moment were fuzzy, like everyone I used to know—school friends, neighbor friends, relatives, teachers, and coaches—was grouped into one big hazy group. And I didn't feel strong emotion toward the group either. Nothing overly good or bad. Neutral, as if my childhood was just fine.

Somewhere in my soul, though, I did have some awful memory. A place or situation I couldn't quite conjure up yet.

Other memories from childhood crept in. I used to love my Star Wars figurines. Darth Vader would take on Luke Skywalker in epic battles in my backyard. I had a Yoda figurine who would offer advice, as well as R2-D2 and C-3PO who were always ready to help. And Princess Leia always needed to be rescued. I even dressed up as Luke Skywalker for Halloween one year, complete with a cool-looking light saber.

I also had He-Man figurines who would take on the Star Wars crew. Wow, these memories were crystal clear. He-Man, Teela, Beastman, and Faker. Skeletor was my favorite. In some of these memories, I was playing with someone else. No, not with my brother. Must have been with some friend.

That got me going on another tangent. A kid who must have been over a lot because I saw his face clearly. He had messy blondish hair and blue eyes and freckles and was a little kid like me. He played Star Wars with me and anything with a ball—basketball, football, baseball. He loved ketchup. Why in the world would I remember a detail like that? I couldn't picture him as an older kid, though. Did he move, or maybe we grew apart? Was he the source of the pit in my stomach? I didn't think so. I felt a happy aura around my memories of him. Matt. That was his name.

And where did I live? I saw blue walls in the space that was mine, space that must have been my bedroom. I had a shelf of trophies and medals, another one with books, and another one with New Orleans Saints stuff—a hat, a couple photos. Oh yeah, I had a large Saints poster on my wall, too. And next to that was a poster of that cute brown-haired girl from *Saved by the Bell*. She reminded me of someone else, someone I actually knew. Hmmm, fuzzy.

My yard was large and had lots of big trees but also open areas perfect for throwing a football or baseball. I remembered the outside more than the inside of my house. I must have been outside a lot, playing and stuff.

Then, like I was walking along the path of my past life, the memories of being a bit older unlocked from the crevices of my mind. I was now a middle schooler. I didn't feel quite as carefree as when I was a little kid. I remembered the awkwardness of having feet too big for my body and lips too big for my face. And zits. Kids weren't as nice. Sports teams were more competitive.

I remembered one middle school field trip where—I don't know where we went, some historical spot or something—the other boys left me out of their group. I tried during the whole trip to be part of the group, to sit with them at lunch, to be together during the tour, to have them laugh at my jokes, but they kept "forgetting" me. At the end of the day, when I went to the bathroom just before the return trip home, they got on the bus while I was absent and didn't save me a seat next to them. I had to sit with the unpopular girls at the front of the bus. That was a bad memory. But still, I sensed that this uncomfortable feeling of not being accepted into a group wasn't the worst memory I had.

And then, oh, the high school days. By then I had discovered girls. That brought a whole lot of angst in itself. I kinda felt like my guy friendships were fine by then. I think I was good enough at sports—I played football and baseball for the school—that the guys accepted me fine. And I got tall enough to absorb the size of my feet. Schoolwork was a bit harder, but nothing that brought undue stress.

Girls, though. They didn't exactly flock to me. At least not the good-looking ones. I remembered a girl named Emily or Amy or something who used to hang near me. She would laugh at my jokes and seem to like me, but I just had a feeling about her. A feeling like she was a bit desperate. I don't think she wanted *me* in particular; she just wanted *someone* to be her boyfriend. She wasn't that cute, and her personality wasn't attractive, so I talked to her enough to not be mean but not enough to encourage her. After a few weeks of this, she had moved on to hanging on some other guy. Part of me felt bad, but not really. I had a certain type of girl in mind for myself.

Oh yeah, I did date another girl for a while. Sara. She wasn't that memorable. I guess she was that *someone* for me to call a girlfriend during high school. We broke up at the end of senior year. Nothing there explained that heaviness in me. I had some worse memory yet to recall.

College. My soul bled at the memory. What memory, though? This was it. Something bad had happened here. A dark visage surrounded the whole thought of my time in Knoxville. My thoughts turned to my immediate surroundings.

I heard soft beeping sounds coming from the left. These sounds had been with me in the depth of the darkness, when I couldn't hear anything else. The beeping didn't come from words or people, but it seemed to always be there, a thing that existed like the unchanging sound of the sea.

Sea. This word sent my mind tumbling into another barrel of images. Pictures were so clear in my head, but it wasn't easy to capture them or to call them what they were. The word *sea* evoked another memory of when I was young. I might have been five years old, making sandcastles with my father on the shore. For some reason my memories of the past were much more clear than those of the present.

It took me awhile before I was able to turn my head and look toward the sound of the beeping, which was what I had intended to do all along.

Moni . . .

Monitor? This word seemed more defined. Though I couldn't think what it was for, somewhere deep in my mind, I could feel the answer. But it squirmed away from me like a worm escaping my fingers, burrowing deep into the cold dirt. Words were tricky, slimy things.

My throat was parched. Parting my lips, I ran my tongue over them and realized they were dry. My neck hurt, and my body felt stiff. What was wrong? I wasn't sure I could sit up but wanted to try.

I couldn't. My arms felt like a heavy weight. Frustrated, I moaned. The kind of half-sleepy growl I'd made many mornings upon waking.

This thought upset me. I couldn't remember when I had last fallen asleep or when it was that I woke up before this.

***

I fell asleep and was not awake for a time. When I opened my eyes, a young woman was standing above me. She had long, wavy brown hair and wore pink. She was scribbling on something, her head down. I sighed, and she looked up at me.

"Josh!" she said. "Are you awake?"

She leaned over me. I tried to speak, but the only sound that tumbled from my lips was, "Un, hunh."

The next thing I knew, I was surrounded by people. Nurses . . . doctors . . . the woman who next spoke to me identified herself as Dr. Robertson.

"Josh, you suffered a fall. Do you remember?"

I shook my head: *no*. But something about what she asked registered with me. A fall. I had an idea of it in my head. Knoxville. The University of Tennessee. A girl. A pretty brown-haired girl. I think she might have liked me. I sure liked her. She was my type, the one I'd been looking for. But the relationship wasn't easy. I always felt unsure; I clearly remembered now the angst of wondering where our relationship was at. I felt a little anxious thinking of her. But there was something else. Something much darker.

I saw a face in my mind's eye. Someone had intentionally hurt me. And not just my feelings. He had tried to . . . kill me. No! I didn't want to go there in my psyche. The pain was too great. Darkness. Agony. Helplessness. But like someone had pressed play on the movie of my life, I couldn't stop the images. One tumbled over the other into the forefront of my mind. The key to my anguish was here, in this memory. I remembered hitting my hips on the balcony as I tumbled off. He pushed me. I thought he was my friend. I was going to die. The horror of free-falling to the ground. A scream. Was it me screaming or someone else? Agonizing pain everywhere in my body for a split second until . . . until today.

The name was clear to me. The young, good-looking face of the popular, athletic friend of mine—crystal clear as well. When I tried to speak, the word that came out was not his name, or not exactly. The bastard had pretended to be my friend! *Preston*. Tears of frustration, anger, and powerlessness blurred my eyes.

"Preets," I said. It was the first word I'd said out loud since, well, since a very long time, ever since I'd gotten to this colorless place. It wasn't what I wanted to say, but it was close. I could tell the wrongness of it by how the strangers around me stared. It felt weird against my tongue.

The doctor put a hand on my shoulder. "Don't try to talk right now. Things probably feel very strange, but I don't want you to force it."

Someone pressed a button, and my bed moved so that I was sitting up.

"You understand what I said?" the doctor asked.

I nodded.

At that moment, a woman who looked like my mother, only much older, came through the doorway.

I tried to speak again, and this time, I was able to manage it.

"Ma," I said.

Tears of joy came to her eyes, which made mine blurry too. This was my mom! Why was she so old?

***

The following days were filled with successes and frustrations.

Though I had to be told several times what happened to me, I remembered the fight on the balcony and being pushed off. What they tried to explain to me wasn't true! I shook my head, but no one understood. It incensed me when people referred to my fall as an accident. I knew better. Trying to speak was difficult, and it was harder when I was angry. The words came out all wrong.

My mother didn't want to leave me, and she talked to me endlessly. Her appearance had changed so much that I worried for her. Someone had explained to me how long I'd been cooped up in this place. Whenever my mind touched upon the idea that I had lost twenty years of my life, I felt sick. It was too big. I brushed the concept away, or tried to. It popped up at times even though I tried to ignore it. So did the memory of the man who had hurt me. Sometimes I cried, and I hated that. Other times I was so happy just to see people coming in and out of my room. People in this place cared for me, even if I couldn't make myself understood. I was grateful.

My mother was there for every meal. They set up a cot for her the first day I was awake, and she was allowed to sleep in a room down the hall from me. Eventually the doctor told her she needed to go home and sleep in her own bed overnight. I agreed with a nod and a slow blink in my mother's direction. The small gesture was enough to reassure her.

Doctors and nurses came and went. It seemed that someone was always coming to check my vitals. The unspoken reasoning behind me being monitored so closely was that they wanted to be sure I wasn't about to slip into a coma again. The medical team wanted to get me started on speech, physical, and occupational therapy right away. I would do speech and physical therapy at the same time, as a stronger overall body would help improve the muscles I needed to speak and swallow. The OT would help me relearn the basics, like how to eat solid food.

The preliminary results were encouraging to the doctors, but not so much to me. They found I was able to follow commands. Speaking was the problem. I couldn't seem to convert my thoughts into the proper words.

My mother gave me some paper, and I found that I could manage writing small words. Some of those came out just as wrong as the words that I tried to speak, but it gave me something to do. I practiced drawing the letter *P*.

The medical staff didn't seem to mind speaking freely in front of me. They knew I was aware but weren't sure how much I was listening. I sometimes thought it was a test, to see if they could get a rise out of me. A couple times they did, and my nurse was all smiles. "See, he gets us!"

The dark-haired nurse, the one who was the first person I had seen when I woke, was my favorite. I couldn't remember what her name was, but I called her Dani. I wasn't sure why, but she responded to the nickname. She allowed me to squeeze her hand.

"You have to understand, Mrs. Middleton," one of the doctors addressed my mother, "with so much trauma, he's doing very well. It will take time for him to speak properly, but it's good that he's trying. Don't make him repeat things. If he wants to do that himself it's fine, but we don't want to stress him. He needs to take that part in his own time. The fact that he's trying to write and draw is very good. We should also expect the occasional setback. Recovery is never a straight line. If he continues as he is, his speech therapist says we can expect him to be able to speak in small sentences and write a down a few words in the near future. He shows a lot of drive to recover, which is the most important thing."

"Preets," I said aloud, focusing on drawing a big, straight letter "P" on my paper.

Chapter Twenty

Tyler Harrington

I was serious when I told Danielle that I wanted her to let me know what was going on with Preston. But after he came back home, she didn't bother to call me back or tell me what his explanation was for having disappeared for two days. Under normal circumstances, I wouldn't have thought of it as my business. But if my brother was still hurting people, it definitely was.

I texted her a couple of times, with no answer. When the story about Josh Middleton broke, I tried texting Danielle again. She had nothing to say. She seemed to want to drop the whole thing and pretend nothing had happened. Maybe she could bury her misgivings about Preston, but I couldn't. Her doubts had only made me certain that something bad was still going on with my brother.

I wasn't sure that Preston had anything to do with Josh Middleton, but it did seem strange that another person he knew was gravely injured. He'd mentioned to me back when it happened that he knew the man. The fact that

Danielle didn't answer my text about Josh made me suspicious.

I hated to think that Danielle was as naïve as all the other people my brother managed to dazzle. She was a smart, beautiful woman. And she was completely wasted on my brother, who couldn't care for anyone but himself. He'd been as fortunate in his married life as he was in his career.

The other thought that worried me was that maybe she was staying quiet about Preston out of fear. I couldn't ignore that as a possibility.

I let a week pass, giving her time to contact me on her own. When I didn't hear anything, I showed up at the house.

I came over on a Wednesday afternoon when I knew my brother would most likely be out but Danielle would be home from work. She set her schedule up that way so she had more time with the twins.

I rang the doorbell and took a step back, waiting. The chime was loud enough that I could hear it toll through the house. It took a moment before I heard footsteps and the door swung open.

Danielle was in jeans and a white T-shirt, her hair pulled back in a loose knot on the nape of her neck. Her eyes widened, and it took a beat for her to speak to me. "Um, Tyler! What are you doing on this side of town?" she asked.

"Just doing some shopping. I'm going to be at the gala this weekend, and Joanna wanted me to get my shopping done before the last minute." She totally knew I was lying, but I didn't care. "Can I come in?"

"Sure." She chuckled, but her mirth fell flat.

"Where are the kids?" I asked. "I was looking forward to seeing them."

"Oh, they'll be back soon," she said. "I'm trying to get them to have their own separate things lately. Isabel's got soccer practice. Ethan's got swimming lessons. Thank God we have a nanny because I don't know how I would manage with all the pickups and drop-offs by myself."

"Yeah. We have active kids in this family, that's for sure."

"Coffee?" Danielle offered. "I just made a pot."

"Sure." I followed her back into the kitchen and took a seat. She pulled down two coffee mugs and poured for both of us.

"You gave me an explanation for why you're on this side of town," she said. "But why are you really here?"

"After what we talked about, I wanted to check on you."

She took a breath and carefully placed her palms flat against the counter. "Have you talked to Preston since?" she asked.

"No. I didn't want him to know we talked while he was gone for those couple of days. You know how he is. He's not going to talk to me unless he has to."

Danielle briefly explained the excuses Preston had given her for his absence. It sounded unreasonable to me, a man saying he hadn't found a moment to call his worried wife. Danielle sounded tired. She was more understanding than my wife, I thought. If I'd skipped out with no phone call for a couple of days, there would be no end to the complaining and sideways remarks I'd hear about it.

"He's tried this with you before," I said.

She nodded. "He has. Since then, nothing strange has happened. I haven't done anything to check up on him, but he's been working and keeping regular hours."

"You know this isn't going away, though. Right?" I told her. "It's what the problem is in the first place. He's never gotten help for whatever is wrong. He doesn't care . . ."

"Look, I'm really not sure what's been going on with him, but I don't feel comfortable going on assumptions. It's difficult for me to base real-world decisions on your memories of him from when you were a little boy."

"You're going to just forget about evidence you've seen with your own eyes because it's inconvenient for you? You're fine with blood droplets and burned clothes in the backyard. Does that sound remotely normal to you? Because when you came to me a couple of weeks ago you didn't think so. It can't be coincidence that anyone who stands in Preston's way fucking gets killed or worse."

"What do you mean?"

"You know very well what I'm talking about. You forget, I knew Josh, and among the guys who knew him, he told everyone that he was head over heels in love with you. Then he ends up in a coma, and you're suddenly with my brother."

"It wasn't like that; I wasn't dating Josh!"

"I never said you were. Just because you didn't want him doesn't mean he didn't care for you. When it comes to you, no man has a chance against Preston."

She blinked and took a step away from me. "I don't want to talk about this anymore," she said. "I think you better leave."

"Fine." I got up. She walked me back to the door. I couldn't help but try one more time to reach her. "Danielle, cutting yourself off from help is a big mistake. If you don't want to talk to me about Preston, find someone else you can confide in. Please, don't go back to acting like there's nothing wrong with him because you're scared. He knows how to turn things around so you feel like you're the one who's crazy. I've dealt with him too long not to know how he operates."

"That's just the point. I don't have *proof*, and if I'm going to do something that could turn our lives upside down, I have to be damn sure." She ushered me outside. "Not to mention, you better stay out of the whole matter. I'm not going to bring this up with you again, and you don't need to bother me about it anymore. You've done nothing for me but complicate an already fucked-up situation."

"You'll always choose him, won't you?" I asked. "Even over your own safety."

She closed the door in my face.

I decided then that if Danielle wasn't going to cooperate, I would find a way to uncover the truth about my brother on my own.

Chapter Twenty-one

Preston Harrington

I was beginning to feel the need for a release again.

It usually started with sleepless nights and agitation. Danielle had forgiven me for my last two-day disappearance. I was relieved that she'd stopped asking questions. Despite that, I knew better than to push it.

I'd have managed a quick visit to the house in the country, but I didn't think it would do me much good. I needed to fulfill the need to kill. At this point, anything less would do little to satisfy the itch.

I was thinking that I needed to find a reason to get out of town for a short while, when one presented itself to me. There would be a small amount of risk, but I believed the gamble would be worth it. I just had to find the right way to sell the idea to my wife.

I brought up the subject to Danielle one night after the kids were in bed. We'd stayed up to watch a movie. We were in the living room, sharing the sofa and a bowl of popcorn. When the credits rolled, I tapped her on the knee.

"I want to run something past you, Dani. Tell me what you think."

She sat up. "Okay."

"I had a chat with Kurt today. We talked about a new sports medicine and physiotherapy center being set up in Colorado. It's very innovative, and he's taken a personal interest in it because a couple of his other clients have sought treatment there. He says they've gotten impressive results."

Danielle nodded. "Go on."

"Here's the thing. They do excellent work, but of course, it's incredibly expensive, especially with the variety of preventive care they offer. There's overhead and salaries to be paid to their therapists, which all take a big chunk of their earnings. Though there are plenty of people trying to get in—they have a waiting list—they won't be able to meet their goal of expanding without a few more solid backers. A celebrity spokesperson would really help them toward their goal. They're hoping to open centers on both coasts."

"You're interested in representing them?"

I nodded. "I would like a new spokesperson gig, especially since my contract with Pop's is coming to an end. This would really be within my wheelhouse. Not to mention, they do work that will have a positive impact."

"What's the catch?"

"I want to make a quick trip out to see the facility for myself, before I make any promises. I have Kurt's word, and I've been through all their literature, but there's nothing like seeing it for myself. I would like to make a quick trip out there."

"Okay, but are you going to be back in time for the Sports Corps event?"

"Sure. If I leave tomorrow morning, I can go to a meeting with their director, do a tour, spend the night in town, and be back home the next day. Even if I were delayed, I'd get here Saturday morning at the latest."

Danielle blinked. "Okay. But you'll call me when you land and when you're on your way back?"

I smiled at her. "Yes, baby."

***

Kurt had approached me with this opportunity a few weeks earlier. I had called him and made the final arrangements. The following morning, I was on a flight. I had two days on my own, without having to worry about Danielle breathing down my neck.

Better yet, I only had to spend three hours at the clinic at the most. Once I was in town, a second flight would get me where I wanted to go within three hours. I would take care of my personal business first and then swing back through to tour the sports clinic.

The business I needed to handle in Tennessee was pressing.

I'd heard about Josh Middleton on the news. It wasn't a big story, but it had generated some mild interest on the news and various sites online. "Coma Victim Wakes after 20 Years." The articles mentioned that he had difficulty communicating. I was irritated at how these so-called journalists were so unspecific about the details. Difficulty could mean anything, from barely being able to say one's own name to speaking with a slight impediment. I would have to find out how bad he was myself. Obviously, the less he could say, the better it would be for me.

The real mystery was Josh's memory. According to news sources, even Josh's physician hadn't gauged how much he could recall. There would invariably be holes in his memory but until he could communicate more clearly, there would be no way to tell how much or what events had been lost to him.

I wondered if he remembered me and those last crucial moments before I shoved him from the balcony. This was one contingency I couldn't have considered all those years ago when I pushed him, but I was prepared to take care of it.

The article had given the name of the facility where Josh was. A quick search on the internet and I had the phone number and address. I called and was greeted by a chirpy feminine voice. "This is Greenview, how can I help you?"

"Yes, my name is John, and I was told that there is a family friend of ours in recovery there. I would like to send him some flowers, and if I can get off work at a decent hour I will be down there to see him," I said, chuckling lightly. "His name is Josh Middleton. Would you happen to have the room number?"

There was a brief pause. "Well, all our flower deliveries go to the front desk, and we have our staff members take them to the patients' rooms. If you ask, I'm sure they will be able to help you."

"Oh, I didn't want to bother anyone, you know, I'll be coming in at the last minute and would like to just go back to see him."

Another phone rang in the background.

Another pause. "Well, between you and me, the names are here on the whiteboard in the front, so if you take a look, you'll see the patient's name listed."

"Thank you."

I started to get anxious while I was on the way there. It had been a long time since I'd been back to Knoxville. My old college was close to downtown, a thirty-minute drive from the outlying airport, but I didn't go toward that part of the city; I had more important business. I crossed the Tennessee River and drove straight to the western suburbs where a broken man was still in the bed that I had put him in.

The thing about any medical facility is that there are many cameras around. I made sure I was wearing casual clothes, including a baseball cap and sunglasses. Luckily, this was a small facility. The nursing home was surrounded by trees and a semicircle garden. The place had a peaceful feeling to it, much like a cemetery.

Inside, the nurse's station was manned by only one employee. I sat down in the waiting room by myself, hat pulled low, waiting and hoping most nursing home patrons were not football fans. I'd been there about twenty minutes pretending to read a *People* magazine when she darted away to answer a patient's call light, which flashed on a board above her desk.

I got up and looked. Standing on the visitor's side of the reception desk, I could see each patient's last name and first initial written on a whiteboard, the column beside it indicating the room number. I quickly scanned for the name I wanted: *Middleton, J. 114.*

I walked slowly down the hall, passing only one harried nurse the whole time, and followed the numbers until I found the right room. The door was wide open.

A man sat in a chair on the left side of the patient's bed with his back to the door. I took a step backward. It was Tyler! Another older woman, presumably Josh's mother, was also in the room. I scooted past the open doorway and ducked into the empty adjoining room beside Josh's and stood behind the door, listening to the two talking.

"It's really nice to meet one of my son's friends. You're the first one to come see him since the coma broke. How exactly did you know each other?"

"We bonded over football," Tyler said. "I was in high school and played in a game against your younger son's team down in New Orleans. Josh had come down to see him, and he ended up congratulating me when my team won. That's a rare thing, you know. So many people get mad when their favorite doesn't win, especially when they have family on the opposing team. They forget it's supposed to be about the love of the game first, no hard feelings on either side."

"Good sportsmanship," Mrs. Middleton said. "My husband and I worked on instilling that in both our sons. So you're a New Orleans boy, then."

"Yes, ma'am. Born and raised. Our high school was just a couple hours away from Josh and his brother's—your son."

Tyler continued, "When Josh came over to congratulate me, we ended up talking, and he really encouraged me in my sport. We kept in touch after that. It just really says what kind of person he is. Josh has always been a stand-up guy."

Listening to all this from behind the door, I almost had to stifle a groan. Josh and Tyler had been *friends*? Not that I ever knew. He was lying through his teeth. Something else was going on here.

"I'm surprised I'm the first to come see him since he regained consciousness," Tyler said. "He had a large circle of friends."

"It's been a long time, and some of those friends may feel odd about it. I can't say I necessarily blame them, when it's been difficult even for some of the family." She sniffed, and though I couldn't see her from my vantage point, I imagined that Josh's mother must have been dabbing her eyes with a tissue. "David, my other son, will be here for a visit next week, and his cousins that live in town have been by to see him, but his dad hasn't made it up yet. I was hoping he would have been back by this time, but what can you say? Maybe when he's well enough to be at home he'll get more visitors, but I expect that's still a ways off for us."

"I see," Tyler said. "You know, I was wondering. Do they think he'll be able to talk soon?"

I perked up at this question, which was exactly what I wanted to know also.

The woman sighed. "He's said a few words here and there. I'm told it could take months or even longer for him to get his speech back. There's something wrong with the way he associates words with things and people. It's all mixed up. I'm sorry that you ended up here while he's sleeping, but he tends to nod off around noon for a couple of hours. He's been doing physical therapy in the morning and it takes a lot out of him."

I was incensed. What was my brother doing here? Tyler did know Josh—they had been acquaintances before I'd met him, that much was true. But Tyler certainly seemed to be stretching the depth of their friendship. What the hell was he doing at the man's bedside? I couldn't think of any genuine reason he would have to look up Josh after all these years. As always, my little brother was fishing for something. This meant trouble I didn't have time for.

"I wasn't there the night he fell," Tyler said. "Sometimes I wish I had been. Maybe if I had been there, or one of his other friends, it could have been prevented."

"Oh, there's no use in thinking like that." Josh's mother sighed. "I know, because for years I thought that way. You know, why did this happen, exactly how did it take place? I wouldn't hope for anything this awful to happen to someone else, but I often wondered, why my boy? No one is perfect, but Josh was a good kid. I know he didn't do anything bad enough to deserve this. In the end, life is really unfair. We have to do the best with what fortune we have and keep moving forward. Otherwise, you drive yourself crazy."

"I guess so," Tyler said.

They chatted for a while longer, but Tyler didn't ask any more questions. Whatever he had come for, maybe his curiosity had been satisfied. I knew I would have to slip away soon. Tyler was saying goodbye.

"I will be in town for another day on business, so I'll stop by and see if I can catch him while he's awake. Even if he can't speak to me, I would like him to know I was here and that I've been thinking about him."

From the doorway crack, I could see that Tyler still had his back to me. I snagged the opportunity to slip out, heading the opposite way down the hallway from where I'd come. Ahead twenty feet, I could see a back exit. Walking like a speed walker, nearly jogging, I scurried around an old lady with a walker to get to the outside door without turning around or calling attention to myself. "Ha-looh!" she called to me in a cheerful voice. I had no time for that and ignored her. Since I had, of course, driven a rental car here, Tyler would never recognize my car, but ideally I would reach it and take off before he could see me.

I walked on the grass around the back and side of the building to get to the front where the main parking lot was. Stopping to take a quick glance before sprinting to my car, I saw Tyler exiting the building about twenty yards from me. Damn! How had he gotten there so fast? Now I had to wait, suddenly feeling conspicuous.

I stood near the corner of the building with only a thigh-high bush to conceal me. I hoped he'd parked on the other side of the lot, but no, here he came strolling down the sidewalk less than a ten-yard first down away from me. I dropped to my knees and dove behind the bush. What was I theoretically doing? Looking for something I'd dropped? Being a groundskeeper? Either way, I kept my head down and acted busy, spying on Tyler the whole time, even as he stopped to sign an autograph. Apparently nursing home people did watch football.

Finally, he got in his car and left. I stood up, nonchalantly walked to mine, and left as well.

***

Danielle Harrington

Preston didn't know it, but I was relieved when he told me that he was going to be away for a couple of days. Though I didn't trust that this trip was for business only, I wasn't about to question him about it. In the meantime, I was going to take care of some things on my own. He was up and ready early in the morning. He told me that he would be stopping by Kurt's office before heading to the airport. I wouldn't have to drop him off for his flight as I'd expected. That made it even better. I kissed him goodbye and wished him a safe trip.

I got back into bed after Preston left but wasn't able to sleep. I got up feeling worse instead of better.

I felt bad for having gotten into an argument with Tyler, but I couldn't help it. I was confused enough without him in my ear, telling me stories that could be half-truths or wholesale figments of his childhood imagination. Tyler had slipped up because for the first time I saw the jealousy Preston was talking about. Yet jealousy didn't necessarily make Tyler wrong when it came to my husband.

His words about Josh hurt me. I didn't want to think that anything I had done, even by extension, had caused the misery he'd gone through. I'd also considered that maybe Preston had wanted him out of the way. The sad thing was I never intended to be with Josh. I was sure about that before I even met Preston.

After I got out of the shower, I texted Tyler a brief message.

We'll talk later. I'm stressed. Not quite an apology, but it was the honest truth. That was the best I could do.

I went about my morning in a daze. It was Thursday. I cooked the kids breakfast, got them ready, and drove them to school before heading back home to get some work done. I felt like I was only half listening to their conversation that morning, but I couldn't help it. So far they had been well protected from the drama in our household, and I hoped it would continue that way.

I didn't check my phone until I got home, and I found a message on my voicemail. It was the doctor's office. I'd gone in on the previous Friday, and they'd taken a blood test while I was there. I hoped it was nothing bad. Usually, they emailed me the results when everything came back normal. I didn't need some kind of health crisis on top of everything else.

When I called the office, I had to wait on hold for the nurse to pull up the results. I waited nervously while classical music played in the background. I was in a bit of a daze when there was a brief silence, and then the nurse's voice came on the line.

"I have some very interesting and hopefully exciting news for you," she said carefully. "After reviewing your symptoms, the doctor asked that we run a pregnancy test. It came back positive. You're expecting."

It took a moment for me to answer. "Um, how far along am I?"

"You're about six weeks."

I pressed my eyes shut for a moment. What was I going to do? Preston and I hadn't planned on more kids! With what was going on with him, was it even fair to bring another child into this mess? I was already trying to wrap my head around the idea of how this might affect the twins. A new baby. A child dependent upon me to protect it, a new little life.

What would Preston say? We'd always been so definite about the fact that we only wanted two children. Ethan and Isabel were the most important things in my life, but I wasn't looking forward to having another baby. I thought the days of diapers, formula, and midnight feedings were behind me; and that would be the least of my problems.

The nurse rattled on about me setting up a series of appointments. "You need to start taking prenatal vitamins, being monitored through the stages of pregnancy. Since it has been so *long* since you had your twins, there is no shame in brushing up with some Lamaze classes when you're further along. Because you're in your late thirties, the pregnancy this time around would be considered a high risk."

"I know that," I snapped. "I also know there's nothing that says I have to sit here with you and set all of this up right now. I'll call you back when I'm ready."

I caught the edge of an exasperated sigh before I hung up.

Six weeks. Conception would have fallen about six weeks after Rob's funeral. Right around the time all this mess began. I tried to remember. I must have missed a pill at some point.

I put a hand on my stomach. Tears came to my eyes. *Did I want to have another child for this man?* Was I willing and able to raise three kids by myself?

Chapter Twenty-two

Sharon Middleton

Dr. Carrey had been Josh's doctor for twenty years. When I first met him, he was a fresh-faced resident. Now, he was an attending with many years of experience under his belt. There were streaks of silver at the crown of his wavy hair, and the sharp planes of his face had grown softer. Over the years, I had met with him in emergency rooms, at my son's bedside, and even had brief conversations on the phone. Only a few times had I met with him in an office, and all those times had indicated some important news. None that I remembered had ever been good.

I tried to calm myself. For years I had lived in an elevated state of worry, but on this morning I was close to panic. I had seen my son earlier, and as far as I could tell, his status hadn't changed. He'd spoken with me a little, but only a few words.

"Hi Ma," was the usual. Josh had told me he loved me a few times and was able to ask, "How's your day?" It was heartwarming and sad at the same time. It was like having him back, but as a little boy instead of the mature man he should be. When I left, he was still scribbling on a notepad, drawing oversized, shaky letters on paper. He frowned while doing this, as if it took him the same concentration another man would spend on a painting or a piece of sculpture.

The doctor's office was small but warm. On his desk were pictures of him and his wife on their wedding day. Another picture showed two little girls with red hair and freckles. The walls were painted in a pale shade of yellow; the couches were beige. As I sank into the visitor's chair, I sighed; it was puffy and meant for comfort. A bonsai tree sat on the left edge of the desk, along with a snow globe.

I wondered how many unsuspecting family members had been told that there was no hope for their loved ones while sitting in this peaceful room. The figures in the family photos stared back at me with smiles and laughter.

It wasn't that I envied people their happiness. It's just that I hated that my oldest son had no such milestones to mark his own life. I would have loved to have some pictures of Josh's wife and kids to display somewhere. I'd have settled for any past that would have included him being alive and healthy all these years, happy and free to live life as he'd have wanted to.

Dr. Carrey flashed me a brief smile. "I wanted to talk to you away from Josh's room. But first off, I need to ask you, how are you doing?"

I took a deep breath. "With all the improvement my son has been doing, I can't imagine what we have to talk about. Unless something went wrong that no one has told me yet."

"Oh, Mrs. Middleton, I'm so sorry. That's not at all why I wanted you here today. First off, I wanted to tell you that the whole team here is so happy with his progress. Just the fact that he's sitting up, writing, and trying to speak;

people will call it a miracle, and it is. Yet a massive part of that is due to his determination. I can't promise you he'll ever be quite the same as he was before, but there's much hope to be had for him."

I sighed in relief. "All right. Then what's this all about?"

"You know there was a fund created to help cover Josh's expenses and it's open to the community."

"Yes, sure. It's never amounted to much, but of course we appreciate every bit of help we can get."

"Well, recently there was a donor. The person wishes to remain anonymous, but whomever they are, this individual is very generous."

The doctor wrote a figure on a piece of paper and handed it to me. It took me a moment to understand what I was looking at. I received an accounting of the fund every year, and on a good year, I could expect a couple thousand dollars from it.

"Oh. This. Wait, this can't be right. You must have added several zeroes too many."

The doctor beamed. "You see why I wanted to make sure that you were told this privately? The clinic administrator will be by to explain it all to you in detail, but since we've known each other for so long, I asked if I might be able to break the news to you. The donor only stipulated that the money be used to help cover his treatment, hospital bills, and anything you need to get along."

I put a hand over my mouth. It was a long moment before I could speak again.

"Nine million . . ." I gasped.

"This will make a big difference for your son. The main thing I wanted to discuss with you is about taking him home. Once this money is in your possession, you'll be able to afford private duty care for him. Of course I wanted to discuss this with you first because I didn't want to assume anything. You've already sacrificed so much for your son, and even with nursing care and therapy at home, his care will require some commitment from you different from him being at the facility."

"I . . . whatever he needs I'm here for. I haven't even really been able to dream of him being at home, but if that's the best thing for him, absolutely. In a completely selfish way, I would love to have him home with me."

The doctor nodded in agreement. "I think it would be the best possible thing. He's been in the hospital for so long, and patients really do their best healing at home. It will help him get accustomed to the idea of normalcy again."

"How soon?" I asked. My mind was already rushing with the possibilities. A few weeks ago, I had lost all hope for my son. Now, I was contemplating a new life, one that involved him and hope for a recovery. There might be some things he could never do, but there were a host of things that he could. My boy was stubborn, a trait he got from both his parents. I couldn't wait to see how far hard work and his attitude would carry him.

"He can still get all of his therapy at home, and we'll get an agency to send nurses out as well. There may be some things you need to change at the house too, to make it more accessible for his current physical limitations. I'd say, give us a week or so to get it arranged."

"Is there a way to keep this transfer of money quiet?" I asked. "I want to make sure that no one bothers Josh and me while he recovers. I don't know how we could keep it out of the press."

***

Josh Middleton

"Pressed," I said.

I whispered it to myself at night, when I was alone. I said it to stave off the nightmares, to remind myself that I could say it. I wanted desperately to tell someone. I had to hold onto that name, even if other words drifted away. It was almost perfect. If I could just master this one word—Preston—I could make sure someone knew that he was the one who had done this to me.

I could recall every moment. The rest of my life seemed to recede into darkness in comparison. I had told my friend that I was in love with Danielle. Next thing I knew I was fighting for my life, only to be pushed off a balcony.

***

The nurse patted my shoulder gently, waking me. "Good morning, Josh. Time to take your vitals. Your mom is already here," she added. "I think she might have gone downstairs for some coffee."

I looked over to the chair where my mom usually sat. She had left behind a bag of yarn and a partially knitted square. I didn't remember my mother being so good with crafts before. In fact, I'd never known her to even try them. I'd managed to speak a brief question. "She. Maaakes. Things?" I asked, pointing to my mom's chair.

"She's always working on something," the nurse said. "Embroidery, crocheting. She's made a lot of quilts and pretty scarves over the years. She even made a baby blanket for my son a couple years ago."

I nodded. My mother had learned how to create things. The pretty nurse had gotten married to some lucky guy and had a baby. So much life had happened all around me, while I remained trapped, unable to live.

It had been two days since I had seen myself in a mirror for the first time. I'd struggled to ask for it. Once I saw myself, I regretted it. Despite the deep sleep that had trapped me for the last twenty years, I had dark circles around my eyes. My ghostly pallor was worsened by the swollen, saggy face that stared back at me. My hair, once a dark blond, had turned into a shiny silver. Even my eyes seemed to have lost something, as if they had grown pale from not being open.

I looked like my father, not the young college student I remembered myself as. I'd struggled to hold back the tears for my mother's sake, and for my own pride. I wept in silence when I was alone.

Everything was so difficult. Still, the staff praised me for every tiny increment of improvement. I was able to eat small meals—mostly broth and gelatin—and I managed to feed myself sometimes even though I still had my feeding tube installed. I had to drink the soup through a straw. My doctor promised that as I kept improving, I would soon get real meals and be able to get rid of the tube.

Food was not only sustenance or pleasure, but it would also help to build my strength again.

I felt that I was beginning to connect words and their meanings a little better. The speech therapist was helping me. Simply learning to hold my mouth and move my tongue in the correct way was frustrating. Sometimes my thoughts found their way to the wrong words, and I would blurt out something different than what I was supposed to say. As much as I hated those sessions, nothing was worse than physical therapy.

The therapist worked endlessly with me on getting from a lying-down position to sitting up and scooting to the edge of the bed. When we first began this exercise, just sitting there for ten minutes with help was exhausting. I couldn't balance without the therapist's steadying hand on me and my hand gripping onto the bed rail for dear life. This simple maneuver that I used to take for granted required the use of core muscles that had not been activated for all those years. It was frustrating to work on baby tasks that should have been easy for someone my age. When I winced and groaned in pain from fatigue, the therapist told me what I was feeling was good. My muscles were learning how to work again, and the pain meant they were waking up. I tried to keep that in mind.

After therapy, I was exhausted. Some days I would fall asleep and not wake until late in the afternoon, when the sun was going down.

On this evening, my mother was back in her chair. This time she wasn't knitting. She was reading a book. She must have felt my eyes on her and looked up.

"Hi, son. How are you feeling?"

"Ohhh-kay," I said. My voice sounded thick, like I was speaking through a mouthful of food, but at least I was making myself understood. I smiled when I saw the sparkle in my mom's eyes.

"That's always good to hear. I wish you had been up earlier. You had a visitor."

I raised an eyebrow. My lips worked to draw together the right word. "Whew?"

"You mean *who*," she replied patiently. "A young man from your school days. Tyler Harrington. I didn't realize you knew him. He's a big-deal football player these days. Very humble young man, though. He didn't even mention his career to me. One of the girls at the front desk told me. Anyway, he said that he would try to come around again when you're feeling stronger."

I felt like someone had socked me in the chest.

"Pressed!" I yelled.

"Pressed?" my mom asked.

"Tie-hur," I struggled. "Tie-hur brother. Press-done!" I slammed my fist against the bedside table.

Chapter Twenty-three

Tyler Harrington

Though I would have preferred not to go to the Sports Corps banquet, there were two reasons I needed to show up. First off, my team would expect me to be there to represent them. I was also scheduled to present a lifetime achievement award to my brother, which was going to be a surprise. When I heard about it, I could have strangled the person who had come up with the idea. I couldn't exactly decline and admit we weren't on good speaking terms. I decided to grin and bear it.

It was only one night, one uncomfortable photo op, and then I would be done with it. At least that's what I told myself the whole month leading up to the affair. Once the evening arrived, I wasn't so sure.

I realized Preston probably wouldn't be happy to see me, but if I had backed out of it and he had found out, he'd have been pissed. There were enough leakers at Sports Corps that I was pretty sure somebody would leak any comment either of us made to the press. Their network was known for solid reporting, but they did televise bits of gossip when it suited them, under the guise of "behind the scenes" teasers.

My wife was looking forward to the celebration. I knew she could tell I wasn't enthusiastic about going. She reminded me that this would be a pleasant night out for us. There would be drinks, good company, and limousine service. The kids would be at her mother's house for the weekend. She'd reserved a room for us at the hotel so we wouldn't have to bother coming home if we didn't want to.

While the room sounded enticing, I didn't look forward to all the bullshit ceremony we'd have to go through before the night was over.

As she was finishing the last touches on her hair and makeup, I got a phone call. I stepped out into the backyard to take it. It was Ed Birch.

The private investigator was brief and to the point. "I have something to tell you, but first I need to know why you were in Tennessee a week ago."

The night air was full of the scent of honeysuckle. The flowers had sprouted all along the back fence, and at night or in early morning, their perfume seemed stronger. Everything was quiet. I could hear crickets chirping and the distant sound of a television playing in the house. I was well out of earshot of anyone in my household, but I still felt the need to keep my voice low. I didn't want to even speak of it inside my home.

"I was there to see Josh Middleton," I said. I told him how I knew Josh, and then how Preston had come to know him. "It's always been something I wondered about, if my brother possibly had something do to with that man tumbling over the balcony. He knew the people who threw the party that night. I don't have a hard time believing he would get rid of anyone in his way when it came to Danielle. I was hoping he would be well enough to answer a few questions. He wasn't."

"It may be safer for him if he can't, at least for the time being. As far as Preston trying to kill this poor guy over a woman, I've seen men do worse for less," Ed said. While I wondered what he could possibly mean by *worse*, the investigator asked me another question.

"You had no other business in town? Did anyone else know you were going?"

"No," I told him. "My wife doesn't know about this mess with my brother. I told her I was away on business. I certainly wasn't going to tell Danielle what I was up to. I did mention to her that I had seen a news story about Josh being awake."

"What was her reaction?"

"She was very defensive."

"All right," Birch said. "You can probably understand my surprise when Preston turned up there, at the facility where Josh is. I followed him. He took a flight that wasn't on his itinerary to do it, paid cash, and didn't report it on his expenses to his agent, either."

"How do you know that?" I asked.

"There are ways to get information; don't worry. It will be included in your bill. Anyway, he was on the premises the same time you were. I was wondering what he was doing there, if he was following you or he was there for Josh. Obviously there were details you've left out of what you told me about your brother."

"All of this has happened so fast," I said. "Josh wasn't a factor in this when you were hired. To be brutally honest, I hadn't thought about his accident in years. In retrospect, it seems more than a little fishy."

"Did you or anyone else think to look into it at the time?"

"Remember, I was younger than Preston. I was still in high school at the time, so I obviously wasn't there. If anyone looked into it, I don't know about it."

"I did some checking into the newspapers at the time, and they all described it as an accident. One never knows when things might have been done quietly and off the books. Not to mention, those were wealthy college kids at that party. Let's just say, the authorities might have wanted to look the other way if some parents put enough money in the hands of the right people."

"You think someone took a bribe?" I asked.

"I'm not saying I know that they did, but I wouldn't dismiss the possibility. From what you tell me about your brother, it sounds like the man is damn near untouchable. What I'm telling you is he's not. He may be the all-American man, but somewhere, there was a slipup. At some point in his life, someone knew about something he's done. Maybe they just suspected it like you do. I'm working on unraveling a few possibilities. Meanwhile, I want you to sit tight because I have the feeling things are about to get messy. If he hasn't made a mistake soon, he will."

"As glad as I will be to put this behind me, I'm not sure I like that."

"You're a wise man then," Birch said. "I won't bore you with the details, but I'll keep you informed. Some of my methods may be slightly problematic for you to know about. This case requires a harder push. If he's doing what you think he is, then he needs to be stopped."

"I agree," I said, taking a look back through the sliding doors and into the house. My wife wasn't anywhere in sight.

I'd read Birch's resume before I hired him. Back in his days with the bureau, he had hunted killers. This was familiar to him, like an old dog returning to a scent that had long alluded him. Birch's voice, usually dry and professional, changed tone to that of an insistent father. His tinge of worry prickled the hairs on the back of my neck.

"It would seem that Danielle hasn't voiced her suspicions, and that's a good thing. In the meantime, I don't want you to utter another word to her about your brother. I'd recommend you avoid the both of them for a while if possible. Whatever you do, for God's sake, don't make him angry, and don't give him any reason to suspect your motives."

"But I don't feel Danielle is safe around him. Who will protect her?" I pleaded, my voice higher than usual.

"I will."

***

Preston Harrington

"Danielle, you look beautiful."

My wife was in our bedroom, studying herself in the mirror. The dress she wore was ravishing: black, lacy, and high-necked in the front, backless and dipping low in the back. She frowned, considering herself from different angles. It was rare for her to be critical of her body, but I could tell she was having second thoughts. Danielle is the kind of woman who can make anything look good, and her body definitely did the dress justice.

"You think so?" she asked. "It's a little more revealing than what I'd usually wear."

"I know so," I said, and kissed a spot of exposed skin just beneath her neck. She sighed. I ran a finger down the column of her spine. She turned and looked up at me. Her eyes were serious.

"We need to talk about something tonight, when we get back."

"Oh?" In my experience, when she wanted to have a "talk," it didn't end well for me.

"It's nothing bad," she said. "Maybe something that can make things better, even." She slipped her arms around my neck. "I want us to be happy."

"So do I." I leaned forward and kissed her lips. I caught a hint of perfume, a light scent that reminded me of white roses. Her cherry lipstick was sweet against the tip of my tongue.

"It's a special night," I told her. "The dress was a good choice. I'm going to enjoy pulling it off of you or maybe even working around it. That sounds like fun."

Danielle gently pushed me away. "Uh huh. Well, we're going to be late if we get into it, and I don't want to have to get ready all over again," she said, smiling.

I sat down on the bed and watched as she added touches to her makeup. She was wearing her hair in an elegant updo, even better to emphasize the long, straight line of her back. I really wanted to bed her. I was proud that every other man at the reception would probably wish they could do the same.

"How are you feeling about your speech?" Danielle asked.

"It's fine," I said. "I learned it about a week ago. I'm going to keep it brief. I'm always irritated when people take forever on stage accepting an award."

"Yeah," Danielle said, looking over her shoulder. "It's your turn in the spotlight, though. You get to stay up there as long as you want. You know a lot of these fucking blowhards haven't done half as much as you have for charity," she continued. "They aren't giving you a lifetime contribution award for nothing."

"Well, I don't mean I'm going to say thank you and walk off," I teased. "I know how to keep it within reason."

"My point is, don't rush," my wife said, skimming her hands over her hips. It was just a little gesture, not made for my benefit, but it made me want to do her right then. I knew she would be genuinely irritated afterward, especially if I tore her dress. I adjusted my crotch and tried to get my mind back on the conversation.

She was right. What she couldn't understand was that I didn't feel anything about it. The time and money I had donated was more about maintaining an image than anything else. Sure, our father raised my brothers and me to believe that those who earned their wealth had a responsibility to give back to the larger community and help those who didn't have good fortune or the opportunities we did. I knew for sure that Greg and Tyler took that to heart.

I didn't feel those sorts of things. It all felt like just another night of socializing with people when I would rather be doing something else.

But I couldn't tell my wife that. She wouldn't understand. It was something I fantasized about—telling her the whole and unadulterated truth about me. It was one desire I knew had to go unfulfilled, but I thought about it often. I'd only seen a glimpse of her reaction the day she'd found the matchbox from Grinder's and that piece of my burned jacket. What would she think if she knew all of it? All the way back to when I was a boy, and all the kills since?

What would she think if I told her the power I felt? It was better than anything. It was like sex, adulation, and sheer thrill all wrapped in one powerful emotion. She wouldn't understand that it was a power unlike any other, the godlike power of choosing when someone else would take their last breath. For as long as I could remember, it was the only real emotion I had ever felt.

I would have loved to see her reaction to knowing. I hated that this was the only thing we couldn't have real honesty about. We were open when it came to all of each other's secrets except this, the most important one in my life.

I knew well that would be dangerous for us both, and not worth the temporary thrill. She had her own code of morals, and I knew that what I liked to do wouldn't fit with how she was raised. If she didn't agree to remain quiet, I would have to take care of her, and that was one thing I didn't want to ever have to do.

I didn't want to be a widower. I preferred my children to be brought up by their own mother, not some other woman who would have to learn her role in their lives and work for their trust. Not to mention, another woman would have to learn her role with *me*.

Once we were ready, the drive to the event was brief. One of the things I enjoyed about Sports Corps is that when they held an affair, they did it right; they rented out an entire luxury hotel for the night. When we arrived, there were cameramen out front taking pictures on the red carpet as everyone entered. Inside, the grand ballroom was decorated with chandeliers, yet the room was somehow comfortably dim. The banquet tables were graced with white candles and orchid centerpieces.

Our table was near the front, and a few choice guests would sit with us, other award winners and their spouses. Once we were seated, a stream of people came up to say hello to us. After about thirty minutes of greeting people and enduring small talk, I noticed that Danielle seemed a bit annoyed.

"Are you okay?" I asked.

"It just feels like . . . a lot of people. It's a little stifling."

"Darling," I whispered. I rubbed her knee, and she managed a small smile. I wondered what had caused her mood to change so quickly. She was usually more comfortable at these functions than I was.

"Preston!"

I turned to see Adam Murray standing only a foot away from us. He was one of the attorneys who had been contracted to work for my old team. Their main job was to negotiate the legal aspects of new deals between teams and players. He was an industry insider who knew everyone who was worthy of notice within the sports world. If you went to any sports-related benefit or gala, odds were nine out of ten that you would run into Adam at some point in the evening.

"How are you, Adam?" I said. He shook my hand.

"I'm doing great." He grinned. "Just made it here in the nick of time," he said. "It took longer to get our son down than expected."

"Oh yes, that's right, you have a new little one. Congratulations," Danielle said. "How's Gina?"

I was pleased. Here it was Danielle who remembered the name of Adam's wife, something I hadn't bothered to recall. Even when she was not at her best, she still managed to put her best foot forward.

"Oh, she's doing fine, thanks for asking. I hope your husband here doesn't take any offense to me saying so, but you look gorgeous tonight, Danielle."

"Oh, thank you," my wife said.

"I feel bad because I meant to say hello to you and Tyler when I saw you at the Meridian Arms last week. I was having cocktails with a new potential client, and by the time I would have been able to come over, you and your brother-in-law were already leaving."

"Oh?" she said, blushing.

"Well, I must go find my wife. She's already threatened to hit the open bar," he said with a wink. "Can't blame her. It will be our first night out since the baby. You two have a nice evening. Congratulations on the award, Preston."

"Yes, thanks Adam," I blurted. When he was gone, I squeezed Danielle's arm, drawing her close to whisper in her ear. "What was that all about? Why were you with Tyler?"

"Nothing. Your brother had just gotten back from a vacation with the family, and I said we should go to lunch so I could hear about it."

"Why?" I whispered. "Did you meet him at a hotel?"

"We met at the five-star restaurant of a hotel. I just wanted to catch up with him and hear how he and Joanna and the girls were doing."

"Oh," I said between clenched teeth, "so do you ever think about propriety? What do you think it looks like when a married woman meets a man at a hotel?"

Danielle's eyes narrowed. "Like I said, it was a restaurant in a hotel. You know I think of him as my brother too. Which, by the way, I don't have siblings, so it might be nice if you paid any attention to either of yours."

"Not the place or the time," I told her. "But we're going to talk about this incident later. And I want the truth, not bullshit."

"Fine," she said. "I'm going to the lady's room."

***

Danielle Harrington

I was already feeling sick to my stomach, and Preston's grilling me about my lunch date with Tyler didn't help matters. I was upset that the stupid lawyer, Adam, had brought it up. Was he trying to make trouble?

The hotel had a plush powder room with high-backed velvet chairs placed in front of the mirrors. I sat down and powdered my nose and refreshed a layer of lip gloss. What I was really concentrating on was breathing deeply, trying to bite back the feeling that I was about to throw up. It was a tricky proposition. Deep breathing wouldn't necessarily prevent me from being nauseous, but it would at least hold it off for a few minutes. How was it I had managed to forget this phase of pregnancy? Morning sickness had popped up all times of the day and night when I was carrying the twins. I barely remember the first trimester, except that I survived on ginger ale, crackers, and rice cakes for most of it.

I sat for a while and began to feel the seasick feeling subside in my stomach. Maybe I would be luckier this time. My obstetrician had said I was less likely to have severe nausea for a second pregnancy, especially if I weren't carrying another set of twins. I hadn't expected I would ever test her theory out.

I had to bite back my anger. How dare Preston talk to me like something was going on between me and his brother? If I was going to cheat on him, I'd never be dumb enough to fuck Tyler. Beyond that, I was deeply insulted because he should know that I would never cheat on him with anyone. It wasn't for lack of opportunity, either. It was just because I loved him, despite all I suspected.

As I concentrated on feeling better, I heard the emcee over the speaker system. The ceremony was about to begin.

I heard a lot of water running and paper towels being tossed into the receptacle by the door. Women hurried out of the restroom, a couple saying that they had to get to their seats. I knew I couldn't move quite yet. To make it worse, I had to worry about my dress. I wasn't sure how much wiggling I could do in this thing without ripping a seam or tripping on the hem. I was afraid that once I stood, my head would start to swim.

"Oh, there you are." I heard a voice behind me. I turned around.

"Crystal," I said. "How'd you know I was back here?" I knew she would be at this party. Between the influx of people rushing to our table and when I started to feel sick, I hadn't even thought about finding her to say hello.

"I didn't, but Preston said you might still be in here, so he asked me to come looking for you. Are you okay?"

I took a quick look around. We appeared to be alone.

"Crys, I'm going to tell you something not even Preston knows." I paused. "I'm pregnant."

Saying it made it more real. I suddenly felt like crying. "Fuck. I don't have time to be hormonal right now," I said and bit my lip. "I don't know why this is the night that I have to get sick."

My friend smiled at me. "I thought you were."

"How'd you know?"

"You've had . . . a glow for a few weeks now. I know you talk about not wanting more kids, but I also know how great you are with the two you have. This new little one is going to be so lucky to have you as a mother. Congratulations, honey."

"Thank you," I said.

Crystal rubbed my back. "And here I thought I was having a bad evening because my boyfriend had to cancel last minute. You definitely have me beat."

I stood up carefully. The moment I was on my feet, the whole room swayed around me.

"Uh, are you going to be okay?" she asked.

I pulled my dress up around my knees. "No," I managed to say before I took off running toward a bathroom stall.

Chapter Twenty-four

Preston Harrington

I was angry, and as the night drew on, my temper only grew worse.

Danielle disappeared for twenty minutes, and even after I sent Crystal to go find her, it took another thirty for the two of them to come back.

Danielle walked to our table slowly, one hand on her friend's arm. I got up to pull out the chair for Danielle. A maître d' rushed over with an extra chair so Crystal could sit at our table. The other couple seated with us, a basketball player and his wife, nodded and greeted the ladies cordially as my wife and her friend took a seat.

"See, I brought her back for you all in one piece," Crystal said with a smile.

"Yeah," I said dryly. "Thanks for that."

I turned my attention to my wife. She looked pale. Her makeup was perfect, but her eyes were watery, as if she had been crying. I thought of asking her if she was okay but decided not to. She obviously wasn't, and I knew the wrong words and she would start crying. Instead, I reached for her hand and squeezed it. "This won't be much longer."

That was a lie, really, because with one hour into the show, I knew there was one and a half to go. I couldn't leave because my award was scheduled to be the last one presented that evening.

A server came by, and Danielle asked for a breadbasket and a glass of mineral water. She saw my frown and managed a shaky smile. "I'm sorry I was gone so long, Pres. Something I ate earlier must have disagreed with me."

"Nothing to be sorry for then," I said. I didn't believe her for one moment. At the best, she had made a stupid choice by being seen at a hotel with my brother. At worst, she had done something unforgivable. I couldn't even begin to think about that because I needed to hold myself together for the remainder of our time in public.

I caught a look between Crystal and Danielle. I wondered what she knew. Had Danielle admitted to her friend that she and Tyler were involved? The idea that my wife might have shared information that I didn't know was maddening.

I didn't like the idea that while they had been in the ladies room, my wife was pouring out her heart to her best friend. I had just accused her of sleeping with my brother. In a way, having Crystal there might have worked for my benefit. I certainly wasn't going to say anything untoward to Danielle in public, but there would be no snippy comments from her either with her best friend right there. I couldn't get a read on Crystal's reaction. She was polite but not talkative.

The night seemed to drag on. I didn't dare take a glance at my watch, even though I wanted to. I was aware that the event was being taped, and they loved to do closeups on people when they weren't looking. Danielle didn't try to smile. She just looked weary and ready to go home. She sat up straight in her seat, legs crossed.

I noticed she hadn't eaten her meal, either. She had a few bits of bread, but her dinner plate was still full when a waiter took it away.

Crystal stole glances between Danielle and me as if she were afraid we were about to break out in an argument any moment. One way or the other, I could see that she sensed the tension between us. What the fuck had Danielle said to her?

On the stage, the announcer was droning on, when he said four words that caught my attention.

"Please, welcome Tyler Harrington."

I watched as my brother walked across the stage, dressed in a tux. He took his place at the podium through a roar of applause. I plastered on a smile and forced myself to clap. It took a few moments for the clapping to die down before he was able to speak.

"Thank you so much," he said. He looked down into the audience, and for a brief moment our eyes met and locked. Then he looked away.

"First off, I'd like to thank Sports Corps for inviting me. As you know, SC has been a big part of any sports lover's life for the last thirty years. For those of us who play, coach, or who are involved in any way with professional sports, the stamp of approval from Sports Corps is a huge commendation. Over the years, SC has become not only a network, but a way of life."

Tyler paused, smiled, and shifted his weight. "Tonight, we're not here to talk about me, or what it means to be a professional football player, or even the love of the sport. We're here to talk about my older brother, Preston Harrington."

I felt it when a spotlight was trained upon me. The crowd gave me a standing ovation. I stood up just long enough to wave and acknowledge the audience. I smiled. I made sure not to look at Tyler again; instead I pulled the notes from my pocket and took a quick glance at them.

After the crowd took their seats again and quieted down, my brother continued.

"There are many things I could tell you about Preston Harrington. It's been a pleasure to be his younger brother, to learn from the example that he and our older brother Gregory set. While you may think I'm speaking of his example as a sportsman, that certainly isn't all. He's a dedicated husband and father. He has always been a perfectionist, someone who strives to be the best in all that he does. Perhaps more important than that, I know him as a man who shows . . . compassion." Tyler paused. He coughed. "A man who shows compassion for the less fortunate, reaching out to those who haven't gotten the best chance in life. Over the last twenty years, Preston has used his platform as a world-renowned athlete to help children all over the world. And now I'm proud to be able to announce that Sports Corps has named my brother, Preston Harrington, the recipient for this year's Lifetime Achievement for Excellence in Philanthropic Giving."

I stood, straightened my jacket, and plastered a smile on my face. I could feel the spotlight on me as I made my way to the stage. Tyler waited for me at the podium. I wondered who in Sports Corps had thought this would be funny. Or maybe they were just stupid enough to buy the story we always tried to sell: the Harringtons, the all-American football family. It played well to both the press and the cameras.

When I reached him, Tyler patted me on the back. "Brother," he said with a nod. He handed me the award and took a step back.

The crowd gave another standing ovation. I scanned the crowd and took in this small moment of adulation. Not as good as the fans at a football game, but close. I looked at

Danielle and saw that her eyes swam with tears. She mouthed the words, "I love you." I wondered if that was true.

When the crowd had settled, I spoke. "Thank you all so much for coming out tonight and for the honor you've given me this evening. I had a speech planned. I am very grateful for the life I've had, both on the field and off. Even more so, I am grateful to have had the privilege to reach out to others. Children deserve a good start in life, and as adults, citizens of this world, we have to do all we can to ensure that happens, no matter where or what circumstance those kids were born into. Again, thanks so much for this honor, and good night."

I exited the stage, with Tyler right behind me. Moments later, the emcee was back at the microphone, making final announcements to thank the audience for their donations, thank the honorees for their participation, and close the ceremony for the night.

"We're going to have a talk, brother," I said, once we were backstage.

"My wife is waiting for me," Tyler said. "Can we make this brief?"

"Absolutely," I said. "Let's you and I have a little celebratory drink."

***

Tyler Harrington

Sports Corps had rented out the entire hotel for the evening, and since most of the attendees had gotten their drinks during and before the banquet, there were few people in the restaurant bar. I sat on the far end of the bar with Preston beside me. The place was suitably dim, and with our backs to the other patrons (a young couple in the far corner of the room who appeared not to notice anyone else) I realized we would be left alone. With a few more people around, he might not feel so ready to talk.

The bartender, of course, recognized my brother right away. I didn't say anything and took a long gulp of my drink. Whenever we were together, I could count on at least a handful of people recognizing him and wanting to talk football with him. When I was recognized, it was never while I was in his presence.

"I heard about your award tonight; congratulations," the young man said. He looked like a college kid, and I wondered if this job was a way to work through school. I always wondered how people managed to do that. College and football were all I could handle back then.

Preston was happy to oblige the bartender's request for an autograph. He scrawled his signature on a napkin. That was enough to send the guy on his way with a smile.

My vodka burned at the back of my throat and going down. As soon as it was gone, I wanted another. Instead of asking for another, I waited to hear what my brother was going to say. I figured I would need it more afterward.

Preston took time with his drink. He sighed, wiped his mouth with the back of his hand, and looked at me with a shitty smile. "You want to tell me what you were doing at a hotel with my wife?" He said it casually, as if we were discussing the volatility of the stock market or unusually warm weather.

I kept my voice low and looked him in the eye when I responded. "First of all, I wasn't doing anything *with* her. I told her that I had just gotten back from a vacation with my family, and she wanted to go to lunch to hear about it. Since the restaurant inside the Meridian Arms is one of my favorites, I told her that we could meet up there."

"What did you talk about?" he asked.

"The usual things we talk about. Your kids and mine. Family stuff. Friends we have in common. Crystal seems to know half of my friends, so Danielle and I talk about acquaintances."

"Crystal is popular," Preston said. I picked up on the implication. I always had the feeling that he didn't care for her as a person, most likely because she was so close to Danielle. Preston preferred to have all the attention, so anyone who stood in the way of that would be a problem for him.

"What I find hard to believe," Preston continued, "is that neither of you thought about how that might look."

"Okay, it was a hotel restaurant, but people can always make something innocent seem dirty if they want to. There was less chance of anyone seeing us there than going out to one of the restaurants in town. You should know that. I would hope you trust me more than that."

"Are you fucking my wife or not?" Preston asked, his voice low and deadly calm.

"Despite whatever you think of me, I wouldn't do that to you. I have my own wife and family, and if I were interested in having someone on the side, she would be far outside the circles my family travels in. You know my wife. That would be the end of my marriage."

"Well, you know, that's a good thing. Because there's not anyone left around who could tell you how things worked out when they tried to get between me and Danielle. It didn't end well for Rob, and it would end worse for you."

Chapter Twenty-five

Danielle Harrington

"Preston carried that off without a hitch," Crystal said.

"Yeah, it was a great speech," I said. I'd gotten teary eyed when he talked about the importance of children. It was all beautifully executed, all down to the part where he pretended not to have carefully rehearsed his speech. No one could beat Preston when it came to putting on a show for people. He was so good at it that sometimes I questioned what I was seeing—the authentic man or the shine of his public persona.

I stood up slowly, a hand over my stomach. I was relieved that I didn't find that I was dizzy again. The nausea seemed to have passed, but I wondered aloud where Preston was.

Crystal locked an arm with mine. "You know what? Preston will catch up. Wherever he is, he's probably saying his goodbyes to somebody or, I don't know, I saw him talking to Tyler. Whatever he is up to, why don't we work our way out of this crowd? You can go out to my car and sit with me, turn on the air. You're not feeling well, and it's going to take a few minutes before everybody can get out of the parking lot."

It sounded like a good idea. I wondered what Preston was up to and what he and Tyler were getting into. There was nothing I could do about it at this point. I didn't know what Tyler might say, but I figured it wouldn't be anything different than what I had told Preston. After all, he didn't want anything to look untoward, and it wasn't like we had done anything. If he admitted anything else, I was determined that I would tell my husband I had no idea what his brother was talking about.

I texted Preston to let him know I would be with Crystal. She moved her car next to ours so there would be no missing us. I wanted to make sure he didn't have any excuse to be anxious or question my whereabouts when he was already pissed.

Crystal and I had been sitting in her car for a few minutes when Preston caught up with us. I could tell from his posture, the stiffness in his shoulders, that something was wrong. As he moved toward us, I could tell that he was upset. But when he got closer, he pasted on an easy smile, as if nothing was wrong. Anyone who didn't know him like I did would have thought everything was fine.

He patted Crystal's shoulder before speaking. "Thanks so much for staying with her. I was talking to Tyler for a few minutes after the ceremony, and people kept interrupting us to congratulate me."

Crystal smiled, said goodbye, and promised to call me later on in the week. When Preston turned his back, she winked at me. I knew how hard it was for her not to gush about how happy she was for the two of us. Crystal had always been good at keeping secrets—but a new baby was a big secret to keep quiet. Knowing her, she would be on the internet shopping for baby clothes and toys as soon as she got home. She spoiled the twins, and I knew this time wouldn't be any different for her. She took her role of auntie very seriously. If only things were so simple and clear cut for *me*.

Telling Preston about the baby should have been a joyous moment for both of us. Instead, I felt tired just thinking about it. I wasn't at all sure how he was going to react, and I could only hope he would be surprised and happy about this. We certainly weren't the only couple who got pregnant one more time than expected. If I had gotten pregnant a year, or even eight months earlier, I wouldn't have hesitated to tell him.

The truth was, no matter how well he took the news, I had serious concerns for all our children and how our family was going to continue. I already knew that I was going to wait to tell him just a little longer. I certainly wasn't going to tell him that night.

The ride home from the Sports Corps event was uneasily silent. I knew that Preston was angry, so I didn't say anything either. I wasn't looking forward to hearing his opinion about the evening or this bullshit about how he was mad at his brother for seeing me at a hotel. I was still feeling sick and only wanted to go home and go to bed. But I knew things were not going to go that easy.

He held back whatever he had to say until we got into the house. The kids were at my mother's for the night, so he didn't bother trying to contain himself. The moment the door closed behind us, he started arguing with me.

"All right," Preston said. "I want the real story of what happened. What motivated you to feel like you had to go to see my brother at that hotel?"

He walked behind me. Though I answered him, I didn't turn back around. I was headed straight for the bedroom.

"I don't know why you're upset like this, but the only thing I can tell you is that it's normal to have a relationship with family members. I know you don't talk to Tyler in that way, but we've always had a friendship. I called him, and he mentioned that he had just gotten back from a vacation with his family. The restaurant inside that hotel is one of his favorites, so we agreed to meet there so we could catch up. Nothing else happened."

As I reached the bedroom door, he spun me around. "You want me to believe that?"

"Why wouldn't you?" I yelled. "I've always been faithful to you! I don't know which I'm more insulted about. The fact that you would ask me why I was with him at a hotel like I had sex with him or the idea that it would even cross your mind. Where the fuck do you get off?"

I pulled away, opened the door, and went into the bedroom. I peeled off my dress and kicked off my shoes. While Preston sat on the edge of the bed and watched me, I walked from the dresser and pulled out a nightgown. As I crossed the room and went back into the bathroom, he followed me. I turned to look and saw his frame filling the doorway, arms crossed over his chest.

"What was it you were so fired up to tell me about before we left this evening?"

Oh shit, I thought. I almost said it out loud. This was not the way I wanted him to hear the news. I brushed my teeth and took my time rinsing. He was waiting for an answer.

"You know, I really don't feel like talking about that right now," I said, reaching for a tie to put my hair in a ponytail.

"Now you're going to play coy?" Preston asked.

"It's not about playing anything. I'm half sick and not in the best mood right now. Can we just do this tomorrow? There's plenty of time to talk about stupid shit, but right now I am going to sleep."

I walked to the door. He didn't move so much as a muscle, and there was no way I could pass him.

"I think we should hash this out now. If you and my brother only talked, what did you talk about?"

"If?" I said. "When did you suddenly start acting like Tyler, or any man for that matter, was competition for you?"

That comment seemed to strike him. There was some change in his eyes, a flash of anger. His blue stare grew coldly indifferent.

"I never said he was competition. I need to know if you've been sleeping with him, that's all."

"No. No. And never. You realize how insulting that is to me? At least give me the benefit of the doubt to not be stupid enough to fuck your brother."

"Then why didn't you mention seeing him?"

"Because it was no big deal. I halfway forgot about it before Adam brought it up tonight."

"All right. I believe you. What did you discuss?"

"His kids, and ours. How being a dad sucks sometimes. He mentioned your parents and that you haven't spoken to them in some time. Tyler went home a few weeks ago, and they mentioned not seeing or hearing from you in several months. He said the fact that they said anything at all means it bothers the hell out of them. We talked about his team and the fact that he's ready to retire if it comes to that. You know. All the shit that you should probably be discussing with him yourself."

"Right," he said, and drew back.

He let me pass, and I sighed in relief. I got into bed and turned on the television. Not that I wanted to see anything, but I wanted noise, some distraction. Anything that would make things feel boring and normal. Lately I missed the feeling that we were like other couples. I hated always questioning what was behind his motives and actions.

With his back to me, Preston undressed. I didn't even look his way. He leaned over and snapped the light off. He grabbed the remote and turned the television off.

"Danielle," he said and sat down beside me. "Look at me. Don't ignore me."

I slowly turned toward him. He put his hands on my shoulders. "Baby, do you still love me?"

"Pres, of course. Yes, you irritate the fuck out of me sometimes. But you know that I do."

He laughed at that. Cupping my face in his hands, he leaned close and whispered. "My darling, you know that I love you. The one thing that I will not accept, above anything else, is disloyalty. Things that happen between us are for us only and not to be spoken about to other people. I believe you when you say that you wouldn't do anything with him. I do think that you might look at sharing information with him as, I don't know, commiserating with your brother-in-law."

"Preston, I don't know what you mean," I said, keeping my voice as calm as I could make it. I was relieved that he couldn't see my expression in the darkness.

He continued as if I hadn't spoken to him at all. "Whatever he might have told you or insinuated, it's not true. I don't really care what he says as long as you're not buying it. He will say awful things about me anytime he gets an opportunity. He's always been jealous of my success in life. He believed that he can tear me down by ruining my reputation. It's the way he's done things since we were kids. Understand?"

"Of course," I said. "We didn't . . ."

"No more about that," he cut me off. He kissed my lips while his hands roamed my body. He pushed me back against my pillow, climbing on top of me.

"You belong to me," he said, pushing my gown up. I felt him leaning over me, his hardness brushing against my skin. He came into me with one push. He moved with me, leaning down so that his face rested against the hollow of my shoulder. I held onto him and wrapped my legs around him. I felt the need to make him sure that there was no one else.

Preston had always been good at stopping an argument by adding sex to the equation. Under different circumstances, it was a good way to make up when we were having a disagreement. But on this night, it was different. He wasn't trying to soothe my nerves or even work out his own aggression. For the first time, I felt like sex with him was more about keeping me in line than having anything to do with love or passion.

Chapter Twenty-six

Josh Middleton

After so many years of being in a coma, every time I woke up, I feared that I might be dreaming. Sweat gathered at my temples. I grabbed the sheets in my fists, gritted my teeth. Then I looked at the walls around me, the sliding hospital bed table, and realized that this was the reality I had come to know. I could look out the doorway and see the hall. Voices of the morning staff were muted, but I was able to hear them as they prepared to help their patients start the day.

It wasn't what I wished for, but this place was very real. I couldn't wait to be out of there. In its own way, the place was as confining as the coma I had been in. I couldn't wait for the time when I would be able to get up and walk again. The few halting steps I had taken were enough to elicit praise from my therapist and doctor, but they weren't nearly enough for me. I wanted to get back to a normal life again, or something like it.

My window was open, and I could see outside. Birds chirped in the sunshine. If I listened hard enough, I could hear the distant sound of cars out in the street beyond the facility.

I had become used to the schedule in this place. Everything was about mealtimes, medication, checks of temperature and blood pressure. Built around those were my therapy sessions. Physical therapy was painful. I had sessions on Monday, Wednesday, and Friday. I'd have taken it every day if they allowed it, though most afternoons the exertion wiped me out for the rest of the day.

Speech therapy was the most frustrating. The only thing I did like was that the therapist gave me exercises that I was able to do between her twice-weekly visits, so with daily practice I saw improvement. Oddly enough, as the words from my mouth became more distinguishable, the ideas in my head seemed to stick better. I hadn't realized that hearing the words come out garbled or wrong had made me more confused.

I was now able to speak more clearly, though it sometimes took much too long for the words to come to me. Sometimes the words seemed to be trying to run from me as soon as I was about to take hold of them. But I was learning to capture them, bit by bit.

I made the decision that this would be the day when I finally told the truth. I might be able to write it, but I was convinced it would be better to tell my story.

The day was an average one. When the nurse came in with my breakfast, I asked what day it was. This was Thursday. That meant my speech therapist, Peggy, would come to see me later. My mother arrived around ten thirty. My therapist came in at eleven.

Peggy was a chubby woman with freckles across her nose and red, unruly hair. Before she had a chance to run me through the usual exercises, before my tongue seized up or I forgot, I blurted out the most painful words. "Preston. Harrington. Tried . . . to kill me."

"Honey, what?" my mother said. She glanced at the speech therapist, the two of them exchanging surprised glances. A moment of silence passed when I feared they hadn't understood me—or worse yet, didn't believe me— but I continued anyway. I'd thought about this moment so many times since I had woken up, but nothing could compare to the reality of finally saying it.

I continued. "Night of the party. Preston. Pussssshed me. From bal . . . bal . . . balcony." I wasn't sure why the last word was so hard for me to say. I could still see the wrought iron railing in my mind's eye, feel the sensation of falling as I hurtled over and off the edge.

"Josh, are you saying someone hurt you?" Peggy asked.

"Yes!" I cried. "Pres . . . ton Harry . . . ton. Football player. He pushed me . . . off," I said, making a forward motion with my hands. "Off the bal . . . cony."

I heard my mother curse under her breath.

"Our coma patients say a lot of odd things when they wake up," the therapist said.

"No, you wait a minute!" my mother replied. "He knows Preston Harrington. His brother was just here not long ago. What he's saying . . . my God, it's entirely possible."

"It's t-t-t-t-true," I said. "Pressed-ton pushed me."

The therapist rubbed my shoulder, and I pulled away. "Not baby," I said. "Do . . . don't treat me like it."

"We should tell the doctor," the therapist said, taking a cell phone from her pocket. She walked out into the hallway.

My mother stood, and I reached for her hand.

"You're sure about this, darling?" she asked.

I nodded. "Yes, Preston pushed . . . me."

"Okay, son. We'll see what they say. But if these people don't call the police, I will."

"Yes, please, Mom."

Sharon Middleton

Dr. Carrey came in and spoke to Josh, and he repeated the same story. It seemed the more he said it, the clearer he was speaking, the better he got at explaining it. After the doctor heard what Josh had to say, he asked me to step outside with him.

"What do you make of it?" I asked. I still had chills. It had never occurred to me that anyone had hurt my son. When he was injured, I had blamed God. I blamed fate. I came to blame my son, feeling that this was an accident that could have been averted if he hadn't been drinking that night. It took years to finally accept my child's injuries. The idea that someone had done this to him and gotten away with it all these years changed everything.

"It's hard to say," he said, shifting uncomfortably. He leaned toward me, dropping his voice to a whisper. "There's still so much that we haven't learned about the human brain, but one thing we do know is that patients can dream while in a comatose state. Sometimes they wake up with delusions formed during the time they were under. The imagination can work overtime, and when patients wake, they can confuse memories with events they dreamed of. You said he actually knew the Harrington brothers before his accident?"

"He did. Tyler Harrington came here to visit him not that long ago, and he talked about how Josh had been friends with Preston. They both studied at the University of Tennessee." I crossed my hands over my chest. "Tell me something. You don't think Tyler is the anonymous donor, do you? I've been thinking about it, and the money was donated to Josh's fund not long after he came to see my son. I don't know anyone who has ten million dollars just lying around. The press interest had subsided by then."

"Josh seems very determined about this. I can't say I know for sure if anything will come of it or if his memory is correct, but I think we should call the authorities. Let them figure out how credible they think his story is."

Later that afternoon, two police detectives arrived to interview Josh. Both middle-aged men, one was six foot two and trim, with a shock of white hair; he introduced himself as Peter Dillard. His partner, who introduced himself as Mack LaCroix, was smaller with thinning wisps of brown hair, a man who looked like he'd eaten a few too many donuts in his life. He spoke with a trace of a southern accent.

Dillard did most of the talking, while LaCroix hung back and took notes. I could tell by their chemistry that the two had been partners for a long time. I listened as they told me how this questioning of my son would proceed.

"Because of what he's been through, we prefer to have you in the room with him as a source of comfort. It's important that you don't speak or give him any cues. His doctor told us what he said, but we will ask him to repeat it. We want to get a fresh account from him rather than hearsay. Just as importantly, we need to be sure that he's very clear on these events, given the situation," explained Dillard.

That bothered me. If my son was correct, would his testimony stand up in court, given all the physical and emotional trauma he had been through? I knew I was getting far ahead of myself. So many years had passed. Any attorney would try to say that Josh was confused about what had happened to him. Since that question was unlikely to have a positive answer, I asked something else.

"Have you done anything like this before?"

The two officers exchanged a glance. Dillard said, "Well, I don't know that we have ever talked to a coma patient who woke up after twenty years. We have interviewed many victims of crime during their time in the hospital and spoken to witnesses who were traumatized. We'll be gentle with him and let him know he can stop and take a break at any time."

I worried that my son would be intimidated by the detectives. He wasn't. I went into the hospital room with them but stood back as the officers had suggested. For the third time, he told his story. It took a little longer for him to speak, but I had the distinct impression that he was going a little slower to make his words clearer. I was so proud that he was standing up for himself and simultaneously furious that he'd had to endure any of this at all.

How had I believed that my son had done this to himself all these years? I should have known he would never let himself get that drunk. I was certain that he had not been suicidal. I remembered clearly how happy he had been in the weeks leading up to his accident. He didn't have a history of depression or anxiety.

My son's halting speech brought my thoughts back to the present.

"Preston . . . and I . . . we were friends. Told him. My secrets. That I loved Dani. We were at the party, upstairs. He pushed me. Off the . . . balcony."

"Dani?" LaCroix asked. "As in Danielle?"

"Yes."

"Harrington's wife," Dillard said. "That's a motive."

"All right. Well, I think we have what we need from you right now, Mr. Middleton."

"What . . . will . . . you . . . do?" Josh asked.

"We're going to get to the bottom of what happened," LaCroix said. "I can't promise it will be easy or quick, but we'll find out what happened."

"Get him!" Josh yelled.

***

Ed Birch

I had been putting one hundred percent of my energy into this Harrington case. I felt an obsessive energy to get to the truth. Good for the Harringtons but bad for my relationship. My girlfriend, Anna, decided she needed time away to "think" about us. I'd heard that one before. It was all just as well, though. I was a couple thousand miles away from her spending endless days following leads. I needed the freedom right now to set my own schedule and not be accountable to anyone. Besides, I now knew about the cancer eating away at the good cells in my body. Save for a miracle cure being developed, I had two to five years left to live. I hadn't told Anna. This knowledge I intended to keep to myself for a while. This Harrington case gave me a much-needed opportunity to focus on something other than my health.

Over the entire time I had worked so far for Tyler Harrington, the football player had never called me directly. I was always the one to reach out. I'd gotten a few text messages from Tyler, but I had the impression that Tyler, like most people these days, didn't do phone calls unless it was urgent business.

So when my caller ID lit up with Tyler's phone number, I knew something was up.

"What can I do for you, Tyler?" I answered.

"You know that piece of advice you gave me the other night?" he said. "About not pissing my brother off? Well, I might have blown that to shit." He chuckled after saying it. I heard the tinkle of ice in a glass. The sound was musical in a way it could only be to a recovering alcoholic.

"You having a drink?" I asked.

There was a pause. "Yeah, yeah. It's one of those days already."

"I'm on speakerphone?"

"Yes, but I'm alone."

"Just pick me up anyway," I said.

Tyler picked up the phone and gave me the short version of the argument between him and his brother.

"What got me," Tyler said, "was not only that he accused me of having an affair with his wife but that he threatened me. He hasn't threatened me with anything since the two of us were kids. It brought me back to what it was like back then."

"What exactly did he say?"

"He said, 'Good things don't happen to men who try getting too close to my wife. It didn't work out for Rob, and it won't work out for you either.'"

"How . . . had you mentioned Rob? How did Preston happen to bring that up?" I tapped my fingers on the table.

"I didn't mention him at all. As a matter of fact, I haven't heard Preston even speak Rob's name since the day of the memorial service. He was there crying and talking about what a good friend he was," Tyler answered. "And then I thought about it, you know? He was probably one of a lot of men who had a crush on Danielle. He flirted with her a bit, but she's a pretty woman; a lot of men do. He wasn't the type to ever do anything about it; at least, I don't think so. Even if he tried it, I know Danielle would have put him in his place."

"You mean your brother's partner, the one who wound up dead in the restaurant he co-owned?"

"Yes."

Fuck, I thought. I cleared my throat and then asked a question. "What's your schedule like for work?"

"I'm going to be off for another month before practice begins."

When I spoke, I kept my voice calm and authoritative. "I'm going to make a very strong suggestion to you. This is the time to plan a trip. If there is anywhere your wife has wanted to go for a while, this is the time to take her. The timetable is going to have to move up on your brother."

"Meaning?"

"Meaning it's not safe for other people that he's out and . . . up to whatever it is that he's doing. I don't think he was playing with you. From what we know of him, I would take what he says as a serious threat. I have been tailing him, but I'm going back to Tennessee soon. I can't watch him here and then keep an eye on Josh, too. I would feel better if you were somewhere far from Preston, preferably anywhere he doesn't know where you are. I'm not saying it to scare you, but it's best if you take preventive steps."

"How close are you to getting something on him?"

"Close," I said. "But not close enough for you to mess around with him these next couple weeks and get yourself killed."

There was silence from Tyler's end of the phone. "Okay."

"As controlled as he is, it sounds like he's obsessed with anyone who seems like they're flirting with his wife. He'll be watching Danielle, so don't speak to her. If she calls you, don't call back. I know we talked about this before, but from now on, she's officially dead to you. Whatever protective instinct you have must be put aside for now, for your sake as well as your family."

"Instinct? To protect Danielle? I don't know what you mean . . ."

"Are you sure?" I pressed. "Many of your questions when this started came out of concern for her. I'm not your therapist and it's not my business what you feel about her. I'm trying to get this done without having another body on my hands."

"What have you learned so far?"

"Enough to be highly suspicious. Not enough to make a case. I could go into the details with you, but I will have more for you in a day or two. I would rather talk about it then. We can theorize all day, but I need to get some facts nailed down."

"If you need anything," Tyler said, "subcontractors, money for expenses to move things along, I'll get you whatever you need."

"Glad you feel that way, because one more person to tail him wouldn't hurt."

Tyler didn't hesitate. "That's done. Whatever you need. You know, for a while now I have been thinking about what my brother may have done. I thought it was suspicious when Rob died, but I had no way to prove it and didn't fully want to let my mind go there at the time. If I'm honest, the idea that my brother killed him scares me more than anything."

"Why?" I asked.

"Because Rob was his best friend. They played on the same team for years; they bonded. Things didn't go as smoothly with the business end of things as they might have liked, but they remained close. Rob was the next best thing he had to family. If Preston would go that far, he would do anything."

Chapter Twenty-seven

Danielle Harrington

Preston was up early as usual, and I stayed in bed as long as I could. He was gone by eight with a kiss on my cheek and a promise to be home around seven. I smiled and watched him go. I was relieved that he was going. After the strange night we'd had, I wanted a little time to clear my head. One moment accusing me of an affair, and less than an hour later making love . . . it was a lot to absorb at once. I was still shaken and worried about what was going on with him.

I didn't bother to ask what his schedule was like, and I decided not to do any checking behind his back to find out. I really didn't want to know anymore. I was more concerned about keeping my family together and figuring out how all of this was going to work out.

I drove in to work and tried to concentrate on what I was doing, but it felt like the day was mostly a loss. I sorted through bills and business statements and went through emails of artists who wanted their art to be featured at my gallery. I decided to answer those when I was in a better mood and less likely to say no to everyone with barely a glance at their work.

Around two o'clock, my assistant peeked into my office. "Did you ever take a break today?" she asked.

I looked up from my laptop, rubbing my temple. "No, and that's probably why I have a headache right now," I said. Reaching for my purse, I motioned for her to come inside. "Would you mind picking up a sandwich for me? I want one from the bakery down the street. Just cheese, though. I'm avoiding deli meat. You know, nitrates and all that," I lied, at least about the reason to avoid deli meat. I didn't want to tell her I was pregnant, but I did want to avoid the listeria risk from processed meats.

She was back with my food in about twenty minutes: Swiss and cheddar on a baguette with tomato and cucumber. The food hit the spot and gave me much-needed energy. I powered on my laptop but picked up my phone. I scrolled through the contacts, feeling like I wanted to talk to someone but not sure who I should reach out to. I thought about calling Josh. I wondered what Preston had said to him, but I thought better of it. If I tried to talk to him and my husband found out about it later, he would take it as confirmation that something had been going on between us. Some part of me feared for Josh's safety if I were to be tied to him in any way.

I wondered if Preston truly believed I was unfaithful or if his apparent outrage was a distraction from whatever he was doing. While I tried to prove my loyalty to him, who knew what was really going on with him? I knew that man better than anyone, and yet I had to admit that he had some parts of his life and his thoughts that he wasn't ever going to share with me. If he was out there hurting people, maybe I was safer when I wasn't trying to find out what was going on.

Two days passed, and he told me that he would need to travel out of town for work. He was going to be doing some commercials and press appearances for the new sports clinic he'd visited a few weeks earlier. I didn't care. It would give me a few days away from him, time to spend with the kids and not have to think about his behavior. He would be gone for about a week.

He explained all of this over breakfast. I was having my coffee and only half paying attention, planning what things the kids and I could do while he was away, assuming my morning sickness stayed at bay.

"Maybe, when I come home, we can plan a family vacation," Preston said lightly. "We haven't gone anywhere together in too long."

"Where do you want to go?" I asked.

He shrugged. "The Bahamas might be nice."

***

Sharon Middleton

For the last twenty years, my schedule had revolved around my son. In a way, it still did. I was the gatekeeper for all the appointments he needed. I spoke to the nurse and therapists to keep appraised of his progress.

Dr. Carrey had warned me that bringing Josh home would place a considerable amount of stress on me. But I found it to be the absolute opposite. Thanks to my mysterious benefactor, I not only had a new home to take care of him in and a car to get around, but I also had as much help caring for him as I wanted.

During the day I had a private nurse, but I opted not to have her live in or stay during the evenings. Josh worked as much as he could to build his strength back, and at night, he slept peacefully. The nurse would be in early to help him.

I liked to sit with him around three in the afternoon—before he was asleep for the evening but late enough for him to have completed his regimen for the day.

"You don't have . . . oth—other stuff . . . to do . . . Mom?" he asked.

I was sitting in a recliner beside his bed. "What else would I do?"

"Some . . . thing," he said softly. "Pl—Play bingo. Go on date."

I laughed heartily. "Personally, I hate bingo, and I don't know anyone I want to date right now."

"Play hock—hockey?" he teased. "Go skiing?"

I shook my head. Other than the stuttering and occasional mispronounced words, this was my son. Right down to the corny jokes. He might be battered and bruised, but this was still my kid. Though I laughed, the realization made me want to cry.

"When I'm . . . up," he said, "you will need to . . . do things."

"I will, son, I promise. For right now, I just want to enjoy having you home. Is that okay? I promise I won't hover forever."

The vowels of the next word he spoke were drawn out, but I could still understand it. "Deal."

I sat and watched television programs. All the shows he liked to watch had gone off the air long ago. I was able to find reruns of one of his favorite comedies, *The Wonder Years,* which was comforting to him. We even shared a couple of laughs over some silliness.

Once he fell asleep, I got up from my chair. Unable to help myself, I dropped a kiss on his forehead.

I went upstairs and answered a couple phone calls from family. As I'd expected, they wanted to come see Josh now that he was out of the hospital.

During a conversation with my cousin, I made a decision. "You and your kids can come up," I promised. "But not anyone else right now. I don't want to overwhelm him with too many people. We still don't know whether or not he will remember everyone. I'm still waiting to see if his father will want to drop in, and I haven't heard anything from the bastard."

I told no one about Josh's allegations regarding the person who pushed him. I sincerely hoped the police would do something about it, but three weeks had gone by without my hearing anything about it. Because Harrington was a celebrity, I didn't want to say anything until the police made a move. Knowing some of my relatives, I didn't trust a few of them not to sell a story about Josh to the tabloids. The juicier it was, the more money would be in it for them. The worst thing that could happen would be for word to get out that this man was being looked at by the authorities before they were ready to make a move.

While I hadn't been able to keep the news about the anonymous benefactor completely quiet, luckily it hadn't gotten picked up in the national papers. The information was around for anyone who wanted to dig for it, but I hadn't encountered any problems. Close family members knew, but I didn't answer anyone's questions about where my sudden windfall had come from. I'd lived without a lot of family and friends around over the last few years, so I found it interesting to see who wanted to come back around now that I had money.

I didn't speak to Josh about it, but I hadn't stopped thinking about Preston Harrington and what he did to my son. I developed a minor obsession with him. I would log onto the internet and read all kinds of stories about him.

Most were glowingly positive. I had expected the great commentary about him during his football career. What really turned my stomach was reading the articles about his life after football: *philanthropist, loving husband and father, businessman, entrepreneur.* All things my own son would have been if the chance had not been stolen from him. This selfish bastard seemed to have the world, but he'd tried to kill my son over a woman. To add to the insult, he'd married her and they'd had kids together.

I closed my laptop and slid under my comforter. I didn't like this bitterness, the hatred that was in my gut these days, but I didn't know what I should do with it. As happy as I was to have my son at all, I could not shake the little voice in my head that demanded to know: *what if none of this had ever happened at all?*

It would be another early morning for me, and my son was resting peacefully downstairs. I told myself that I should get some rest. When I did drift off to sleep, with my television playing in the background, I had troubling dreams of being chased through the woods by a creature without a face.

Preston Harrington

I started the week with one objective: to clean up the mess I had left behind in college.

Twenty years ago, one week after Josh's fall, I had gone to see him in the hospital. I stood at his bedside, hands in pockets, watching him. He was breathing on his own, but that seemed about the only thing he was capable of. He had broken bones in his arm, leg, and a broken rib. His nose was broken, which gave him two black eyes. I would have liked to kill the man right then but hadn't found a private moment to do it. Nurses constantly came in and out, and at that time, he hadn't been out of ICU for more than a day or so. He was being watched closely by the medical staff. When a nurse asked, I said that I was Josh's brother. She nodded and went away so we could have time alone.

Still, the nurse's station was visible from a glass window in this room. There was no way to kill him without being seen. I had heard a rumor, nothing confirmed, that Josh had suffered a significant amount of brain damage. Looking at all his injuries, I believed that to be true; I couldn't imagine how the damage to his brain would be anything less than catastrophic. If he ever did wake up, his family would likely be facing a worst-case scenario. He'd be brain dead or so severely disabled that he'd be completely useless.

Knowing this made me feel secure. Even if he did remember what had happened, who would believe him? How would anyone ever prove a crime when the only witness was both physically and mentally traumatized?

I stood there for maybe twenty minutes before leaving, content that Josh would not be waking up anytime soon. I promised myself that if the man ever did, I'd simply come back and take care of the problem.

All these years later, I was going to make good on the promise I had made to myself back then.

Internet research gave me two invaluable pieces of information: Josh had been moved out of the skilled nursing home facility he'd lived at for so long. The local news had briefly mentioned his move, as well as a note stating that the family wanted privacy while Josh continued his recovery. No statements had been made about how much he had recovered or whether he was able to speak or remember his life before the accident.

The fact that Josh had moved home demonstrated a level of improvement. Another search gave me an address of a new property bought under his mother's name. It was the only thing she owned, but she had literally purchased it within the last month. According to public records, Josh's mother, Sharon, had lost everything in bankruptcy many years earlier. Surely, this new house had to be where she intended to bring her son to heal. A real estate site listed the date the house was sold, as well as the address and a brief description about its four bedrooms, two and a half baths, etc. The place was located in another suburb of Knoxville a little farther out from the nursing home where Josh had spent the last twenty years. I knew the family was originally from somewhere near New Orleans, but I guess you spend twenty years in a new place and it becomes home to you.

Researching through Google Maps, I was able to determine that the house was located off a private road a half mile from the interstate and surrounded by wooded acreage. A privacy fence ran the length of the back of the property, but no barriers guarded the front. Apparently no one thought much about security.

I drove my Corolla up to Knoxville—Danielle thought I was leaving it at the airport—and then made myself as inconspicuous as possible. Always careful to wear a baseball cap, sunglasses, and a grungy T-shirt and shorts, I rented a room in a seedy, no-name hotel where I could pay cash and no one cared who I was. I grabbed meals and snacks at gas stations or drive-thru fast-food joints, lamenting over the pounds I might gain but knowing I had to do what I had to do.

I had to be very careful and form an airtight plan. I decided to drive over to check out Josh's place in person. I hid my car along a seldom-used old dirt hunting road in a wooded area off the service road and trekked through the trees to reach the back of his house. I was able to find a large knothole in the fence that allowed a perfect view of the place. The surrounding woods made for a perfect cover. No one ever walked back here. I kept up this routine for several days without ever being seen by anyone.

After a few days of watching at different times of the day and switching my vantage points to various holes and cracks in the privacy fence—or even using the thick brush as cover to view the driveway in front—I learned the schedule. Several people came in and out each day. A private-duty nurse left every evening around six. She drove her own car and always wore scrubs. At least two therapists came each day as well. I was able to tell what agencies they were with by the company cars they drove. These people were always gone by evening also. I staved off boredom by eating granola bars and fantasizing about ending Josh's life.

I wondered how Josh's family could afford all of it: the new house, medical staff, and people coming in and out every day. All I knew was that this needed to come to an end as quickly as it had started.

Josh was alone each evening from the time the nurse left just after suppertime. Apparently he slept through the night, or was at least well enough that his mother left him alone. She had a bedroom upstairs, and her light stayed on in her bedroom window without blinds until quite late— later than I was willing to stay and deal with the mosquitoes. She went to her room and didn't come back down. I wondered if Josh had a panic button or something like a baby monitor in his room. It would make sense; his mom wouldn't feel secure in her room unless she could hear any sounds of distress. It was funny, really—this grown man being handled like a damn baby. It was all his fault. If he had left Danielle alone and moved on, none of this would have happened to him.

I figured a Wednesday night would be the best time to do it.

Josh's room was on the main level and toward the back of the house, where the windows looked out onto the yard and the wilderness beyond. I noted that a sliding glass door in the rear center of the house opened onto a deck and then into the backyard. Wearing camouflage clothing, I entered his yard through the unfenced front and circled around to the back of the house. Because of the contrast between the light in his room and the dusk of evening outside, I could see the edge of his bed through a slit in his blinds.

I always planned ahead. After my second day of surveillance, I'd been concerned about how I would get the sliding glass door open. I found instructions on how to do it, looked up the tools I would need, and purchased them before I took my next trip up to the house. In the end, I didn't even need them.

As fate would have it, everything was perfectly choreographed for my entrance. Because of the gentle breeze that evening, the sliding door had been left open an inch. It wasn't even open enough for me to see the gap until I was standing right in front of it. Dumping my tools quietly on the deck, I simply slid the door open and stepped inside.

Immediately inside was a dining area with an oval-shaped table and four chairs surrounding it. The kitchen to the left was lit only by a small light shining down from the microwave onto the stove. A carpeted living area was directly ahead, past the dining room. I found the light's intensity easily enough for me to navigate around a few moving boxes scattered in the dining and living room areas.

Now that I was here and getting through the door had been so easy, I considered expanding my goals. I could get two for the price of one. I chuckled inwardly at that thought.

I stepped onto the carpeted floor in search of a staircase going up. Because Josh's bedroom was on the main floor, I knew that his mom was alone upstairs. Locating the stairs, I took them two at a time to reach the upper level. I mentally calculated which of the three upper bedrooms faced the back of the house, knowing that one was the mom's.

Pausing outside her open door, I heard a fan whirring—I could relate to her need for both a cool breeze and white noise. Hearing no other sounds, I stepped into her room. Light from a nearly full moon streamed in the window, and I could easily see the woman sleeping in her bed. She slept on her back, with ugly, uneven snoring sounds ruining the otherwise peacefulness of the setting. I crept closer, staring at her, willing her to open those eyes so I could give her the fright of her life. The moment she woke, I'd approach slowly, staring directly into her eyes with each step before grabbing her throat and snuffing out her worthless life.

I stepped closer, still staring directly at her eyes, but the stupid woman refused to wake up. Not feeling that killing a sleeping person would be nearly satisfying enough, I drew my attention to the trinkets in the room. Maybe I should pocket some jewelry or something else valuable to her. Naw, I was losing focus. What satisfaction would I gain stealing a trophy from someone still living?

I turned around and stepped out of her room, enjoying the freedom of exploring a house I'd never entered while its inhabitants slept only yards away. And if anyone decided to wake up or interrupt me? Well, I held full power over that scenario.

I stepped into one of the front bedrooms and brazenly flipped on the light. I had no fear whatsoever of being caught. In fact, that would only make my life better. This room had apparently been set up as Josh's memorabilia room. *Soon-to-be "shrine,"* I thought, as soon as I was finished dealing with Josh. I glanced around at the various trophies, some going all the way back to Pee Wee baseball and flag football. He hadn't seemed like much of an athlete to me, but apparently he had tried soccer and swimming somewhere along the way also. And even a high school musical. Ha! Now that was a Josh I could imagine.

I studied a picture of a college-age Josh with a group of friends. Lucky for him, Danielle was not in the photo, or his impending murder would turn into a torture session. Who knew? Maybe it would anyway.

Deciding what treasure to swipe was difficult in this room laden with options. It didn't have to be anything valuable, just something to give me a memory. I settled on a football trophy small enough to slide into my coat pocket. Josh did love football. Then, at the last minute I decided to also grab the photo of Josh and his college friends. I slipped the photo out of the frame, folded it, and shoved it in my pocket next to the trophy. This one was more a move to show his mom who was in charge. At some point she would notice it missing and be extra freaked out that I had been this close to her while she snored away in the other room. Now I was ready to put an end to Josh's miserable life.

I made my way back down the stairs, through the living room, and to the short adjoining hallway that I knew led to Josh's bedroom. A few steps later and I was on the threshold of a wide-open door to Josh's room. I smirked and even let out a barely audible chuckle. This was too easy!

Intellectually, I knew that Josh had changed. I had seen a picture in the paper and knew that twenty years of illness had necessarily had a profound effect on him. But I still imagined him the way he had looked when we were in college together, like he looked in that photo.

I scanned the room. A television mounted on the wall opposite Josh was playing a rerun of the 1990s sitcom *The Wonder Years*. The volume was low but audible enough that I could hear faint laughter in the background. I remembered that show. I chuckled internally, remembering the secret crush I had on the brunette, Winnie Cooper. The TV provided ample light for me to see everything in the room.

What I saw on the hospital bed facing me was a gaunt middle-aged man with no muscle on him. He slept on his back, like his mom, so I could clearly see the planes of his face that were far thinner and sharper than I remembered. His hair, once dark blond, looked platinum but was actually silver. He breathed evenly and his eyes were closed. He was the perfect picture of peace. I loved it. That peace would soon change to its polar opposite.

As I had guessed, a baby monitor sat on the nightstand next to Josh's pillow. I noted that it was a good brand—Infant Optics, the same system Danielle and I had used for the twins. The camera next to Josh would show up on a video screen in his mom's room. "Infant." That was hilarious. Josh the infant. I crept over and, with one gloved finger, pressed the mute button on the front bottom of the device.

I retraced my steps back to the foot of his bed and stared directly at Josh's eyes, willing him to awaken like I had his mom. Hopefully he was more in tune with my brain waves than his mom had been. And then, success! Not more than a minute later—although it felt much longer because I was restless to get my work done—he opened his eyes.

For a moment, he simply stared at me. He probably wondered if I was a ghost. "Who are you?" he asked.

"Really?" I said, using the low timbre of my voice. "You don't remember me?" I moved to the left side of his bed and took a step closer, then stopped. "Your mom said it was okay if I came by for a visit."

He squinted and pushed his hands flat on the mattress, as if he were trying to sit up straighter. The pupils of his eyes grew large as he focused on my face. The hospital bed had him in a semi-sitting position, but he wanted a better look at me.

"I can't say I blame you for not recognizing me. Twenty years is a long time, and it changes a man. My brother came to see you recently—Tyler. But I guess it doesn't count as a real visit when you were asleep."

"Preston," he said. His voice was clear but almost a whisper. His damaged mind was grasping the true danger he was in. His body was now quivering. He had no doubt about what was coming. I wouldn't have even had to turn off the baby monitor, I thought with a quick chuckle; in Josh's terror, he couldn't think coherently enough to even glance at the device.

"Yes," I said, savoring the moment. Josh's eyes widened, and his mouth grew small. He seemed to be struggling to form words, as if the fear had rendered him speechless. He knew me and, more importantly, fully remembered what I had done to him.

"I had to come see you," I said, keeping my voice low and taking another step closer. "You're a rare breed. Not everyone just wakes up after being in a coma for twenty years." I casually motioned with my hand on the words "wakes up" as if we were chatting like old friends. My gaze never left his face.

His lips were working, though no sound came from them at first. "No," he said, and then again, "No." He raised both hands in a defensive pose. Then he tried again. "Preston," he said. He breathed hard, like a man who had been running. His horror must have been magnified by the realization that with his personal boogeyman present, his wasted legs wouldn't even support him long enough to stand, much less run away.

I recognized and was thrilled by the absolute distress in his eyes, the way he shivered as he tried to figure how to beg for his life when he couldn't even spit out the words. I smiled and took one more step closer, never taking my eyes off his dark pupils, our faces now separated by mere inches.

"Why me?" he asked. As terrified as he was, he wanted to know why. I nodded. There was dignity in asking such a question when he could have simply continued to beg for his life instead. He must have known it wouldn't do him any good.

"Because you wanted Danielle and you wouldn't leave her alone. I couldn't have that. A weak and pitiful man like you. You reeked of pathetic. No way could I have even let Danielle waste any more of her time with you."

I let my words sink in, enjoying the moment too fully to commence the final act. The final act of his midlife school musical. From behind me I heard the canned laughter coming from the television. The changing pictures created weird and shifting shadow patterns on the wall.

"But you . . . got . . . got her. N-n-not me."

His stuttering was precious. "Yeah. I did, didn't I?" I smiled. "I got everything. Let's see: fame, fortune, a family, the girl. And what did you get? Hmmm. Twenty years asleep. A regular sleeping beauty. Except no beautiful princess came to wake you up. And you know what? She . . . never . . . will."

With a swift movement, I yanked the pillow from behind his head, covered his face with it, and pressed down with my full upper body strength. I was surprised at the fight he put up. He tried to grab my hands and push them away, clawing to pry my fingers from the pillow. I was glad his legs were tucked under the covers or I would have had four unruly limbs to deal with. In the chaos, he managed to get his fingertips on my wrist, between the edge of my glove and my sleeve. I stopped his pathetic attempt with two even harder pushes. I felt him choke on his last breaths, smothered beneath the soft pillow. His hand on my wrist went limp.

Once I let him go, he crumpled toward the left side of the bed, so I grabbed him by his dead arm and situated him back in the middle, replacing the pillow behind his head and retucking the bottom sheets that indicated his previous distress. His eyes were already closed, thankfully, and the color was already slipping from his face, leaving a grayish pallor. I left him in the same prone position he'd been in when I'd first entered the room. No one would ever know what happened to him. Everyone would think that he simply slipped back into a deep sleep and his heart stopped—which was what should have happened to him all those years ago.

I re-pressed the mute button on the baby monitor, making sure it was on as it had been a few moments before. I crept out of the room, made my way back down the hall, navigated the dining room, and slipped back out the sliding door, leaving it only one inch open, the way I had found it. With full clarity of mind, I remembered to retrieve my bag of tools from the deck. I swung around to the front of the house to get around the fence, trekked back through the woods to my car, and hopped onto the interstate. I wouldn't have any need to go back.

All of this was Josh's fault for being stubborn, but I would have no more trouble from him. Now that I was rid of him, my emotion gurgled up into full-out laughter. I even snorted and made myself laugh even harder, slapping my hand on my knee in giddiness. Maybe I would even stop at a Dairy Queen to celebrate with a Dilly Bar.

My only regret was that it couldn't have lasted longer. He had died knowing who I was and why I was about to kill him. That was the best ending I could have given him and the only one he deserved.

Chapter Twenty-eight

Danielle Harrington

"Wait a minute. You still haven't told him?"

Crystal and I were in my backyard. The kids were playing ball, and we were sitting at a table beneath an umbrella, drinking iced tea.

"I've only known for three weeks now. He was in a shitty mood after the awards ceremony, and he left for business not long after. He's been gone since a couple days after that on business. It's not exactly the kind of news I wanted to give him over the phone."

"Well, yeah, there's that. When's he supposed to get home?"

"Another three days," I said.

I didn't want to get into an explanation about the fight I had with Preston, but Crystal didn't ask. "Well, maybe you should do one of those corny reveals women are doing now, where they have a cake made."

I laughed. "That's a gender reveal, not a pregnancy reveal," I said.

She shrugged. "Could work the same way. Congrats, Daddy, you're having another baby."

"Why does that sound dirty when you say it?"

"Because most things do sound that way when I say them." Crystal grinned. "You have plans for when he comes home?"

I glanced at the kids before answering. This state of happiness without Preston at home wasn't going to last. I felt a little guilty that I felt good without him around. I'd spoken to him over the phone a few times since he had been away and sent a couple of texts. None of it was substantive; we were just checking in with each other. He was doing it because he knew I expected it. The sad thing was that I was replying to him for the same reason. I didn't want to break the status quo and make him uncomfortable.

"We need to hang out at your place more often," Crystal said. "You guys ever do anything back here? You've got a lot of land."

I bit my lip. I wanted to say: *Yeah, my husband comes back here and burns up shit for no apparent reason.* Instead I told her, "The kids get the most use out of it, but Pres and I aren't in the yard much, except when he plays touch football with them."

It was exhausting to pretend to be normal. But what other choice did I have?

The doorbell rang, shaking me from my thoughts.

I was in shorts, a tank top, and flip-flops. I wasn't expecting company, but I had it in the back of my mind that it might be someone delivering a package. I was always ordering things for the kids or myself, and at times I forgot items were scheduled to arrive.

I ran inside and got to the door just as the bell rang once more.

I stumbled backward when I saw who was waiting for me. "Tyler."

"Hey, Danielle. Can I come in for a minute?"

"Sure," I said, stepping aside. I closed the door behind him. We stood in the foyer for an uneasy moment.

"I won't take much of your time."

"Well, that's good. Preston's not home, but Crystal is here." We were both whispering. I hated that it felt like being near Tyler was some sort of clandestine thing I should be ashamed of.

"That's fine, I won't keep you from your company."

"You took a big chance coming here," I told him. "Preston is probably still angry at you."

"I know," he said. "He made that very clear. I had it on good authority he wouldn't be here today, so I thought I would try to see you."

"Why?"

"I can't tell you what to do or how to feel about my brother," he said carefully. "You've always been so loyal to him, and I respect that. When you make the decision to stay with him, despite what he's done . . ."

"What he may have done," I corrected.

"What we know he did," Tyler pressed. "Women have left men over a lot less serious shit."

I wasn't going to fight him on that point. I crossed my arms over my chest. "And?" I said.

"It's not just you, but it's the kids too, Danielle. I can't help but worry about your safety and theirs. I know you don't believe he would ever raise a hand to you or your children, but most women who have violent men in their lives don't see it coming."

"I'm not abused," I said. "What do you want?"

He took out his phone. "I'm sure you would have heard this on your own, but I wanted to be certain you didn't miss it," he said, scrolling through his screen. He handed the phone to me. "Look at this."

It was a news story. The headline made my heart skip.
Coma Victim Who Woke after Twenty Years Dies

Joshua Allen Middleton died sometime yesterday evening, according to authorities. He'd recently been discharged to his mother's home to recuperate after waking from a coma. Middleton fell from a second-story balcony at a house party twenty years ago and had been in a coma up until two months ago.

Though he has been under a doctor's care and was seen by a nurse on the day of his death, he appeared not to have any condition serious enough to contribute to his demise. While the preliminary cause of death is listed as a heart attack, Middleton's mother, Sharon Middleton, has requested an autopsy to determine an exact cause of death.

I handed the phone back to Tyler, trying hard not to release the tears gathering in my eyes. Until Josh woke from his coma, I hadn't thought of him in years. So much time had passed while he remained lost. I wondered how his family was handling him being tragically snatched away after having him back for such a brief time.

"Tyler," I said. "Wait a minute. You don't think Preston had something to do with this? He couldn't!"

"Wouldn't he?" My brother-in-law took a step closer. We were already speaking in whispers. "He's out of town. Do you know where he was when this happened?"

I shook my head. "That would be too cruel . . ."

"Is anything really too cruel when he needs to cover up what he did before? You know him. He's a meticulous man, but he's driven by jealousy. You are and have always been his most prized possession. I believe he pushed that man over the railing at that party to keep him away from you. Once the coma broke, he went back to make sure the job was completed this time. You really think he would let anything stand in the way of keeping his secrets? Are you so sure there's anything he won't do, even when it comes to people he claims to love?"

I took a careful step back. I knew that I was very close to the wall.

"You said it yourself, those are your beliefs. You have no evidence of such a thing, and you've always believed the absolute worst about him in any situation. You can go now."

Tyler swayed back on his heels, hands in pockets. "Yeah, I can go now," he said sadly. "At least you won't be able to say I didn't try. You remember that."

I closed the door behind him. My hands were shaking. My husband could be violent and jealous, but to commit such a calculated murder? No. This was the man I'd had children with, a man I'd built my entire life with. I knew my husband. And yet . . .

***

I didn't sleep well that night.

Preston didn't call, but he did text. I was relieved that I didn't have to hear the sound of his voice. I would only ask the wrong questions, trying to figure out what was going on with him by analyzing the sound of his voice or the expectant pauses between phrases. I had too many things I wanted to ask him that couldn't be done over the phone.

By text, I could more carefully monitor my tone. It took several tries, typing, erasing, and editing myself before I came up with statements that seemed reasonable enough to send. He didn't have to hear the break in my voice when I spoke his name or hear the hollowness of the anger in my chest.

The last thing I wanted was a fight. Well, maybe I did. But I wanted it in person. A good old-fashioned screaming match. As dangerous as that might be, I'd reached the point where I felt that it was absolutely what I needed.

Preston asked how the kids were doing. I said that they missed him but were otherwise fine. The truth was that they were getting more used to his absences and didn't ask so many questions about him being gone any longer. I wasn't sure if I should look at that as a good thing or not. I'd grown up close to both my parents. It was the one thing in my own childhood that I could always depend on, and I'd hoped to pass that same stability onto them.

But I missed him. Not the Preston of the last few months, but the one who had wooed me and claimed my heart what seemed so long ago. We'd been living a dream, and I'd been given more than any woman could ever hope for. Was I greedy? Did that keep me from seeing what I didn't want to see?

Preston ended our brief conversation with a text saying, *I love you, good night.*

Of course, I answered in kind. What was I going to say? You sonofabitch, when have you ever really loved anybody but yourself? Is it really so much fun for you, having a family for appearances sake? Is it just convenient for you, Preston? Was it all about the fucking? And by the way, your brother thinks you're a murderer, and he thinks I'm blind. Oh, and I know you're busy with your scheming and planning, but I'm pregnant, and for the first time, I'm not sure I want this baby.

My fear, probably the one that was more realistic than Preston hurting me, was that he would listen to what I had to say and then he'd make me feel foolish and unfaithful. How do you accuse your spouse of terrible things and then take them back if you're wrong? Preston was a master for making others feel like they were to blame. Why should this be any different? He'd tried it before, after all. Even when I had presented him with the evidence I'd found, he had acted like I was the one who was confused. I would never admit it to Tyler because I didn't want to admit it to myself, but I was beginning to feel unsafe with Preston, and I didn't want to bring another baby of his into the world.

Chapter Twenty-nine

Ed Birch

At one point in my life, after I was pushed out of the FBI, I felt like I might have lost my knack. Not until I reestablished myself years later did I begin to see that my ability to find the truth in any situation had not left me. It had only been covered and distorted after the pain of the death of my child, the divorce, and alcohol. Without those distractions that wrongly impacted my judgment, I believed that my prowess as an investigator matched up to the best in my field.

Knowing that, I didn't take Preston's skills for granted. It takes a master manipulator to live a double life for so many years, to convince people in both public and private that he was a loving family man. His skill on the gridiron was the only thing that was real about him, but even that was tainted by what he did in private.

When Tyler first came to me with his suspicions, I had maintained a cool demeanor and tried to remain impartial. My gut told me that the whole situation was too strange not to be true and that Preston's life appeared too perfect. Upon closer inspection, I always found that what appeared flawless had its share of cracks and fissures.

Following Preston came with a few challenges. The one plus was that since Preston had retired, he didn't travel with a security entourage.

I couldn't do all the tailing myself. I had to hire a couple of detectives I knew, short-term subcontractors who I paid off quietly and gave only the minimum of details. I let them assume we were stalking the famous football player because he was cheating. Tyler had asked that I pull out all the stops, and that was what I was doing. Someone was in place who watched Preston's residence at all times. And another man tailed Preston whenever he drove around town. This allowed me the job of tailing the former player myself when I got word that the man would be leaving town.

Though I hadn't been with the bureau in years, I was still able to do certain things that, as a private citizen, might be viewed as slightly outside the law. Some of my best leads came from being able to access real-time credit card information and purchases. It was the kind of information only federal authorities could get their hands on, and in most cases, required a warrant.

But Preston wasn't stupid. He bought little with his credit card. Although for certain exceptions, like his plane ticket for an upcoming business trip, he didn't mind charging. It didn't matter to me. Withdrawals of cash also were of interest. Preston never made any withdrawal less than twenty thousand dollars, but I had noticed a pattern in Preston's intervals for taking out money. He always made some kind of move right after.

One could assume that a married man who was supposed to be in one place for work but drove into another state might be trying to cover up an affair.

My instinct, however, told me that nothing Preston did was ever so innocent. I tailed him all the way to Knoxville. I knew how to follow someone and remain undetected. Preston had history in Tennessee; it was where he had spent his college career. Maybe he was simply visiting friends in the area—a comfortable place for him, somewhere he was happy to return. The moment I realized where exactly Preston was driving, I felt a lump in my throat. One quick exit off the freeway, and I knew who Preston was headed to see.

I had previously driven past Josh Middleton's new home. It looked like a peaceful place: a two-storied home shrouded by trees and a privacy fence that snaked its way around the back of the property. Following a surreptitious distance behind Preston, I observed him park his car on a nearby road. After I passed him, I then witnessed him sneaking into the woods in the direction of Josh's house. I was disgusted at how Preston was likely stalking Josh by watching the comings and goings of who was on the property from somewhere behind the back fence.

I couldn't linger without being seen, so I continued down the main road. Once I was a few streets over, I parked my car and punched a number into my cell.

My call was answered on the fourth ring. "I need a really big favor."

***

I still had a few friends left at the bureau, and when I needed them, I could depend upon a small favor. Getting an audience with the local police was one of those. It took about an hour for the correct people to be notified. I went into the local police station, showed my identification, and was asked to wait in a small conference room. Two police detectives joined me about thirty minutes later.

I could tell the pair had been partners for a long time. Dillard was the taller, more talkative one, LaCroix on the stocky side.

"Sorry for the wait, Mr. Birch," Dillard said. "I was told you have some concerns about Josh Middleton."

"I have some very serious concerns for his safety," I replied. "I was hired by someone who believes that Josh Middleton's college buddy, Preston Harrington, may have something to do with his fall and could be out to make sure he doesn't talk."

The partners exchanged a look.

"We can definitely talk about the mystery surrounding Middleton's fall," Dillard said as I took a seat. "But first, what makes you think he's taken steps to hurt him again?"

I scratched at my cheek. "Well, we could begin with the fact that he's watching the man's house."

***

I followed the creep, Preston, for four days of him stalking Josh. But tailing without being discovered was getting more difficult in such a remote area. I did what I could to avoid discovery by twice switching to a rental, or even parking a distance away and walking past Preston's car.

On the third day, since I was already on foot anyway, I carefully made my way into the woods to get a better handle on exactly what Preston was doing. I knew where Josh's house was but not where Preston would be, so I took a wide loop to avoid suspicion. I had plenty of experience doing stakeouts, but usually these were done from a car and not on foot through a wooded area.

I would take a few steps, pause, listen, and then take a few more steps. Covering the half-mile distance took a long time this way, but eventually the fence behind Josh's house came into view. Preston had wisely dressed in earth-tone colors, but I had my high-powered binoculars with me to identify him from afar.

After several minutes of searching from my concealed position behind a grove of trees, I finally spotted him. He looked so comfortable, it made me sick. He would chomp on some wrapped snack and spend several minutes at one hole in the fence before moving to another vantage point. What did he think this was? A picnic?

I was certain he planned to kill Josh Middleton. What was taking those jokers down at the police department so long to arrest this guy? Did someone else have to die before they could gather enough evidence to get him off the street? I didn't want him to get nabbed for the lesser crime of stalking or I would have called in the two police detectives. No, I wanted him caught red-handed for murder.

I felt helpless to protect Josh. Memories of that other victim I had failed to protect flashed through my mind, but I shook them away and laser focused on the case at hand.

Preston seemed to be following a pattern of arriving midafternoon and then leaving a little after six p.m. Once when I drove through the neighborhood in the early morning, I spotted his parked car at that time as well.

On the fourth day, he broke the pattern. I drove past periodically between morning and afternoon, but either he had parked in a completely different spot or he stopped stalking in the short term.

I drove back to town to grab some food before I would once again check out the Josh Middleton neighborhood. After a satisfying dinner plate of eggs and hash browns, I retraced the route that had grown so familiar to me over the past few days.

I was a mile from the exit to Josh's house when I heard a giant popping sound and the car reared sharply to the right. No! Not my tire! Why hadn't I chosen to rent a car today of all days? I pulled over to check the damage, and it was bad—completely flat. I couldn't drive even a mile on it without destroying the rim. I opened the trunk to grab out the spare but found it flat as well. I now remembered that I had given myself a mental reminder to fix the spare, but the importance of completing that task hadn't seemed pressing at the time.

I yanked out my cell phone and dialed AAA. After waiting on hold an exasperating fifteen minutes, the lady assisting me assured me that someone would soon be there to tow me to a shop that would get me all fixed up.

"Soon" wouldn't come for over an hour. I waited helplessly by the side of the road until the guy finally showed up, loaded my car onto his flatbed trailer, and towed me back into town to a place right next to the restaurant where I'd eaten my dinner. Luckily the tire was easily fixed with a plug, but by the time I paid the tire shop and got out of there, it had already been dark for nearly an hour.

I raced down the road to Josh's neighborhood, but as I expected, since I was so late, Preston's car was nowhere to be found. I drove past Josh's house too, but it looked quiet and peaceful. I decided I'd return to my hotel and continue the surveillance the next day.

But I never made it back. While en route the next day to Josh's neighborhood, I got the call from Dillard that Josh had been found dead.

I clicked the button on my phone to end the call and then pounded the steering wheel and screamed at the top of my lungs. "AHHH! You bastard! AHHH!" No words could describe the torment I felt.

I pulled over as tears of shame and helplessness streamed down my face. I had failed again to protect an innocent victim.

***

Later on the day I heard about Josh's death, I drove past his house again. The anguish in my soul at failing to protect the person I *knew* would be killed was eating me up.

The boy's—man's—mother would be inside, grieving in a way only a mother could. Cars were parked in the driveway. Relatives and friends, probably. She'd have plenty of support until the funeral. And then she'd have to face her demons alone.

I parked up the street in an area with no houses, pondering what I was even doing here. For some reason I couldn't leave. My guardian angel instincts were kicking in. What a lousy guardian angel I was, though. But for some reason I felt a kindred spirit with the mom, Sharon. We'd both failed to protect her son.

I considered knocking on Sharon's door. I felt that somehow I had to explain what I knew to her. But would that make things better for her or for me . . . or much worse? Did she have information I needed to know? Not really. I had zero doubt that Preston had killed Josh. She would know too, soon enough. And if she somehow thought her son had died of natural causes, maybe that would be easier for her to mourn through. No one to point the finger of blame at and experience the frustrating, out-of-control rage that families of murder victims often faced.

I slapped my face with my hands a couple times to get myself out of my stupor. I really wanted a drink. But no, my purpose had to be a laser focus on catching that fiend, Preston. And I realized that sitting here in this neighborhood was counterproductive. I needed to return to

New Orleans and keep tracking that SOB. My moment of self-pity over, I turned the car around and headed out of town.

He would *not* harm another victim under my watch.

Sharon Middleton

I don't remember much about the first few days after Josh's death. My sister and a few friends stopped by to see me. My younger son, David, took a plane out to visit.

Now that Josh was gone, really gone this time, I couldn't quite grasp the reality. Whenever I was left alone, I stayed in bed and couldn't get ahold of myself. I'd get up to put on a brave face for the well-wishers, but internally I was a mess. I couldn't get myself to shower or put on makeup for a few days, and I existed in a uniform of frumpy sweatpants and an old T-shirt.

When David came, he tried to cook for me, but I wouldn't eat much. I know he was frustrated, but I was beside myself with emotion. When he would leave to buy groceries, I would take advantage of the alone time to scream at the top of my lungs. By the time he returned, he'd find me sitting in silence staring out the window. For some reason, I couldn't get the tears to come.

The anger was the worst of it, on top of the sadness. Maybe I could have accepted it better if I had believed that Josh's fall was an innocent accident and that, after all these years, his heart had finally given out. I would like to have believed that he came home and that maybe that was all he truly wanted, that my son was pleased with that short respite of time and had gone on to find peace.

But instead, in my gut, I believed my son had been murdered. Most likely by the same person who had pushed him from the balcony to begin with. The Harringtons had something to do with it, I was sure.

I didn't bother voicing my opinion to David or other family members because I knew how they would react. And though talking might have made me feel better, in the long run I would get dozens of questions about how I was going to handle my son's passing and speculation about whether I was simply hysterical. I expected to get plenty enough of that treatment from the authorities.

I demanded an autopsy. Once that was done, we were finally able to bury my son. But not until after the funeral did I learn the official cause of death. The coroner ruled that Josh had died from suffocation. His broken nasal bone added to the proof. David had gone back home by then. That was better for me. I needed to mourn alone.

The investigators, Dillard and LaCroix, requested to meet with me down at the station. I shoved that report into my purse and took a cab because I was too shaky to drive.

Once I arrived, they gave me a cup of coffee and had me sit in a room for a few minutes before one of the detectives came in. This one was LaCroix. I remembered him from the day he and his partner had visited Josh in the hospital.

"Have you even heard about my son's death?" I demanded, standing up. "Are you people doing anything about it?"

The detective raised his hands in a posture of surrender, which only made me angrier.

"Ma'am, my partner and I were just discussing this today," he said. "We're working in conjunction with another police department to find out exactly what happened. Other than that, all I can tell you is there is an investigation into your son's death. I wish I could go into more detail about the situation, but I can't."

I took a step backward. LaCroix gently helped me into a chair. And for the first time since my son had died, I cried.

"It's being treated as a murder?" I asked.

The man paused. I realized I was probably making him risk his job by telling me. "It's not a natural death," he said carefully. "We're trying to find out what exactly happened. I really implore you, Mrs. Middleton, not to tell anyone. I can't promise you what will come of this, but we will do our very best to find out what happened to Josh."

When I returned to my home, I continued my mindless routine of sleeping, staring out the window, and occasionally screaming. I honestly felt a little better knowing that the detectives were probably viewing my son's death as a murder, but it still didn't bring back Josh. Throughout the twenty years Josh was in a coma, all hope for his future had slowly slipped away. I had learned not to expect a daughter-in-law, grandchildren, or to be proud of my son's successes. But the door had been opened to hope in the last few weeks, so to have it slammed shut again—this time nailed and boarded over, never to be opened again—was murder on my emotions.

I wandered the house in my dispirited existence. We hadn't lived in this place long, but in our short time here, the memories we'd created were enormous. So much hope. Josh had been improving every day. Hope was something I had completely lost over the twenty years of coma. I had visited the unconscious Josh out of love, duty, and routine, but this home had finally embodied hope.

In my excitement to rehabilitate Josh, I had set up his trinkets and trophies in one of the upstairs rooms. I had even found a couple Star Wars posters to hang up, these from the more newly released Star Wars movies. I had wanted to coax out the memories of his happier years, to remind him of who he used to be . . . and still could be. He was happy, talented, and athletic. He'd had friends, hobbies, and goals. I had gotten him to come up here only once. He had still been so weak, and besides, we would have plenty of time to relive memories . . . or so I had thought.

Ever since his death, though, I hadn't wanted to enter the room with Josh's memorabilia. But one day, for some reason, I felt strong enough to do so. I ventured in, pausing. I had to let the despair flow through me if I were ever to heal.

The bed was neatly made up with decorative pillows where a face would go. I wondered who had made the bed so nicely. I guess my various visitors had needed something to do while I was unresponsive to their aid and comfort.

I turned to the shelf with his various trophies, letting in the memory of one award at a time. I picked up a soccer trophy and forced myself to smile at the figurine of a young soccer player making an amazing shot. Josh had played soccer as a boy, until football swallowed up his interest by middle-school age. I set that one down and picked up a swimming medal. He had been a good swimmer; maybe he could have competed well in high school. But swimming was also a distant memory by the time the teen years hit. Football trophies took up the bulk of space on his shelf. I scanned the lot. Why were they oddly spaced? I was sure I had set them up evenly spaced from each other but noticed an odd gap between two of them. Maybe someone had removed the trophies to dust and replaced them differently than I'd had them. I adjusted the spacing and then turned to the nightstand by the bed.

On this piece of furniture I had displayed several photos: Josh and his brother, Josh with me and his dad, Josh with his friends from various stages. I had always loved the picture of him and Matt displaying the fish they had caught together. The two of them with their goofy little-boy smiles on the dock with their fishing poles next to the shimmering water, so carefree and proud of their prize. I smiled at the memory before my face crinkled with a gush of pain. I laid down on the bed to calm my emotions and took several deep breaths before continuing to scan the room.

Off to the side the closet was open. I'd put many of Josh's clothes there for safekeeping until he could sort through the ones he wanted to keep versus throw. Above me the ceiling fan was off. I noticed how dusty it was. I made a note to take care of that some other day.

Sitting up, I glanced again at the photos on the nightstand, and this time I noticed something was off. The wooden frame in the back—it was empty. I'd had a picture in there, hadn't I? Yes. But what was it? I scanned my memory. Oh yes, I remember that it had been the picture of a happy-looking Josh with his friends the way he looked right before the acci—attempted murder. I picked up the frame to see if the picture had simply slipped down or fallen on the floor. But when I realized the back of the frame was tightly sealed up and no picture lay on the ground, chills went up my spine. Someone had removed the picture. There was no other explanation. Someone had been walking through this house. And I rarely left the house, which meant . . . the someone had taken it right from under my nose.

With shaking hands, I sent off texts to David, my sister, and the only other couple of friends who had entered this house to care for me after Josh's death, inquiring if any of them knew anything about the picture. My sister and friends responded immediately that they knew nothing about it. David would respond later with the same answer, I knew. The health care workers wouldn't have taken it. But someone who had entered this house to kill my son—Preston—would have.

I slunk down onto the bed with the empty frame in my unsteady hands and wailed.

Chapter Thirty

Preston Harrington

After I got rid of Josh Middleton, I still had two more days on my business trip. I caught a flight from Knoxville to Denver. I wore a dark-haired wig, a baseball cap, glasses, and loose-fitting clothing on the plane. Then I pretended to sleep during the whole flight so no one would bother or recognize me. I needed to do a couple promotional shoots and photo ops for the new physical therapy center I'd pledged to support. Not only was this a great reason to be away from home, but all aspects of the venture were promising. The idea was to woo other sports players to this clinic. Having my face on the advertising would give them the credibility to handle elite clientele who needed the best care under the highest discretion.

I kept in touch with Danielle, enough to determine that she and the kids were all right. I mostly sent text messages, but the one time I did speak with her, she seemed distracted. It was understandable. I could hear the twins playing and the television on in the background. I knew they could be a handful, but the thought crossed my mind to wonder if something more wasn't going on. When I asked her about work, she mentioned something about an upcoming show, a new artist she had high hopes for. I could never tell my wife that I found her love of the art world boring and pedantic. It wasn't something you would say unless you were looking to start an argument. And I could sense lately the growing importance of not getting tangled up into too many disagreements with her. Since she had confronted me with the piece of burned jacket and the matches from Grinder's, I'd made it my priority not to fight her on anything.

Once I was done with my work for the new center, I flew back to Knoxville to pick up my car and then make the nine-hour drive to New Orleans but didn't go directly back home. I wanted to visit the farmhouse.

Whenever I visited, I always felt an odd sense of returning to where I was supposed to be. Something there always seemed to need care. Since I couldn't trust anyone else to be around my prized possessions, the upkeep of the place fell to my shoulders. We had a maid who came in twice a week at home. I wondered if Danielle would be surprised to see me vacuuming, dusting wood tables, and spraying down counters. I was amazed at how the dust seemed to come out of nowhere.

Oddly, I found a small pleasure in it. Once I was done, I grabbed a beer from the fridge, dug through my luggage to find my coat, retired to the living room, kicked off my shoes, and turned on the television. I found a series on one of the cable stations with in-depth interviews from current and former sports figures. This episode was about a woman who had won an Olympic medal in track, a first for the small country in South America from which she hailed.

My mind swirled as I half watched the show. I should receive a medal myself, I thought. Did anyone give medals for wielding the most power? For possessing control over whether the ones around you lived or died? I laughed aloud at the thought. I was like Thor, or maybe more like his dark brother Loki. I knew no one like myself. Even those others whose books graced my upstairs shelves weren't in the same league as me.

I felt satisfied with my life. If only I could share my accomplishments with the world and receive the accolades I deserved! But the stupid imbeciles on this planet would never understand. They thought my athletic abilities were my best asset. If only they knew!

Reaching into my coat pocket, I brought out the football trophy I'd swiped from Josh's room. I sat back and enjoyed the beer, fingering the trophy and feeling relaxed and a bit bored when the credits rolled and the next program came on.

I ran my thumb across the letters of the trophy that was a 3-D rendering of a young male football player catching a pass. U12 was the team Josh had been on when he'd won this thing, back when he had hopes that his life would turn out well. I also remembered the photo and dug a little deeper into my coat pocket to find it. It had a crease through it now that happened to fall directly across Josh's neck. Fitting, I thought.

My upstairs room, the one where I held my trophies, called to me. I had two more to add to the collection.

Danielle Harrington

My morning started out like any other, but my brain was in a complete fog from sleep deprivation and stress. I needed to get the kids together for school, and nothing seemed to be going right. Ethan misplaced his backpack, and I spent twenty minutes running all over the house hunting for it. Turns out he had left it in the back seat of the car. Isabel was being more fretful than normal. She wanted

Apple Crunch and we didn't have any. I told her toast and eggs would have to do. How I hadn't managed to get another box of her favorite cereal when I last went shopping was a mystery. I focused on the mindless, on the everyday to avoid dwelling on Preston.

Once the kids were off to school, I decided to go into the gallery. I had been working from home often lately, but still some things were best done onsite. It bothered me lately that everything seemed to be on the back burner. Whatever was going on with my husband, I couldn't afford to walk around in a haze.

In need of a lift, I ordered the largest coffee and a blueberry muffin from the coffee shop directly across the street from the gallery.

As usual, the line was long, and I found myself staring out the window, daydreaming. The edges of sleepiness and a dark mood were still pulling at me. I wanted a vacation from my life, somewhere secluded where no one knew my name. I thought of the first time Preston and I had gone to Bali—the greenness, the beauty, and the serenity of it. You could sit outside all day by the water and get lost in the quiet and believe, at least for a short time, that terrible things didn't happen.

"Ma'am?"

I felt the light pressure of a man's fingertips against my back. I turned, instinctually moving away. My first thought was that this stranger wanted to pass me. My second was that he was after my bag. I clutched my purse closer, frowning as I looked at the guy who was barely taller than me.

"I'm sorry?" I said.

The man leaned forward, not moving out of my space. "Mrs. Harrington, I'm sorry to have startled you. Is there somewhere we can talk in private?"

"I don't know who you are."

He spoke softly but with authority. "My name is LaCroix, and the business I need to discuss with you is very sensitive and has to do with your husband. It's best if we don't discuss it here." He flashed a badge at me.

I nodded. "You mind me getting my coffee first?" I asked. "We can speak in my office."

He nodded. "I was hoping you'd say so. I wouldn't mind getting a cup myself."

I'd only suggested it because I needed a moment to think. With each passing second I felt myself beginning to panic. Were Tyler's suspicions of Preston true? And had my husband done something to put the police on his trail?

What did this man want from me? Of all the possibilities I had considered, this hadn't been one. I'd never thought what it might be like when the authorities came with questions for me. Would they think I was complicit or just a stupid woman who had no idea what her husband did when he was away from her?

I got my coffee and muffin and waited for LaCroix to get his coffee and pastry. Then he followed me across the street. I felt half sick thinking about a coming interrogation. Maybe he was coming to tell me my husband was in custody and had been charged with murder. Maybe I was losing my mind.

It was still early and my assistant wasn't in yet. I locked the gallery door behind us and showed him to my office. Even to my eyes, my desk looked untouched. No papers were scattered on the desktop, only my laptop and a pencil cup—nothing for me to pretend to be distracted with while LaCroix laid out his reasons for this visit.

He sat across from me and quietly began to speak. "It's my understanding that you were acquainted with Josh Middleton."

"Briefly, in college."

"What was the nature of your relationship?"

"Friends."

"You didn't date him?"

I paused and took a sip of my coffee. "No. We were just friends."

"You weren't there the night that he was injured?"

"I wasn't. I was studying for an exam that night. I always felt bad about that."

"How so?"

"Just . . . maybe I'd have kept an eye on him if I had been there. No one seems to know exactly what happened."

"Funny you should say that. You are aware that he woke from his coma a few weeks back. He died recently."

I nodded. "Yes, I heard."

"How did you find out?"

I tucked a strand of hair behind my left ear. "I saw the story on the internet."

"All right," LaCroix said. He took out his phone and typed something. He was taking notes. I wondered what he was writing. I even wondered if he was recording me without saying so. The police weren't supposed to do that. Rather than to ask him and appear paranoid, I didn't say anything.

"Back when you were in college, was Preston friends with Josh as well?"

"They were acquainted. I think they had drinks occasionally and probably watched some football together. That's all I can remember of it."

"Well, then you have a good memory indeed; that was some twenty years ago," LaCroix replied. "I talk to people all the time who can't remember what they had for dinner two nights ago, much less what their friends were up to that long ago. Mrs. Harrington, do you remember exactly when you and Preston started dating?"

"I'm sorry, but what's the use in questioning me about this? Josh is gone now."

"I was wondering if you and Preston got together before or after Josh's accident."

"What does one thing have to do with the other?" I demanded. I was trying to keep calm, but my nerves were slowly making me lose my manners.

"If you would answer my question, my reasoning will become clear to you."

I sighed. There was no way to avoid the answer, and it was obvious to me that he knew the truth about this already. A good detective would have verified the facts before seeking me out.

"It was after Josh's fall that we started dating."

"And there weren't any other young men you were seeing around that time?"

"No, there weren't. I took my studies very seriously. I made it through school on scholarships and work. I didn't have the luxury of time many of my classmates did."

"And that's only to your benefit," the police detective said with a nod. "Not everyone rises from such humble beginnings to be as successful as you are."

"You said the reason for your questions were going to become clear to me?" I said. "So far I'm still lost."

"When Josh Middleton had his fall, the detectives working his case were under the impression that he didn't have any enemies and that no one had anything to gain from him being out of the way. But if he were competing for your affections, that theory becomes patently untrue."

"Competition? What are you saying?"

LaCroix stared at me for a long moment before replying. He nodded his head to the left slightly, as if to ask me if I really expected him to believe what I was saying. He took a moment before speaking again. "All right. Let me ask you about something else. What do you think happened to your husband's friend and business partner? The relationship between those two went through a lot of ups and downs, didn't it? From what I understand, Rob was considering leaving the business to go out on his own. Your husband had something to lose if he did."

"That's not true," I said. "They were so close. I mean, yes, they had disagreements, but the business was solid. Rob had told me about some of his new plans for the restaurant not long before he died. He was excited about a new menu."

LaCroix put his phone down on his thigh. "You didn't know?"

"Know what?" I snapped.

"Rob and your husband were parting ways, as far as business goes. He'd already had a lawyer draw up the paperwork. It wasn't complete, and from what we were able to find, it looked like Rob expected Preston to contest his wishes. He wanted to buy your husband out, making the restaurant solely his own. I suppose he was excited about changes he would make, seeing as it was going to be his sole enterprise soon. Preston didn't tell you?"

I crossed my arms and leaned back in my chair. "My husband has a lot of business ventures. He doesn't tell me every single detail of what goes on with each one. Knowing Preston, he wouldn't mention it if he thought he still could talk Rob into changing his mind."

This part was the truth, and I thought I did a good job of selling it, but I was upset. Preston wouldn't have liked the idea of his name and influence no longer being important for good business; he would have seen it as a shame, an embarrassment. Once the paperwork was signed off, the sale would have become public knowledge. He would have hated it. He would have viewed not retaining the restaurant, even if he didn't care about it anymore, to be a failure. If there was one thing he couldn't stand, it was anything that made him somehow feel like he'd lost. He couldn't tolerate the appearance that he could be wrong about anything.

Of course, he hadn't minded selling the place once Rob was dead. Everyone expected that. No one questioned his motives or insinuated that maybe it was because the business had been doing poorly in the first place. My mind flipped back to the mysterious package Rob had brought over before he died. It must have had to do with selling the business.

I could feel the heat in my cheeks move along the back of my neck. I knew I was blushing. Some part of me had long accepted that my husband was capable of violence against strangers, enemies. What LaCroix suggested was something different. Rob's death had been brutal. The idea that Preston could kill someone so close to him, who had been a part of his life for many years, was a possibility I had never considered. My belief had always been that he took out his aggression on strangers. I tried not to shake but felt my ankle twitching beneath my desk.

"I don't know what exactly you're suggesting, but I don't like it," I said, keeping my voice as modulated as possible. "I think you need to go. If you have anything that you want to discuss with my husband, I suggest that you do it with him directly. This is nonsense. I doubt he will waste his time with you the way I have."

"Is that true, Mrs. Harrington?" the detective pressed. "Because these are simple questions, and if he doesn't want to answer them, then there are other ways we can go about making him answer."

LaCroix stood, closing the button on his jacket. "We may be talking to your husband very soon. Until then"—he reached into his pocket and drew out a business card—"if you should remember anything or decide to share information, give me a call. It may be for your own benefit. You wouldn't want to find yourself implicated in anything that Preston may be responsible for or on the wrong end of his rage."

I stood up, wanting to say something to defend my husband but not finding the words. I had probably said too much. Yet silence felt like agreement.

***

After the detective left, I'd worked until two in the afternoon. I sent my assistant home and drove out to the marina, where I watched the moored boats gently rock in their slips. I sat in my car and thought about everything that had gone on in the last few months. I was about to go home when I got a text from the nanny saying that Preston was back from his trip, earlier than expected.

I should have gone home, but instead I went to a restaurant and sat alone. I ordered a nice meal for myself, or more importantly, for the baby. Roast beef with vegetables, mashed potatoes with gravy. I ordered iced tea instead of wine. If not for the baby, I would have drunk myself into oblivion.

I was able to get down a little less than half my meal. Despite how good it tasted, it sat inside my stomach like a knot. I couldn't quite digest it, but I didn't feel ill enough to bring it up, either. A sensation of light-headed dizziness came over me that I tried to shake off. *Must be the hormones combined with stress.*

I kept telling myself that it was time for me to come to grips with what Preston might have done. The police were looking into it. That meant there was reason to believe that he might have been involved. All the doubts and questions I'd wrestled over the last months were founded. I worried about what else was out there that I had yet to know about.

Chapter Thirty-one

Preston Harrington

By the time I drove back home, I was feeling good about things. I had accomplished what I needed to and was happy that I would never have to worry about the Josh situation again. I was pleased. Everything seemed to be going well. No one would have to know about my detour or what I had done there. I'd been careful not to do anything that would draw attention to my famous face.

When I got home, the kids were there with the nanny, but Danielle wasn't back yet. The nanny said that my wife had called and said she would be a couple of hours later than usual and that she'd instructed her to go ahead and cook dinner for the kids. That was unusual but not unheard of. Maybe she needed to catch up. She had been spending a lot of time with the twins lately. It had to take a toll on her work, whether she owned up to it or not. Feeling the need for some private time with my wife when she got home, I sent the kids home to sleep at the nanny's house. The nanny knew a nice-sized bonus came from spending extra hours with our children, so she readily agreed.

Danielle came home that night just before ten. I was waiting for her in the living room.

The lights were off, and as she came in the doorway, her figure was a silhouette against the outside lights. Once the door closed behind her, I couldn't see her.

"Babe?" I called. I stood up.

Only the television was on, but I knew she could see me in the pale light given off by the screen. She seemed to hesitate, her hand gripping the doorknob, as if she might want to go back out.

"Preston . . ." Her response was emotionless. So many times I had come home to her—late, early, expected, by surprise—and I had never heard her say my name quite that way.

Danielle closed the door. I noticed then that her steps weren't quite right. She seemed to have a difficult time negotiating the floor, as if it were moving underneath her. She went as far as the archway that opened into the living room and leaned against the wall.

"Are you *drunk*?" I hissed.

"Before you say anything"—she raised her hand—"the doctor said no wine, so I didn't drink, but I am feeling a little light-headed."

I took a few steps toward her. "Why did you need to ask your doctor about it? You're usually a lightweight, but damn." I didn't believe for one second that she hadn't been drinking. I wondered how many drinks it had taken to get her loopy. She was definitely walking like she was tipsy but not outright drunk. I still didn't like it. Not for any wife of mine. Danielle knew I didn't like her to drink too much. Perhaps it was more of a pattern than I realized, when she met Crystal for lunch. Two hens gossiping and getting stoned.

"Um, nothing, never mind," Danielle said. "I thought you were coming home tomorrow," she said, bending at the waist to recover from her tipsiness, I guessed.

"We wrapped up a day early, so I wanted to get back to you and the kids. Did you have a bad day?" I normally would have closed the distance between us and placed a comforting hand on her shoulder, but I felt the ire building in me and remained standing where I was.

"You could say so," she replied softly. Righting herself and stepping carefully, she made her way to the couch. She sat down and undid the straps on her shoes.

"What happened?" I usually would ask out of the need to appear caring. This time I was curious.

"Nothing but people stopping by the gallery uninvited and wasting my time," she said.

"Aren't those usually your customers?" She was hiding something. "Is something else bothering you?"

Danielle shook her head, guarded. Once she had her shoes off, she curled her legs under her. "I don't want to talk about it. Boring anyway. Tell me about your day."

"The trip was good. I got home hours ago, expecting you to be here, but I came home to the nanny caring for the kids. So I sent the kids home with her for the night."

"You what? I like the kids to sleep here!"

"Well, then I guess you should have been here."

"Preston, that's not fair. You come home late all the time. And I can't stay out late one evening?"

"Apparently not, because then you're irresponsible and come home drunk."

"I'm not drunk! I wasn't even drinking. I'm just a little dizzy and light-headed."

"Mm hmm. And who were you out with? Tyler? Or was it some other man this time?" In my heart of hearts, I didn't truly believe Danielle was cheating on me, but her staggering into the house late had turned my pleasant mood on a dime. I felt irrationally irritable, and she was the most convenient one to vent on. Too bad I didn't have a dog to strangle.

"I am NOT cheating on you! I was by myself! I can't believe you're even accusing me of such a thing!" A bucket of tears poured down her face. Her crying seemed excessive compared to normal. Was she truly guilty of something? She grabbed a tissue from a box the nanny had left in the living room, blew her nose, and dabbed at the mascara streams clouding her eyes.

"Well, I guess the nice, relaxing night I'd envisioned spending with my wife has gone to hell."

"Stop it! You're so unfair! I had no idea you were finally home and wanting to spend time with me." She blew her nose again.

"How about you enjoy that nice, big bed without me tonight?" I opened the nearby chest where we stored blankets and grabbed out a couple, indicating I'd be sleeping here on the couch tonight.

"Preston!"

I merely stared at her, waiting for her to move off the couch so I could make my bed for the night. After a few moments of more quiet sobbing, she slowly got up and retreated to the bedroom.

Danielle Harrington

I awoke from a restless night to find two messages on my phone. One was from Preston. He'd texted me earlier in the morning to say he'd be gone for the day. How lame was that? Couldn't he at least have left a handwritten note? Or, better yet, waited to tell me to my face?

The other message was from that football friend of Preston's with kids the same age as ours. Apparently her kids were asking to spend more time with ours. I groaned at the thought of having the kids away for longer, but another part of me felt too drained to properly care for them today. I arranged for our nanny to drop off the kids at her house. They would stay the night, and I'd pick them up tomorrow.

The next order of business was to get food in my stomach to stifle the nausea I felt coming on strong. I plopped two pieces of bread in the toaster and heated water for ginger tea. I slumped down at the kitchen table, trying not to think about the awful argument with Preston. But the more I tried to think of anything else, the more the memory came flooding in. A torrent of tears came once again. My hormones were working overtime.

After eating, I attempted to do a short workout video, but my body was too exhausted to cooperate. I quit halfway through. With nothing else pressing my time for the day, I retreated to bed and the soothing, mind-numbing sleep of a woman in her first trimester of pregnancy.

A full three hours later, I rolled out of bed feeling clearheaded. A thought that had come to me during the clarity of my slumber was about that GPS I'd placed in Preston's car. The first order of business, however, was food. While chomping on some slices of Parmesan cheese, a handful of grapes, and some heated-up leftover roast beef and sweet potatoes (thank-you, nanny!), I opened the door to the garage to see which car Preston had left behind. I danced a little jig of joy when I saw the Corolla parked in its usual spot.

Shoving another forkful of potatoes in my mouth, I found the keys to the Corolla in their usual dish on the counter and pressed the button to open the trunk. Upon examination, nothing appeared to have been rearranged in the Corolla's trunk, and I removed the phone and battery pack that were still hidden underneath the blanket.

I felt a new burst of energy at the data I held in my hand. But on the tail of my high spirits was the realization that this was my husband. I didn't truly want to find anything inexplicable.

I ate a few bites of strawberry yogurt to finish off my meal and clicked on the GPS app to see all the places this car had been.

Starting at the beginning of the app's history, I found that Preston had visited places around New Orleans. I recognized restaurants, gas stations, and friends' houses. Nothing earth shattering. I calmed down, realizing that my paranoia was for naught. But as I continued scrolling through, I saw something that sent shivers up my spine. My knees went weak, and I sunk into a chair, on the verge of fainting.

He'd gone to Knoxville. And I didn't know the exact date of Josh's death, but Preston's trip was right in the ballpark of the same time frame. He had no legitimate reason that I knew of to go up there. And he'd never mentioned it. If he'd gone to visit friends from college or to do some event, he would have said something.

I felt a cold sweat coming on and nausea in my gut. But this was different from pregnancy sickness. The cold air coming from the air conditioning vent was suddenly freezing. I shivered, and my teeth chattered. And then I scrambled to the toilet and threw up my lunch.

I lay on the cold tile next to the toilet writhing in pain from the nausea and the instant headache I'd developed. My very soul ached. My husband was a killer. He'd killed Josh. The man I loved was the worst kind of human on this planet. And I was pregnant with his child.

The minutes ticked by as I waited for the next round of nausea to hit. I knew the routine. I never threw up only once. Once I started, I was in for several hours of vomiting.

I spent the afternoon snoozing, crying, and retching until I had nothing but stomach acid to bring up. At some point, Preston texted to let me know not to expect him back until the following day. I didn't even send a return text.

Finally, in the early evening, I felt the burst of energy one has after finally feeling well again after an illness. I knew I needed to eat again to replenish the nutrients for my unborn baby and to stave off the jitters from low blood sugar.

As I heated up more leftovers, I felt the courage to hit up the phone's GPS again. I scooted past the Knoxville trip and found another destination—this one on the outskirts of New Orleans—that I didn't recognize. It looked like a residential area. I zoomed in and then changed to satellite mode. Yes, this was definitely a house. But I had no idea who lived out there that Preston might visit. Did he have a girlfriend? Was it a football buddy's house? But I knew all his close friends and approximately where they lived. No one I knew lived out in this area.

My private eye mode returned in full force. Realizing I had a rare opportunity with both the kids and Preston gone for the rest of the day, I finished my meal, grabbed a sweater since the weather looked like it could turn, packed some saltines in my purse for later, and buckled myself into the Corolla to find out what I could about this mysterious residence.

Before I left, the more cautious side of me felt the need to tell someone where I was going. Who could I tell? The detective? No. This house could simply belong to some friend of Preston's that I didn't know about. No need to escalate things if I was just being crazy. I scrolled through my contacts, found Tyler's name, and quickly typed: *Going out for a drive to check on a house Preston visited recently. Not sure who lives there or what I'll find. Can we talk in a half hour? CALL ME.*

I didn't add that I was afraid or that a detective thought Preston was a murderer. Or that my mind was swiftly cruising toward that accusation as well. For some reason, I still felt that loyalty toward my husband, the need to protect his reputation. Whatever the truth was, it would eventually be revealed. Soon. I set the GPS coordinates to the unknown house in the country and took off.

I cruised west on Route 90 into territory I'd never visited. At some point I exited the highway and continued on a two-lane country road. I passed farmland, canals, and sparsely located houses. The sun was setting as I pulled off onto a dirt road and followed the GPS's last direction. In the dim light of sunset, I had trouble finding an address but reasoned that since this was the only property within sight, I had to be in the right place. I parked along the road, not feeling brazen enough to pull into the driveway. The semidarkness gave me a bit of confidence to be able to check out the place without being seen. A white stucco wall with peeling paint hid whatever residence was behind it. I slipped on the sweater; locked my purse in the trunk; slid the keys under the passenger floor mat; grabbed my phone and a handful of saltines to munch along the way; and began my trek down the dirt driveway. The wind was beginning to pick up, and I clutched my cardigan tighter around me.

Once I reached the wall, I noticed that the place had a gate blocking the entrance. It had been so obscured by the trees and bushes surrounding it that I hadn't noticed it at first. The keypad on the gate was exactly like the one we had on our own garage door at home. I absentmindedly punched in the month and day of our anniversary, the same code we had at home. I jumped upon hearing a slight electrical buzz. The gate clanged as it powered open.

What? Only Preston would have set a code like that! Did he own *this place? Did he keep a harem of women out here or something? A secret love nest?*

I stepped past the beckoning gate, ate a saltine to calm my butterflies, and checked out my surroundings. The landscape was natural and desert-like, the type that would require minimal upkeep. I hurried down the path, my feet crunching on the loose dirt, knowing that when the sun finally did set all the way, I'd be left in darkness. The house appeared to have white siding with a darker trim color, maybe green or blue. A swing on the front porch made the otherwise desolate place look homey.

I didn't want to knock on the door. Who would answer anyway? No one appeared to be here, and I certainly had no explanation to give Preston for why I was here. Now that I was here, I wasn't even sure of what I was hoping to find. I began a loop around the exterior of the house, to see if anything would give me a hint about what this property was all about. On the east side of the house, the windows appeared to be completely covered up from the inside. Odd. Someone—maybe Preston—was awfully secretive. The backside of the house looked out on the woods. I could smell stagnant water somewhere in the distance.

While making my way back toward the front on the west side of the structure, my phone rang. Tyler. I clicked the button to answer, but before I could even say hello, the dark form of Preston appeared directly in front of me. Hands shaking, I slipped the phone into my pocket.

Preston Harrington

As upset as I was at my wife, I knew I couldn't spend the day with her. I'd made myself an early golf appointment, gone out for a long brunch with a few guys I used to play football with, and then played a whole other round of golf. I missed the kids but didn't have the energy to deal with them today. Danielle would figure out how to get them home and cared for. Knowing I didn't want to go home to her quite yet, I texted to let her know not to expect me until the next day. She didn't respond.

By the time my second round of golf was over, happy hour was starting at the bar many of the NFL guys frequented. I enjoyed a nice dinner and some drinks. Just when I was about to pack it up and leave, a new bunch of guys I knew came in, so another couple hours passed easily. By early evening, I was itching to leave—itching to go visit my secret property.

I picked up some electrolyte water at a convenience store nearby to help clear my head after the afternoon of drinking. I wasn't by any means drunk but wanted to stave off any possible headache that might develop in a few hours. Then I took off down Route 90.

The wind was picking up and the temperature dropping as sunset approached. I flew down the route I knew like the back of my hand, exiting the freeway but maintaining my speed, kicking up dust on the country road. I slowed as I approached my second home.

Seeing a car parked on the road outside my home, my anger flared up, sudden and sharp. "What are you doing here? This is *my* place to be alone!" I shouted at nobody. "This may turn out to be a very bad night for you. You just ticked off the wrong guy!" I continued my tirade.

Drawing closer, I was rendered speechless. This wasn't just a car. It was *my own* car! The Corolla. Danielle was here? Someone else? No, it had to be Danielle out here snooping around. But how? No one knew about this place. My irate thoughts immediately focused on Tyler. He had to be involved somehow. Sticking his nose into my business. Danielle wouldn't have brought the kids, would she?

I pulled up behind the Corolla and got out to peek in the windows. Nothing was on the seat—no purse or coat or any hint about who had driven it here. The doors were unlocked. I found the car keys underneath the floor mat and took them with me.

With darkness soon approaching, I figured I now was the one with the element of surprise in my favor. I turned to walk down the driveway, hoisting myself over the gate instead of risking the noise of having the gate open mechanically. The swirling winds assisted me in not making enough noise to be detected.

The sun's last lingering rays lit up the place enough that I could clearly see that no one was in front of the house. The porch swing rattled a bit as the wind whipped it from side to side. I decided to circle the house starting on the west side. I had just turned the corner when I heard a phone ring and saw the form of Danielle only three yards away.

"Danielle! What are you doing here?"

Danielle Harrington

This was the worst possible scenario. My mind went blank. I hadn't even thought up a good lie in case he caught me at this place. "Uh . . . ," was all my terrified brain could come up with.

Preston grabbed my elbow to guide me toward the front of the house. He didn't hold me with a heavy grip, yet the way his body was angled between me and the woods, I was completely shielded from escape.

I decided to skip the part about how I'd found out about this house. "Well, I found out that you'd been out here, and curiosity got the better of me. I decided to come check it out. Why do you have this house, Preston?" I attempted to go on the offense.

"HOW did you know I had this house is the question." His loud, hissing voice tone terrified me. I thought at this point that the truth might be best.

"I hid a GPS in your car. I was going out of my mind with your unexplained absences."

Preston stopped as we rounded the corner back to the front of the house. The porch swing that, by daylight, promised loving embraces and warm Hallmark movies was now a sinister, screeching ogre. Pictures of creepy one-eyed Chucky doll faces, a hooded scythe-bearing grim reaper, and blood-dripping zombies flashed through my mind.

But knowing I had to keep my mind about me, I sucked in some deep breaths of the swirling air. *He's not going to do anything bad,* I told myself. *He's never shown any aggression to me or the kids. And it would be too suspicious. Preston is careful. And he loves me. He does love me.*

Even as I tried to think positive thoughts, doubts crept in. *I bet Rob never thought that Preston would raise a hand to him, either.* I closed my eyes for a moment, fighting back the image of the crime scene photos from Rob's demise. I made my right hand into a fist and squeezed until my nails bit into my palm. My stomach was doing somersaults.

"Well, as long as you're here," Preston replied, sounding strangely bright, "let me give you a tour." He guided me to the front of the house.

Chapter Thirty-two

Preston Harrington

Danielle seemed surprised at my change in mood. She'd managed to connive her way to finding out about this place. I would use the circumstance to my advantage.

She pulled her sweater closer as the wind whipped the unbuttoned panels. Not only did she not want to go inside, she looked like she wanted to run back to the road. The neighbors were too far away to hear if she screamed. Certainly she'd never make it far enough down the road for anyone to see her.

Guiding her by the elbow, we stepped onto the front porch, moved past the swing, and paused as I unlocked the front door. I then commenced a charade.

"Surprise! Here we are!" I called out. I gave the biggest fake smile I could muster. Danielle hesitated a moment before crossing the threshold. I grabbed her hand. She had a look on her face that vaguely reminded me of our daughter, Isabel, who was a smart kid, capable of figuring out many things on her on, but every now and again her teacher would approach her with some new thing that left her stumped. That was the expression Danielle had: wide eyes, slightly parted lips, and brows drawn in concentration.

"Do you want to let me know when you bought this house?" she asked, tentatively looking around after I flipped on the lights.

I stood still, making my reply as cool and polite as I could. "Not long before we married."

"Why didn't you ever tell me about it, Preston?"

"At the time I didn't think you would like it, so far out in the country, and it's not exactly a mansion.

"Come on. Let me show you around." Now that I had gotten over my surprise at her being here, I was honestly excited to have her. I had wanted for so long to let her into my life . . . my real life. Hopefully she'd be able to understand—well, maybe not exactly understand, but to commiserate, to comprehend how I had these urges . . . and had to act on them. Like an itch that needed scratching.

She seemed to relax as I took her through the downstairs rooms. I felt downright giddy. Everything was normal like any house would be—a living room, kitchen, dining room, and den. She only nodded as we moved from one room to another. I even got her a glass of water and insisted that she take a sip, which she did. When it was time to show her upstairs, I hesitated.

"No one has been living here, have they?" she asked.

"No. I visit infrequently. Some men have a man cave. I have a separate house. But if your question is about women, I've never invited any here. You know that, don't you?"

I lifted her chin with my forefinger. "There's never been any other woman but you. We've had this conversation before, and I thought you believed me."

"Sometimes I feel like I don't know you enough. Why'd you feel you needed this house? Or that you needed to keep it secret? There's nothing in here that you don't have at our house. I just don't understand."

I took her hand and squeezed it. "I'm actually pretty glad that you made it out here. There are things I've needed to tell you for a long time. I decided recently that I didn't want to have secrets from you anymore. There are things that I've never told you. Never told anyone.

"The only way to move forward is to let you know about my past. It's time I let you in."

"Pres," she said, "what exactly are you talking about?"

"Come upstairs. I'll show you."

I started up the steps, walking a bit slower than I needed to. She had to come of her own will. I wouldn't hurt my wife, no matter what. But she had to come up. I was dying for her to be in on this with me. I needed a partner in every aspect of my life. Not that I expected her to join me in my . . . activities . . . just to admire me on some level for my power. How could anyone not be impressed by the strength I wielded?

I was near the top of the stairs when she finally caught up to me.

"Am I going to regret this?" she asked. In the dim light of the hall, shadows hung around her eyes. I noticed her hand gripping the banister, the veins standing up against her pale skin.

"I don't know," I said lightly. "Let's hope not."

***

Danielle Harrington

I was having trouble breathing by the time Preston opened the door into a converted office—cozy but masculine. The massive desk, which took up the back wall of the room, was made of heavy mahogany wood. The matching guest chairs that flanked it were heavy, dark leather pieces that looked as if they'd never been sat in. This was his other life, the one I knew nothing about. I glanced around the room, evaluating each object like my life depended on it. Which items were within reach to either defend myself or take the first whack at Preston? Possibly the football trophy on the desk. But that was on the other side of the room from me. Maybe I could pick it up later.

The bookcases lining most of the other walls, redolent with the perfume-sweet scent of aging paper, would normally have made the room instantly inviting. The odor brought me back to my college days and the many hours I'd spent in my favorite nook of the library, poring over research or studying. The days when anything felt possible and I'd never considered that my husband could be a murderer.

Paper hanging on the wall to my left fluttered from the whoosh of wind the opening door produced. Preston smiled, his eyes dark, as he noticed me ascertaining what I was seeing. The paper was cut into long, thin strips with an occasional black-and-white photo—newspaper clippings.

"Make yourself at home. I'll be right back," Preston said lightly, leaving me alone.

I drew closer to examine the articles, feeling like I was now in the midst of a surreal crime drama. The headline Tyler had once shown me grabbed my attention first, about the coma victim who had died after twenty years. Josh's smiling, twenty-year-old face made me nauseated. I had killed him. In befriending him, I had killed him.

But the article about Josh was surrounded by dozens of others. I stepped back to take in the enormity of what was clearly Preston's obsession, possibly even his pride and joy. From this past year, an article about Rob's brutal murder.

No! Was this the proof? Was Preston truly capable of killing one of his best friends? Or did he just have a fascination with death and collected articles about it? Even faced with all the proof, I couldn't imagine how a person could kill anyone. How could Preston ever kill someone like Rob when the two of them had shared so much life together? I missed Rob's crooked smile and playful demeanor.

Another article reported on the assault and slaying of the guy outside Grinder's. The guy had a name: Steve Bishop. Maybe Preston had a macabre attraction to people he knew who died.

I glanced around the room and wondered where Preston had gone. With a silent gasp I remembered my phone. I snuck a quick glance at it. It was still on the call with Tyler, but the battery was now at only nineteen percent. A creaking of a large branch whipping around in the wind spooked me, and I slipped the phone back away before Preston could catch me with it. He just might be insane enough to kill me if he caught me on a call with Tyler.

Then an intense but short-lived burst of light outside was followed quickly by a piercing crack of thunder. The lights in the room blinked a couple times and then went off. My stomach was so queasy and my legs wobbly, I feared I was on the verge of fainting. I tried to call Preston's name, but my tight vocal cords were paralyzed and wouldn't emit a squeak. I instinctively placed my hand on my pregnant stomach.

Then without warning the lights flashed back on again. I sunk to the floor to gather my strength. After taking a few deep breaths, I rose and took a closer look at the wall of clippings in front of me. This time I noticed others: From five years ago, a girl who went missing in Detroit. Another one from ten years ago about a girl whose beaten body was found in San Francisco. Another guy slaughtered in Tampa Bay—all cities where Preston had played away games during his career.

I stepped closer to examine the date on an article about a girl murdered in Dallas. The slaying had taken place the weekend we were in Dallas! How? I covered my mouth as I gagged back vomit. The fine hairs along the back of my neck stood on end. I scanned the other dates and found one all the way back to 1995—this one about a five-year-old killed in a house fire in Preston's hometown; arson was suspected. The little boy's face had been circled with a black marker and the name "Jim" scrawled next to it, accompanied by a smiley face.

No! Not a child! I was sickened. And all the others as well? There was no way Preston could have committed so many heinous crimes. Why was he so mesmerized by news about murders? I still had trouble getting my mind to fully wrap around the truth—that my husband was the worst kind of person on this planet, a serial killer.

Maybe the articles themselves would give me some clue as to what they all had in common. The one about the girl in Detroit was unsolved. She'd been beaten but not sexually assaulted. Her smiling predeath face resembled . . . no, she didn't . . . yes, she did . . . the girl looked like me. The girl from San Francisco—also beaten and left for dead; I couldn't ignore that her hair, eyes, and face shape also reminded me of a younger version of myself. The guy in Tampa Bay—beaten as well. At least he didn't resemble me. These were not just quick deaths these victims had experienced. Someone—please, not Preston, no—had taken out his wrath on these people. The article from Denver showed a similar female victim with eyes that resembled mine. Why? What had they done wrong other than look like me? Tears stung my eyes.

The victims varied in age, but most of the female victims who had a picture attached to the article had a face, hair, and eyes like my own. The male victims—I couldn't immediately notice a pattern with them. It seemed so cruelly random and inexplicable.

The weight of what I was viewing sunk in. These people had families, loved ones. Each single death affected the lives of so many others. I normally felt a heaviness when I heard about someone's life that ended abruptly. But to have so many articles about murder victims displayed so callously—like, like *trophies*. As if the person displaying them was *proud* or at least enthralled. These clippings were arranged with the pride of someone displaying a hobby. A lump caught in my throat. How could I have lived with and loved a person who could do such things with a sense of *pride*?

Then a folded-up picture on a small pedestal table caught my attention. In this room where everything else was so tidy, it looked out of place, like it had been recently placed there on a whim. With trembling fingers, I picked up and unfolded the photo to see a picture of Josh the way I remembered him, happy and with a group of friends. A bolt of terror shot through my body. Preston had traveled to Knoxville. Years ago, he had pushed Josh off the balcony, and then he'd gone back to finish the job.

How could I have been so foolish to not know this dark secret about my husband? He was so smooth, so athletic, so generally well liked. I'd given him my heart, my soul, my body. Shame coursed through my veins. My entire adult life was based on a lie. From the very first date in college, he had set me up for ruin. Even my kids were tainted with his blood. I didn't want this. I wanted to run from my messed-up life and never see anyone I knew again.

I turned away, on the verge of collapse, when Preston, who had at some point reentered the room and was watching me, caught my arm and steadied me.

"I see you've found my little wall of history. I've wanted to let you in on this part of myself for so long. Ahhh, what a relief that I can now open up to you about all the things I've kept inside for so long." He sighed happily, his features relaxing. "Come, let's sit down."

As I set the picture down and dragged my heavy feet to the center of the room, Preston's hand firmly on my elbow, I couldn't help but glance back at the door, calculating how long it would take me to sprint out and down the stairs. The smart thing to do would be to run, but he would catch me. I couldn't compete with him on the playing field. Besides, my legs felt like cement; I didn't think my shocked brain could have even given them the signal to move, let alone quickly. I had to be smart. I had to somehow prepare myself for what was about to come.

Preston smiled and beckoned to me. "Have a seat in this chair." He was thoroughly enjoying this. I wondered how long he'd planned on telling me, and if my real reaction was as satisfying as the one he'd envisioned.

He indicated one of the desk chairs, and I sat down across from him, leaving space between us in case I had no option but to escape. My mouth was so dry, the inside felt sticky and thick. I felt oddly like a guest, someone who wasn't supposed to be in this place but was being allowed there for some reason. Preston's comfortable demeanor in the face of my terror made my whole body shiver. So deep was the chill I felt, my teeth even started chattering even though the room was far from cold. I had never met this man before, this murderer, this *butcher*, this man I'd been married to for fifteen years.

I wondered again exactly how often he had come here. How many times had he been late or missing that he'd spent in this alternative home? I held little hope that the authorities or Tyler knew of this place. What became crystal clear in my mind was that my own life was in danger to be alone in a desolate house with this madman. No matter what he might say, he knew the huge risk in revealing all this to me. He would no doubt deal with me like all the others if he felt threatened.

Now that I was closer to the trophy on his desk, I saw that it was a youth football award. Odd. Odd because Preston had a lot bigger, more important awards to display since he'd been in the NFL. As I glanced down at it to avoid meeting Preston's eyes, I could clearly read the name on it. *Josh Middleton.* Why was it here? Clearly the same reason that the photo of Josh was here. Another wave of nausea came over me, and I gagged, automatically reaching up to cover my mouth.

I looked up to see Preston reaching into his pocket. I gripped the arms of the chair and made a barely audible gasp. Would his weapon of choice be a gun? A knife? Something to beat me with? He removed a ring of jangling keys that he held up before me with a glint in his eye. He then bent over and used them to open the bottom drawer of the desk. I could barely register the little metal box he removed, which also was locked. He shoved Josh's football trophy to the side to make room for the box, which he opened with another key. My nose was assaulted by something like dust. I detected another smell too, something familiar and coppery.

Time stood still. I was aware of the wind howling and whipping through the pine trees outside the window. The latch on the window shook like a ghost's chattering teeth. Flashes of lightning continued to periodically light up the sky.

"In this box are a few little things that are important to me. Some of the most important mementos I have, you could say. Souvenirs. Items I've collected. I've never showed these to anyone before."

I guessed what was in the box before he even showed me. Things he kept to remind him of his crimes. My only hope was that Tyler was still listening, and that he could somehow get here in time to rescue me before I became little more than a trophy in a metal box.

Preston sorted through the objects in the box, handling each one with a tender expression on his face. He was enjoying these memories. I once again felt on the verge of throwing up, but Preston was in his own world at that point and barely seemed to register my presence.

"When I was very young, I used to have these thoughts"—Preston began, sounding eerily like the confessional before a crime—"about what I would like to do when people crossed me. These things didn't seem wrong. I realized that other people would think differently. I knew the way I viewed the world was . . . was exceptional." His voice was low and rumbly, like the voice of the devil himself. "For many years, it confused me, how much people placed values on other people's feelings and wishes. I couldn't find any meaning in such things. It's disconcerting, realizing that you're so different from the time you're young. I soon came to realize that the way I looked at the world was a gift."

I knew my life depended on using my brain. I somehow found my voice and adopted a comforting tone, almost like a counselor. "Everyone has troubling thoughts, Preston. Everyone." I tried to assuage him, to make him feel like he was telling me a story and not confessing. And how was I to react? Shocked? Supportive? Which version of me would he believe? Nothing else mattered, except correcting the wrong I had made when I stepped into his car to drive out here.

"You don't understand. It's not about empty thoughts. I learned from watching others that if you didn't assign value to people and their feelings, you were viewed as abnormal. By the time I was nine years old, I realized how important it was to blend in. If you didn't, you could be punished and wouldn't be able to conduct your life the way you wanted. I hid my real self."

I tried again to access the part of his brain that wasn't demented. "I know the real you, Preston. Do you think we could be married this long, have children together, and that I wouldn't realize that you were different?"

He smiled, but not the kind smile of a husband and father. This was the irrational expression of a man I did not know.

"Norms are probably what the psychologists would call it. Sometimes these things do fall under the heading of religion. My parents were WASPs, but who's to say how much they really believed in any of that? We showed up for church on Christmas and Easter, but they didn't talk about their faith, if they had any. What I'm really talking about are the rules we live by in society."

"Do unto others?" I asked.

"Do not kill," he countered. "Do not steal. Though I'm not sure why those things are even considered separate. Killing is just a very high form of theft."

I was so still, I was aware that I was short of breath. I'd held it without knowing. I again tried to calm myself enough to suck in some air.

"What are you saying?" I asked, trying to keep him talking. "What is it you want to tell me? Or is now not the right time? We could drive home. You could sleep on it. This doesn't need to be game day. This can be practice." I tried to appeal to the professional in him, the one who watched hours of film and practiced the same routes over and over with his receivers. He wasn't impetuous. He was a planner. If he hadn't put thought into this play, maybe there was still time to turn back.

Preston reclined in his chair, his arms dangling loosely by his sides. The metal box was open between us, but I didn't dare lean in to look at the contents. Besides my chattering teeth, I barely moved at all.

Instead, I stared at Preston's face. I gazed into his pale blue, emotionless eyes and wondered how I'd ever thought I'd seen joy or love there. Maybe I had projected these emotions onto him because it was what a normal human being should have felt.

"I'm saying that despite how I was raised and what was expected of me, I've always been free of those kind of beliefs. I'm not bound by labeling things good or bad. I do what I feel."

"That's not true," I blurted. "You're a man who has always prided himself on being a responsible person."

"As a father, a husband, yes." He nodded. "Certainly in my career this is so. But I have never been afraid to take charge of a situation. I don't mind when things are messy. In some cases, I prefer it."

"I understand," I said, even though I didn't. *Why had I driven out here alone? Did I really think that Tyler, miles away, could somehow save me? The truth about my husband was so clear, but I'd refused to assemble the pieces until now. I'd held onto hope, and now it was going to get me killed.*

"Do you?" He sighed. "You were always a good girl. You've never done or experienced the kind of things I have."

"Okay. Then tell me. I want to understand what you're feeling. Isn't that what a spouse is for?"

He paused for a second and then launched into a story. "When I was young, there was this kid a little older than me, Jim, who lived in my neighborhood," he began, running his hand across the top of the desk. He spoke slowly and clearly, drawing out my terror with his narrative. I recognized the name Jim from the marked-up newspaper clipping. "We used to ride bikes together when we were young. I even remember playing capture the flag with him and a bunch of the other neighbor kids. I didn't think much of him. He was just another kid. When we got older, he played football against me, for the other middle school in the area. I thought we were merely opponents, but I found out one day who he truly was. Yes, he revealed his true colors one day." Preston's eyebrows slanted and his eyes squinted, his face dark with some vivid and painful memory. But then he suddenly chuckled. "Oh yeah, he definitely regretted messing with me.

"I'll tell you what I've told no one else before. What this failure, loser, little bastard did to me. He made me feel small, Danielle, as if I didn't matter. He humiliated me."

I listened with rapt attention that wasn't an act. I had never heard this story before.

"He waited after school for me one day. Him and a bunch of his friends. They cornered me—a group of older boys all taller than me at that time. They knocked my books out of my hands, and then they took turns beating on me. One after another. Sometimes more than one at the same time. Four on one. They bloodied my face and blackened my eyes.

"But that wasn't the worst of it." He paused and looked off in the distance, as if looking directly at my face during this recounting was too difficult. He continued in a quieter voice. "They dragged me to a hidden area and removed my pants. I was forced to bark like a dog." He paused again and closed his eyes, the shame and pain palpable on his face. "But after I barked, they didn't give me back my pants. They ran off, and I had to walk a whole block to get home . . . with my ass and privates exposed to the whole world."

"Preston," I said, placing my hand on his, "I'm so sorry. That's terrible."

"And, something else." He paused, looked down, clearly letting in a flood of pain from some repressed memory.

"This part is really hard to tell. I've never even come close to telling anyone before. Never thought I would."

I squeezed his hand, wondering what this awful memory was all about. He continued to look down as if he didn't have the confidence to look me in the eye while reliving this horrible event. I could only imagine what was so awful that caused this otherwise emotionless man to feel shame.

"Some guy was back there . . . in the woods behind the houses." He spoke slowly, carefully.

"He must have seen me coming. He was an adult, huge, with a goatee and mustache. I'd never seen him before. But he grabbed me and . . . and . . . touched me all over. For many long minutes, I couldn't escape." He was barely whispering now.

"Preston, that's awful."

"I should have tried harder to get away. Maybe he thought I liked it. But I didn't. I hated it. He took something away from me that day . . . part of my manhood.

"We were in the woods behind the houses, so I don't think anyone else saw. But I always wondered. Whenever anyone would look at me with an odd smile, I would wonder if they knew something. If they thought I was into guys or something. Back then, it was the worst thing you could be.

"If Jim hadn't have done what he did . . . none of the rest would have happened. He was the leader, the instigator." Preston's eyebrows narrowed, but his voice now became stronger again, as if he could quickly shake off the pain of that beating and humiliation.

"I'm so sorry," I repeated. Now his eyes met mine again.

"One thing I did know was that if I didn't defend myself against them, it would just keep happening. More than that, I wanted Jim gone. Jim was the one who deserved to pay. And so . . . I burned his house down." Preston said it like anyone would have come to that conclusion.

I didn't speak. The words stuck in my throat, like jagged stones. It hurt to breathe, to swallow. But I managed to smile, to nod in comprehension. His story from his past was clearly awful, and I felt compassion for the little boy who'd had to suffer such a disgrace. Clearly the incident had changed something inside him. But my reality was that Preston would easily repress that memory again, only the residual rage would remain, and I was about to become his next victim.

The longer he kept talking, the better. Time was my friend. Preston would call it knowing how to use the clock to your advantage. Taking longer in the huddle, waiting for the last second to snap the ball. Playing the sidelines. I knew him. I knew his language. I just had to be smart and not give in to stupid panic. Fear kept squeezing me in the chest and churning my insides. I wanted to get up and run away.

Preston continued his narrative, the molestation now forgotten and his thoughts focused fully on his hatred toward Jim.

"Jim and his parents weren't home at the time, but his little brother was. I didn't find out until later that he was inside."

He motioned to the newspaper articles pinned on the wall. "You probably saw the clipping. It was my first, uh, reckoning. I was in my early teens at that time."

"I'm sure you regretted it," I said. "You didn't mean for this child to pay for what his brother did to you."

"No," Preston replied coolly. "I didn't. I guess you could say he was an unintended victim, a casualty. I've never thought much about him, though. All I can tell you is his family left town that same week and I never saw Jim again. I consider it an accomplishment. I got what I wanted."

"Did you ever tell anyone?" I said in such a small voice that I wasn't sure he heard me.

"No one," Preston replied. "No one but you. Just now." He smiled at me oddly. In his twisted mind, his revelation was a compliment to me.

"It was so long ago. None of it matters," I said. "None of it matters. I love you. Do you hear me? I love you. This won't change anything." I lied to save my life. I hated this man more than anyone I had ever known, with my entire being.

"It's not the only thing in my past," he said. "As you can see, that was just the beginning."

Chapter Thirty-three

Preston Harrington

I saw an unfamiliar look in Danielle's eyes; it wasn't quite shock. Betrayal? Disbelief? It had never occurred to me what kind of emotions she might have once I told her the truth. I only knew that it was necessary that she understand the truth in order for us to continue on. I understood what I wanted. A partner on my journey. Someone to share my experiences with. I hadn't realized it before, but Danielle was the missing piece. I needed her to be a partner in this part of my life as much as any other.

"How many more accidents were there?" Danielle asked.

"Several. And they weren't accidents," I clarified. "They were all planned, though some with more care than others. Do you want to hear? Or would you rather not know? I can take you home and we can pretend like tonight never happened. If we do that, understand that there will be certain things you can never ask me again. I don't want it to be that way. I haven't enjoyed being secretive, but it's been a necessity. I had to be sure you were ready before I even considered telling you."

Danielle got up and began to pace the room. I saw her eyes stray to the bookcase and the titles there. Sure, some people were obsessed with serial killers the way others read presidential memoirs or the lives of famous chefs. But few people could say that they killed other humans. And if they did—soldiers and policeman among those expected to kill—how many of them could admit that they enjoyed watching the light pass out of someone's eyes?

She turned to me. "I want to know. We're a team."

Excellent. I could sense her pride in me, that she revered me.

"Sit down," I said.

She came back to her seat, but this time she tilted her body back, just a little farther away from me. I saw her glance briefly toward the door. She may have been trying to figure if she could make a run for it—a natural reaction but one I couldn't allow. I wasn't worried. I could easily overpower her, and we both knew it. Then I would have to redirect her. I couldn't harm her. She was the only one on the planet—besides my kids—that I wouldn't hurt. It never occurred to me that she might not understand that I was different. I needed to ensure she stayed convinced that I was almost superhuman.

"Have you killed anyone we know?" Danielle swallowed, her eyes widening slightly.

I hated that she looked at me with fear, even though she tried to hide it. Did she believe she could outmaneuver me? And at the same time, part of me was intrigued by it. I liked to see her try to stay in control. No, I wouldn't hurt her, but I wasn't beyond playing with her emotions a bit.

"I killed Josh Middleton. See, this here belonged to him." I held up the small football trophy.

I could see her quick intake of breath. She was careful with her next words. "You pushed him off the balcony? Why?"

"He loved you and he wasn't going to stop trying to get your attention. I did what I could to let him know it was a bad idea. Introduced him to other girls. Told him that you weren't interested. Once I realized he wasn't going to stop, I had to put an end to him."

Danielle clutched the arms of the chair. "He was only a friend to me," she said quietly. "I was never going to date him. You and I were barely acquaintances back then."

"I knew that I was going to make you my wife. It didn't matter what obstacles I had to get out of my way. That's the difference between him and a man like me. I'm willing to do what it takes to get the results I need."

"The fall didn't kill him, Pres," she said. "You didn't hear; he just died recently."

"I know," I said. "You're not really listening to me, are you? After all those years, he woke up, and I couldn't tell how much he remembered. It was important that I finish the job. Then I hung the clipping about his death on my wall."

"No one would have believed him," Danielle said. "You should have told me before you made a move like that."

"And what would you have said?"

"I'd have suggested paying him off," she replied. "No one was going to listen to a coma victim with a head injury twenty years after the fact. You're famous now. He could have just latched onto your name."

"Payoffs always lead to blackmail. What if he got greedy? Then he'd have to be silenced anyway. I took care of it last week. It's over. He didn't suffer, if you're wondering."

"Who else?" she asked.

"Well, you know how I was always faithful to you?"

She nodded. It warmed me to know she'd never doubted me.

"Still, certain women—they, they tempted me. Women will throw themselves at a famous quarterback like me. Some looked and sometimes acted like you. The others didn't even turn my head. But the ones that were beautiful like you, I couldn't let them continue living. So I rid them from this world to eliminate the temptation."

Danielle nodded again, her eyes a bit glazed over.

"Then there was the man who was found dead at Grinder's."

"Why?"

"He got in my way. He thought I was a fake and that Tyler was the unsung talent in our family. It might have only turned out to be a fistfight, but things went too far. I strangled him. And then to be sure, I hit him with this." I reached into my desk and brought out my favorite tool: the length of pipe that I'd used to kill. My wife stared at it but didn't speak for a long time. I let the quiet grow between us. She was the first to break it.

"I need to know about Rob," Danielle said suddenly. There was a resignation in the way she said it. She knew. Only the details were a mystery.

Chapter Thirty-four

Danielle Harrington

I wanted my husband to tell me he had nothing to do with Rob's death. And I wanted to believe him. The other murders, as awful as they were, I could almost understand. No, I couldn't. His reasoning and justification were dizzying, irrational, and insane. Killing to justify not cheating? I would have preferred him to cheat on me a thousand times rather than be a killer.

But those people were strangers, men and women Preston had a grudge against. He'd seen Josh as competition. If only he'd understood that I'd never wanted Josh. He was just a sweet guy with a crush on me. Would that have stopped Preston? Or were his violent tendencies too deep?

Killing Rob would have crossed a line. Preston was closer to Rob than either of his blood siblings. I needed to know Preston could never hurt me or the children, never hurt anyone he cared about. I had the weird thought that this was the way mob wives lived. The rationalizations one made to stay with a violent man and protect the family. My children didn't deserve the media onslaught that would follow them for the rest of their lives.

Foolish me, I wasn't ready to let everything go. "You had your arguments, but Rob still loved you like a brother."

"Rob betrayed me," Preston said, his eyes cold. "He was fighting me for the restaurant. Wanted it all for himself, with as much time and money as I had already put into it. At first I wanted to be a silent partner and would have been happy remaining one. I'd have been there to support him in whatever decisions he needed to make for the business."

I thought back again to that package Rob had dropped off for Preston.

"But he got greedy. Since he wanted me out, that would mean legalities, paperwork, and eventually media scrutiny. I met up with him one night at the restaurant and we had an argument about it. When I asked him why he suddenly wanted the change, he unloaded on me, about not being in my shadow anymore. He even said that one day you were going to wake up and see that I was a self-centered asshole."

"You beat him with that *thing*?" I asked.

"We shoved each other, and then I grabbed a knife that was lying around the kitchen. I had the pipe with me, and I used it to finish him off."

"Oh my God! Preston . . ."

"I knew you wouldn't understand," he said. "I wanted to give you the chance. If you can't be with me anymore . . ."

"You don't understand," I cut him off. "I have something to tell you too. A police detective came to my job today. He wanted to talk about Josh. They suspect you in his death."

"What are you talking about? When did this happen?"

I took in a deep breath and quickly told him about the detective who had cornered me earlier in the day. I tried to hide my feelings and project the mask of the supportive wife. But the horrific thought kept entering my mind: *He'd killed Rob. And so cruelly.*

"And you weren't going to tell me this!" he yelled.

The harshness in his voice ripped through me like a thousand shards of glass. *Be smarter. Be smarter. Choose your words more carefully.*

"Of course I was going to tell you. I was trying to decide how. I wasn't sure if it was some bullshit or he was really onto something. I told him I knew nothing and that he should talk to you."

"That's good," he said in a calmer voice. "That's exactly right."

We were both silent for several seconds.

"What happens now?" I asked.

"We have to leave," he said. He stood up, and I did too, like a dog following her master. What was wrong with me? I needed to grab something, anything that could serve as a weapon. Kill him before he killed me. Or the kids. I saw no way to grab the trophy without Preston knowing, and I couldn't get to anything else in the room. I had to keep clearheaded and plan as the rest of the night unfolded.

Preston put the items back in the box and locked it, then put it back in the desk drawer, along with Josh's football trophy, and locked the drawer as well. He tucked the keys back in his pocket. Why did he feel the need to keep such mementos? Evil. Insane. There were no other words for it.

He led me back downstairs to the main level. Through the window, I saw the reflection of headlights going down the main road. Probably a neighbor, but in this neighborhood the houses were far enough apart that you would probably never see them. And they wouldn't be able to hear or see a woman in trouble. I hoped Preston hadn't seen, but he immediately stiffened.

"Come on," he said, grabbing my arm. "We don't have time to waste."

"Where are we going?"

He picked up the glass I'd drunk water out of moments earlier. His calm response chilled me to the bone. "To get rid of any evidence that you were here."

Preston turned off all the lights and tugged me out the door, down the driveway, through the gate—which in his haste he left open behind us—and out to the street. He directed me into the passenger side of the SUV before dashing around to the driver's seat. "Oh, by the way, I have these." He dangled the Corolla keys in front of me and then pocketed them. "You can never be too careful." A sliver of hope faded as he climbed into the driver seat.

He maneuvered around the parked Corolla and then sped a short distance down the country lane before he suddenly slowed down. We had traveled no more than half a mile down the road. The patchy cloud-covered sky was now pitch black; a few stars glowed, and the wind continued to shake the bank of pine and oak trees surrounding the desolate road.

"Aren't we going home?" I finally said. Preston waited for a beat before answering, as if needing to decide which lie he was about to tell me. After what I'd learned, I couldn't accept anything he told me as truth.

"A quick diversion," he said. "And then back home."

He craned his neck left and right, seemingly looking for landmarks, and then navigated the SUV a few feet to the right, bringing the vehicle to a stop on the shoulder. He took the keys from the ignition but left the headlights on. "Give me your phone and wait here."

I reached into my pocket, felt for the power button to turn it off, but found no need. The battery had drained. "Here," I said. "You can trust me. We've built too much together for me to ever let it go."

Did he believe me? Probably not. Or he would have left the keys in the ignition. He was giving me a chance to run, knowing I couldn't find my way back to the road if I tried. Soon I'd get lost, and he'd catch up to me. He knew this place. That's what this little stopover was all about. A test.

Preston got out of the car, taking the drinking glass and my phone with him. I watched as he walked to the edge of the clearing. The moment the door opened, I could smell the dank odor of the stale, unmoving water. There was a swamp down there. I wished I had the Corolla keys with me. I wanted to drive away and leave him here. I could go straight to the police and tell them that he had confessed everything to me.

Would anyone believe me, or would I only end up making Preston into an enemy? I knew he could never forgive me for being disloyal. He was already testing me by telling me the truth. If I failed, I would end up one of his victims. And then what would happen to our children? Could he pass whatever darkness dwelled inside him onto them? Or worse yet, would he engineer a way for them to conveniently "disappear"?

He thought I was weak. That I didn't understand his thirst for killing. And I didn't.

But I was a mother who would do anything to protect her children. I touched my stomach absently.

I couldn't play his game. I needed to change the rules. One day he would kill me. If not, he would get careless and the police would arrest him. Everything would come out. With enough money, luck, and public sentiment behind him, he might avoid prison. But again my thoughts turned to my children—forever marked the spawn of a killer. I shuddered.

Through the open car door and a momentary break in the howling wind, I heard the distant sound of a splash.

He'd gone all the way down to the swamp and thrown my phone in—evidence that I'd been here. He was preparing to kill me too.

Acting on pure instinct, I opened my door and took off running in the opposite direction of the swamp. I leaped like a madwoman across the gravel shoulder and down into the ditch, and then encountered the waist-high grass that slowed my run to a wade. Bushes with sharp points scratched my arms, and adolescent trees ripped at my clothing. Still I pushed on in the darkness. I could barely see a foot in front of me. I ran with my hands blocking my face so my eyes wouldn't get ripped by an errant branch. Suddenly, my foot caught on a root and I fell in a heap on the ground.

Wiping my sweat-streaked forehead, I burst into tears. What was I doing? And worse yet, what was the future for my kids? Would Preston hurt them? Could he? He wouldn't be the first parent to harm or kill his children. Right now I believed Preston was capable of any and all evil deeds.

Much as I wanted to get up and continue running, to escape, I knew in my sobbing wretchedness that I needed to go back. I paused for one more moment of freedom before aiming back toward the car, its headlights a beacon in the desolate night.

Now I feared that Preston would have returned in my absence. If so, he would catch and kill me. Creeping closer to the car, I didn't see him inside or anywhere near it. *Think, think.* He was stronger than me, but I was smarter than him. I devised a plan B.

Approaching the open driver's door, I reached down on the floor next to the seat, yanked on the hatch release, and heard it pop. I went to the back of the vehicle and raised the hatch door. Lifting the carpeted cardboard that concealed the spare, I grasped the tire iron on the side of the well, hugging it tight to my body.

Ever so carefully, I quietly latched the hatch and returned to the passenger's seat. My hands were shaking. All of me was shaking. Sweat dripped into my eyes. I was filthy and had scratches on my arms. Would Preston notice? I took a deep breath and set the tire iron between the side of my seat and the inside of the passenger door so it was not visible. And I waited.

When Preston returned and slipped into the seat beside me, I could read the irritation on his face. He didn't expect to find me waiting for him, the dutiful wife. He'd wanted me to run so he would have a clear reason to doubt my loyalty; then he would have had the thrill of hunting me down. By his reaction, I knew I had been right to return. I felt the smallest sense of having the upper hand, which boosted my confidence and momentarily gave me a sense of power. I noticed he was covered in mud.

Preston Harrington

"What happened?" my wife asked, her words slurred. I assumed she was referring to my muddy shoes and wet shirt.

"In the dark I couldn't tell exactly where the swamp started, and I accidentally got filthy when I walked through the muck. But I got rid of your stuff." This last part I said with a noticeable brightness to my tone.

I didn't really need to get rid of her stuff. She wasn't going to die. But I had to admit I was enjoying lording over her the power of death over life, of evil over good. Toying with her was just too satisfying.

I turned on the ignition but paused before continuing to drive. "That swamp area is downright creepy—the perfect place for a crime!" I got a good laugh out of that one.

"This life must have been difficult for you," Danielle said. "You worked so hard for your . . . your totems that you showed me . . . Are they like Super Bowl trophies? Do they mean that much?" Danielle must have been trying out the supportive wife role.

"More," I said. "My memorabilia. Each item is a symbol of a life snuffed out. In each case, I had the power over them. I made the decision about whether they would live and how they would die. Can you understand?"

"Yes. And the feeling of killing? What is it like?"

She was good. Reenacting the feeling of killing in my mind did lessen my need to do it in real life—and she assumed she was the obvious victim. I was enjoying this night immensely.

"It's the ultimate release. Like sex, but far more intense. I can ride that high of having taken a life for some time. When the need returns, it's strong and hard to ignore. Anyone standing in my way finds themselves in a very bad place."

She gasped so loudly, I chuckled internally and envisioned pounding on my chest like Tarzan.

Danielle Harrington

I reached down in the dark car and gripped the tire iron with my right hand.

He spoke so calmly, as if he were discussing the plays of a football game. What had caused him to be this way? I thought again about the article I had read. Multiple head injuries. A family that was loving but distant. Clearly mental illness. Maybe there was a predilection to violence too, a feeling that this was simply a man's way of solving problems.

My husband was missing some necessary component in his brain—a sense of empathy. I'd been fooled for years.

He'd duped me into believing that he had real emotions. Maybe it wasn't even possible for him to love, not in the way normal people did. I'd bought the act, the smile and athleticism, the all-American man with his doting family. Was this the definition of a psychopath?

I waited for him to turn slightly, to yank on the seatbelt before he started driving again, which blessedly stuck, like it had often over the last few months. Thank God I'd never had that fixed. Those few seconds were all the time I needed to convince myself to strike. I had to do what I could to rescue my kids. I launched the tire iron into his cranium with all the force I could conjure up in that cramped space. That first blow wasn't very hard, but I'd caught him by surprise. He yelped and clutched the bloody area of his head. In the chaos, I screamed and hit him twice more, the thud of iron hitting his beautiful eyes and nose.

As I wound up to hit him again, he grabbed my left arm with both his hands. He had a surprising amount of strength left in him, considering the damage my hits had done. But this was a man accustomed to playing through pain.

"You'll never get away, Danielle," he bellowed. "Your strength is no match for mine!"

I opened my car door and attempted to flee, but his fingers reached farther up my arm. Using my entire body strength, I attempted to yank my arm free. "Yaaahhh!" I screamed and, still holding the tire iron, dug the fingernails of my right hand into his arm. I gritted my teeth and dug in deeper, knowing I had to be drawing blood. As I dug in, I constantly wriggled my trapped arm. Preston let up for one instant and then tried to grab me again. But the adrenaline kicked in, and I was faster than him this time.

As I dashed out of the SUV, something prevented me from running. Something was caught. My sweater! Preston had it in his grip. Thinking quickly, I straightened my arms behind me, holding the tire iron flat against my arm, and twisted to shed the garment. Once free, I ran, this time in the direction of the swamp. I was aware of him chasing after me, but he had to make it around the car first, which gave me a bit of a head start. I didn't dare take the time to glance back.

Taking care not to stumble as I had before, I ran at a constant but slow pace. Once again, the dark trees rushed up and threatened my face. Dodging branches in the dark, I hustled down the steep, forested bank.

But what would I do once I got there? Even injured, Preston was still stronger than me. I thought again of Ethan and Isabel and the unborn baby. My motherly instincts kicked in. I had no choice but to eliminate the threat.

I paused behind a large tree and tried to calm my loud breathing. The loudness of the wind helped conceal me but also made hearing my pursuer difficult. As Preston got closer, stumbling down the embankment in his rage, our SUV's headlights behind him in the distance clearly revealed his dark, shadowy presence.

I wound up, waiting for the precise moment to strike. The instant Preston passed my hiding spot, I struck him with all my might in the back of his head. But I hit poorly this time. It barely fazed him and, instead, simultaneously enraged him and revealed exactly where I was.

"DAN—IELLE! You . . . should . . . not . . . have . . . done . . . this!" he roared in an ungodly voice.

He grabbed me and threw me to the ground. My upper leg landed on a sharp tree root and my face got scratched by sharp twigs on a bush, but in my terror, I barely felt that pain.

"No, Preston! I was wrong! I love you! You know I do!" I shrieked from my prone position. Tears stung my eyes. Preston's body glowed around the edges from the distant headlights shining on him. A distant blackbird cawed. The wind howled, spreading the foul swamp smell everywhere.

But instead of immediately striking me, he broke out into laughter. He laughed louder than the wind whipping through the woods. And it only increased in intensity. I'd never seen him laugh this hard at any comedy show or event—ever. The lone blackbird cawed a couple more times. Preston threw back his head like the scene before him of his wife in horror lying prone on the muddy ground was the funniest thing he could imagine.

I took advantage of his insanity by slowly crab-walking backward. But I couldn't inch away fast enough.

"NO!" he snarled and reached down to grab me.

"YAAAHH!" I screamed and kicked with all my might, scrunched my eyes, and braced for the blow.

But instead, I heard a loud clunk and then the thud of Preston's body falling inches to the side of me.

I screamed even harder, not knowing what was going on, and instinctually got up and began running the opposite direction from the now-prone Preston. When someone grabbed my arm, I shook it off like a madwoman and kept fleeing.

"Danielle! Danielle!"

Someone was calling my name, but all I knew was that I had to get away.

"Danielle!"

Someone again grabbed my arm. I turned and dug my fingernails into his skin.

"Ouch! Danielle, stop! It's me, Tyler!" He grabbed me with both arms, placed both hands on my face, and forced me to look at him.

"Tyler? What? Why?" I lost all rigidity in my legs and sunk to the ground.

Tyler Harrington

I held up Danielle by hooking my arms under her armpits and forcing her back to a standing position.

"I'll explain later, but we've got to get you out of here. I knocked out Preston with a shovel, but he's not dead."

"No, no."

She shook her head. Her body alternated between rigid and slumped. Danielle was beyond shock. I could tell she could barely understand what I was telling her. What terror had she been through to reach this point?

I half walked, half carried her shivering body through the brush and trees uphill toward the deserted country road. We were making great progress and were only ten yards from the car when she stiffened and pointed. Only a gargling sound escaped her lips. I followed the direction of her finger and saw Ed Birch half hidden in the brush.

I started to explain to her that it was OK, that I knew that guy, but she was inconsolable. She muttered about Preston doing bad things, that he was a killer, but I could only understand half of what she was saying. I realized that she was trying to warn me.

"I heard a lot of your conversation before the phone went dead," I told her. "I heard what he said about Josh and about Rob."

Her only response was to nod and sob quietly.

Danielle and Preston's SUV remained parked on the dirt road, the headlights still shining. Behind them was my Audi. She was now snuggled against my shoulder, barely standing and crying uncontrollably. "Danielle, Danielle," I tried to snap her back to the present. "I'm going to put you in my car. Danielle."

"No!" She jerked, each limb flailing. I nearly dropped her when her arm swung at me, barely missing my right eye and connecting instead with my forehead. "No!" she repeated.

"Ouch! Damn it. Danielle, it's OK. It's me, Tyler. You're safe here, but I need to go back down and deal with Preston before he wakes up. You'll be safe here in my car."

"No! Not in the car. I'll wait here next to the car."

"OK. I'll be right back."

I hated to leave her, but I had to deal with my brother. As I took off back down the hill, I glanced back to see her pacing, looking in every direction, as alert as a cat on a hunt.

Danielle Harrington

I realized that Tyler had come to my rescue. How? I had no idea but was too jumpy to ponder anything other than my own safety. Every creak of a limb, every chitter of a nocturnal animal, and every faraway blackbird call seemed intent on warning me that my life was in danger. The wind was finally calming down a bit, but it kept blowing my hair into my eyes. I heard a footstep on the gravel behind me but turned to find nothing there. No way would I be a sitting duck in the car, though. At least out here I could run if anything threatening came my way.

Why was Tyler taking so long? What was he doing anyway? My body was still shaking horribly and my teeth chattering. I wondered if they'd ever stopped chattering since leaving Preston's awful secret house.

And then my mind took off on a more terrifying trajectory. What if Preston got to Tyler *first*?

"No, no." I said it aloud to force down the awful thoughts.

A man-sized object on the edge of the tree line caught my attention. Was it a person? It was the right size and shape to be a person, with hands visible to its side. No. Of course it was a tree. I forced myself to look away and then back. Had it moved? Did it look different now? I became hyperaware again, the sound of crickets sounding like screeching in its loudness. Suddenly my mind flashed back to something similar I'd seen in the woods when Tyler was carrying me up the hill. I'd seen a man!

Hadn't I?

But who would be in the swampy woods this time of night? I couldn't remember clearly. The memory was already fuzzy. The man I saw was probably as much a man as the figure I now saw on the wood's edge.

Tyler Harrington

I left behind a frantic Danielle, but I had to meet up with Ed. A bird call alerted me to his position.

I felt like I was making an enormous racket in tramping down the hill. I didn't think the blow to Preston's head would keep him down for long, with his apparent determination to kill. And to kill his wife, Danielle? What kind of insane idiot was he anyway?

I moved in the direction of the bird call and then made out the shadowy form of Ed. He pointed in the direction of the unconscious Preston, who was beginning to thrash about. Any second now and he'd wake up.

"I'm glad you called me," whispered Ed. "This nonhuman doesn't deserve to live."

I was a little surprised by his passion but glad also that someone felt as strong a hatred as I did toward my brother.

We formulated a plan that I agreed to, and less than half hour later I was headed back to Danielle.

I found her exactly the way I'd left her—pacing on the road, never still for more than a couple seconds. "Danielle!" I called out so I didn't spook her further. I did anyway.

"Ahhh," she screamed and then popped her hand over mouth when she saw it was me. "Sorry. I'm pretty fragile right now."

"I'll take care of you. You're going to be OK. No one is going to hurt you. Get in the car and I'll take you home. I'll come back for your car later."

"But, Preston . . ."

"Everything is taken care of. He'll never bother you again. Or anyone else, for that matter. As far as the world knows, he disappeared. We can talk now, but afterward, we must never speak of this night again."

Danielle was quiet for several minutes while we began the drive to her house. "Tyler," she finally broke the silence, "how did you ever find me? Did you know about this house of Preston's?"

"No, I sure didn't. You were a smart one when you left your phone on. I could hear parts of your conversation and knew you were in trouble. I used the GPS to locate you."

"Oh, Tyler." Now she let down her guard, and the tears gushed. She sobbed and sobbed, her body contorting in the release of emotion. "I nearly d-died tonight." A fresh wave of tears came.

I reached over to grab a container of Kleenex from the glove compartment and handed it to her.

"He did kill Josh. You were right. And Rob. And others." She paused to once again gain her composure. "He was horrible. He was a monster. And I was *married to him*."

"Now don't you go there. He fooled us all. He was a charming guy—one side of him anyway."

We drove in near silence for a while, and I pondered our next steps. "So, Danielle, where are your kids?"

"The kids?"

"Yes, where are Ethan and Isabel? Who is staying with them?"

"Uhh, they're not home. They're staying at a friend's house."

"OK, how about this? I drop you off at home. Then, when Joanna gets back tomorrow with our kids, how about

I pick up your kids and bring them to our house for a couple days . . . just until you are ready to take care of them again. They could use a little time with their cousins, don't you think?"

"Sure." I didn't know Joanna wasn't home but didn't care about that detail right then.

"And then tomorrow I'll arrange to get your car back to you."

"OK," she whispered.

We drove up in her driveway, and she hopped out to press the code to open the garage door. I walked in with her to make sure she was as settled down as possible.

When Danielle turned to look at me under the bright lights of the kitchen, she gasped. I looked down at my clothing and hands and saw the blood stains everywhere.

"Uh, that doesn't look too good," I whispered.

"Go ahead and take a shower here and then grab some of Preston's clothes to wear home."

I did as she suggested, finding a basic T and shorts in Preston's closet that looked similar enough to ones I had at home. While the hot water poured over me, I tried to calm my shaking hands. What had I done? I had tried to kill my brother, my own brother. My salty tears washed down the same drain as the blood from my blood-stained hands. I took a little extra time to straighten out my emotions before I rejoined Danielle.

"Now," I said as I left, "the world will believe that Preston has simply disappeared. You will be able to grieve openly. Figure out a story to tell your kids, and know that anything is better than them knowing the truth about their dad. You'll be questioned, so stick to the truth as much as possible. Except about tonight. Tonight you went to bed. Period. We will never talk about tonight again. Anything comes up, call me; don't text. You'll be fine. Everything is better this way."

I kissed her on the forehead and left.

Chapter Thirty-five

Danielle Harrington

It's been two years now since that awful night when my famous husband almost killed me. The public and my friends felt sorry for me and flooded me with cards, flowers, food, and support. All any of them know is that he disappeared, and I'll never say anything different. I played the part of supportive, grieving wife perfectly. The grieving part wasn't difficult, only that the loss I felt was for what could have been, what I thought was our life. People assumed that I was the supportive wife, grieving a man who had done me wrong. And their ideas weren't entirely false. I had loved my husband right up until the time I discovered what he truly was.

Fortunately, the police have stopped coming around to question me. They believe he has fled, disappeared into the wind, very much a wanted man.

Few others suspect the truth. The detectives believe they know the truth about some of his crimes but lack the evidence to convict.

20/20 did a show on Preston. I declined to be interviewed for it. They concluded that he may have committed a handful of crimes and is likely living a clandestine life on some remote island. After all, several eyewitnesses have "spotted" him from time to time. I shake my head whenever I hear those stories.

Sharon Middleton went to the press accusing Preston of killing her son, but she was dismissed as a crackpot. Last I heard, she has breast cancer. Preston's fans posted so many pictures and videos of the smiling, charming, children's-hospital-supporting, all-star football player that it would be the persona most people remembered. Anyone who dared say an unkind word against him or question possible criminal allegations got dragged all over social media.

Internally, I compartmentalize that last night and even my whole life with Preston. I won't let my thoughts go there. I have a script I tell the kids about how their dad loved him, was a wonderful man, and a great football player. If they ever ask any other questions, I'll think up lies for those as well. I encourage them to look at his photos and web posts and to watch tape of his old games. "That's Daddy," I say. "That's Daddy." In my mind, he never truly existed. That's what I have to do to keep on living.

The kids seem to have accepted that their dad is gone. They don't understand it, but who does? Of course, one-year-old Zack never even met his dad. Having a new little life to care for greatly helped me in my healing, and I got Ethan and Isabel some professional counseling to help them work through their issues.

Preston's body has never been discovered. Rumors about his disappearance and suspected foul deeds still occasionally make the news cycle. Authorities could never prove anything without his confession or some DNA evidence, so his murder victims' cases remain open. Only

Tyler knows what really happened and where that body is, but he'll never tell. As far as most people know, he was asleep in his bed the night Preston was last seen. His wife Joanna had been gone with the kids and her parents on a quick Disney trip on that fateful day, so not even she knew Tyler wasn't home.

Someday they'll find that house in the woods, the one I'm not supposed to know about. Then they'll be able to put together some evidence and solve Preston's crimes. My emotions are mixed on whether I want this to happen. I know the victims' families would like closure, but I have my own kids to think about. How would they react, even years from now, if they knew their dad was a serial killer?

Tyler and I have stayed tight to our agreement and never speak about that night. I will never betray him. He's finally out of his brother's shadow. He's had his best season ever, has won a third Super Bowl, and there is now talk that he might go on to become one of the greatest players of all time. He understood that Preston had to go. I feel content knowing that we will each keep this secret forever.

Tyler Harrington

I was questioned by the police about that night soon after it happened, but I was asleep in bed, I told them. I knew nothing about his disappearance or about his alleged crimes. The reason I'd gone to visit Josh Middleton? Simply friendship.

I felt uncomfortable with people treating me like we'd suffered this great loss. The end of Preston was, truthfully, the most freeing day of my life. But I was cordial and acted like I was grieving, at least in public. My wife knew I'd not been close to him, so at least I didn't have to put on a show at home.

At one point, I did some research on that house—Preston's secret house. According to the official records, the owner is anonymous. That guy had his tracks covered, for sure.

I saw Danielle the other day at a family get-together. She pulled up in the new minivan she got soon after that night. The SUV held too many memories and potential evidence, so she exchanged it for new wheels. She also sold the Corolla. After all, she didn't need two cars around anymore. Our two families and even the extended family have grown closer since Preston disappeared. The cousins get together occasionally to play, with Greg's kids in the mix also, and my parents are more doting and attentive with the grandkids than they ever were with us. I'm grateful they have no idea what kind of person Preston was. I don't think my mother could survive it.

Danielle and I are cordial but always keep our conversation to the basics. Joanna says that Danielle is difficult to get to know on a deep level. I understand the woman's demons but can't explain to Joanna, so I just remind her that Danielle has been through a lot in her life and is therefore guarded.

I sense that Danielle views me with jaded eyes. I catch her staring at me sometimes from across the room with a glazed-over expression in her eyes. She gazes without seeing me because she's deep in thought at these moments. I feel she views me as guilty, and I want to defend myself. But I let it go.

I remember our agreement to never speak of that night. And we never will.

Chapter Thirty-six

Ed Birch
Two Years Earlier

I could feel my blood pressure rising as I listened on the phone to Tyler telling me that Danielle was in trouble. She was apparently alone in some remote area with her husband, who was going off the deep end and threatening her life. I told him I was all in, just tell me where to show up.

Visions of that other pretty, doe-eyed girl that I'd failed to protect flashed through my mind. They were joined by thoughts of the helpless kid who'd been pushed off the balcony and then murdered right under my nose. No way in hell was I letting another person under my watch become a victim. I had as much energy as a kid on crack. I had one last opportunity to right the wrongs of my life.

I plugged the address Tyler had given me into my GPS and drove like a maniac. It led me to a dark, remote area far outside the city limits. I was almost to the location, checking address markers of the few and far-between residences way out there, when I reached the one with that number. The gate was wide open, so I drove in and parked.

Strangely, I saw no other cars in the driveway, although I had noticed one parked on the street.

I jogged up to the unlit house and was reaching out for the door handle when I was startled by what sounded like a scream. The sound seemed to be coming from the woods, though. Definitely not from inside the house. *Danielle! No!*

I needed to get there, and fast. Judging the best way to quickly cover territory to be by using the road, I set off on foot back down the driveway, past my parked car and then the one parked on the street, the dirt and sand crunching under my feet. I'd traveled about a hundred yards up the road when I heard another scream. That could only be Danielle. I raced faster than I even knew I could run. I had to reach her in time. I had to!

The road took a sharp bend to the left, and that was when I saw the two parked cars ahead of me. One had headlights on that were aimed away from me; the other I recognized as Tyler's. I delved into the woods in the direction I'd heard the scream.

Only ten yards into the thick foliage, I stopped to ascertain the movement I was seeing. With the shadowy light of the headlights, I made out the form of Tyler. He was carrying something. A person with dark hair. It had to be Danielle. No! What had Preston done? The monster! A stream of rage and depression ran through my soul. My life was meaningless if I couldn't do this one thing right. If I had failed to protect Danielle, I could not go on living.

I rushed toward him so he could see me, but didn't speak. He saw me and put up his hand to signal me not to come any farther. Then he gave me a thumbs-up and motioned with his head that something or someone was farther down the hill. Danielle stirred in his arms and even appeared to open her eyes for a couple seconds before succumbing to slumber, unconsciousness, or whatever. I was so relieved to see she was alive that I felt a momentary release, like tears were about to come. I squeezed my eyes and shook off the feeling. I wasn't a crier.

I took a deep breath to clear my head and continued gingerly down the hill, expecting to find Preston. But I had no idea of his condition. Was he dead, alive, waiting to ambush me? The wind helped cover the sound of the twigs I was snapping, but it also prevented me from hearing what I was heading toward.

I caught myself sharply when I nearly tripped on Preston's foot. I almost lost my balance and fell right on top of him. I shot back, concealing myself behind the foliage to determine what condition he was in. He seemed to be still, and I knew he wouldn't be unless he were knocked out.

I turned my attention to Tyler, who was making his way back down. He must have left Danielle in the car. I didn't like the thought of her being alone, even if the predator was down here in my sight. I retreated to meet him so we could discuss the plan.

"He's just ahead in the clearing," I explained. "I—"

I felt the jar to my lower back as what felt like a ton of bricks slammed into me from behind. In my unceremonious fall forward, I took Tyler down with me. I twisted and squirmed, thrashing both arms and legs to get out from underneath Preston's grasp. I must have smacked Tyler a couple times in my efforts to free myself, and he connected elbows and knees with me also in his haste for freedom. Preston, even with his strength, was weakened from whatever had been done to him before I got there, and he couldn't keep both of us down.

I don't know how Tyler got free, but suddenly all I knew was that Preston and I were engaging in a two-way hand-to-hand combat, with him at a clear advantage by being on top. I yelped when I took a fist to the face, but when he wound up to strike me again, his hand stayed stuck in midair. I couldn't see what was holding back his arm but used the opportunity to grab a handful of loose sand from the ground and smear it into his eyes. With the double whammy, Preston loosened up momentarily. I wriggled free just in time to see Tyler slam a shovel into Preston's back.

Preston cried out in pain but managed to flip around to face his attacker. His head was covered in blood. "You! I always knew you were so jealous of me. And now you think you can hurt me. I'll come after your family! Consider your wife dead! Your kids are good as dead!"

He leaped up and plowed headfirst into Tyler in a full-on football tackle. Tyler went down like an unprotected quarterback.

I scrambled for the shovel. Grabbing and lifting it over my head, I saw Preston whip around. He took advantage of the opportunity to attack me while my arms were up and my midsection exposed, like a wide receiver stretching up to catch a pass. His bloody head connected with my sternum, blasting me back on the ground. At my age, my lower back couldn't handle too many more of these takedowns. The shovel went flying somewhere behind me.

Preston, much more limber than me, clambered over me to get to the shovel. But at the same moment, Tyler leaped, his full body extended in midair, to catch his brother before he reached the weapon. The two of them now tussled just inches to my left, but this time Tyler had the upper, more advantageous position. He slammed his fist into Preston's face, and blood squirted from his nose. But Preston landed a knee kick into Tyler's groin, rendering the man temporarily helpless. Preston rolled out from underneath Tyler and wound up to deliver another punch to the face.

My back ached, but Josh's face flashed before my eyes. He deserved justice. I thought of Danielle, who deserved freedom. And then I relived the raw memory of that other doe-eyed brunette girl from so long ago. A murder conviction and serving time was too good for Preston. Anyway, I knew how these things worked. Preston would get all spiffed up for court, wear a blue tie that made him look honest, get all kinds of character witnesses to say what a great guy he was, and, lacking substantial evidence, likely go free. I could not let that happen. I would not fail again! I had to protect the innocent.

With a surge of adrenaline, I grabbed the shovel. "Die, Preston!" I shouted and struck him in the back of the head. He fell heavily with his head crashing into Tyler's chest, his limbs sprawled at awkward angles. Tyler broke free and came at me, yelling, "Give me the shovel! Give it to me!"

"No." I twisted so my back was to him and he couldn't reach the shovel.

He grabbed me from behind and attempted to yank the shovel from my hands.

"No. Tyler, stop. Stop! I've got this. Tyler! Move out of the way!"

He stepped back, and I slammed the shovel down another time on the still unmoving Preston.

We both paused for a few seconds, sucking in breaths of air, and staring silently at Preston's unmoving carcass.

"It's time for you to go, Tyler," I said in a calm, fatherly voice. "I've got this. You're his brother. You need to go."

His shoulders slunk and he nodded but didn't move.

"Go now. Danielle is waiting for you up there."

He kept nodding like he was trying to figure out what to do. I let the shovel fall to the ground and grabbed Tyler by the shoulders. "This is mine now, all me. Go to Danielle. He'll be out of your life now. He'll never hurt anyone again."

My suggestion finally registered with him and he left.

I sat alone in the woods, leaning against a tree near Preston, thinking he was probably dead but a little too spooked to check for sure. I didn't observe any movement in his chest, so I took a first step by kicking his foot. No response. I moved on to cautiously taking a pulse in his wrist. Nothing. More bold now, I flipped his blood-spattered body over and checked the neck, then felt for air coming out the nose. This guy was dead.

I paused for a moment to realize that I felt a sliver of hope to be living in a world without Preston. I'd done my part to save Danielle. Finally, I'd been in the right place at the right time and done my job. A surge of emotion flooded my head. But taking a deep breath because I didn't have time for that, I planned what to do next.

Obviously, I had to get rid of the body. Closer to the swamp was an area with more grasses than trees, so I determined it to be the best place to dig. I dug a few shovelfuls but came up with water each time. Huh. Stupid. Of course. This was New Orleans, the land of swamps, nothing like the terrain of the north that I was more familiar with. I realized I'd have to work *with* the water or it would be working against me the whole time.

I could easily dump his body in the swamp, but it would float. I'd need something to weigh it down. Looking around, I determined that I could use several heavy fallen tree branches on top of his body to get it to sink.

Making my way back to the body, using the light on my phone to guide me, I nearly tripped on a whiteish branch sticking out of the ground. Chiding myself to be more careful, I took no more than three more steps before seeing other similar white branches, although these weren't as much of a tripping hazard. My curiosity getting the better of me, I stooped down to observe what kind of branch was such an odd light color. What I saw shook me to my core. These weren't tree branches; they were bones. Dozens of them, by the looks of it. And I knew from my forensic training that they were human.

Now alert to the fact that I was surrounded by bones, I searched for more. My eyes were opened to the vast number of human bones in this area. Many human bodies—impossible to estimate how many—had apparently been buried here, but the swamp was giving them up. Was Preston responsible for this? Did he have a partner in crime? Or was this the work of some other fiend? I had no way of knowing, but the possibilities sickened me.

Reaching Preston's body, I went through his pockets. I kept the cash from his wallet but would bury the wallet with him. I found two sets of keys and kept them in case they'd come in handy later. His phone? I'd keep it to see if I could gather any evidence.

I dragged his limp body down to the swamp's edge and filled his pants and pockets with stones. Then, adjusting his shirt, I tied it up so it resembled a sling and weighted it with more rocks. I grabbed a couple large but manageable branches from the woods and placed those on top of the body.

With all that weight on him, I had to go first into the water and drag him in. His body scraped a line in the wet dirt that oozed in with fresh mud as I tugged him farther into the swamp. I pictured the lucky alligator that could make several meals out of this freak of a human. The wind had calmed down by this time, and besides my grunting as I pulled the dead weight along, the only sounds in the swamp were of the crickets and an occasional plop into the water of a frog, turtle, or some other creature. My feet sank into the dense swamp floor, and I had to release the suction with each new step. I thought how no other circumstance on the planet would have gotten me to take a midnight plunge into a murky New Orleans swamp infested with who-knew-what kind of organisms.

Preston's body disappeared beneath the surface with each step until he was fully immersed, as if replicating some twisted baptism. No one would have cause to visit this area for years to come, and by then his body would be long decomposed, eaten by hungry swamp beasts, and I would be dead.

My job here complete, I retrieved my phone, Preston's phone, the shovel, and both our sets of keys and made my way back up the hill to the road, following it back to the house. My waterlogged sneakers and muddy, saturated clothing would have made me quite a sight if someone would have seen me.

Back at the house, I had a second wind and a desire to know what was inside. I threw the shovel in my trunk, removed my muddy shoes, and slipped on a pair of sleek rubber gloves, then, trying each key on each of Preston's keychains, I found one that unlocked the door and stepped inside. The place was stuffy, as any non-air-conditioned New Orleans structure would be, but quite neat. I didn't see so much as a used drinking glass out of place, as if no one had lived here recently. The main floor living room, dining room, and kitchen all appeared quite ordinary, with furniture and a television ready to handle nonexistent guests.

I decided to do a check of the upstairs. I flipped on the light in the first bedroom and saw that it had no furniture. Same with the second bedroom. But all the way in the back was a bedroom converted into a fully furnished office. The room's dark, heavy furnishings spoke of this being a male hangout. Even the bookcases had a masculine feel to them.

I was drawn to the section of wall on my left that was different, the one that featured something other than bookcases or a window. Stepping closer, I could read the text of the newspaper articles Preston had chosen to display. I recognized the picture of Josh Middleton and those of the friend Rob and the guy who'd recently been murdered outside a local bar—all the ones Tyler had suspected his brother of having some involvement in. But alongside those were at least ten others, of varying ages and whose deaths took place in various locations. Several good-looking girls smiled at me from the yellowed clippings. I noticed they all had a similar look. What was it? As I scrutinized further, I realized they all reminded me of Danielle.

I unpinned the one about Josh to read it more clearly and was surprised to find a different article underneath it. Curious, I removed another article and also found a different one under it. I removed the whole top layer, not caring if I ripped some newsprint here and there. Every story in the second layer was different from the first. I kept going. I uncovered a whole third layer—all separate stories. By the fourth layer, the newsprint was sticking together and I couldn't read the stories so well. Preston had killed all of these?

The investigator in me kicked in. The keys from Preston's pocket had to unlock something other than the front door. I checked the desk and found a bottom drawer that opened with one of the keys. Inside was a metal box, which I set atop the desk and opened with another key. I drew back from the stench of the box. Inside were small personal items—jewelry, small clothing items, a football trophy—likely memorabilia from the twisted killer. So many crimes. So many lives cut down prematurely and families destroyed.

Taking another look in the drawer, I found a youth football trophy. This one had the name Josh Middleton on it. I set it on the desktop next to the box.

Something else in the drawer caught my attention. Underneath where the metal box laid was a three-ring binder—the standard kind you would buy at Target. I removed and opened it to find a neatly drawn grid with headings that read Date, Name, Location, and Reason. The first entry was dated October 3, 1995. The name was Jim Davis, location New Orleans, and the reason, "because he beat me up." The next entry wasn't until 1998, but then the entries piled up, with several each year. Locations were all over the country—all in or near towns with NFL teams, I noted. Reasons were as inane as "she tempted me to cheat on my wife," "drove purposely slow in front of me and caused me to be late for practice," "flirted with Danielle," and "embarrassed me in front of my teammates." The first page had more than twenty entries.

My heart beat faster. I'd known of serial killers in my days as an investigator, but twenty murders was a lot.

I turned the page to find twenty more. The next page had the same number. On this page were primarily male victims. I continued to scan the reasons. "A known bully in the neighborhood," "Witnessed him making fun of a shorter kid in the bar," and "Court didn't convict him of molesting young boys, so I did." When I reached the end, I'd counted more than eighty. I swiped my dripping forehead with the back of my hand. This guy was the worst of the worst. And to never be convicted of any of them?

At least half had taken place within a hundred-mile radius, which is how he'd amassed such a collection of bones. How? How could so many deaths not ever be connected?

I thought back to Preston's smiling face on the television, how the announcers and fans would heap adulation on him simply because he could play a game well. Did anyone ever question his character? He had an "in" to dozens of settings across the country and an "out" to any investigation due to his fame.

The other crimes In Preston's carefully recorded book took place in locations throughout the country: Denver, San Francisco, Baltimore, Dallas, Charlotte.

Charlotte. The place I used to live. Charlotte was nothing but a dark memory to me—a place I didn't go in my mind except on my worst days. The place where the loss of kids we never had sucked the life out of my soul. The place where a girl got murdered under my watch. The place where I lost the job I'd been working toward for years. The place where my wife left me alone to wallow in my misery.

Even though Preston's book sickened me, something within prompted me to take a closer look. In my spirit, I felt an ugly, dreadful emotion welling up. This emotion wasn't directly connected to Preston. It was my own. It was . . . I recognized it . . . as guilt. My own culpability. But why? A drip of my sweat landed on the desk. I smeared it with my gloved finger and wiped it completely dry with the bottom of my shirt.

I scanned the records of Preston's crimes, somehow knowing what I'd find but not wanting to let in the full realization. But there on the third page back, I found the evidence. *Charlotte, North Carolina. 1992. Katy Dupont. Reason: a temptress who looked like Danielle.*

No! No! The guy I could have caught that night so long ago. The serial killer I'd missed because of my drinking. He had been the one to kill the doe-eyed girl. And all these dozens of crimes that had happened since then. I was responsible. My incredible stupidity and weakness had caused so many families pain. The enormity of the weight pressed on my chest. I could barely breathe.

I slumped to the ground in a fetal position as darkness closed in on my very soul. I could hear the taunts of my demons. I literally felt the cancer inside me multiplying, replacing good cells with bad. I didn't deserve to live. I was a failure. I belonged on the floor with the rats, mice, and other rodents that likely infested this place.

A deep depression filled my being. I sat in silence, unable to move, willing myself to die so I'd never have to face anyone ever again. Shame's cold fingers gripped my beating heart. The slow hands of time ticked my miserable life away for several long minutes.

But then a sliver of light trickled into my being. Preston was gone. He would never hurt anyone again. I willed myself off of the ground, grabbing hold of that hope and counseling myself with that truth over and over again. I had to. My very life depended on that tiny stream of hope.

He was gone. Forever. I'd done something right. Far, far too late, but I'd righted the wrong. This black stain of humanity was in the past. I'd have to live forever with the now-uncovered consequences of my lapse in judgment from that dark, lonely night. But I could build on that optimism now circulating through my veins. I could be a new man who would never stop protecting the weak and innocent.

I sat back and pondered what to do, breathing more deeply now. The world needed to know about Preston's crimes, but Danielle needed peace and for her kids to live with the untruth that their dad was a nice guy. Myself? I could easily get off on self-defense, especially with all this evidence.

But no one, except Tyler, even knew I was here. This case had been so hush-hush that I'd told no one about the particulars of it, just disappeared off the grid—not that I had much of a social circle anyway. The guys I'd hired earlier to follow Preston didn't know me well and had assumed Preston was just having an affair. Tyler would never tell anyone about this night, I was sure.

I knew what I needed to do. I decided to protect the doe-eyed girl. I'd failed the one from years ago. But the one who'd had the misfortune to marry Preston would live a life free from courtroom drama and the shame of association with him. I'd done my research and knew Preston did not have his name on this property. The search for a vanished Preston would not lead here.

Thus resolved, I replaced the three-ring binder, locked the metal box, and secured them both away in the desk drawer. I took the keys with me. I would check through Preston's phone and then toss it in a dumpster miles from here. Yes, I'd get questioned because authorities would find out Tyler had hired me, but I knew how to answer questions.

I took a final look at the place, a scene I would never again return to. In my mind, I sealed up the memories of this night. Yes, I still felt like a chastised child, like a man who would forever carry a pit around in my stomach, a part of my heart forever deadened. But I had a mission, a purpose. And that was enough for now.

I checked to see that no one was coming down the road before shutting the gate and locking it. The sun's rays were not yet beginning to lighten the earth, so escape without detection was easy.

I made my way to the freeway and took off.

About the Author

Blake Rudman enjoyed a former, successful career in executive management, building his own companies from the ground up.

Success or not, Blake's heart has always been in the written word, and the myriad ideas he spent much of his spare time jotting down in notebooks, Post-Its, and scraps of paper whenever the inspiration hit him.

Now a breakout author of five noir thriller novels – all to be published in 2023 – Blake's destiny of becoming a writer of some renown is well under way.

When he's not working diligently on his next novel, Blake spends quality time with his family and tropical fish.

Follow Blake's blog at: https://blakerudman.com
Facebook: @BRudmanThriller
Instagram: @BRudmanThriller
Twitter: @BRudmanThriller

For all Blake's books, visit him at:
www.hellboundbookspublishing.com/authorpage_rudman.html

Blake Rudman

Blake Rudman Novels from HellBound Books:
Available in Kindle, paperback, hardcover, and audiobook.

The Gentleman's Choice

"Caught in a whirlwind of adverse publicity following a viewer's death, the streaming show, The Gentleman's Choice becomes the target for a sadistic killer – and it's up to PI Vanessa Young to put a stop to it before more young women are murdered."

A sleazy internet dating show blamed for a viewer's death, a host with a dark, secret past, and a killer with a sadistic grudge…

Someone is kidnapping and murdering previous contestants from the popular streaming show *The Gentleman's Choice* – a strictly-for-adults hybrid of *The Bachelor* and *Love Island*. Private Investigator, Vanessa Young, is hired by a victim's family to infiltrate the show as a contestant to expose and capture the killer.

Vanessa and the show's charismatic star, Cole Gianni, begin to fall romantically for each other, until Vanessa's plan goes terribly awry when they're drugged and taken to a remote location to take part in their captor's own brutal, ultimately fatal, version of *The Gentleman's Choice*.

With the clock ticking toward their fateful final night, Vanessa and Cole are forced into a battle of wills to survive their tormentor and escape with their lives before it's too late…

Dark Beauty

Tessa and Kristin Morgan are identical twins, exquisitely beautiful, and have the world at their perfectly pedicured feet; they are also profoundly different beneath their stunning facades.

Tessa is the laser-focused academic with her eyes firmly fixed upon a career in neurology, while Kristin exploits her striking looks and undeniable power over men to carve out a single-minded path to fame and fortune as a model and actress; an ambition she also holds for her sister.

But, on the night of the pair's debut as top-tier models, and with a high-profile movie role in the bag, tragedy strikes the twins in the form of a cruel acid attack by an unknown assailant. Thus, a gruesome chain of events begins - one that leaves a trail of blood, death, and devastation behind both Tessa and Kristin.

As Tessa fights to rebuild her life and uncover the truth behind the attack, she finds herself getting closer and closer to an uncomfortable truth about her sister and her search for the truth turns into a nightmare struggle to stay alive.

Goodbye Stranger

"As with *American Psycho*, Blake Rudman's *Goodbye Stranger* has a wealthy, successful man whose wonderful family life masks a much darker side. Throw in a once-trusting, increasingly suspicious wife, and the stage is set for twists and turns you'll never see coming!"

Danielle Harrington has the life many women envy: She's beautiful, rich, has two wonderful children, and is married to *the* Preston Harrington - the handsome, charismatic, retired quarterback who won two Super Bowls.

Unfortunately, something is very wrong with Preston. Having suffered more than his fair share of injuries and concussions, he becomes quiet, withdrawn, and distant. As Preston spends more time away from his family, Danielle begins suspect an affair without realizing her husband is involved in something much, much worse...

Following a series of tragic incidents and the return of an old nemesis from the past, things begin to spiral out of control for Danielle as Preston's dark side puts her and their children in terrible danger.

Redline

"If Lee Childs' Jack Reacher or Clive Cussler's Dirk Pitt tackled a terrorist scheme that utilized subliminal messaging to sow social and economic chaos on a global scale, it would look a lot like *Red Line*." Baltimore Police Detective Mitch Wilson wants a nice day out with his wife and son. Instead, they are all caught up in a catastrophic terrorist attack that has repercussions across the USA and triggers events that could alter the course of civilization.

Having lost everything, Mitch sets out to seek justice – and revenge and stumbles upon a global conspiracy.

On the other side of the world, renowned linguistic professor, Yasaman Karami, flees her native Iran for the freedom of the west; she holds one of the keys to defeating the terrorist organization.

Yasaman and Mitch's worlds collide as, alongside federal agents and allies, they race against the clock to hunt down the terrorist masterminds and prevent worldwide catastrophe.

Kutri

The Slow Plague killed billions of women and girls worldwide. The gender-targeting infection without cure drove the remaining, sparce female population into an insane supply and demand situation in which they are treated as valuable commodities.

Though their "market value" is high, paradoxically, women's rights take a nosedive as they have become more desirable than the most precious jewels. Women are objects avarice, awe, and worship – to be owned or won in high-stakes games.

Kutri Chandigarh, one such "prize" and a rare beauty, is shipped from her native India to Los Angeles, a shattered metropolis barricaded behind a radiation-repelling wall. Within the city stronghold, a bleak, broken society comprised mostly of men is mesmerized by the stupefying programs pumped out by Little Angel Studios: an endless parade of reality TV shows.

The studio's #1 hit is "Good Breeding", in which a bevy of ethnically "pure" young women compete to marry a chosen suitor and produce a family in the spotlight of the public eye.

Like all women, Kutri has dreamed of wining the competition since her early childhood. But, when she arrives in LA and meets Jakob Freeman, her assigned matchmaker, the fantasy is turned on its head. It quickly twists into a horrific nightmare that extends far beyond Kutri and the man she chooses for herself.

As Kutri tries to escape the fate she once coveted, Jakob is swept up in events that threaten him body and soul and spark memories of a past he has deliberately tried to forget.

www.hellboundbookspublishing.com

Follow Blake's blog at: https://blakerudman.com
Facebook: @BRudmanThriller
Instagram: @BRudmanThriller
Twitter: @BRudmanThriller

For all Blake's books, visit him at:
www.hellboundbookspublishing.com/authorpage_rudman.html